TABITHA TENNANT

The Sons of Prophecy

Tyg Tennant
x

A CIP catalogue record for this book is available from the British Library.

Map illustration and family tree by Tabitha Tennant and Mark Swan.

First edition

ISBN: 978-1-0369-0019-9

This book was professionally typeset on Reedsy.
Find out more at reedsy.com

To my uncle, Chris, for his unwavering love and support.

"In an age of brutal passion, the affectionate care Jasper bestowed upon his fatherless nephew throws into relief the hideous ferocity that surrounded him."

H. T. Evans

England and Wales
1456 - 1485

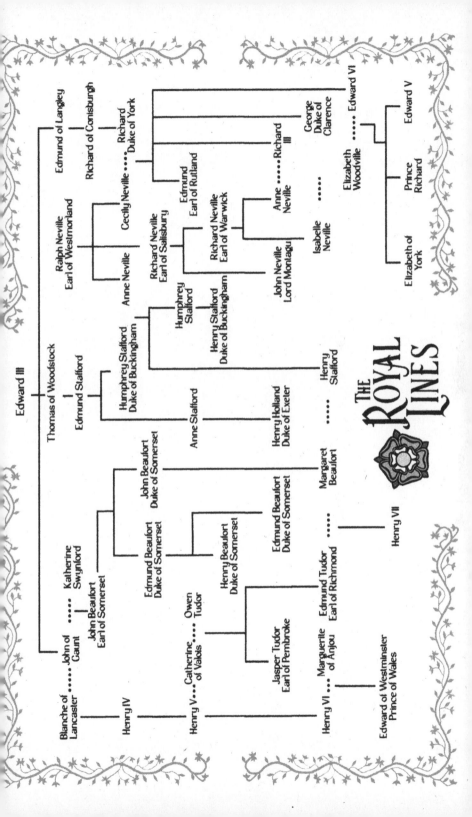

THE ROYAL LINES

I

Part One

1456–1461

"Jasper will rear a dragon for us, the fortunate blood of Brutus is he ... he is the hope of our nation. Great is the gift of Jasper's birth, a pure spear of Cadwaladr's line..."

—*Dafydd Llwyd o Fathafarn*

1

November 1456

The wind howled through the trees, bending their limbs close to breaking. Icy rain, in sheets, lashed down unrelentingly. Beneath the branches, a lone horse raced dangerously fast along the old Roman road, its rider bent low against the weather. A week on the road had turned Jasper's once-fine cloak into little more than a sodden rag. His dark hair was plastered against his head and rainwater ran like small rivers down his face, intermingling with the tears that seemingly refused to stop.

His horse spooked slightly. It could sense the turmoil raging within him, the grief that threatened to overwhelm. More like twins than brothers, Edmund had been the one constant in Jasper's life, anchoring him when their father was imprisoned and they were sent away to the Abbey. And now he was dead. How could someone with so much life in them be gone?

Jasper struggled to believe it. He'd desperately been trying to secure his brother's release ever since he'd heard of Edmund's imprisonment in early August. He had tried everything, used all his connections and charm. He'd even petitioned King Henry to send a force to free him, pleading with his half-brother in the name of their late mother,

Queen Catherine of Valois. But the king's position had been shaken by the Duke of York's attempt to seize power, and he could offer no assistance. Jasper clenched his fists around the reins. To think he had once trusted York, regarded his attempts to instil good governance while the king was incapacitated by illness as admirable. Even after the battle at St Albans, he'd truly believed there was still a way to resolve the rising tensions diplomatically; calling for leniency while the likes of Northumberland and Somerset, men raised up prematurely to their dukedoms by the swing of York's blade, demanded vengeance for their fathers. Well that naivety was long gone now, buried deep in the cold ground with Edmund. The letter said it was the plague that had taken his brother from this world, but given everything, Jasper couldn't dislodge the suspicion that York's supporters had had a hand in his death.

Shaking his head, he spurred his horse on, finding release in the speed as he galloped along the uneven road, his heart pounding fast. Jasper was no stranger to death. Though only twenty-five, he had already seen his fair share. But the despair he felt for Edmund was like none he had ever known. And yet, despite his grief, he was angry. Angry at himself, angry at the injustices that had brought such devastation to his family. But burning hotter than either, and the reason he found himself risking his neck on such treacherous roads, was the anger directed at his brother. For it was not just him Edmund had left behind. There was his wife, now a widow, abandoned in an unfamiliar country, heavy with her dead husband's unborn baby, and she barely more than a child herself. Jasper cursed. Edmund never should have married her in the first place.

He could remember the argument, how their raised voices echoed off the walls of Pembroke's hall. He had tried to convince his brother to wait. What need was there to rush, he'd challenged Edmund. They'd held Margaret's wardship for two years already; what difference would another few make? But there had always been a darker side to Edmund's ambition, and in his eyes, Margaret was the key. Her Beaufort inheritance would guarantee his future, and only marriage could secure it for certain. And now, just a year later, Jasper was riding to protect his thirteen-year-old sister-in-law from the simmering unrest that would surely soon catapult the country into all-out war.

* * *

Riding purposefully beneath the gatehouse arch into a large courtyard, Jasper allowed himself a moment to appreciate the elegant haven he had arrived at. Hidden amongst the wild Pembrokeshire hills, there was an almost spiritual serenity to Lamphey Palace, no doubt a product of its role as home to the bishops of St David's for centuries.

Grimacing against the pain in his protesting joints, he swung a leg over the neck of his mount and leapt down onto the cobbles. He had assumed he would need to announce himself – he'd told no one of his journey, concerned for the danger such knowledge might have created – yet there was no look of surprise on the face of Bishop Delabere, who materialised at the palace's great oak doors. He smiled consolingly as Jasper took his hand and pressed his lips to his episcopal ring. "Warm greetings on this cold day, my Lord of Pembroke. May God bless you for your endeavours."

"Your Grace," Jasper replied tightly. He had little desire to discuss the details of his grief with a stranger, even if that stranger was a man of God.

The Bishop sensed his reticence and motioned him inside. "The Countess of Richmond has been told of your arrival and is waiting to receive you."

Jasper nodded and allowed himself to be led into the heart of the palace. Conscious of his dishevelled appearance, he had hoped for the chance to make himself more presentable, but it did not appear he would be offered such an opportunity. He supposed in the end it did not much matter. If the last weeks had taught him anything it was that there were more important things in life and so he resigned himself to greet his sister-in-law in his current bedraggled state. If nothing else, it would at least convey the urgency with which he had undertaken his long journey.

As they entered the hall, the first thing that struck Jasper was how young Margaret looked. He had aged her in his mind, but in reality there was no escaping the fact she was more girl than woman. The second was the swell of her stomach. Grossly disproportionate to her small frame, it was physical proof of the worst parts of his brother's character, and despite his grief, Jasper could feel his anger flare at the sight, making a muscle jump in his jaw.

"My Lord," Margaret said, lowering herself into an awkward curtsey, one hand supporting the weight of her stomach.

"My Lady," Jasper replied with a bow. When he lifted his gaze, his eyes met Margaret's. "I'm sorry—" his voice cracked, "I'm sorry for your loss."

"Our loss," Margaret replied softly.

Jasper nodded stiffly, swallowing against a spike of emotion. Out of the corner of his eye he noticed Delabere slip quietly from the room and felt a sudden wave of gratitude for the kindness of the old bishop. Clearing his throat he continued. "Forgive my unannounced intrusion, I have come to take you to Pembroke. To my home." He attempted what he hoped was a small smile of reassurance. "You'll be safe there – both of you."

Instead of returning his smile, Margaret hesitated, and in that moment, the conviction that had propelled Jasper from London faltered. He had thought only of her safety, not for once entertaining the notion that she might not want to go with him. That she was his ward once more and therefore legally unable to object did not lessen the impact of the realisation. He silently cursed his foolishness. It was clear that, though scared, Margaret was not suffering the same intense grief at Edmund's passing that he was. And why should she be? She had not chosen to marry him, nor to carry his child. Why then had Jasper assumed she would willingly go to a strange castle with a man she barely knew, and who she no doubt held partly responsible for her current situation? He wanted to tell her that he understood; that he had no wish to add to her distress, but words seemed incapable of conveying such a sentiment.

In the silence that stretched out, Margaret watched him with her clear blue eyes as though weighing up the decision before her. There was a steeliness to her stare that belied a hidden strength. A child she may be, yet there was a poise to how she conducted herself. Under her scrutiny, Jasper ran a hand self-consciously through his hair and decided then that he would not force her to come with him. If she were to join him in Pembroke, it would be of her own volition.

As though she could hear his thoughts, Margaret at last gave her reply. "Thank you, my Lord, I am most grateful for your generous offer. I— we," she corrected, running her hand protectively over the bump, "will be much safer in your company."

Relief washed over Jasper. Without a second thought, he dropped to one knee, his head bowed. When he spoke his voice was thick with emotion. "I swear on my honour, as kinsman to the king, as Earl of Pembroke, and as your brother, that from this day on I will protect you and your child in any way I can. As God is my witness, I pledge my life in service to you both."

Uncertainly, Margaret stretched out a hand. It seemed strange to have a man such as Jasper kneel before her. Unsure of what was expected, she placed her hand on his still-damp curls. "Thank you. I know in my heart that with you here to guard his family, Edmund will rest peacefully."

Another wave of grief clenched Jasper's chest at her words, and he kept his head bowed lest Margaret should see the tears that sprung to his eyes. After taking a moment to compose himself, he rose to his feet.

"Will you take refreshment, my Lord?" Margaret asked, aware that she had been remiss in her duties as host.

"Thank you, but no," Jasper replied. "I fear if I rest now, I may not rise again. Better to wait until I am home." He cast about the room. "I do not wish to hasten your departure, but we would do well to be within Pembroke before nightfall. Do not worry about your belongings," he added. "I will ensure they are delivered safely."

"That is very kind, though I have little in terms of possessions. I barely spent enough time with my husband to get to know him, let alone create a home together. Yet, it will be a comfort to have those few treasured items with me at Pembroke," she continued quickly, noticing the sadness that flickered across Jasper's face.

"Very well, I shall make the necessary preparations."

* * *

The rain that had marred his earlier journey had mercifully ceased and, by the time Margaret emerged from the Palace, the courtyard was bathed in golden autumnal light. Jasper had thrown himself into preparing for their departure, relishing in the distraction it offered – shouting out orders as he strode about. He paused when he caught sight of Margaret, his demeanour visibly softening. Bundled as she was in multiple layers to protect from the bitter November chill, she struggled to navigate the slippery cobbles and Jasper quickly stepped forward to offer a guiding hand, which was accepted with a small smile.

"Forgive my earlier silence, my Lord," Margaret began. "Your offer took me quite by surprise, and my hesitation was merely evidence of that rather than of any reluctance. Since I heard— since I heard of my husband's death, I have received no letters of condolence, no words of support or advice, not even from my mother, though it was naive to expect any different from her."

Jasper's brows furrowed in concern. "I am sorry you have felt so alone. I should have written of my intentions but there seemed little point when I would have most likely arrived before any such note reached you. And please, call me Jasper," he added. "We are family after all."

"Jasper," Margaret repeated.

"Though the journey ahead is not a long one, I would ensure you are comfortable." Jasper motioned to a sturdy-looking pony, with a groom standing by with a lead rope.

Margaret stopped, a frown lining her young face. "I am more than capable of riding on my own," she said curtly.

"I do not doubt it. But it is not your skill as a horsewoman that prompts my caution, rather the condition of the roads themselves. The rain has wreaked havoc on them, and it would be remiss of me, after so recently swearing to protect you, if I did not see you delivered safely within Pembroke's walls." He gave one of his charming smiles. "Please, indulge me in this request, sister."

Colour rose in Margaret's cheeks. "Of course."

"Thank you."

As if to cement her embarrassment, it took the assistance of both the groom and Jasper to see her settled in the saddle. If her struggle was proof of Jasper's argument then he had the good grace not to point it out. Instead his focus was entirely on checking she was secure atop her mount. His strong hand encircled her slender calf, guiding her foot into the stirrups. Though there was no intended intimacy

9

in the action, it still made Margaret start to have a man touch her in such a way. Ever observant, Jasper's grey eyes noted the reaction. He dropped his hand and took a step back, re-establishing the distance between them once more.

"I hope this is comfortable enough for you, Margaret; as I said, it is only a short journey."

"I am stronger than I look, you know," Margaret responded, unable to keep the annoyance from her voice. Jasper's eyes widened slightly in surprise. "But, I— I appreciate your thoughtfulness," she continued quickly, smoothing her skirts in an attempt to regain her composure. Jasper inclined his head, a smile playing on his lips.

With an effortlessness Margaret envied, Jasper leapt up into his saddle. Spinning his horse around, he called over to the captain of the guard. "Lead on."

* * *

The sun had almost set by the time Pembroke came into view. Positioned imposingly atop a high rock promontory, the castle's grey stone walls that towered above the landscape were silhouetted against the darkening sky. Surrounded on all sides, bar one, by water, a traveller first setting eyes on it would be forgiven for thinking it a cold, unwelcoming place but to Jasper it was the home he had worked hard to create. There was an awe-inspiring beauty to its scale and even in his grief-stricken state it still made his spirits rise to see it once again. Glancing over his shoulder, Jasper tried to gauge Margaret's reaction as she took in the place that was to be her home. It surprised him to realise that it mattered to him what she thought of Pembroke, he who so rarely cared what others might think. She seemed content enough, though in truth he could decipher little from her expression.

Unbeknownst to Jasper, it was not Pembroke that Margaret's sharp blue eyes assessed. She had grown up in enough castles to be immune to their grandeur, and in any case there was something of far greater interest that drew her gaze. Measure a man by the way he treats his inferiors, that was what the scriptures instructed, and she would know the character of the man who had come to rescue her. So as Jasper led the procession into town and down the main street, Margaret watched the faces of those who had assembled to welcome him home; the men with weather-worn skin who removed their felt caps, the women with full lips and ample chests who smiled coquettishly, and running alongside, the children of various ages, their cheeks red from the cold. It was to these that Jasper paid the most attention, leaning down over the neck of his horse and placing coins into their eagerly outstretched hands.

But it was not just Jasper who the townsfolk had come out to see. No sooner had their lord passed by than their focus turned to Margaret, their eyes widening as they first took in her condition and then her age. Margaret did not need to understand Welsh to know that the whispered comments that swept through the crowd like the wind through wheat were directed at her. Jasper, however, could; his smile slipping as the words reached his ears. Reining in his horse, he purposefully positioned himself next to Margaret. They rode the last few hundred yards up to the gates side by side, and under his stern gaze the gossip was silenced, at least for a moment.

Once within the castle's outer ward, Jasper jumped down from his horse, handing the reins to a groom. Above the heads of fussing attendants, the grizzled constable of Pembroke, John Vernon, caught his eye. It was clear from the seriousness of his expression that the rest Jasper so longed for was to be yet again delayed. For now though, he motioned for Vernon to wait and turned his attention to Margaret. Offering his hand, he helped her dismount. He noted the grimace of pain as she did so but said nothing, remembering her

11

earlier admonishment.

"Welcome to Pembroke, Margaret. I recognise it is not as luxurious as Lamphey, but it is secure, and I hope you will find it a comfortable alternative." He called over a buxom woman with a kind face. "This is Joan. She will show you to your rooms. I regret the castle is somewhat lacking a female touch. If there is anything you need, anything at all, ask Joan, and she will make sure you have it." Jasper glanced distractedly at Pembroke's captain. "Now, if you'll excuse me, there are pressing matters I must deal with." Bowing formally, he strode away.

"My Lady." Joan bobbed into a quick curtsey. She had a soft, lilting accent that was immediately reassuring, banishing the memory of the staring townsfolk. "If you'd like to come with me." Margaret gave a quick glance in the direction of Jasper's retreating figure before following Joan into the castle.

* * *

Hours later and finally alone in the solar, Jasper felt some of his tension melt away as he watched the flames of the fire flicker. His wolfhound, Ianto, was stretched out by the hearth, gently snoring. The country may be teetering on the edge of an uncertain future, but there remained something comforting about being within Pembroke's formidable walls. Not for the first time, he wondered whether he could hide behind them forever.

He rubbed his brow while turning his conversation with John Vernon over in his mind. He was reassured to hear the improvements he had ordered to Pembroke's defences had been carried out, but in his heart, he knew it wouldn't stop what was coming. Jasper sighed deeply. Hiding in Wales wasn't going to mend the divisions that were starting to pull the country apart. It was only a matter of time before he'd be called to assist the king. Absentmindedly, he rubbed his left arm where a long scar ran across his bicep, a souvenir from St Albans. Almost two years later, it still ached occasionally, a reminder of what had already been sacrificed in defence of the Crown.

Jasper took a sip of the brandy he had been nursing, his thoughts turning to Margaret. The journey had clearly been taxing for her. She had politely declined his offer to dine with him, opting instead to eat in her rooms. He hadn't had the chance to spend much time with her when she was married to Edmund but he was impressed by how she'd handled herself today. He was ashamed of the reactions of some of the townspeople, and had made a point of telling Vernon that he would not have his sister-in-law disrespected in such a way, though he was consoled by the fact that Margaret had seemed little troubled by it. She seemed more mature than he remembered. Yet beneath her resilient exterior, he knew there was still a frightened child. Whatever happened next, he'd been right to bring her here.

The warmth from the fire enveloped the room, the orange glow of the flames making shadows dance on the wooden vaulted ceiling. Leaning back into the chair, Jasper could feel his eyes becoming heavy. Almost a fortnight on the road was finally catching up with him, a dull ache building in his muscles that would no doubt make it hard to move in the morning. He put his hands to his face, emotionally and physically exhausted. The adrenaline that had been coursing through his blood ever since he had received the news of Edmund's death was slowly ebbing away, giving way instead to the heaviness of grief that weighed on his chest like a stone.

2

January 1457

I t felt as though the wind was intent on tearing the castle apart. Lightning flashed across the sky as rain lashed against the stone. But Pembroke's walls had never been breached, and they weren't about to be defeated by the weather. A more superstitious person would say it was an omen; that nothing good could come of a night such as this. Normally, Jasper would roll his eyes in response to such mutterings, but tonight that educated reasoning held little sway, and he found himself shivering involuntarily as Mother Nature hurled herself against Pembroke's ancient defences.

Deserted by his usual calm composure, Jasper paced in front of the fire like a caged animal. He was too agitated to sit, so he walked to release some of the tension. Back and forth, back and forth, over and over again, watched all the while by Ianto's doleful eyes. Jasper was surprised by his own emotion. It had taken him some time to adapt to Margaret's presence in his life, and she too had initially struggled to find her place in Pembroke, where she was neither its mistress nor its guest. Not that that period lasted long. Incredibly self-assured and confident, Margaret was unlike any thirteen-year-old Jasper had ever met, and she had soon made her mark on the castle and on him.

There was a maturity to her demeanour that was at odds with her age. Jasper's father, Owen, had described her as an old soul when he'd visited for a subdued Christmas, Edmund's absence still painfully conspicuous. Yet for all her emotional maturity, her body was really still that of a child. As her stomach had grown, so too had Jasper's unspoken fears, and now across the castle Margaret was fighting for her life as she struggled to bring another into the world. Not for the first time that night, Jasper cursed his brother and his ambition.

Margaret had entered her confinement a few weeks before. As a man, he'd naturally been kept far away, but he had given strict instructions that he was to be informed of any developments. Jasper had hoped that, for Margaret's sake, it would be a quick ordeal. He'd been told this morning it wouldn't be much longer, but the sun had long since set, and it seemed they were no closer to the arrival of a child. Jasper knew the dangers of childbirth well enough. He could remember his confusion and his father's anguish when his mother had died shortly after giving birth. A time that should have been filled with joy quickly turning into one of agony and heartbreak. If a dowager queen in the prime of her life could die following the birth of her fifth child, then what hope was there for a thirteen-year-old in this isolated part of Wales? Jasper shook his head and said a quick prayer to his mother, asking her to watch over Margaret. Lost in thought, he started when the door to the solar opened.

"It's just me," his father said, raising his hands. Jasper sighed, turning back to the fire.

Owen Tudor stepped into the room, closing the door quietly behind him. Wiry, with dark hair tinged by grey, his Welsh accent was still strong despite his years in England. Closing in on sixty, he still possessed the same rugged handsomeness that Catherine of Valois had fallen for many years before. Gregarious and amiable, Owen was a man who relished life and delighted in the quirks of fate that had made him husband to a queen and stepfather to a king. Ianto, who had been occupying his usual spot by the fire, padded over to Owen, receiving a scratch behind the ear by way of a greeting.

"Do you mind if I—?" Owen asked, gesturing to a small table where a glass bottle filled with amber liquid sat.

"What?" Jasper glanced over his shoulder. "No, go ahead," he said, waving a hand.

Owen poured himself a measure of brandy and then settled into one of the chairs facing the fire, which crackled and spat in the silence. Eventually, Jasper spoke.

"I was just thinking about Mother."

"She was a truly wonderful woman," Owen smiled in reminiscence. "You know, the first time I saw her, it seemed as though an angel had descended from heaven – I'd never seen such beauty."

Jasper nodded absentmindedly in agreement. Usually he loved to hear the stories of his parents' courtship; of an illicit romance played out in secret away from the prying eyes of a court who feared the power his mother held. But tonight he was too lost in his own thoughts and so silence fell between them. Owen took a sip from his cup, his eyes watching his son intently. He could always tell when Jasper needed to vent his worries, and knew not to prompt him. Better to stay quiet and wait until he was ready to speak. As usual, he did not have to wait long.

"I pray God is watching over Margaret tonight," Jasper said, sitting heavily in a chair beside his father. "In truth, I fear for her and the baby. Not just for this night but for the future." He leant forward, resting his elbows on his knees, his voice rising with suppressed anger. "The country is in turmoil. A line was crossed at St Albans. Politics – if that was ever the true motivation – is irrelevant now. It is about personal vendettas; sons avenging fathers, fathers mourning sons." Jasper sat back. "And unless Henry retains his composure," he continued more

16

quietly, weariness overcoming him, "there's no knowing where this will end. York has tasted power; he won't give it up now without a fight. And I— I—"

Reaching across, Owen gripped Jasper's shoulder. "Look at me." Jasper dragged his gaze from the fire, focusing on his father's. "Life is full of uncertainty. Peace, war – it does not matter – we can never know in which way Fortune's Wheel will turn. All we can do is try to live with honour and in God's grace. Margaret is safe because of you. Her child will be safe because of you. Loyalty has always been your greatest virtue. In the trials to come, that is what matters."

Jasper took a deep breath. *"Diolch,"* he said simply. Owen squeezed his son's shoulder and then settled back in his chair. Taking a slow sip from his cup, Jasper rested his head back on the chair as the warmth of the alcohol spread through his body. He was just letting himself succumb to the warmth of the fire and brandy when a loud knock on the door jerked him back to full consciousness. From his spot by the hearth, Ianto looked up, alert.

"Enter," Jasper called.

A servant entered the solar and bowed deeply. "My Lord. The Countess of Richmond has been delivered of a boy."

Jasper slapped his leg, grinning widely at his father. "That is truly wonderful. And the countess, how is she?"

"Tired, my Lord, but in good spirits."

"Praise God."

"My Lady wished me to tell you," the servant continued, "that she has named him Henry, for the king."

"I had hoped for Edmund—" Owen began, but Jasper cut across him.

"It is a fine name," he declared. "Please tell the countess of our joy at this wondrous news. If there is anything she needs, anything at all, she is to have it. I hope she will permit me to visit little Henry in the morning."

"Of course my Lord," the servant replied with a bow and slipped quietly from the room.

Shaking his head in disbelieving joy, Jasper picked up their cups and refilled them from the bottle. Handing one to Owen, Jasper raised his high in a toast. "To Henry."

"Henry," his father echoed, drinking deeply.

Jasper collapsed back into his chair, relief flooding through him, banishing the tension he had been carrying. He felt tears pricking at his eyes. His happiness for the new arrival seemed to amplify Edmund's absence. He should have been here to celebrate the birth of his son. He felt hands on his shoulders. Glancing up, he saw his father standing behind him. He, too, had tears in his eyes. Jasper placed a hand on his father's. Neither spoke as they watched the fire die down to embers, both deep in their memories.

3

February 1457

Jasper had thought the arrival of a baby would disrupt the rhythm of life at Pembroke. Yet as he sat in the great hall with Margaret, the two of them enjoying a simple supper at one end of the long table with Ianto sprawled at their feet, it seemed very little had changed, though he had to admit that he was so busy that there hadn't been time to notice if it had. Even now he was still in his travelling clothes, dog-tired from another long day in the saddle. As he had suspected, he'd not been allowed to enjoy the sanctuary of his small corner of Wales for long. His summons arrived soon after Henry's birth, along with well-wishes from the king for his new half-nephew and namesake. Though it had only been a couple of months since he had last been at court, arriving at Coventry where the king had decided to hold his Great Council felt like entering another world – one Jasper would have rather forgotten for at least a while longer. Even at the best of times court felt like a bear pit, but with the simmering tensions it was nearly unbearable. Jasper found himself physically tensing every time the Duke of York came into his vicinity, a reaction that did not go unnoticed by the arrogant Earl of Warwick who followed his uncle like a shadow. Though Jasper tried to control his emotions, it made his blood boil to see such men striding free, unrepentant for the devastation they had wrought. At least William Herbert, the man who had confined Edmund to the dank cell which had become his coffin, was not amongst their number – Jasper would not have been responsible for his actions if he had. There was vengeance to be had there, and he would not be satisfied until he had achieved it.

"You are unusually quiet this evening," Margaret commented, interrupting Jasper's brooding thoughts.

"Am I?" he asked, wearily shaking the images of Herbert's leering face from his mind.

"You have barely spoken all evening."

"Forgive me, I am still much occupied with matters at court."

"Anything that we should be worrying about?" Margaret probed.

Jasper sighed. "The same issues we have been worrying about for the last few years. The king's illness and York's greed. I had thought the king would use the Great Council as an opportunity to administer long-overdue justice, to treat York and his supporters with a firm hand. Yet the only punishment my blessed half-brother seemed capable of mustering was to re-appoint York as Lieutenant of Ireland," Jasper replied, unable to keep the frustration from his voice.

Margaret frowned. "That does not sound like a punishment."

"Exactly my point, it is not. God knows what possessed him to make such a decision, though I imagine it would have been because the queen sees it as akin to exile. And for most she would be right. But for York? From the sly look in his eye when he accepted the position, I do not imagine it will be long before he is plotting again."

"At least he can do us little harm from there."

Jasper shook his head. "I would not be so sure. Keep your friends close but your enemies closer, that is what my father has always taught me. If anything, being away from prying eyes makes York more dangerous."

"Then you should have raised your concerns with the king," Margaret pressed.

"I did. Not that it achieved anything. He merely dismissed them with a wave of a hand, as if they were no more than irritating flies, and then asked me to join him in prayer for York's soul."

"Well, that decides it then," Margaret announced abruptly, her expression serious.

"Decides what?" Jasper asked, bracing himself for the battle he could feel brewing. Margaret's headstrong nature had become even more pronounced now she had Henry's future to consider and he rarely emerged the victor from their verbal clashes.

Margaret took a deep breath. "It is time I took another husband—"

"No, absolutely not," Jasper cut across her, his voice rising, causing Ianto to look up warily. "It's too soon. You're supposed to be in mourning for my brother!"

"I am well aware of what society expects of me. You on the other hand? I had mistakenly believed you would be on my side rather than sitting there and presuming to teach me about grief," Margaret responded sharply.

"That is not what I'm trying to do," Jasper said exasperatedly. "I'm just saying it may be more appropriate to follow protocol and take a year before—"

"What use is protocol? In a year, we could all be dead!"

Margaret's voice echoed around the hall. Ianto, now fully awake, padded over to his master, nuzzling his arm in concern. Jasper ran a hand through his thick fur as Margaret took a sip of wine, recovering her composure.

"And what of your feelings?" Jasper asked, consciously managing the tone of his voice.

"My feelings are irrelevant," Margaret replied dismissively.

"You do not wish to find love?" Jasper asked, genuinely surprised.

21

"Love is for fools," Margaret admonished.

Jasper raised an eyebrow. "Even you cannot truly believe that. You are too young to possess such cynicism."

"Am I wrong, though?" Margaret pressed. "What woman has ever chosen marriage for love?"

"My mother did," Jasper replied simply.

"Your mother was the Queen of England!" Margaret volleyed back.

Jasper lent back in his chair, letting silence fall once more between them. "I do not wish to argue with you on this. Despite what you may think, I am far from naive. I know affection usually factors little in such arrangements and I concede my mother had the standing to make such a choice. But I saw the love my parents shared, grew up in the light of it, and I only wish that you may one day feel the warmth of such a bond. God knows you did not experience it with Edmund," he added, more to himself than anything else.

"He was not cruel to me," Margaret reasoned, caught off guard by Jasper's candidness.

"Neither was he kind," Jasper said sadly, swirling the contents of his cup. "You may say love is for fools – I disagree. It can and should be found in marriages, even if it is not there at the start."

"You speak of love as if it is some jewel to be cherished," Margaret scoffed.

Jasper smiled quietly to himself. "You may be wise beyond your years, Margaret, but in this there is still much for you to learn."

"If that is true, then why are you resistant to the idea of me remarrying? I'm hardly going to learn of the love that can exist between a husband and wife as a widow!"

Jasper considered his sister-in-law, unable to find a retort for such undeniable reasoning. "Because I had hoped you would wish to wait a little longer," he admitted with a sigh. "Not because I care about protocol or believe you in some way owe it to my brother," he explained, noting Margaret's expression. "Rather because I wished for you to have time to be with Henry and enjoy, if only for a moment, a life free from duty."

"Those are luxuries we can ill afford," Margaret replied quietly, the sadness in her voice unmistakable.

"And I am not blind to that reality," Jasper agreed, leaning across the table and taking her small hand in his. "Just know that my only wish is for you to be happy. You may not be a queen as my mother was, but this decision will be yours to make and no one else's. I am not too proud to recognise when I have lost an argument – if you are certain of your intention, then I will prepare a list of candidates for your consideration."

"I am, and I already have a list," Margaret said quickly, presenting a small roll of parchment.

Jasper shook his head, unable to keep the smile from his face. "Why am I not surprised?" Taking the roll, he purposefully took his time unfurling it and reading the names, enjoying the obvious effort it was taking Margaret to control her impatience. There were no more than half a dozen names on her list, but each represented a potentially advantageous alliance and spoke to the author's keen understanding. Of all the names, one in particular caught Jasper's attention.

"Henry Stafford," he read, raising an eyebrow. "A good choice. I know his father, Buckingham, well. He's one of the most powerful noblemen in the country and, most importantly, loyal to King Henry. I cannot foresee him objecting to you marrying his son. As far as I'm aware, Henry Stafford is an honourable man, although obviously, as a second son, he's not destined to inherit."

"That is precisely why he is a good choice," Margaret replied eagerly, clearly prepared to defend her choices against any questions Jasper might pose. "His position means he has valuable connections but is far enough removed from the dangers of court to be immune to sudden shifts in power. He will offer me security and comfort, and that is all that I can ask for."

"As ever, Margaret, your astuteness is remarkable," Jasper smiled, raising his cup in a mock toast. "I will write to Buckingham in the morning and arrange for us to visit him at Newport. If his son meets your approval, then I will be happy to give my consent to your marriage."

"Thank you."

Jasper nodded, taking a sip of his wine. "And what of my nephew? Where does young Henry feature in these plans?"

"I am doing this for him!" Margaret said vehemently.

"I do not doubt that, Margaret," Jasper said placatingly. "I am merely asking the question. I'm not your enemy."

"I'm sorry, I know that, it's just—" Margaret waved a hand, communicating what her words could not. She paused. "Joan will look after Henry while we're away," Margaret continued, her tone more measured. "As for once I'm married, I will request that the king grants you Henry's wardship." She placed a hand on Jasper's arm, looking at him intently. "Though it will break my heart to be parted from him, there is no one else I would trust with my son's life and there is no safer place for him than here in Pembroke."

"It would be my honour, Margaret," Jasper said sincerely. "I only wish to make sure you're certain."

"I know my mind, Jasper."

"Yes," he chuckled as the servants entered the hall to begin clearing the table. "That you certainly do."

4

March 1457

Greenfield Manor was a simple yet beautiful building positioned on a gently curving bend of the River Ebbw. While smaller than Newport Castle, located just three miles downriver, Buckingham had suggested Greenfield because of its greater privacy, something that Jasper was grateful for. The hundred-mile journey from Pembroke had been long and tiring, and it was a relief when they finally arrived in the modest courtyard. Jasper had been tense for the whole journey. The roads were dangerous at the best of times, but in the years since St Albans, lawlessness had increased tenfold. Men had come to believe they could take whatever they wanted without repercussion. And take they did. Encouraged by Yorkist landowners like William Herbert, the man who had imprisoned Edmund, raiders had left the roadsides littered with evidence of violent attacks. Fortunately the heavily armed retinue accompanying them had been enough to deter even the most daring of gangs and the miles had passed by uneventfully. For Margaret, still recovering from Henry's birth, the journey had been equally unenjoyable, though as ever, her stubbornness meant she refused to show her discomfort.

Buckingham strode out to meet them as they dismounted. He was a formidable man, his loyalty to the king unwavering. One of the most powerful magnates in the country, he had fought alongside Henry V in France and, following the king's death, had played a prominent role in the royal council that governed the country until his son reached his majority. His face was badly scarred, a visual reminder that even three arrows at St Albans could not turn his loyalty. At fifty-five, he showed no sign of slowing down, and he grasped Jasper's outstretched arm with surprising strength.

"Pembroke! I trust your journey was tolerable?"

"It was, my Lord. I had feared Herbert might attempt some sort of attack, but it seems he stayed away, though I look forward to the day when I can face my brother's captor."

"Ah yes, Black William. He was once your trusted councillor, was he not?" Buckingham asked. Jasper nodded stiffly. "It just goes to show," Buckingham sighed, "how much this feud has torn the country in two; brother against brother, friend against friend. Herbert, just like all those other Yorkist sympathisers, will need to be brought to heel sooner or later, and when that day comes, you will get your justice. But," Buckingham clapped his hands, "there will be time later to discuss such matters." His eyes settled on Margaret, who was standing a few paces behind Jasper. "This must be the girl you intend my son to marry?"

"Yes, your Grace." With a smile, Jasper gently took Margaret's hand, ushering her forward. "May I introduce my sister-in-law, the Countess of Richmond, Lady Margaret Beaufort?"

Margaret dropped into a low curtsey, her head bowed. "Your Grace."

"Welcome to Greenfield, Lady Margaret. You must be tired after your long journey. Your mother arrived this morning, and I believe she is anxious to see you."

Margaret smiled. "My mother has always been very attentive in her care of me," she replied smoothly.

Jasper tried to suppress his laugh with a cough. He'd met Lady Welles, as she was now called, only once before, at Margaret and Edmund's wedding, but he had heard enough from Margaret to know there was little fondness or maternal love between mother and daughter.

"And when will I meet your son? I am keen to make his acquaintance," Margaret continued, ignoring Jasper.

"Henry is busy with business in Newport at the moment. He will return in time for supper, and you will be able to meet him then. In the meantime, I imagine you may want to rest after your journey." He waved forward a servant. "Rooms have been prepared for you, and I hope they prove to be to your satisfaction."

"Thank you, your Grace," Margaret replied, bobbing into a curtsey before following the servant into the house. Jasper made to follow, but Buckingham intercepted him.

"I'm afraid, Pembroke, I must keep you from your rest for a while longer; there is much that we need to discuss, this marriage and William Herbert amongst them."

* * *

"She seems an impressive young woman," Buckingham remarked, settling into a chair in his study.

"She most certainly is," Jasper agreed, joining him by the fire, quietly hoping that whatever Buckingham wanted to discuss would be brief. He was exhausted and desperately wanted to bathe before the evening's meal.

"And you have not considered marrying her yourself?" Buckingham continued. "Not to disparage my son, but you are a more eligible choice of husband."

"You sound like my father. I am flattered you think so, but no. Her safety is the priority, and your son can offer her protection that I cannot. My proximity to the king leaves me too exposed, as it did my brother. Not to disparage your son either, but she will attract less attention being married to him."

"There are certainly advantages to being the second son. Not that I imagine you benefit from them any more, if you ever even did – you always seemed the elder, even when Edmund was alive."

"At times I felt it too. Then again, I wonder how much that was symptomatic of the situation we found ourselves in. It is hard to live as a carefree second son when your father is imprisoned and your only other family is the King of England."

"Indeed. Even more so when that king has been incapacitated. I wonder, has that been cause for resentment?"

"You question my loyalty?" Jasper bristled.

"Not question, challenge. As I must do any man since St Albans," Buckingham explained.

Jasper considered the duke. "In that case, there is nothing for me to say save that I believe my actions both before and since that dark day speak for the truth in my heart. And what of you?"

"I admit I am frustrated at the lack of action since St Albans," Buckingham replied candidly, showing no surprise at having the question turned on him. "The violence unleashed there cannot be brushed aside, whatever our peace-loving king may wish. I would counsel him to action."

Jasper nodded. "I share those frustrations, yet if we advise him too strongly does that not play into York's hands? It is not the king he seeks to usurp but those of us that advise him."

"Come now, you do not really believe York will be content to stop with the king's advisors?" Buckingham chided.

"You think he desires the crown?" Jasper asked aghast. He had been harbouring the same fears, but to hear the words spoken aloud, and by someone so central at court, still shocked him.

"And you do not? Think about where we find ourselves, Pembroke. Old Somerset, God rest his soul, was the one who York singled out as the focus of his ire. And now he is dead, and does York sit quietly satisfied with his work? No, he stokes up support, riles men to anger – lets the likes of William Herbert loose on the unsuspecting and believes he does not have to answer for the consequences."

"You do not need to remind me of that," Jasper replied curtly.

"Of course. I meant no disrespect. Merely to prove the point. Never forget, traitor's blood runs in York's veins, and blood will out."

"If it is as you say, then how can it be resolved? Despite everything, the king loves York and will not let him be dismissed, whatever the queen might wish. While York remains in the king's grace, how can we move against him?" Jasper pressed.

Buckingham spread his hands with a shake of his head." We cannot. We can only bide our time and wait for the moment that York puts a foot wrong. When he does, we must be ready to act."

"You make it sound as if we are at war."

Buckingham assessed Jasper sadly with eyes that had seen too much. "That is precisely where we find ourselves, and I fear it will tear this country apart before it is resolved."

* * *

During supper, Margaret watched Jasper intently, captivated by the change in him. She had only ever seen him in Pembroke. There, in the seclusion of his own castle, he had a relaxed and easy countenance, an informality that endeared him to those who served him. But here, surrounded by other noblemen, Jasper was a different man. He held himself with an understated yet undeniable confidence. Sitting alongside Buckingham at the head of the table, Jasper looked every inch the brother of the king.

"Margaret?"

Margaret pulled her eyes away from Jasper, turning her attention to Henry Stafford, her future husband. She had been shocked when she first saw him, for he looked so much older than she had expected, with receding hair and thin lines marking his face. But as the proverb said, eyes were the windows to the soul, and Stafford's were honest and kind.

"I'm sorry, my Lord, my thoughts were far away," she said, smiling apologetically.

"I was just asking what you enjoy doing with your time?"

"You wish to know the things I enjoy?" Margaret replied, failing to disguise the surprise in her voice.

Stafford chuckled softly at Margaret's expression. "Yes, of course. If we are to be married, I would like to know what you enjoy so I may be able to make you happy."

"Well, um," Margaret could feel herself blushing. "I like to spend my mornings in the nursery with my son."

"Ah, of course, young Henry. Tell me about him."

"He is wonderful. Truly, he brings me so much joy." Margaret's face lit up as she spoke. "Just the other day, he smiled for the first time! Jasper is, of course, utterly besotted with him. The way he dotes on Henry," she shook her head with a smile, "you would think him his son and not only his nephew."

"It is hard to lose a sibling, especially one with whom you have been close," Stafford remarked thoughtfully. "I'm sure having Henry eases Jasper's pain at losing Edmund so suddenly. That uncle and nephew have such a strong relationship will surely make it easier when you come to leave Pembroke?"

"Yes, I suppose it will," Margaret replied, bitterness creeping into her voice.

"Forgive me; I did not mean to upset you. Henry will be lucky to have a man such as Jasper as his guardian. But," Stafford placed his hand gently on Margaret's, "I want you to know that Henry will always be welcome at Bourne. When we are married, what is yours will be mine, and what is mine will be yours, and that includes your family. I would hate for you to feel like you had to keep the different parts of your life separate."

"Thank you, my Lord."

"Henry, please."

"Henry," she repeated, wondering if she would ever be able to say her future husband's name without first thinking of the son she had been forced to leave behind.

* * *

The windows in the low-beamed room were wide open, letting in a cool breeze carrying the tang of sea salt. Breathing deeply, Jasper leant back in his chair, allowing the sound of gulls and shouts of fisherman from down on the quay to wash over him. He'd been in Tenby for the past few days inspecting the progress of the improvements to the town's defences. The old walls, though impressive, had been built nearly two hundred years before, when arrows, not cannon, posed the greatest threat. To better protect the port from the realities of modern warfare, Jasper had ordered the walls be raised and reinforced. Even with the town's merchants begrudgingly covering half the expense, the work was still costing Jasper a small fortune. But, as he reasoned with himself, it would be worth it in the long run. Tenby's port provided valuable trade links to Europe, and if Fortune's Wheel was to turn, it would also serve as an effective escape route.

Leaning forward again, Jasper surveyed his desk, which was a mess of organised chaos. Resting on top of the varied assortment of papers and letters was an ornate certificate affixed with a large seal. Jasper sighed as his eyes scanned the document confirming papal dispensation for Margaret's marriage to Henry Stafford. He'd put it off for long enough; he needed to tell Margaret.

He found her reading quietly in the parlour, her face turned towards the sunlight streaming through the window, with Ianto laid out at her feet. Jasper had invited Margaret to Tenby, hopeful that the colourful town would lift her spirits. She'd been unusually taciturn on their journey back from Greenfield, and in the weeks since, she'd become more withdrawn, spending most of her time in the nursery with Henry. It had been six months since Jasper had swept into Lamphey's courtyard in a cloud of grief, and Margaret was almost unrecognisable from the girl who had stood quietly as he swore his impassioned oath to protect her. Though still petite, she'd grown taller in that time, and her figure had become more womanly. Dresses that used to hang limply now revealed the gentle swell of her breasts and hips, not that Jasper focused on such things. To do so brought back unwelcome memories of the conversations he'd had with his father shortly after Edmund's death about whether he should marry his brother's widow. Jasper had flatly refused. He'd told Buckingham it was for her safety that he had made such a choice, but it was more than that. His brother may have had few qualms about wedding and bedding a girl barely out of childhood, but he certainly did. It was a decision he had not once regretted, not even now the small, unexpected family they had made was about to be ripped apart.

"Confirmation of papal dispensation for your marriage to Stafford has arrived," Jasper announced, trying to keep his voice light. Margaret merely nodded, barely acknowledging his presence.

"I thought you'd be pleased?" he persevered. Still, he was met with silence.

"Margaret?"

"Thank you for bringing me the news," she responded quietly, closing her book, still avoiding Jasper's gaze. She stood, smoothing her skirts. "Now, if you'll excuse me," she continued, making for the door.

"Margaret, wait," Jasper said, reaching out to catch her arm as she passed him.

"You've barely said two words to me since we left Greenfield. Something is troubling you. I wish you would talk to me," he implored softly.

"What do you want me to say, Jasper?" she replied sharply, pulling her arm from his grip. "That I want to stay in Pembroke with you and my son? Is that what you want to hear? It serves no purpose for me to voice such thoughts aloud." Hot tears pricked her eyes, but she refused to let Jasper see her cry. "As soon as my year of mourning is finished, I will marry him. There is no other option for me, so do not dare tempt with visions of an impossible future." She fled from the room, leaving a bewildered Jasper standing alone.

Jasper rubbed his forehead. *"Duw helpa fi,"* he muttered to himself, slumping into a chair. Try as he might, he did not know how to soothe Margaret's anguish. What words had he for a mother soon to be separated from her child? This next chapter of her life was one she must undertake without him, and Jasper despaired at how useless that reality made him feel.

Behind him, the floorboard creaked. Standing quickly, he turned to see Margaret in the doorway, her cheeks wet with tears. "I'm sorry," she said simply.

"Come here," he gestured, pulling her into a tight embrace.

"Pushing you away is the last thing I wish to do," Margaret mumbled into Jasper's shoulder.

"It will take more than that to push me away," he chuckled admonishingly, quietly relieved that the tension between them had melted away.

5

August 1457

I t was peaceful inside Carmarthen's old Franciscan church. The air was cool, and the lingering smell of incense reminded Jasper of his childhood at Barking Abbey. He'd arrived in Carmarthen just a few hours before on his first official visit since his appointment as the castle's new constable. Once the initial formalities had been dispensed with, he'd slipped discretely away, leaving his clerk to deal with any urgent matters. It had been a year since Jasper had watched his brother march away for the last time. A year with grief as his constant companion, ever-present even in moments of happiness. Yet standing in the church where Edmund was buried, Jasper finally felt some sort of peace come over him, though not the complete closure he might have hoped for. That would not be achieved until William Herbert was brought to justice. For too long, he had allowed Herbert the freedom to incite unrest in South Wales, unable to come to terms with his former councillor's betrayal. But no longer. If Herbert was not willing to present himself at court to answer the charges laid against him, then Jasper would happily drag him there himself. Carmarthen was just a stopping point on his journey east towards Monmouthshire and Herbert's home. Apparently he'd been hiding nearby in the Black Mountains since spring, afraid of what was coming for him, not that that made any difference to Jasper. He'd already vowed not to return to Pembroke until he had his brother's captor in chains, and he'd scour the whole of South Wales if that's what it took. Lighting a candle, Jasper said a prayer for Edmund's soul, and then, with a final glance at his brother's grave, strode out into the summer heat, his mind focused on the task at hand.

* * *

Rising up ahead of them like a crown upon the ridge, there was a magnificence to Raglan that was almost breathtaking. With the sun beating down on its pale sandstone walls, it made Pembroke seem bleak by comparison, and only served to increase the anger burning inside Jasper's heart. How dare Herbert enjoy such grandeur while Edmund had lain dying in Carmarthen's dank dungeon? Crossing the bridge over a deep moat, Jasper reined in his horse with a look of boredom as two guards stepped out to halt their progress through the great gates. He could tell a man's experience with weapons just from how he held them, and judging by the stance of the two guards before him, Jasper doubted that either had ever had much cause to use the long pikes they carried. Still, they did their best to project an air of authority, as the burlier of the two demanded to know what business they had at Raglan.

"I am the Earl of Pembroke, half-brother to King Henry," Jasper responded. "We are not here for violence, merely to speak with Lady Anne."

"We were not told of your visit," the guard called back.

"No, it was unplanned. Still, I imagine Lady Anne will want to hear what we have to say," Jasper explained, rapidly losing patience.

"I'm sorry, my Lord," the guard stammered. "We were told not to admit anyone."

Jasper clenched his jaw in annoyance. "I said we were not here for violence, but make no mistake: we will resort to it if that is what is needed to ensure we are heard," he replied, the hand not holding the reins flexing around the hilt of his sword hanging from his belt.

The guard gulped and shared a glance with his companion before shrinking back against the walls. "Right decision," Jasper muttered, leading his men past the guards and through the gates into Raglan's cobbled courtyard.

While the others watched the horses, Jasper beckoned his captain follow him into the shade of the entrance hall. What he had said to the guards had been the truth: he had no intention of bringing violence within Raglan's walls. Yet Herbert's family made him vulnerable, and after weeks of scouring most of South Wales without sight or sound of the man, it was time to exploit that vulnerability. He'd already shown more restraint than he knew Herbert would have exercised had the situation been reversed.

Ignoring the servants that tried to intercept them, Jasper and his captain made their way through the castle. They found Herbert's wife waiting for them in the great hall. With her children gathered around her and her dress cut to draw attention to the swell of her stomach, she appeared the very picture of feminine innocence. But Jasper knew it was all a ruse. Indeed, when Lady Anne saw who her uninvited guest was, she shooed her children away with their nursemaid and fixed Jasper with a steady gaze. "I wondered how long it would take you to come here."

Jasper spread his arms as he crossed the room. "Lady Anne, how wonderful it is to see you again after so long," he announced with a saccharine smile. "Clearly I must congratulate you on the happy news of your condition. Another child to fill your expanding nursery, William must be overjoyed."

Lady Anne regarded him as she might a beggar on the side of the road. "Save your platitudes. He's not here."

"Rather too conveniently, it would seem," Jasper replied, dropping the pretence. "Not to be indelicate, but it appears he was here more recently than my reports suggested."

Lady Anne shrugged. "I cannot speak for your spies, only myself – and he has not been at Raglan for some weeks now."

"Then where is he?"

"You came all this way without knowing where he is?" Lady Anne asked with mock incredulity. "My Lord, forgive me, but that seems rather short-sighted. What a pity that the effort of such an arduous journey is to be wasted."

"Do not test me, Madam. You will find my patience has already worn thin."

"I cannot possibly fathom what you mean."

Jasper took a step forward. "Do you think me a fool?"

"My Lord?"

"A fool, Lady Anne, do you think me one?"

"No, sir."

"Then why do you play these games? You forget that I know you. That I know your husband also. And so I ask again, where is he?"

"I play no games, my Lord. I do not know where he is."

"You expect me to believe he left you here, in your current condition, and did not mention when he might return?"

"I expect you to believe it, because it is the truth."

Jasper smiled tightly. "You'll forgive me, madam, if I do not take your word for that. The William I knew would not have abandoned his wife like this."

Lady Anne lifted her chin. "Well then, maybe you do not know my husband as well as you thought you did?"

Jasper's grey eyes met her stare. "No, I can't have, otherwise my brother might yet still live," he replied, his voice menacingly low.

Lady Anne swallowed, her hand moving unconsciously to cover her stomach. "I do not know where he is," she repeated quietly, devoid of her earlier bluster.

Jasper considered the woman before him for a moment. He could feel the anger simmering within him, demanding to be heard. Another man might have felt justified to take some vengeance, here in the serenity of Herbert's home. But not Jasper. He'd already allowed his emotions to push him beyond his usual boundaries; he would not let them lead him any further astray. Taking a conscious step back, he noted with a sense of shame the way Lady Anne relaxed now that there was distance between them once more.

"Whether he is here or not, the fact remains that your husband must answer for his crimes. He cannot hide forever. You may tell William, when you next see him, that justice is coming for him, as sure as day follows night." With that he left Lady Anne to consider her husband's fate in the grandeur of Raglan's great hall.

He caught the sleeve of his captain as they walked back into the sunshine. "Watch the castle," he whispered in his ear. "Herbert will hear of our visit soon enough, if he hasn't already, and when he does he will be compelled to check his family remains safe. That is how we will ensnare him."

* * *

Sat in an upstairs room of some small village inn, Jasper had to admit he was near breaking point. Herbert should have appeared by now, but over a week had passed since their visit to Raglan, and there was still no sign. He'd put all his faith in this plan; if it didn't work then he wasn't sure where that left him. True, Herbert couldn't hide forever, but the more time that passed since Edmund's death, the less interest others had in trying to bring his captor to justice. Jasper could already sense in the slow movements of his men as they prepared their horses for yet another day of fruitless searching that their resolve was beginning to wane. If he didn't find Herbert by the end of the summer then the chance would be lost forever.

Jasper rubbed his face. What he would give to be back in Pembroke, sitting with Margaret and Henry in the solar. He missed them more than he had ever thought he would. Now that Margaret's wedding date was set, the months seemed to be flying by, and Pembroke would certainly be an empty place without her. But at least there was always Ianto, who, at this moment, was lying loyally next to his chair, his great head resting on Jasper's foot. With a sigh, Jasper returned his attention to the scout's report he'd been studying.

Suddenly there was the sound of a commotion in the courtyard, shouts ringing out. Ianto was immediately alert, a low growl reverberating in his throat. "Easy," Jasper murmured as he stood, his hand instinctively going to the dagger at his belt. He spun quickly as one of his men burst abruptly through the door.

"We've got him, my Lord!" he exclaimed excitedly, his words almost drowned out by Ianto's barking.

"*Taw!*" Jasper said sharply in Welsh, and the wolfhound fell quiet. He turned back to the man in the doorway.

"We've got Herbert, my Lord," the man continued, breathing heavily. "We discovered him trying to sneak back into Raglan, just like you said he would. The men rode him down as he was trying to escape!"

"Where is he now?"

"They're bringing him into the village now. I rode ahead to give you the news."

"When he arrives, bring him up here straight away," Jasper ordered.

"Yes, my Lord, of course," the man replied, running from the room.

Jasper ran a hand through his hair as he paced the room, his mind whirring. He had a few minutes to compose himself. He needed to handle this in the right way. He couldn't let his emotions get the better of him. Coming to a halt, he focused on his breathing until his pounding heart returned to a steady rhythm. Voices sounded on the stairs. Jasper turned towards the door, ready to face his brother's former captor.

William Herbert was escorted into the room by two guards, his hands bound before him with rough rope. Leaning back against the table, attempting the nonchalant air of someone fully in control, Jasper assessed the man before him. Despite the reports, it was clear Herbert hadn't been living rough in the mountains. His clothes were too smart, his hair and face too clean, though there was a trickle of blood running down from a small cut above his eye. Conscious of Jasper's gaze, Herbert drew himself up to his full height, jutting out his chin.

"Tudor," he drawled arrogantly, as though it were Jasper held captive.

"Seems as though your luck has finally run out, William. The comforts of Raglan must feel like a distant memory. It is time you answered for my brother's death," Jasper said, his voice even and cold.

"I had no hand in it, he was alive and well when I left Carmarthen," Herbert retorted sarcastically, his eyes wide with mock confusion.

"As alive and well as your wife was when I left her at Raglan?" Jasper asked, satisfied by the wild panic that filled Herbert's eyes.

"What have you done to her?" he demanded, struggling against the guards' grip. "I swear to God if you've done anything to harm her I'll—"

"You'll what? I think you'll find it is you in chains, not I," Jasper replied. "In any case, your wife is perfectly fine. Unlike my brother."

His panic relieved, Herbert's sneer returned, and Jasper silently cursed himself for not prolonging his distress.

"What do you want me to say?" Herbert asked. "That it was pathetically easy to take the castle? That I'd expected Edmund to put up a bit more of a fight?" Herbert paused, his eyes sparkling with delight at the obvious effort it was taking Jasper to control his rising anger. "Or would you prefer me to say that it was exactly as I expected?" he continued more slowly with a smirk. "After all, with a servant for a father and whore-queen for a mother, Edmund was never going to be—"

In a few quick strides, Jasper had crossed the room. He grabbed Herbert by the collar and slammed him against the wall. "How dare you speak in such a way?" he snarled, his face only inches from Herbert's.

"What are you going to do, Jasper? Kill me? Is that what you do to old friends?" Herbert asked, still smirking despite the pressure on his windpipe.

The thought flashed through Jasper's mind. It would be so easy. No one would know. His men were utterly loyal to him and wouldn't lose any sleep over one less Yorkist sympathiser. The familiar weight of his dagger on his belt seemed to taunt him, but Jasper shook his head.

"Do not talk to me of friendship. You showed where your true loyalties lay when you attacked my brother. And no, William, I will not kill you," Jasper replied, his voice now dangerously quiet. "I have too much respect for your wife to make her a widow. You will be sent to the Tower. I hear the Duke of Exeter is constable now, and you know as well as I how much he hates traitors."

Jasper smiled in satisfaction as all the colour drained from Herbert's face. "Th— Th— the king will show me clemency," he stammered, fear overcoming his previous swagger.

"He may, and if he does, then he is a better man than I," Jasper said with a shrug. "But the king is a busy man," he continued, his voice hardening. "I wonder, will he consider your wellbeing a priority after the disdain you showed for his half-brother's?"

With a shove, he released his hold on Herbert, leaving him slumped against the wall. Stripped of his previous swagger, Herbert cut a pathetic figure. "Please. Jasper," he began to plead. "Have I not served you well over the years? Edmund would not want—"

Jasper rounded on him. "Do not speak to me of what my brother would have wanted! You lost that right when you left him in that godforsaken cell." With a click of his fingers, the guards stepped forward to restrain Herbert once more. "You'll be sent to London in the morning. Do give my regards to Exeter when you see him. I hope he leaves at least something for your wife to recognise you by." With that, Jasper turned his back on Herbert, ignoring his pleas as he was dragged away.

* * *

"I let him rile me, Margaret. I knew he would try to get under my skin, and yet I was incapable of resisting it," Jasper said, throwing his hands up in exasperation. The two of them were sitting in Pembroke's solar. For once, the great stone fireplace was cold, the windows thrown open to let in the summer evening air. In one corner, Henry slept peacefully in his cot, which Jasper had ordered be placed in the room so that Margaret could spend as much time as possible with him in her last remaining months at Pembroke.

"You're being too hard on yourself," Margaret responded, putting down the needlework she had been concentrating on. "You faced the man responsible for your brother's death, and you let him leave with his life. If you'd really lost control, he would have been dead as soon as the words left his mouth."

Jasper looked at Margaret, his eyes wide with surprise.

"Oh, do not look at me like that, Jasper," she admonished. "I am well acquainted with the ways of men."

"Oh really?" Jasper smiled, wandering over to Henry.

"Yes, really, and you are amongst the most honourable I know. You let Herbert live, not because you're weak but because you are strong. Strong enough to let your head rule even when your heart was demanding to be heard."

Jasper shook his head. "When did you become so wise, Margaret?"

"I'm not the scared girl you rescued from Lamphey any more."

"No, you most certainly are not," Jasper chuckled.

"What will happen to Herbert?"

"The king will pardon him, of that I am certain," Jasper replied, absentmindedly rocking Henry's cot back and forth. "Punishing Herbert would only strengthen York's hand, and the king's position is already weak enough. Even the people are beginning to voice their support for York."

"But why? Do they not see how faithfully the king has served them for the last thirty or more years?"

"The people do not see him like we do, Margaret. Whereas we see his faith and compassion, they see only a frail and powerless king. They're afraid. Afraid that his perceived weakness emboldens our enemies across the water. If Henry cannot keep the peace within his own court, then how can he possibly defend the country from France or Spain? But, enough of politics," Jasper said more brightly, walking back over to where Margaret sat by the empty fireplace. "How about another game of chess?"

6

January 1458

B asking in the winter sun, the red sandstone of Maxstoke Castle seemed aglow. With its intricately landscaped garden petrified in a thick layer of sparkling frost, Margaret had to admit she could not have chosen a more beautiful location for her wedding. The rain threatened by the previous day's thick clouds had mercifully never materialised and the morning was bright and crisp. Margaret watched as her breath curled in the cold air. She'd escaped from her domineering mother to enjoy a moment of solitude before she became a wife once more, and the freedom she'd enjoyed in Pembroke was lost forever.

Margaret raised her eyes to the heavens and let out a deep sigh. To think this would be her third marriage. Well, technically, given she was seven at the time, the first one to John de la Pole did not truly count but nevertheless, it was not a tally she'd ever expected to reach, let alone before she turned fifteen. At least this time she knew what to expect. She shuddered slightly at the memory of her wedding night with Edmund and said a silent prayer that Stafford would show her more kindness in their marital bed. There was a sound behind her and Margaret spun around quickly, an excuse ready on her lips. But instead of her mother coming to berate her, it was Jasper, cradling a sleeping Henry in his arms.

She had been adamant that Jasper and Henry would accompany her on the journey to Warwickshire. They'd been a sort of family, the three of them together in Pembroke, and the last few months had been some of the happiest she had known. But despite her joy at hearing Henry's first words or the satisfaction she'd felt when she'd finally beaten Jasper at chess, the preceding weeks had been tinged with sadness. She wouldn't be there to see Henry's first tottering steps or be able to sit up late into the night putting the world to rights with Jasper. Tomorrow, after her wedding night was over and the remnants of the banquet had been cleared away, she would have to stand at Maxstoke's gate and watch Jasper and Henry ride away. Even the thought of it made her eyes well with tears.

Jasper, ever observant, took a step towards her, his brow furrowed in concern. "What's wrong?"

"It's nothing," Margaret replied, forcing a smile as she brushed away the tears. She held out her hands and Jasper passed Henry to her. It felt right to have her son in her arms. She still marvelled at every inch of his little body and the love she felt for him was almost suffocating.

Jasper gently stroked Henry's head, his downy hair soft beneath his calloused hand. "You know you never have to hide from me, Margaret."

Margaret hesitated for a moment. She didn't want Jasper to think her weak but if she could not confide in him then who else was there? She took a steadying breath. "I know I was the one that instigated this, yet I have to admit that now the day is upon me I am nervous."

"I would be concerned if you weren't," Jasper said reassuringly. "You are a truly remarkable woman, Margaret. I remember how you looked when you walked out from Lamphey." Jasper smiled at the memory. "Even with your world crumbling around you, you still held yourself with such poise and bravery. Stafford is lucky to have a woman such as you for his wife," he continued, squeezing her hand. "Just as my brother was," he added, more softly. "If Henry has inherited even an ounce of your strength then he will be a force to be reckoned with."

Margaret lifted her head to look at Jasper, surprised to see his eyes were also filled with tears.

"Thank you, Jasper," she replied, her voice thick with sincerity. "For everything. I could imagine no one better to be Henry's guardian. He already adores you, and I know you will raise him to be a man of whom his father would be proud."

As if understanding he was being spoken about, Henry began to stir in his mother's arms. Margaret chuckled. "I think that's a sign we should be getting back. My mother will be starting to worry I've run off."

Slowly, the three of them began to make their way back along the path to the castle. "I wouldn't be surprised if, in a few months, he doesn't even remember who I am," Margaret said, trying to sound carefree but failing to hide her distress at the thought.

Jasper stopped. "Do not talk such nonsense, Margaret. He will remember you because I will tell him about you. And in any case, the gates of Pembroke will never be closed to you. It is as much your home as it is mine. Once you are settled into your new life as Lady Stafford, it would be my pleasure to host you and your husband."

"But with everything that's happening—" Margaret trailed off.

"These are uncertain times, Margaret, there's no point denying it, and I fear the future will be even more precarious. But that need not impact our relationship. I have come to love you, Margaret, as a brother loves a sister, and I will always do everything in my power to keep you from harm's way, even if from a distance. You will be safe with Stafford and, in time, I hope you will be happy." A smile returned to Jasper's face as they continued walking. "Who knows, he might even let you win at chess!" he joked, playfully elbowing her in the ribs.

* * *

Like the wedding ceremony earlier in the day, the evening's banquet had been a truly extravagant affair. Dish after dish of beautifully presented food, each more delicious than the last, had been brought out from the kitchens until the long tables had groaned under the weight of them. Up in the gallery, musicians played, and the hall was filled with the hum of dozens of conversations.

Jasper was positioned a few seats away from Margaret on the top table, looking out over the assembled guests. She looked resplendent in her wedding gown, and the jewels around her neck glowed in the candlelight. He was pleased when he glanced her way to see how animated she was, a smile never far from her lips. Her voice had rung out clear and unwavering in the chapel when she said her vows, solemnly committing to obey her new husband till death parted them. Jasper had smiled at that. The words obey and Margaret did not belong in the same sentence, save when it concerned God. Stafford had been incredibly attentive to Margaret all evening, refilling her cup and engaging her in conversation. It embarrassed Jasper to remember how Edmund had behaved at his own wedding banquet. How he'd barely acknowledged his young wife, choosing instead to drown himself in ale.

Jasper stifled a yawn. The hour was late, and tiredness was setting in. Though he wanted to, he could not excuse himself before the bride and groom departed for the night. A passing servant tried to fill his cup with more wine, but Jasper placed his hand over it. He had a long ride ahead of him, and did not need to contend with a pounding head at the same time.

A hush descended amongst the guests as the new Lord and Lady

Stafford rose from the table. Jasper caught Margaret's eye as she stood, giving her a small smile and an almost imperceptible nod of reassurance. Taking a deep breath, Margaret returned his smile. Threading her arm through Stafford's, the new couple processed from the hall. As the doors swung shut behind them, Jasper felt the curtain fall on an unexpected chapter in his life.

JANUARY 1458

7

March 1458

T he noises from Brook Street floated up into the bedchamber. Jasper stretched. Next to him, Jane, the maid from the inn stirred, her auburn hair glowing in the early spring sun that reached like fingers through the windows. Absent-mindedly, Jasper gently stroked the soft strands, enjoying the feeling on his skin. He'd already been awake for what seemed like hours, the thoughts whirring around his head making it impossible to go back to sleep despite his best attempts. London seemed a world away from Pembroke. It had a unique energy that Jasper relished, though he was always thankful when he managed to escape back to Wales. It was sixteen years since the king had brought him and Edmund to live at court. He could still remember the combination of fear and excitement he'd felt when they'd arrived in London for the first time; how it had made his palms clammy and stomach jump. Compared to the tranquillity of Barking Abbey, court had been an assault on the senses, and it took a while for Jasper to adjust to his new surroundings. Back then, hushed whispers had followed them wherever they went. It wasn't long, though, before Jasper's quick wit and skill with a sword had won over the other boys at court. Soon enough, even those at the highest levels of the peerage had come to respect his intelligence and astute political understanding. By the time he and Edmund had been officially recognised as King Henry's half-brothers and raised to the rank of earls, they were both well-respected members of court, and the snide comments about their unusual parentage had long since abated. To think how much had changed in the years since then. The betrayals and allegiances, the good men taken too soon from this life, his brother amongst them. Even now, he still felt Edmund's absence when walking through Westminster's corridors. Jasper rubbed his eyes. It did him no good to dwell on the past, especially not today.

After Margaret's wedding, he had returned Henry to Pembroke and then almost immediately set off again for London. He'd now been in the city for nearly two months, awaiting the culmination of the reconciliations the king had hoped to achieve when he called all the nobles to attend another Great Council. The fact violence had not broken out between the heavily armed retinues accompanying many of the nobles was a small miracle and one that Jasper gave thanks for. The dozen or so men he had brought with him paled in comparison to the six hundred soldiers the Earl of Warwick had brought from Calais. All dressed in red and wearing the earl's bear and ragged staff badge, they looked more like a small army than peaceful retainers, and Jasper could only hope they continued to stay away from the Percy brothers' similarly large force. There would be no chance of reconciliation if a fight broke out before they even made it to St Paul's. The tension was palpable, and understandably so. Even he had been unable to hide his incredulity when he'd first received the king's summons. Of course, his loyalty to his half-brother was unwavering, but he still couldn't fully swallow the idea of parading through the streets of London hand in hand with York and his allies as though the last few years were merely a bad dream. Jasper pinched the bridge of his nose and sighed. It was going to be a long day.

Pushing back the covers, he swung his legs over the edge of the bed and stretched. He felt a hand on his back. Looking over his shoulder, he smiled at the sight of Jane, her brow furrowed with sleep.

"Is it not still early, my Lord?" she asked, her voice gravelly. "Come back to bed."

Jasper leant back for a kiss. Her lips were soft and warm, and he had to pull away before he lost himself in them entirely. "Not today. I'm expected at Westminster."

Jane flopped back onto the pillow in defeat, an arm thrown over her face. "You're always expected at Westminster," she complained, as Jasper began to dress.

"That is rather the point of my being in London in the first place," he chuckled. "It would be more surprising if I weren't."

"I suppose," Jane conceded. "Still, I'd prefer you stayed in bed."

"As would I. Believe me. A day with you would be infinitely more enjoyable than traipsing through the city with York and his cronies."

"I should hope so! What is the point of that anyway?" Jane asked, propping herself up on an elbow. "It seems an odd way to resolve a quarrel."

"It is less the act itself, more what it represents. What better way to demonstrate unity than former enemies walking hand in hand," Jasper explained, buttoning his new doublet. "And it is more than a mere quarrel. The scars of St Albans cut deep, though this parade might yet heal them."

"You think it will?"

"If the king believes it, then so must I."

Jane scrunched her face. "You don't sound convinced."

"Is it that obvious?" Jasper replied with a grimace.

"Nothing a smile won't fix. In any case, you look the part," she commented approvingly as Jasper appraised himself in the looking glass.

"Let us hope it is enough," he murmured quietly at the stony-faced reflection staring back at him.

* * *

Westminster Hall, the beating heart of court for nearly four hundred years, was alive with activity as elaborately dressed nobles and knights thronged beneath its hammer-beam roof. Yet despite the extravagance of their dress, it was not jubilation that filled the hall but a distinct sense of unease coupled with simmering violence. Everyone was on edge, and Jasper flinched when a strong hand slapped him on the shoulder.

"Looks like I'm with you, Pembroke."

Turning, Jasper took in the pinched face and tight smile of Sir John Neville, the Earl of Warwick's younger brother. The same age as Jasper, he held himself with an arrogance that was seemingly a prerequisite for being a member of the Neville family.

"Sir John," Jasper nodded in acknowledgement, consciously drawing himself up to his full height. If Neville's penetrating eyes noted the movement, then he said nothing, turning instead to look at the rest of the group.

"Well, this is a disaster waiting to happen," he remarked, his voice dripping with disdain.

Scanning his eyes over the other pairs, Jasper could see his point. The queen was barely able to disguise her disgust at having to stand next to York, while Henry Holland, the Duke of Exeter, looked like he wanted to run Warwick through with a sword. Luckily for all those present, weapons had been forbidden. Meanwhile, the king, standing alone, bedecked in his royal robes and crown, looked serenely untroubled by the tension that hung heavy in the air. Jasper had to admit that, compared to the others, he'd been fortunate with his partner. While their relationship was now strained, he and Neville had been friends once, back in those early days at court, and the two of them had been knighted together in the same ceremony at Greenwich.

Once the participants were set, it was Neville's grey-haired father, the Earl of Salisbury alongside the young Duke of Somerset who led them out through Westminster's Great Gate onto King Street and towards St Paul's, as bells tolled out across the city. Of all the pairs, theirs was the most symbolic. With almost four decades between them, the two men reflected the range of generations caught up in the hostilities. At just twenty-two, Somerset was a man hungry for revenge. Seriously wounded at St Albans, he'd watched helplessly as his father was brutally murdered by York's supporters. Holding Salisbury's hand in a vice-like grip that conveyed none of the companionship King Henry hoped to encourage, Somerset epitomised a generation unleashed by violence.

Towards the back of the procession, Jasper's eyes constantly surveyed the crowds lining the streets, wary of any sudden movement. The majority of those gathered were armed soldiers, with only the bravest of Londoners risking a glimpse of the spectacle. Without the familiar weight of his sword on his belt, Jasper felt vulnerable. It was not a feeling he was comfortable with. The dagger hidden in his doublet gave him some small comfort, but he highly doubted he was the only one who'd taken such precautions. For the most part, he and Neville had kept up a relatively amicable conversation during the procession. However, once inside St Paul's, the small talk soon gave way to silence as they stood to listen to Thomas Bouchier, the Archbishop of Canterbury, deliver the Sacrament of Penance.

Jasper shifted uncomfortably. He was wearing too many layers for the warm spring air, and he could feel a trickle of sweat running down his neck. Distracted, he stared up at the vaulted ceiling. Anyone watching would think he was taking a moment for private contemplation, when in reality he was trying to understand how such seemingly delicate stone ribs were preventing the whole roof from collapsing in on them. He could feel his eyes become heavy as he let the Archbishop's monotonic Latin wash over him. Jasper's head lolled forward, starting him. Next to him, he heard John Neville scoff. Right then, Jasper would have liked nothing more than to wipe the smile off Neville's face, but he resisted the urge, turning instead to look at his half-brother, who was listening intently to the sermon, his face filled with hope. Despite his best attempts, Jasper could not share the king's optimism. Resentment at the lack of justice for Edmund's death still gnawed at his heart, and if the anger shining in Somerset's eyes was any indication, he was not alone in harbouring feelings of revenge.

As if reading his thoughts, Archbishop Bouchier raised his voice, the words of John's Gospel echoing around the Cathedral; *"Quorum remiseritis peccata, remittuntur eis: et quorum retinueritis, retenta sunt."* Whose sins you forgive, they are forgiven; and whose sins you shall retain, they are retained. Jasper shook his head, smiling ruefully at the hollowness of the whole spectacle.

8

April 1459

After days of unrelenting rain, the sun streaming through the branches made Jasper's soul soar as it warmed his face. All around him the wood was a riot of colour, the yellow of daffodils standing out against the vibrant green of new leaves. Jasper let out a contented sigh. Here in the countryside around Pembroke was one of the few places he could truly allow himself to relax. Usually, he would have raced through the trees, whooping in exhilaration at the thrill of galloping at breakneck speed. But he'd discovered a new type of enjoyment, walking steadily with Henry perched in front of him. There was something comforting about the weight of Henry's little body leaning back into his chest as they rocked in time to the rolling gait of his father's old warhorse. As constant as the mountain lakes for which he was named, Tarn plodded along the worn path, his large hooves never faltering, unfazed by the tugs on his thick mane from Henry's tightly balled fists. Ianto loped alongside them, occasionally bounding off into the undergrowth in pursuit of some new, intriguing smell.

Even though Jasper knew the land like the back of his hand, riding out with Henry was like seeing it through a new pair of eyes. At the age of two, Henry was an inquisitive toddler, eagerly pointing at the birds that flew past. He chatted away happily in a garbled mix of English, French and Welsh that even Jasper struggled to understand and called out hello to any and every passer-by. The people of Pembroke had accepted Henry as if he were Jasper's own and indulged him accordingly, slipping him sweet cakes when Jasper pretended not to look. The fierce love he felt for the small bundle nestled in front of him had taken him by surprise. His days, when not filled with politics, were devoted to his nephew. He'd instructed the local Benedictine monks, just across the river at Monkton Priory, to prepare themselves to begin Henry's education, not that he was in any particular rush to send him into their care. Jasper enjoyed sitting with Henry before he went to bed, reading to him like Catherine had once done for him and Edmund. It was in those quiet moments that Jasper's thoughts would turn to Margaret. Though he kept her fully informed, he knew she missed her son terribly. He had hoped she would have visited by now, but then again the journey from Lincolnshire was not an easy one. He was pleased, though, to hear how well Margaret had settled into her new life. He'd been confident that Stafford would treat her with nothing but kindness. Nevertheless, it made him happy to hear of the freedoms Margaret had been afforded, and of her excitement at running her own home.

By the time they got back to Pembroke, the fresh air and soothing rocking of Tarn's rolling gait had lulled Henry into sleep. Taking care not to wake him, Jasper gently passed his limp body down to Joan. Dismounting, Jasper sneaked Tarn an apple before letting the stable boy lead him away. Shivering slightly in the cool evening air, he rubbed his hands together and headed inside to the solar where he knew his father would be waiting for him.

Over the preceding months, Owen had taken up semi-permanent residence at Pembroke. Though the king had granted his stepfather various properties over the years, Owen preferred to spend his time in this secluded corner of Wales. For his part, Jasper enjoyed the long evenings they spent together sitting by the fire in the solar, although Owen had been somewhat distracted in recent days. The arrival of a new half-brother had taken Jasper completely by surprise. At twenty-eight, he should have been the one having children, not his sixty-year-old father. Nevertheless, he couldn't begrudge Owen's excitement. Edmund's death had dulled some of his father's characteristic spark, and with the birth of little David Owen, Jasper could tell it was starting to brighten once again. The boy's mother, Beth, was a local girl, not much older than Jasper himself. Jasper had watched how his father treated her and could tell he cared for her, but even now there was a child, he doubted his father would take any steps to make their relationship official in the eyes of God.

"There's a letter there for you," said Owen, nodding over at the carved table by the window before returning to his papers.

"No doubt another instruction to attend to some far-flung dispute," Jasper replied with a resigned sigh. Picking up a small knife, he leant against the table as he sliced through the royal seal. He quickly scanned the scrawled writing, and then read it again to make sure his eyes weren't playing tricks on him. He hurried over to his father in excitement.

"You recall King Alfonso of Spain died a few months ago?" he asked.

Owen nodded absentmindedly, still engrossed in the papers he was reading. Jasper pressed on. "Well, his death means there's a vacancy in the Order of the Garter."

Jasper paused to let the news register with his father and was satisfied when Owen looked up, visible shock on his face. "This is a summons from the king. I'm to be invested at the end of this month."

Owen clapped his hands together, "Oh my boy, that is brilliant news, although I would have expected nothing less. It is time your devotion to the king was properly recognised. Let us call for some wine – a moment such as this should be celebrated."

* * *

Jasper's footsteps echoed off the stone floor as he followed a servant down the long corridors of Windsor Castle and out into the spring sunshine. Leaving the upper ward behind them, they made their way down the hill towards St George's Chapel, eventually coming to a halt within the galilee porch before a pair of ornately decorated ironwork doors.

"Please wait here," the servant said before scurrying away.

Had he been alone, Jasper would have indulged the urge to run his hand over the intricate metalwork and marvel at the craftsmanship. As it was, two other men stood within the porch, and instead he inclined his head to each in turn. "Dudley. Berner."

"Pembroke," they replied, acknowledged him with a nod. Like Jasper, they had dressed in their finest clothes, with tailored doublets made from richly coloured velvet. Both had fur-trimmed cloaks around their shoulders, though in Jasper's mind it was far too mild for such things. It struck him then, the difference in age between him and his companions, and for a moment he felt self-conscious of his relative youth. These were men who had proven themselves over a lifetime; Dudley had even accompanied the old king's body back from France. In comparison, what had Jasper done, save being born to this king's mother? Then again, Jasper reasoned to himself, he represented the new order; a generation that had never known another monarch, committed to defending the Crown whatever the personal cost.

They stood for a moment in anticipatory silence, before Berner leant forward, almost conspiratorially. "Have you heard the news from the Channel?" he asked.

"No?"

"Warwick has been attacking Spanish merchant ships, claiming he does so under the king's prerogative. It's been all the talk at court, by all accounts the ambassador could be heard shouting from outside the presence chamber, so incandescent was he with rage."

"That makes no sense," Jasper countered. "Warwick is the Captain of Calais, why would he start attacking the very ships he is meant to be protecting? Surely it is in his interests to keep the Channel free from piracy?"

"From others, yes, but that garrison he's amassed must be costing him a small fortune, and it's not as though he's receiving any funds from the crown."

"That is not a garrison," Dudley scoffed. "Nearly a thousand men? It's an army and everyone knows it."

"Indeed," Berner nodded eagerly, "and none more so than Buckingham. As Warden of the Cinque ports, he has responsibility for the coastline stretching from Hastings to Sandwich. Warwick's piracy undermines that position, making him appear weak."

"What does the king say?" Jasper asked.

"He's recalled Warwick to court, not that the earl shows any indication of obeying," Berner explained.

Dudley shook his head. "What has this country come to if an earl does not heed his king's summons? His father would never have stood for such a thing, old King Henry would have had Warwick strung up for such insolence."

"Yes, well this Henry has never shown any inkling of his father's spirit, has he?" Berners cut in. "No, too much of the mad French king's blood runs in his veins."

"It is no more than runs in mine," Jasper volleyed back, fixing his cold stare on the Baron.

Berners blanched. His eyes darted to Dudley appealing for an intervention that might alleviate the strained silence which had fallen.

Dudley cleared his throat. "So where is Warwick now?"

"If what I've heard is true, he's retreated to his northern heartlands," Berners replied, grasping the chance to move the conversation to firmer ground.

"To what end?"

"To prepare for war," Jasper said quietly, thinking back to his conversation with Buckingham at Greenfield.

"Exactly," Berners nodded.

"And what of York?" Dudley asked, voicing the question at the forefront of Jasper's mind.

"Ludlow," Berners confirmed. "Doing the same as his nephew. Mark my words, before the summer is out, we will have seen another unleashing of violence. And this time," he added quickly as trumpets began to sound from the other side of the ironwork, "it will gouge a division in this country that no amount of hand holding can heal."

With the ominous weight of those words still hanging in the air, the great doors finally swung open to reveal the splendour of St George's Chapel. Home to the Order of the Garter for more than a hundred years, the chapel was a riot of colour, bedecked with banners, each depicting the crest of a knight. On a day such as this, the stalls beneath the banners should have been filled, yet as Jasper cast his eyes around the chapel there seemed to be a large number of absences. The stall beneath the Duke of York's banner was unsurprisingly empty, but so too were Shrewsbury's and Fauconberg's, and even Norfolk was missing. No wonder the barons felt they could speak so candidly: not a single Yorkist supporter was in attendance, and as Jasper gazed at their banners he could not help but wonder for how much longer they would be allowed to hang in this hallowed place.

He forced himself to concentrate as the king approached him. "Your Grace," he said, bowing deeply.

"Brother."

Jasper looked up to see the king smiling at him and was aware of Berners shifting uncomfortably next to him, no doubt wondering whether his earlier insolence would be relayed to the king. Though frail, Jasper was reassured to see that his half-brother seemed lucid and his eyes had regained their usual spark. Beside the king stood several servants, all holding cushions bearing the knights' items of the Order. The Duke of Buckingham was also there, ready to assist the king in dressing Jasper in the vestments of the Order. First, a deep purple mantle was draped over his shoulders and fastened with elaborate cords. Next came a black velvet cap with a plume of feathers. Finally, Buckingham stepped forward to place the heavy gold collar around Jasper's neck. Composed of intricate heraldic knots, an enamelled figure of St George on horseback slaying a dragon was suspended underneath.

Once the collar was secured with white ribbons, the king spoke softly and slowly.

"Do you swear loyally to keep and observe the statutes of this Order as far as within your loyal ability is able?"

"I do so swear," Jasper responded, his voice clear.

"Kneel," Henry commanded.

Jasper sank onto his right knee as the king picked up a small blue strap which had the motto *Honi soit qui mal y pense* (Shame on him who thinks evil of it) embroidered in gold thread. The Chancellor of the Order's voice rang out as the king tied the garter above Jasper's left knee, his hands shaking slightly as he did so; "Wear this as the symbol of the most illustrious Order never to be forgotten or laid aside; may you stand firm, valiantly fight, courageously and successfully conquer."

Cheers went up around the Chapel as Jasper's banner was raised alongside the others. Composed of the royal coat of arms boarded in blue with golden martlets, it was a visual reminder of Jasper's connection to the king, and it made Jasper's heart swell with pride to have it suspended there for all to see. Whatever happened next, he knew on which side he would be standing.

9

November 1459

Usually a sanctuary for Benedictine monks, the chapter house of St Mary's Priory in Coventry was abuzz with the organised chaos that was Parliament. The room itself was a sea of red; scarlet parliamentary robes trimmed with ermine fur keeping the assembled lords warm in spite of the icy November rain lashing against the towering stained glass windows. The room was tightly packed with people, and as Jasper looked around it was clear almost all the lords loyal to King Henry, both temporal and spiritual, were in attendance. There was Buckingham whispering quietly with the Earl of Oxford, no doubt discussing the impending marriage of their children. To the left of them, Lord Clifford stood with his brother-in-law, the Earl of Devon, while, in an opposite corner, the Duke of Northumberland looked uncharacteristically jovial as he waited for confirmation of the punishment his family's great enemy, the Nevilles, would receive. Not that their sneering faces were there to hear their sentence. Berners had been correct in his ominous prediction. The oppressive heat of long summer days had indeed re-ignited violence, shaking the country from its restless slumber. The outcome had been less certain, and Jasper imagined it was one that the old baron might well be disappointed with.

York may have drawn first blood, but after all the anxious antic-ipation, it was not he who found himself on the ascending side of Fortune's Wheel. With his forces routed outside his castle at Ludlow by an indomitable Buckingham, York had been forced to flee. His supporters, Salisbury and his sons amongst them, had not been far behind. Supposedly, York was on his way to Ireland, no doubt eager to rekindle the relationships he'd forged during his time as Lieutenant. Once again Jasper was uneasy about the false sense of security offered by the Irish Sea. Fortune's Wheel was not bound by loyalty, it could turn against them just as quickly as it had against York.

Jasper shook the thought from his head, his eyes focusing on the figures presiding over the scene. Seated atop two gilded thrones were the king and queen. While Queen Marguerite sat ramrod straight, her husband was slumped slightly in his seat. Jasper was shocked by the change in his half-brother since he'd last seen him, at his investiture ceremony. The lucidity he had been so relieved to see then was gone, replaced instead by a vacant stare. But at least he was in attendance, Jasper reasoned, forcing himself to see some positives as he said a silent prayer that the king would not succumb to his illness once more.

Jasper pulled his attention back to the lectern as Sir Thomas Tresham, the Speaker of Parliament, cleared his throat. "My Lords, I thank you for your input. We will now adjourn for a moment before a decision is taken."

The room quickly descended into a cacophony of noise as multiple heated conversations began about the various merits of the proposal. Jasper smiled as Henry Beaufort, the Duke of Somerset made his way through the crowd. Dark-haired and handsome, at twenty-three Somerset had the knowledge and experience of a man at least a decade older.

"Congratulations, my friend," Jasper said, grasping Somerset's arm in welcome. "Captain of Calais? I do not imagine Warwick will give that title up without a fight!"

"No, I should not think he shall. Especially not now. From what I hear he is on his way there now with York's son Edward, Earl of March. Your uncle, the Duke of Burgundy has apparently already offered his support."

Jasper laughed ruefully. "Why am I not surprised? My mother always said Philip was only driven by his own self-interest, Now I suppose I have the proof. Interesting that Edward did not go to Ireland with his father. I hear York fled so quickly, he left his wife and two younger sons alone at Ludlow Castle."

Somerset shook his head in disgust. "I always knew the man lacked honour, but even I could not imagine his cowardice would bring him so low. Buckingham found Duchess Cecily standing in the main courtyard with her younger boys hiding behind her skirts. Maybe that is why Edward chose to accompany Warwick? To escape the shame of having such a father."

"Maybe," Jasper shrugged. "Regardless, it is fortunate that Buckingham found them and not his men. Cecily is a formidable woman, but those soldiers were hungry for a reward. I doubt they would have made any distinction between a Duchess and a serving girl that night," he added, though his concern for York's wife seemed to fall on deaf ears.

"Fortune's Wheel is an unpredictable mistress is she not?" Somerset continued as if Jasper had not spoken. "For those few days after Blore Heath, I admit I thought our cause was destined for failure, so decisive was Salisbury's victory. But then the rout at Ludlow? That will teach me to underestimate the loyalties of common Englishmen."

"Or more likely, the persuasiveness of a pardon and a heavy bag of coin!" Jasper added, with a wink.

Somerset laughed in agreement. "Which way will your vote fall?"

he asked, his face becoming serious once more.

"Obviously I will vote to punish York and the others. They are traitors and there can be no other recourse. The failure of the Loveday truce has proven that. But attainder? It will be as though they are dead. No – it will be worse than that. Their bloodlines will be corrupted. With a few strokes of the pen their families will be left with nothing; no income, no inheritance. Is it right to make innocent children suffer for the sins of their fathers?"

"Was it right that I was made to watch as my father's life was mercilessly taken?" Somerset spat vehemently, his eyes shining with anger.

Jasper held up his hands placatingly. "Peace Henry, I meant no offence. You are right of course, there are no innocents in this," he replied.

Somerset was silent for a moment. Jasper waited, only guessing at the horrors playing across his friend's mind. Once the duke had regained his composure he continued. "In any case, the king says he will try to keep the estates mostly intact, ready to be reclaimed if they submit."

"Maybe some will, but I doubt it. There will certainly be no pardon for York, not now, not ever, and he knows it." Jasper sighed. "In truth, Henry, I fear that rather than resolving the issue, this course of action will only worsen the divisions tearing this country apart. What incentive does York have now? If he is attainted we will have backed him into a corner. Either he fights or he lives in poverty and exile for the remainder of his years. You and I both know him well enough to know which of those options he will choose. Mark my words, York will return to wreak his vengeance on us."

"Well then, we will have to be prepared for when he decides to unleash his fury. I for one—" Somerset broke off as Speaker Tresham returned to the lectern. Around the room, conversations ended in

67

hushed silence.

"My Lords!" he declared, the acoustics of the room carrying his voice. "The question is that, should Richard Plantagenet, Duke of York, and twenty-six of his followers, the Earls of Salisbury and Warwick amongst them, be attainted for acts of treason committed against the Crown?" Speaker Tresham paused, surveying the room before he continued. "As many as there are of the opinion, say Content." Jasper joined in as every lord assembled called out in unison, the confirmation echoing off the stone. Speaker Tresham nodded. "And of the contrary, Not Content." The room remained silent. Not one person raised their voice in response; the only sound the wind howling outside.

"It is clear," Speaker Tresham proclaimed triumphantly. "The Contents have it, the Contents have it!"

Somerset leant in to Jasper. "Well then, we have made our move; now we must wait to see how York will respond."

10

May 1460

As it transpired, nothing was York's response, or at least nothing yet. And that was why Jasper found himself on a hillside in North Wales, squinting against the spring sunshine at one of the prizes York had carelessly abandoned in hasty retreat.

"It won't be long now," he called above the deafening roar of the cannon.

"You said that two weeks ago!" Owen shouted back.

Jasper smiled grimly. What had been intended as a quick assault had become a brutal war of attrition. They'd known the castle would put up resistance, but even their most pessimistic estimations had not anticipated it would withstand so many weeks of besiegement. It had been just after Christmas when the king had announced his decision to grant Jasper the Lordship of Denbigh. It was a great honour, and further recognition of the crucial role Jasper was playing in holding Wales. Yet it was the decision that he should hold the position jointly with his father that made the appointment truly special. Not even the not-so-insignificant matter of the castle being in Yorkist hands could dim the happiness Jasper had felt seeing Owen's excitement when he learnt of the news. But that had been back in January, when they'd still been riding the high on the Lancastrian success at Ludford Bridge, and York was still laying low in Ireland nursing his wounded pride. Now spring was in full flourish, the rumours of a Yorkist resurgence gaining greater traction, and still Denbigh held out against them. The castle itself was positioned intimidatingly on a naturally defensible rocky outcrop. Encircled by high curtain walls, the fortification was a formidable sight, and one that Jasper did not relish having to attack.

Jasper's men had set up camp a little under a mile away from the castle. Over the past few weeks the collection of tents had taken on the feel of a small village. The men took it in turns to venture into the nearby woods to hunt, the handful of women who accompanied them from Pembroke turning whatever the men managed to catch into surprisingly delicious meals. That morale was generally high also helped to prevent any unsanctioned excursions. Jasper been explicit in his orders that the neighbouring settlements should not be attacked, and so far it seemed his men were obeying his directive. The long-term benefit of such restraint far outweighed whatever bitterness some of the men felt about being deprived the spoils of battle. Jasper needed to ensure that, when he finally took control of the castle, the locals would be, if not overtly supportive, begrudgingly accepting of the change in leadership.

Deep in thought Jasper did not notice his father walking over to stand beside him. "Here they go again," Owen remarked, close enough that he no longer needed to shout. Jasper looked up as yet another group of his men advanced and were then repelled back from the castle walls. With each approach they were getting closer but progress was painfully slow. Jasper sighed. God only knew how much money he had sunk into the venture or how much more it would require. No doubt he would be paying back the loans for a while to come. If he was honest with himself, there had been times when he had questioned whether their energies should not be used elsewhere. Across the sea in Ireland, York was becoming increasingly bold, while in Calais his son and Warwick were clearly preparing to launch some kind of attack. But, as Jasper had reasoned with himself, Denbigh was a strategically valuable prize. Victory here would help secure the north of Wales for Lancaster.

"What troubles you?" Owen asked, his brow furrowed with concern.

"Everything," Jasper replied with a tired laugh. "Sometimes, Father, I wonder about the purpose of this all. I do not mean just this campaign but rather the feud that has engulfed our country. Fighting against it seems like an almost Sisyphean task."

"Of course there is a purpose to it," Owen countered. "It is about securing a future for my grandson. More importantly, it is about defending what is right."

"That is exactly the question I grapple with. What is right? I thought I used to know. But now? It is as though my life has been split in two and St Albans is the axe that struck the dividing blow. Try as I might, I cannot reconcile the two halves." Owen opened his mouth to reply but Jasper shook his head. "Ignore me. I am simply in need of a good night's rest—"

Jasper broke off as a lone rider came racing towards them. "The outer wall has been breached my Lord," the man called out as he came to an abrupt stop, his horse rearing slightly in protest.

Jasper felt his mood immediately lift. Next to him, Owen clapped his hands in triumph. "Finally!"

Jasper clicked his fingers and his steward came hurrying over. "Prepare my horse," he commanded. He turned to Owen, a grin stretched wide across his face. "Come, Father, let us claim our prize."

The outer defences may have been overwhelmed, but the castle had not yet fully capitulated. Not willing to surrender, Denbigh's garrison had retreated inside the gatehouse. One of the most architecturally complex Jasper had ever seen, it was not a single structure but rather a triangle of three octagonal towers. Determined in their resistance, the enemy's arrows continued to fly, striking down those who, premature in their celebration, failed to recognise the continued danger. But as Jasper's men flooded through the walls, the futility of their defiance became increasingly apparent. By the time Jasper and Owen arrived, it had petered out to nothing, the final men dragged out unceremoniously to await their fate. The roar when the Yorkist banner was finally lowered was deafening. Owen embraced Jasper in jubilation, father and son watching proudly as their Tudor colours were raised above the gatehouse.

Once the flag was fluttering in the spring breeze, Owen turned to Jasper. "Now for the hard part," he remarked.

Jasper groaned. "I thought we'd just done that."

Owen chuckled as he shook his head. "Taking the castle means nothing if we cannot win over the people. Only once we have their loyalty can we truly claim this as ours."

* * *

Nearly two months later, Jasper sighed contently as he stretched out on a large bed, a blanket thrown haphazardly over his legs, enjoying the warmth of the summer sun through the window and the feeling of soft hands on his body. As it transpired, winning over the people had not been nearly as arduous as his father had implied, though he doubted this was how Owen had imagined he would go about it. Jasper jumped slightly as a hand swept over his side. "*Gofalus*, Arwen," he warned, "that tickles."

Arwen looked up at him with a mischievous glint in her dark eyes. The daughter of a prominent local merchant, she was one of the reasons Jasper was in no rush to leave Denbigh, though judging by the glare he'd been given by her father this morning, that time would come soon enough. Jasper smiled to himself; he couldn't win everyone over.

"Do they hurt?" Arwen murmured, tracing the scars that marked his skin like silver threads.

Jasper shook his head. "Not anymore."

"Can you remember where they all came from?" she asked, continuing to swirl her fingertips over their uneven patterns as she moved up his chest.

"Some. It depends."

"This one?" she queried, her feather light touch skating along his right collar bone.

Jasper glanced down. "An arrow. Cutting it out was the more painful part."

Her fingers moved across to his left bicep. "And this?"

"St Alban's. A lesson in the importance of not losing concentration."

Her hand continued down his arm to the line snaking around his wrist. "And which battle was this from?"

Jasper smiled softly. "Hmm no, no battle. That was my brother."

Arwen looked up at him aghast. "Your own brother did that to you?"

Jasper chuckled at her expression. "Not exactly. It must have been when I was seven or eight, we'd been at the Abbey for a year or so. Edmund said I was too much of a baby to climb to the top of the old apple tree in the centre of the orchard. I wanted to prove him wrong."

"And did you?"

"No, I fell as I was reaching for the last branch. Broke my wrist. The orchard was off limits after that. I never did make it to the top."

A small smile played across Arwen's lips as she lowered them to the scar. "Well then, we'll just have to find you something else to conquer."

Jasper grinned widely as he snaked an arm around her waist and flipped her easily onto her back. "I think I already have."

11

September 1460

Apart from a few sputtering torches, the castle was shrouded in complete darkness when the new arrivals made their way through the gates, the sound of hooves striking stone echoing eerily. Their journey had been long and arduous, and the horses' heads hung low with exhaustion. Jasper was waiting expectantly in the outer ward, a cloak pulled tight around his shoulders to protect against the early autumn chill. The tension he'd been holding for the last weeks melted away as the ghostly figures dismounted, helped by servants that seemingly materialised from the shadows. The first figure lowered its hood and Jasper swept into a bow as Marguerite of Anjou stepped into the torchlight. "Your Highness, welcome to Pembroke."

"Come now Jasper, surely you've known me long enough to call me Marguerite," the queen chided, her French accent drawing out the last syllable of his name.

"Of course, my apologies — Marguerite," Jasper replied with a smile.

Marguerite stepped closer, grasping his hands in hers. Jasper was surprised to see there were tears in the queen's eyes. "Thank you for opening up your home to us," she said simply, a magnitude of emotions bound up in those few words.

"Do not think of it. I am honoured that you chose Pembroke as your refuge." He tried to keep his voice light, but his head still spun to think how quickly their fortunes had changed.

Barely four months had passed since Denbigh, though it might as well have been a lifetime ago. Caught up in the excitement of King Henry's return to strength, he, like many others, had allowed his usual caution to waver, dismissing the fears he had shared with his father as mere paranoia. It had proven a costly mistake, one made no less painful by the fact that he was not alone in making it. If York had launched his attack from Ireland, then the effort spent on securing Denbigh might well have been worth it. But the duke had never been a man motivated by securing personal glory on the battlefield. Power alone was his goal, and he proved content to hang back and let others risk their lives to secure it. So while Jasper and the rest of the Lancastrian nobles focused their attentions on Ireland, they overlooked the greater threat lurking over the Channel. To hold the capital was to hold the very heart of the country, and so London found itself on the receiving end of the first wave of violence. Warwick landed in Sandwich in late June, sweeping through the countryside and overwhelming the capital with thousands of Kentish men spoiling for a fight. With London secured, he continued north, meeting the king's army outside Northampton. In torrential rain, Buckingham put up a valiant final fight, but even he was unable to keep Warwick and York's son, the Earl of March, at bay; his name added to the ever-growing list of great men cut down in service to their king. A king who was now a prisoner.

When York himself arrived there was nothing left to do but process victoriously through the streets of London with King Henry paraded behind him, as if he were an exotic animal to be gawped at. It made Jasper's blood boil to think of his half-brother humiliated in such a way, a feeling only mildly soothed by the arrival of his wife and heir, and the knowledge that, for now at least, they were safe within Pembroke's thick walls.

Jasper's thoughts were interrupted by a small figure hurtling through the group. A young boy came to a screeching halt next to Marguerite, tugging at her cloak impatiently. *"Maman, j'ai faim,"* Prince Edward whined.

"Oui, mon cherie." She looked up at Jasper expectantly.

"Of course, there is food waiting in the great hall," Jasper replied, dropping into flawless French. "If you would like to follow me."

Marguerite might be on the run, but she was still the queen, and certain standards needed to be met. As such, Jasper had personally overseen that every inch of the castle was ready to receive the royal family. Walking into the great hall, he was pleased to see a fire was roaring in the hearth and the table was laid with the best silver. Owen was waiting for them in the hall with a tall, fair-haired man standing next to him. Henry Holland, the Duke of Exeter, was the same age as Jasper, but that was where the similarities ended. In contrast to Jasper's courteousness, there was a cruelty to Holland, a ruthlessness honed in the torture chambers of the Tower. Yet, while Jasper could not say he liked the man, he could not fault Holland's loyalty to the House of Lancaster. That it was born out of his own sense of self-entitlement and belief his claim to the throne was superior to York's, mattered little to Jasper.

"Ah, Holland. I wondered whether I would find you here," Marguerite said by way of welcome.

"Your Highness," Holland replied, bowing with an unnecessary flourish. Unlike previously, Jasper noted the queen made no move to correct the duke's formality. Seemingly already bored of Exeter's preening, Marguerite's gaze shifted to the older man next to him.

"So you are the man that seduced a French queen?" she asked, one eyebrow raised.

A smile tugged at the corners of Owen's mouth. "Yes, your Highness, indeed I am," he confirmed playfully.

"Marguerite, please," she corrected.

"Marguerite," Owen repeated, a twinkle in his eyes. Behind the queen's back, Jasper turned his own eyes heavenward, despairing at his father's cheek. "And this must be Prince Edward?" Owen continued, nodding at the small figure haring around the room.

Marguerite caught her son by the arm, forcing him to stand still. "Edward, show our hosts some more respect."

"Sorry. Thank you for welcoming us to your home," he mumbled, before running excitedly over to where Ianto was dozing like usual by the fire.

Owen chuckled. "My boys were just the same when they were young," he said, slapping Jasper on the back. "But they turn out all right in the end."

Jasper felt the colour rising in his cheeks. "Marguerite, may I show you to your seat?" he asked in an attempt to change the conversation.

Marguerite smiled and sat on the chair Jasper pulled out for her. Once the three men had settled into their places around her, the servants set about filling plates with food and cups with wine. It was only when the queen had taken a few mouthfuls and the conversation began to flow more freely that Jasper was able to relax slightly, satisfied that his hosting abilities had so far passed muster. Jasper caught sight of Joan, Henry's nursemaid, hovering by the door and waved her over. She bobbed into a nervous curtsey, her eyes darting between Jasper and the queen.

"I'm sorry to disturb you, my Lord," she stammered. "Henry is feeling much better this evening and wanted me to ask if you would take him out on Tarn tomorrow?"

Jasper smiled. "*Diolch*, Joan," he said, slipping into Welsh. "Tell

Henry goodnight from me and I will come to see him in the morning." Joan nodded before scurrying away.

"Is Henry your son?" Marguerite asked, taking a sip of wine.

"No, your Grace, Henry is my nephew," Jasper said.

"Of course, your nephew. I remember now. My husband still speaks of Edmund with great fondness," she added, addressing Owen, who inclined his head in acknowledgement. "And what of his mother?"

"Lady Margaret Beaufort. She has since remarried and now resides at Bourne with her husband, Sir Henry Stafford."

"Dear Buckingham. We still feel his absence keenly as I'm sure his son does too. And it must be doubly hard for her. Supporting her husband through his grief while she is away from her child. I could not imagine being separated from my Edward," she said, looking adoringly at her son, who was over-enthusiastically pulling at Ianto's ears. Normally a gentle giant, the young prince was testing even Ianto's patience, and with a low growl, he stalked away to the safety of Jasper's chair.

"I hear York has re-called Parliament," Marguerite continued her voice hardening. "I wonder how many of those who previously claimed fealty to my husband have already turned their coats?" There was venom in her voice.

"Do not despair, Marguerite," Owen reassured her from across the table. "Fortune's Wheel may have turned against us, yet that does not mean it will not spin in our favour again. Patience may be bitter, but its fruit, when it comes, is sweet."

The queen cocked her head to one side as she considered Owen's advice. "Hmm, there is merit in what you say, though I admit I do not possess your optimistic outlook."

"Do we not owe it to those we've lost to be so?" Owen replied softly. Though his comment was directed at the queen, his gaze was fixed on his son. Jasper swallowed painfully against the sudden lump in his throat, grateful for the distraction offered by the arrival of the musicians who would provide the evening's entertainment. As the music swelled, the conversation turned to happier subjects, and for the rest of the meal the hopelessness of their situation was forgotten.

* * *

But it would have been foolish to think the reprieve would last, and a few days later, reality returned to Pembroke. In the depths of night, when the majority of the castle was asleep, an anguished scream brought Jasper running to the queen's rooms. He burst through the doors to her chamber, his heart pounding, to find Marguerite standing in the middle of the room, a letter screwed up in her hand. Her maids had retreated to the edge of the chamber for safety. She marched towards Jasper, thrusting the crumpled paper at him. "As if laying his hand on my husband's throne wasn't insult enough!"

Marguerite began to pace back and forth as Jasper quickly skimmed the letter, a sense of dread building as he read. "York has disinherited my son," she shouted. "Named himself as heir, and has the audacity to claim my husband is the one who authorised it! How could Parliament have let this happen? We cannot stand for this." She jabbed a finger at her chest. "*I* will not stand for this."

Jasper watched mutely as the queen raged about the room. He had no words. His mind, that had only moments before been close to sleep, struggled to comprehend the news. He turned as Henry Holland raced through the door.

"What is it? What's happened?" he asked frantically. The duke's usually slicked-back hair was stuck up in all directions and his crumpled shirt fell down below his belt, evidence of the haste with which he had dressed. Jasper passed him the letter without explanation, as he focused his attention on the queen who was still pacing the room.

"He is scrambling, Marguerite. Scrambling to save face. Parliament rejected his claim for the crown himself. He went too far when he placed his hand on the king's throne. He knows that. He cannot kill God's anointed king, not yet at least." Marguerite looked up sharply, her eyes burning with anger. "I'm sorry, Marguerite, but it is true," Jasper continued, raising his hands defensively. "For the moment, this is his next best option."

"And you still have many loyal men by your side," Holland added. "Men who will lay down their lives in defence of Lancaster."

Jasper winced as the queen rounded on Exeter. "And where are these men?" she demanded, unleashing her fury. "Scattered to the four winds, that is where. Meanwhile, our enemies grow stronger and more emboldened with every day that passes." She bunched her hands into fists in frustration before releasing them with a deep breath as she attempted to regain her composure. When she continued, her voice was more measured, though anger still burned bright in her eyes. "It is true what you say, Holland," she conceded. "There are indeed still men loyal to my family. But if the battles of the last years have taught us anything, it is that they alone are not enough. Besides I need my nobles to hold their own lands. York may have taken London but there are still large swathes of this country who swear affinity with Lancaster and they must be defended. No," she continued, "if I am to assemble a force capable of defeating York, I must look elsewhere for support."

Marguerite turned to address Jasper. "I know I have already taken advantage of your kindness but I must call on it again. I need a ship and I need some of your men."

"Your Highness?" he asked, unsure of where Marguerite's train of thought was heading.

"I am going to Scotland. I will ask King James to lend me his support," she explained.

"And what will he ask for in return?" Holland challenged. "He is no fool, he will recognise the desperateness of our position and use it to his advantage."

"I am well aware of that, I would do the same if I was in his position," Marguerite replied. "But I have no choice. It is because I am desperate that I must go to him for help."

"Northumberland will not thank you for such an arrangement," Holland continued, with a hint of patronism. "The Percys have a long history of hating the Scots."

"I am fully aware of the hostility with which many of this country's people, especially those in the North, view the Scots," Marguerite cut across him. "Unless you have an alternative suggestion, I cannot think of where else I can turn."

"I can give you thirty of my best men and a ship to take you from Tenby," Jasper offered. "I wish I could give more—"

"Do not think of it," Marguerite interjected. "You have already given much in defence of the Crown. My husband is fortunate to have a man like you on his side. I will set out as soon as your men are ready. Holland, you will accompany me." The duke inclined his head in acknowledgement of the order. Marguerite turned back to Jasper. "Let us hope, my friend, that when we meet again it is under more auspicious circumstances."

* * *

Four months later, the fire was doing its best to banish the creeping January cold from the solar. Jasper sat next to it, weighing a letter in his hand, relieved by its heaviness. Taking his knife, he eagerly sliced through the seal and was reassured to see the scrawled words running across multiple pages. He'd received the triumphant news the day before, when the queen's messenger had raced through Pembroke's gate, the noise of hooves on icy cobbles punctuating the still January morning. The letter, written in Marguerite's flowing hand, had been painfully brief, stating simply: the traitor is dead. The elation he had felt at those four words had been immense, yet their brevity was cause for annoyance. It had been a frustrating wait for further news.

Jasper did not turn as Owen entered the room, Ianto following closely behind him. "More news?" his father enquired as he settled into his usual seat.

Jasper glanced up. "Yes, a report from Sir Richard Tunstall. Thankfully much more detailed than the queen's."

"Well go on then, speak it aloud. I did not drag myself up those stairs just to watch you read."

"As you wish, but no interruptions," Jasper replied. "I know what you're like."

Owen held up his hands in silent acquiescence. Jasper paused for a moment, letting his eyes adjust to Tunstall's uneven hand, then clearing his throat he began:

"My friend, the field is ours. The Duke of York is dead." Even though he'd had time to process it, the finality of those words still flooded Jasper's blood with excitement. "The queen and her forces overwhelmed him at Wakefield and now his head sits on a spike atop Micklegate Bar, alongside that of his son Edmund and his brother-in-law Salisbury. Someone affixed a paper crown to York's head, which is no less humiliation than that traitor deserves. I cannot say why York left the safe confines of Sandal castle. There are rumours he was deceived, but by whom the whispers do not say. More likely the harsh winter left their provisions depleted. York knew he would have to face us eventually; maybe in the end it was impatience that made him act so rashly. Our forces were swelled by Scotsmen given to Marguerite by King James. She gave him Berwick in return, a price—"

"That will not be popular," Owen muttered. Jasper glared at him. "Sorry."

"A price which will have to be reckoned with once we return to London," Jasper continued. "The battle itself was short but fierce. Somerset, Northumberland and Clifford, all made fatherless by the brutality of St Albans, led the charge, sweeping through York's forces with a terrifying vengeance. No mercy was shown. York himself was slain in battle. His son, the Earl of Rutland escaped the field but Clifford hunted him down. I admit the look in his eyes when he re-entered camp with the boy's severed head held triumphantly in his hand, made my blood run cold." Out of the corner of his eye, Jasper could see his father shaking his head. He ignored him and carried on reading, trying to keep his voice measured. "Perhaps it was some small mercy that York was not alive to see it; Clifford would have drawn it out longer if he had been. As for Salisbury, he was dragged out from his hiding place and killed by a mob of his own tenants. York's death has not sated the queen's appetite for vengeance. She intends to scourge his entire house. We now continue our march south to meet the Earl of Warwick, who holds the king as his captive. After that, we will retake London. To that end, she commands you to gather your men and join us. Godspeed, my friend."

Jasper put down the letter and grinned at his father. "This is it. The time has come to secure justice for our House and the wrongs inflicted against it."

12

February 1461

Pulling back the tent flap, Jasper stepped out into the crisp morning air. The ground seemed to sparkle from the heavy frost that lay upon it, and he watched as plumes of his breath curled in the cold air. Normally the sight would fill him with a childish sense of wonder, but not this morning. Anxiety clawed at his chest and he could feel the weight of tiredness in his bones. The anticipatory fervour that had gripped the men as they'd left Pembroke had long since abated, ground to dust by the long miles of hard marching. But it was in that frenzied excitement that Jasper had made his first mistake. Grief is a powerful motivator, and in underestimating the fallout from York's death on his eldest son, Jasper had inadvertently placed himself on a course to disaster. The Yorkist army had seemed to materialise from thin air, in an instant turning his steady progress across Wales into a frantic race to avoid being cut off. Yet, despite their best efforts, each day the reports from the scouts had brought more bad news, until the previous night when Jasper had finally been forced to call a halt and ready his men for battle. The fight he'd so desperately wanted to avoid was now inevitable. They needed to cross the River Lugg if they were to have any hope of meeting up with the queen. To do so, they would have to go through Edward, Earl of March, the new Duke of York.

Jasper rubbed his hands together, blowing into them in a vain attempt to regain some feeling in his fingers. Behind him, the tent flap opened again and his father came to stand next to him. Owen had ignored Jasper's pleas for him to stay at Pembroke. They'd argued about it late into the night before they'd left but his father was determined to repay his stepson's kindness. "I owe it to your mother," he had said quietly, in the silence that followed one of Jasper's impassioned pleas. He had realised then the futility of trying to dissuade his father. In truth, he had enjoyed his company on the long march through Wales, and now on the dawn of battle, he was thankful for his father's reassuring presence.

Jasper nodded at James Butler, the Earl of Wiltshire, who had just emerged from his own tent, waving him over to join them. A favourite of Queen Marguerite, Jasper could still remember how the earl had fled from St Albans, his loyalty to the king giving way as soon as the first arrows flew. Despite his disdain for Butler's cowardice, Jasper couldn't fault the earl's ability to raise men. His own had been significantly reinforced by Butler's large contingent of Breton and French mercenaries, as well as retainers from his Irish estates. The presence of such battle-hardened men gave Jasper more confidence for what lay ahead, but he still could not shake the gnawing sense of dread that he was trying to suppress.

Butler grasped Jasper's arm in greeting. "What news of the York pup?" he asked, an unmistakable Irish lilt to his voice.

"The scouts report he's set up camp a few miles off, near the road to Ludlow," Jasper said, lifting open the tent flap and motioning the other two inside. "He's had the benefit of a shorter march but we have superior numbers. I would have preferred to go around him but with your mercenaries, Butler," he continued, speaking with a confidence he knew in his heart he did not possess, "the odds should fall in our favour."

"And the terrain?"

"Complicated," Jasper conceded, motioning to a large map that had been unfurled on a table, its corners weighted down with stones. "As you can see, the road on which York has positioned his men has the advantage of a slight rise. The river running along the western boundary narrows our approach."

"And what of the ground to the left," Butler queried, pointing at the map.

"A thicket of bushes and brambles. The scouts assure me it is too dense to offer a viable route of attack. Given the river on the other side, the only option is a head-on attack, which is where our superiority of numbers should pay dividends."

"A fair analysis," the Irishman agreed. "On that basis, what formation do you propose we adopt?"

Jasper took a breath. The decision he made now would determine whether those around the table and gathered in the camp would live to see another dawn. He'd wrestled with it much of the night but now it was time to commit. "I propose we split our forces into three. I shall lead the vanguard. Father, you will take control of the rearguard." Owen nodded, his brow furrowed in concentration. "Which leaves the centre for you and your mercenaries, Butler," Jasper concluded, watching the other man's reaction closely. Although not his primary motivation, he hoped positioning Butler in the centre would make it harder for him to flee should the tide of battle turn. If the earl sensed Jasper's reasoning then he showed no sign of it, his face remaining impassive.

Satisfied, Jasper pushed back off the table and turned to face his father. There was something else that had occupied his mind throughout the night, though this at least had brought more joy than had battle plans.

"You're going to need a title if you are to lead my men," he announced. "And in my opinion it is one that is long overdue," he continued, drawing his sword with a smile. A gift from his half-brother on his investiture as the Earl of Pembroke, the blade was inscribed with his mother's motto. His father looked at him quizzically before his eyes widened as comprehension dawned. Despite his protesting joints, Owen knelt on the cold ground before his son, his head bowed. Jasper placed the blade on his father's shoulder.

"Owain ap Maredudd ap Tudur," he said, using his father's full Welsh name. "As proxy, and by the divine authority of His Grace, King Henry VI, I raise thee to the rank of knight banneret."

Returning his sword to its scabbard, Jasper held out a hand to help his father up. Once standing, Owen reached his hand up to Jasper's neck and pulled him close so their heads were touching. The two of them stayed like that for a moment, silence conveying what words could not, until gasps from outside broke them from their reverie. Looking up sharply, Jasper hurried from the tent, his father and Butler following closely behind. All around the camp, men were falling to their knees, crossing themselves fervently. Jasper pulled a nearby soldier up by his collar. "What is going on?" he demanded.

The soldier, wide-eyed with shock, raised a shaking hand to point at the sky. Above them hung three perfect shining suns. Jasper had to shield his eyes with his hand to stop himself from being blinded by the spectacular rays that reached, like outstretched fingers, through the frosty air.

"It is a sign," Butler proclaimed, making the sign of the cross in front of him. "God is against us."

"Be quiet," Jasper hissed.

Butler was not accustomed to being spoken to in such a manner. He opened his mouth to protest but thought better of it when he saw the fury burning in Jasper's eyes. Raising his voice, Jasper addressed the cowering men. "Do not be afraid," he instructed, even as the unease encircling his heart solidified into fear. "We fight for the divinely appointed king. Trust that God is on our side. Now go, prepare yourselves. Be ready to form up within the hour." At first no one moved, but then slowly the men began to stand, wandering off to collect their weapons and muttering amongst themselves as they went.

Owen caught Jasper's arm as he turned to walk away. "Do you really believe that?" he asked, his voice low.

"I do not know what to believe. God is for Lancaster, of that I am certain. But three suns?" Jasper's brow furrowed. "What clearer sign is there that He has bestowed His blessing on the three sons of York?"

* * *

As the shout of 'Forward' reverberated around the field, Jasper felt his heart leap in his chest as, as one, the men began their march towards the enemy. He'd forgone the option of his horse to be better part of the action and there was something exhilarating about the sense of unstoppable motion around him. Reaching up an armoured hand, he pulled down his visor, his world suddenly reduced to what little could be seen through the small slit. The accompanying claustrophobia was worth it for the protection it offered. This was only his second experience of battle, and he said a quick prayer that he would survive the ordeal, if only so his nephew wouldn't lose another father.

Step by step they moved across the field, the mass of men on the rise before them coming into focus. Mercifully, the cold had left the ground frozen and there was no mud to slow their progress. Inside his helmet, the sounds of their advance were weirdly muffled, the clanking of armour drowned out by the sound of his own breathing. Then suddenly, above it all, came the unmistakable twang of thousands of bowstrings. But rather than from in front of him, as he would have expected, the noise came from his left. A cold sense of dread spread through his veins; the scouts had been wrong, they were surrounded. Even though he knew it was futile, he roared out a warning to his men as their ordered progress descended into chaos. Jasper forced himself not to look up as the first volley of arrows descended like a black cloud on the assembled lines. All around him men fell to the ground as if God himself had struck them down. But there was no time to regroup, as in front of him the first of the Yorkist lines launched their attack, exploiting the gaps left by the arrows. The intensity of the battle was all-encompassing, its brutality unavoidable as the violent struggle of life and death for thousands played out all around. Jasper swore as he saw Butler flee the field.

"Fucking coward!" he shouted after the earl's retreating figure. Thankfully, it seemed most of Butler's mercenaries were too engrossed in the battle to follow him.

Gritting his teeth, Jasper channelled his anger into the fighting around him, cutting down the poorly armed men who made up the bulk of the Yorkist force with ease. The two armies were now fully engaged, any semblance of the previously ordered lines lost in the mêlée. Danger could come from any side, and at the edge of his vision, Jasper saw a flash of steel, and shifted to the left just in time to avoid the deadly blow. Pivoting, he swung his own blade around, slicing deep into the man's side. His attacker crumpled to the floor and was soon trampled underneath the feet of his friends.

Looking across to the right-hand side of the battle, Jasper could see where the rear of the Lancastrian forces, led by his father, were attempting to encircle the Yorkist left flank. Yet even from this distance, he could tell they hadn't pushed far enough, the course of the river hemming them in. He roared in frustration as he watched his father's troops crash into the enemy, who didn't even seem to break step. They were soon swallowed by the frenetic chaos of battle. In that moment, it took all of Jasper's restraint not to send his own men in after his father.

Grappling with emotion, he focused his attention back to the action before him. Amongst the advancing troops, Jasper recognised the Earl of March. A head taller than most of those around him, his armour was coated in blood. The teenager moved in a terrifying frenzy; cutting through men in a grief-possessed rage and Jasper shuddered involuntarily at the sight. Breathing hard, he had to call upon all his strength and years of training as he slashed his way through the enemy, parrying blows that came from all directions. Suddenly, he felt a hot, searing pain in his leg. A soldier on the ground had lashed out, catching him underneath one of his armoured plates. Gripping the hilt with both hands, Jasper plunged his sword into the man's chest with an enraged roar. Yanking it out again, he looked desperately over to where a small band of men, his father amongst them, continued to withstand the Yorkist onslaught. Their persistent effort against the left flank was just enough to disrupt the rhythm of the men now pressing upon his centre, but Jasper knew it couldn't last. He could feel the battle's momentum beginning to shift. Imperceptible at first, but building as a palpable and unmistakable panic set in amongst his men. If he didn't take control of the situation all would be lost. Pride counted for nothing now. Better to accept the inevitable, and live to fight another day. With a heavy heart, he called over one of his captains. The man was exhausted, leaning heavily on the hilt of his sword as he tried to catch his breath.

"Signal the retreat," Jasper commanded, his voice tight with pain. Visible relief washed over the captain. "And get me a horse," he added, trying to suppress his shame.

The captain nodded, before disappearing into the mass of fighting men. It didn't take long for the order to take effect. All around him, men began disentangling themselves from the crush of battle. Jasper flexed his grip on his sword as he watched the Yorkist soldiers, emboldened by the relief of pressure on their lines, dart forward, cutting down men as they turned to run. Finally, out of the chaos, a squire appeared leading a spare horse. With his last ounce of strength, Jasper pulled himself up into the saddle, ignoring the pain radiating down his leg. Throwing a glance over his shoulder to where he had last seen his father, he spurred his horse into a gallop, leaving his men behind him. He rode hard and fast away from the field, hoping to outrun not just his pursuers, but the guilt pounding in his ears.

13

February 1461

The last rays of sunshine had ebbed from the sky, leaving it a dark, inky blue by the time Jasper paused to rest. Progress was slower than he would have wanted, but that was the trade-off he had to accept for avoiding the dangerous main roads. Amongst a copse of trees, he'd found a small stream from which he drank greedily, scooping the icy water with his hands until they were numb. Jasper splashed some water on his face in an attempt to fight the exhaustion trying to drag him down, like an anchor, into the depths of sleep. He was physically spent after the exertion of battle and mentally drained by the feeling of being hunted down like a dog.

The sharp pain in his leg had given way to a dull throb. With effort, he began to remove his armour. He needed to tend to his injury and the stiff plates were making that impossible. Usually the task of a squire, by the time Jasper had divested himself of the heavy plates, he was sweating and his teeth were gritted in pain. Glancing down, he could see his breeches were still wet with blood, but mercifully it seemed as though the bleeding had slowed. He probed the area gingerly with his finger, gasping at the pain that made his head swim. He sucked cold air into his lungs in an attempt to banish the dark shadows that clouded the edges of his vision. Taking his knife to his breeches, he cut away the fabric to get a better look at his injury. The soldier's dagger had left a curved, jagged gash around the top of his calf. In the dim evening light, it was hard to tell if it would need stitching, but regardless, it could have been much, much worse. He'd been lucky. Luckier than the rest.

Jasper could feel his mind beginning to wander; to his father and the fates of the other men left behind. With difficulty he pulled his focus back to the task at hand; there would be time to reflect when he knew he was out of danger. Scooping some more water from the stream, Jasper cleaned the wound as best he could, then bound it with a length of material he'd ripped from his shirt. Picking up his discarded armour, he hid it in some nearby bushes. It pained him to be parted with something so beautiful, and with such sentimental value, but it would only draw unwanted attention. Although he was in unfamiliar territory, Jasper at least had a general idea of where he was heading. He'd realised when they'd set up camp, that one of the Duke of Buckingham's residences was relatively nearby in Hay, a small market town nestled on the banks of the River Wye. It was a useful kernel of information but not one Jasper had ever imagined needing to rely on. Now it was his main hope of escaping his pursuers. He had a vague memory that the castle had been badly damaged the year before, not that he cared. He'd happily sleep in a stable, so long as it was on safe ground. It was just six months since the old duke had been killed at Northampton. His loss had been a terrible blow. Buckingham had always been staunchly loyal to the king and his absence was even more conspicuous now the title was held by his four-year-old grandson. In his place, Margaret's husband had taken on the responsibility of administering his nephew's estates. Jasper smiled ruefully to himself as he walked back over to his horse; he'd never thought he'd have cause to be grateful for Margaret's marriage to Stafford. Ignoring his objecting muscles, Jasper slowly heaved himself back into the saddle, and with a click of his tongue, headed off once again into the darkening gloom.

* * *

It was the depths of night when he arrived on the outskirts of Hay. The last quarter moon had just risen, giving the quiet streets Jasper walked through an eerie glow. Ahead of him, the castle stood imposingly atop a hill, at odds with the small town it overlooked. Silhouetted against the sky, Jasper could tell part of the outer wall had collapsed, but to his relief, he could see torches flickering by the main gate. Dismounting, he led his horse up to the entrance and hammered a fist against the wood.

He stepped back, waiting to hear the scrape of bolts being drawn aside, but none came. Off in the distance, an owl hooted. He knocked again, this time with more force. A window in the door opened and a pale face peered out. "What is your purpose?" the face asked cautiously.

"My name is Jasper Tudor, the Earl of Pembroke, and I request safe haven in the name of my half-brother, King Henry," Jasper declared.

The face disappeared. Jasper heard whispered voices and then after what seemed like an age, the thick door swung open and he was quickly ushered inside.

The owner of the pale face stood before him in the courtyard. He was a stout man with thinning hair. "Welcome to Hay, my Lord. My name is Thomas." He glanced nervously at the sword hanging at Jasper's side. "We were not expecting anyone, especially not this late."

"Forgive the intrusion," Jasper said, running a hand through his hair, suddenly conscious of how he must look. "I've just come from the battlefield at Mortimer's Cross and need somewhere to lay low for a few days. The late duke was a friend of mine and his son Henry is married to my sister-in-law, Lady Margaret."

Thomas smiled, his demeanour visibly relaxing. "Of course, my Lord, any family of Lord and Lady Stafford are more than welcome here. If you'll give your horse to Dai there he'll see to it that she's well looked after." A gangly teenager took the reins from Jasper's outstretched hand and led his horse away to the stables. "Now, what is it that we can do for you, my Lord?"

"Some food, warmth and a place to lay my head."

Thomas nodded eagerly. "Of course, my Lord. The castle is not as it was, not since the attack last summer, but if you follow me, I can show you the way."

Jasper smiled gratefully and let himself be led into the castle. Mercifully, he was only required to climb one flight of stairs; any more and he was certain his legs would have given way. Reaching the top, Thomas motioned to a door at the end of the passageway. "Here you are, my Lord. I hope the room is to your satisfaction. Had we known you were coming, we would have made better arrangements. I have no warm food to offer you, but I can have some bread and ale sent up."

Jasper shook his head. "Food can wait till I have slept. As for the room, I will be content with whatever you have given me. Thank you, truly, your kindness will not be forgotten."

"My Lord," Thomas bowed.

The doorway to the chamber was low and Jasper had to duck to avoid hitting his head. Straightening up, he surveyed the room. A small bed was pushed against one wall and there was a solitary chair positioned by the fireplace. The hastily lit fire gave out a cosy glow, though it had done little to relieve the chill in the room. It may have been simple and sparsely decorated but at that moment, Jasper felt as though it was one of the grand chambers at Westminster. Without bothering to remove his boots, he collapsed onto the bed, giving in at last to the oblivion of sleep.

* * *

Jasper awoke with a start to a knock on the door. From the way the sun was streaming through the windows, he must have slept through most of the morning. Grabbing his dagger, Jasper silently crossed the room to the door. The knock came again, more impatient than the last. Slowly Jasper opened the door, to reveal a servant girl holding a large pail of steaming water. Her eyes widened at the sight of the dagger in Jasper's hand.

"Sorry," he said, tucking it into his belt, "you can never be too careful. Please come in," he continued, stepping aside.

Staggering in, she set the pail down in the middle of the room, a cloth bobbing in the water. Straightening up, she rolled her shoulders to ease the strain from her heavy load.

"There are clean clothes in there," she said pointing to an old chest by the window, "and there will be food down in the main hall whenever you're ready." She gave a shallow curtsey, leaving before Jasper had a chance to express his thanks. A laugh escaped Jasper's lips. Still caked in blood and mud, his hair a tangled mess, he must look like some sort of wild man. No wonder the girl had left so quickly.

Standing next to the pail, Jasper eased his shirt over his head, wincing as the fabric pulled at his grazes. Looking down, he could see his torso was mottled with blossoming bruises. Taking up the cloth, he began to wipe the dirt and grime from his body. Rivulets of muddy water ran down his skin, tracing the contours of his muscles. Pulling off his boots and stripping off his breeches, Jasper turned his attention to his wound. A scab was already starting to form and it seemed it would heal all right on its own. Nevertheless, it made Jasper flinch when he cautiously dabbed at it with the cloth.

Once his skin was as clean as he could make it and the water had turned an unappealing dark brown, Jasper padded barefoot over to the chest leaving a trail of wet footprints behind him. Lifting the lid, he found a pair of breeches and a shirt. They smelt musty and looked as though they'd be a few inches short, but they were clean and Jasper wasn't in any position to complain. He stepped into the breeches and gently pulled them up, trying to avoid the rough material touching his wound. He retrieved his belt from the heap of rags that had been his clothes, dunking it in the water to remove the worst of the mud. As he was fastening it, there was another knock at the door. "There's a messenger for you, my Lord," Thomas' voice called out. "He says he has urgent news."

"Send him in." Jasper grabbed the clean shirt, quickly tugging it over his head as the door opened and a man, dirt clinging to his cloak, stepped into the room, breathing heavily. Jasper recognised him as one of the men that had been in his father's division.

"You fought alongside my father?"

"Yes, my Lord, I did," the man confirmed.

"Did you see what happened to him?"

The man nodded, wringing his cap between his hands. "He was taken, my Lord, captured by the Yorkists. They took him to Hereford along with the other prisoners—" He trailed off, looking awkwardly at his feet.

"And?"

"H— he, he's dead my Lord," the man stammered.

Jasper felt like he was falling, as if the ground below him had given way. His throat seemed to be constricting, making it hard to breathe. "How?" he asked, his voice strangled.

"Beheaded— by Roger Vaughn— in the marketplace. I do not think your father thought they would actually go through with it. It was only when his head was on the block that the realisation seemed to dawn on him." The man gave a tight smile. "He kept his humour, my Lord, even till the end. With his last words, he joked that his head lay on the block like it used to lie in Queen Catherine's lap."

Jasper felt a lump rising in his throat. "I'm grateful to you for bringing me this news."

The man took a step towards him, pulling a small bundle from the folds of his cloak. "There is one more thing, my Lord. Your father trusted this to me before— before they took him away," he explained.

Taking it, Jasper removed the damp wrappings to reveal his father's ring. He had to bite the inside of his mouth to hold back his tears. Stamped with his father's crest, it had been a gift from his mother on their wedding day. In the more than three decades since, it had never left his finger. Until now. A part of Jasper wanted to throw it across the room, to deny the evidence of the messenger's news. But a greater part wanted to hold it close, and it was that side that won out as he slid the ring onto his little finger. He cleared his throat, focusing again on the man standing in front of him. "If you go down to the kitchens, I'm sure they'll be able to find you something to eat."

"Thank you, my Lord. I'm sorry, your father was a good man." With a bow, he left the room, leaving Jasper alone with his grief.

As soon as the door shut, emotion overcame him. Jasper sunk to the ground, his head in his hands.

"No, no, no," he keened. Sobs racked his body as tears streamed down his face. He wanted the world to stop; to rewind time. He should have gone to his father's aid when he saw their lines overwhelmed; better yet, he should never have let him join him in the first place. First Edmund, now his father. What more would this war take from him?

"Henry," Jasper gasped. He needed to get back to Pembroke immediately. For all he knew, his enemies could already be on their way. Jasper wiped the tears furiously from his eyes; he could do nothing for his brother and father, but he alone could keep his nephew safe.

* * *

Flecks of white foam flew from his horse's mouth as Jasper raced into Pembroke's outer ward. Jumping down from the saddle before he came to a full stop, he flung the reins at a bewildered stable hand, then set off at a run towards the keep. He swept up the winding stairs, taking them two at a time and burst into the nursery. Joan started at the sudden intrusion, but Jasper ignored her, his focus entirely on the little boy playing by the window. Henry looked up, smiling widely in excitement at his uncle's unexpected arrival. In one fluid movement, Jasper bent down and scooped him up into a tight embrace. Joan retreated quietly from the room, as Jasper's tears fell into Henry's soft brown curls.

14

April 1461

"**T**he heralds estimate over twenty thousand dead—" Sir
Richard Tunstall trailed off as Jasper spun sharply round,
shock showing clearly on his face.

"Jesu, and what of their commanders?"

"Somerset and Exeter fled the battle. The Earl of Northumberland
was slain. It was a massacre."

"And the king?"

"You have not heard?" Richard asked warily.

Jasper stepped closer to him. "No. What happened?"

"King Henry has been deposed, Jasper," Richard explained slowly,
as though it might help soften the blow. "He and his family have
fled north. It is Edward, the new Duke of York, who now sits on the
throne."

Jasper slammed his fist against the wall. With one sentence, all he
had worked for since St Albans came crumbling down; years and
lives reduced to worthless dust. Richard watched quietly as Jasper
wrestled with his anger. A trusted member of the king's household,
Richard's friendship with Jasper stretched back to when they were
teenagers. He closed the gap between them and placed a hand on

Jasper's shoulder.

"Sit." Richard motioned to the chairs by the fire. "I will call for some ale and cold meats. Discussing such matters on an empty stomach will do us no favours."

Jasper nodded and, still in a daze, settled into one of the two chairs by the fire. Richard rang a small bell, instructing the servant who immediately materialised before taking up his position next to Jasper. The low-timbered room had none of the grandeur of Pembroke's solar, but it was warm and the furniture was still comfortable. After returning from Hay, Jasper had retreated to the winding streets of Tenby, finding solace in being surrounded by the frenetic activity of the bustling port town. Pembroke seemed a lonely place now his father was gone, and even Henry's childish enthusiasm couldn't banish the grief that seemed to hang in the air.

Before long, a jug of ale had been placed along with a platter of meats and cheese on the low table between the chairs. Jasper smiled gratefully as Richard passed him a cup. "You must think me a hopeless host, my friend?"

"No, not at all. The news I've brought has shocked you, as it would have me, had I not witnessed it firsthand."

"Was it really that terrible?"

"It was worse than you could imagine. It was as if we were in Hell itself. Every other battle I have fought in pales by comparison. God was punishing us for fighting on such a holy day, I am certain."

Jasper leant forwards. "What can you tell me of the battle itself?" Richard shifted in his seat. "If it is too painful then—"

Richard waved a hand. "No, it's good to speak these things out loud. Besides, you've always been a good listener." He took a breath to steady himself and then began.

"We had assembled the greatest army I have ever seen. Tens of thousands of men, all loyal to King Henry. Somerset had command of the army, and Northumberland led the centre. The idea we could be defeated, and so decisively, was incomprehensible. But they seemed to have the Devil on their side. We fought in a snowstorm like none I've ever known, even in the depths of winter, let alone on Palm Sunday. I could barely see the man in front of me. We were completely blind, not knowing from where the next blow would come. The falling snow seemed to soak up any sound from the enemy. It masked the noise of their arrows and they dropped from the sky without warning, like a black cloud of death. There was no respite. We fought on and on, standing on the bodies of the dead and dying. Even the snow that usually hides all manners of sins betrayed us, stained crimson by the blood of fallen men. There was a moment when I thought we might have gained the upper hand. The enemy was bone-tired and I could see the defeat in their eyes. But then Edward appeared." Tunstall shook his head. "You should have seen him, Jasper, he prowled the field like a lion. Deadly yet graceful. He fought with a terrifying ferocity, shoulder to shoulder with his men, throwing himself into wherever the fighting was thickest. It galvanised those around him, even when only moments before it seemed as though they'd fall from exhaustion." Tunstall gazed into the fire, lost in his thoughts. "Would it have inspired our men if the king had been alongside them like Edward was for his?" he wondered aloud. "Who can know? But if he had, he would almost certainly now be dead. Instead, Somerset was able to warn them. By the time the enemy marched through Micklegate Bar, the royal family were long gone."

Richard fell silent. Jasper watched his friend, unsure of what to say. He had participated in just one of the battles that had been fought in the months since Marguerite swept down from Scotland. Richard meanwhile had survived three; each one ageing him so that he appeared older than his thirty years. There was no sign of the optimism Jasper had read in the letter recounting York's death in the man who sat before him. The devastation of Towton made that triumph seem like a distant memory. If there were words that could soothe what Richard had witnessed then Jasper did not know them, and so the silence stretched out. Jasper fiddled with a loose thread on the arm of his chair, his mind struggling with the feelings of guilt that had plagued him since the defeat at Mortimer's Cross. Guilt for his father's death, for his inability to reach Marguerite with the men she had so desperately needed when London's gates had remained firmly shut against her, and for the losses that had flowed from it.

"I was sorry to hear about your father," Richard said quietly, breaking the silence. "He was a good man."

Jasper felt hot tears spring to his eyes. He shook his head, a wave of grief leaving him speechless. Wordlessly, Tunstall reached out a hand and squeezed his shoulder. "We have had our fair share of trials, you and I. It sometimes makes me long for those seemingly endless summers we spent together at court."

Jasper nodded in agreement. "Back when life was simpler," he remarked, a hesitant grin spreading slowly across his face. "Do you remember that time you gave Richard Neville a bloody nose? How Edmund had to hold him back to stop him from going after you?"

"Ha. I do not think he ever did forgive me for that," Richard chuckled.

Jasper relaxed back into his chair, grateful for the chance to reminisce with his old friend. "Where will you go now?" he asked, once their laughter had subsided.

"I'm not sure." Richard swirled the ale around in his cup. "Edward no doubt intends to scourge the country of any Lancastrian loyalty, but I imagine he'll bide his time, strengthen his position. For now, I'll lay low till the options are clearer." He looked over to Jasper. "And what will you do, my friend? Will you go to the king?"

Jasper shook his head. "Not unless he calls me or I'm left with no other choice. It will take time to build back to a strength that can challenge Edward. Until then I will stay in Pembrokeshire. There are people here who depend on me, my nephew foremost amongst them."

Richard smiled. "How is Henry?"

"Growing up fast. I cannot believe he's already four. He's a bright and curious boy, but I must admit he can be stubborn when he wants to be."

"Sounds rather like someone else I know," Richard replied with a wink.

"Careful," Jasper warned him jokingly.

"Well, my friend," Richard declared, raising his cup, "let us hope we can secure him a future more stable than our own."

Jasper nodded, knocking his own cup against Richard's. He leant back in his chair as the conversation turned to other things, letting Richard's description of his home and family in Lancashire distract him, if only for a moment, from the stress of his own reality.

15

August 1461

J asper was bent low over his desk, which was littered with an assortment of papers, some of them stained with ink from where he had carelessly knocked over the pot. The candle next to him sputtered and then went out in a wisp of smoke. Jasper sat up and flexed his aching hand. It felt like he'd been working for hours, his writing becoming an almost illegible scrawl. A stack of letters was balanced precariously on one corner of the desk, patiently awaiting his seal. They were addressed to the captains of his main strongholds, instructing them to reinforce their garrisons. In particular, he'd warned Harlech and Denbigh to prepare for a siege. After Towton, while most of the other nobles had bent a knee to the usurper, Jasper had continued his campaign of disrupting Yorkist influence in Wales. It had taken time for the Pretender Edward – Jasper still refused to call him king – to feel secure on his stolen throne, and Jasper had used this small reprieve to his advantage. But now after four months, the inevitable backlash was coming and he needed to be sure his men were prepared for the worse.

Putting down his pen, Jasper rubbed his face with his hands, trying to banish the tiredness creeping into his mind. Leaning back in his chair, he stretched until his shoulders gave a satisfying crack. Picking up the final letter, his eyes scanned what he had just written. He was finishing signing 'Pembroke' at the bottom when there was a knock at the door.

"Enter."

Sir John Scudamore, who had replaced John Vernon as the Constable of Pembroke, walked into the solar with a grim expression on his face.

"Is it true? They've given orders to seize your lordships?" he asked directly, without any preamble.

Jasper looked up, one eyebrow raised. Scudamore was a skilled veteran with a wealth of military experience, but he lacked his predecessor's tact.

"Sorry— my Lord," he added, correcting himself.

"Yes, it's true," Jasper sighed. Even admitting it out loud felt a defeat, and he could still feel the remnants of the anger that had consumed him when he'd first heard the news. "At least my title remains secure, although I doubt for much longer," he continued, reaching for his cup and draining it in one.

Jasper could tell Scudamore desperately wanted to speak up, yet he waited quietly, no doubt trying to make up for his earlier impertinence. Jasper stood up from his chair and went to refill his cup.

"I cannot say Edward, the bastard that he is, doesn't have a wry sense of humour. He's granted them to William Herbert, who I imagine will already be making preparations to come here. I'm sure he'd love to be the one to hand me over to this usurper. But I won't let him have that satisfaction. I'll be long gone by then."

"I'd like to see him try to take Pembroke," Scudamore grinned, showing his crooked teeth.

Jasper did not return the smile; instead, he remained stony faced. "You will surrender the castle." Scudamore looked at him in disbelief.

He opened his mouth to speak but Jasper held up a hand before he could interject. "And that is an order," he said firmly. Scudamore made little attempt to hide his incredulity. "I know it offends not just your principles but also the very oath you swore to me," Jasper continued more gently, pouring the other man some wine. "But I will not allow the lives of the people within these walls to be sacrificed just so I can cling to something I never expected to own."

"Where will you go?" Scudamore asked, taking the cup from Jasper's outstretched hand.

"It's better if you remain in the dark. It's not that I do not trust you," Jasper added, noticing the offended look on Scudamore's face." But Herbert will doubtless question you about my whereabouts, and at least this way you can answer him truthfully."

Scudamore nodded, clearly still not happy with the idea but choosing not to challenge Jasper.

"What will happen to Henry? Will you take him with you?"

Jasper shook his head. "Alone I can travel anonymously, but with a child? It's too conspicuous. As much as it breaks my heart to do it, I will leave him here. Herbert will do nothing to harm him. Henry's wardship is a valuable prize, and one he will want to secure for himself. I've sent a letter to Margaret explaining the situation. Edward has just pardoned Stafford for fighting against him at Towton, so at least that will protect Margaret, though I am sure she is far from thrilled at her husband's acquiescence to the usurper."

Jasper fell silent. Though he was trying to exude calmness, he felt completely overwhelmed; the momentum of Fortune's Wheel was truly against him. In times such as this, he felt his father's absence acutely. Owen would have known whether he was making the right decision. They would have sat up late together thrashing out different options and planning their next move.

A question from Scudamore brought his attention back to the solar.

"When do you leave?"

"Tomorrow at first light. I'll slip away before the castle is awake. I do not want any grand goodbyes, it's better if I go quietly and unseen."

Jasper surveyed the room. God only knew when he would next experience such comfort. He sighed deeply. "My time will come again," he said quietly, more to himself than to Scudamore. "And I look forward to when I can ride through these gates once more without a price on my head."

"I'll drink to that," said Scudamore, raising his cup and knocking it against Jasper's.

Jasper glanced over to the fire where Ianto was occupying his usual spot.

"Look after Ianto. Though our bond is closer than even that which Argos and Odysseus shared, I do not believe he will be here when I finally return."

At the sound of his name, Ianto's tail started to thump loudly on the rug. Jasper smiled. The tempo increased as Jasper walked over and knelt down next to him. Taking Ianto's great head in his hands, Jasper looked deeply into the eyes that had always seemed too knowing to belong to a dog. Though they were beginning to cloud slightly with age, they still spoke to something in Jasper's very soul. As he stared intently at the hound he'd raised from a pup, and who had followed him like a shadow ever since, Jasper thought he saw a glimmer of understanding, a recognition that this time he would not be coming home. Jasper leant down so his head was resting on Ianto's. "Goodbye, my friend."

* * *

Engaging in battle had been a last throw of the dice by desperate men. Jasper had known that from the moment they formed ranks in that godforsaken field. So too had Henry Holland, the Duke of Exeter, who was now crammed next to him in a small boat, shielding his face from the sea spray. Yet though it achieved nothing, Jasper was still proud of their last act of defiance. It had been a parting warning for the usurper Edward and all those who followed him that the House of Lancaster would not go down without a fight. That he hadn't simply rolled over and surrendered, like so many other nobles, made the defeat somewhat easier.

Jasper looked over his shoulder to the retreating shape of the Welsh coastline. He imagined Henry sitting in his nursery, waiting patiently to hear his familiar footsteps on the stone steps. Would he still be asking Joan where he'd gone? It had been two months since he'd left Pembroke. No, not left – fled. The word made his cheeks burn with shame. There were still times when he questioned the decision, usually late at night when the campfire had been reduced to embers and his stomach was growling with hunger. But he knew in his heart it was the right one. Vernon had stayed true to his word and surrendered Pembroke. No blood was shed, no lives wasted. If fleeing like a common fugitive was the price he had to pay to protect his people then it was one he would willingly give again.

It was a small miracle that they'd been able to talk their way onto a boat from Caernarfon, though the heavy pouch of coin Jasper pressed into the captain's hand certainly did no harm. The town had been crawling with Herbert's spies and it was only once they'd made it out of the port that Jasper felt he could breathe again. While the captain of their little vessel seemed competent enough, Jasper did not have the same confidence in the ship itself. They were being tossed about by the waves, the boat pitching alarmingly, sea water sloshing over the rails. Jasper was already soaked to the skin. Rain ran like rivers from his hair and down his face. The cold seeped deep into his bones, making his teeth chatter till Jasper feared they might fall out. Next to him, the Duke of Exeter didn't seem to be faring much better. What little Jasper could see of Holland's face through the assortment of material he'd pulled over himself, was tinged a sickly green and his eyes were screwed tightly shut. Luckily, the voyage to Ireland was not a long one. From there, they'd sail to Scotland, to King Henry's court in exile. Queen Marguerite, always a step ahead of her enemies, had managed to spirit her husband away to the north after Towton. Jasper could remember her anguish when the king had been captured after the battle of Northampton. He'd come face to face then with her tempestuous anger and had not doubted her resolve when she'd sworn she wouldn't let Henry fall into the enemy's hands ever again.

All that Jasper had in this world, he owed to the king. How different would his life have been had his half-brother made a different decision all those years ago? If he'd decided to disown them and leave Owen to languish in Newgate rather than raising them up? He lifted his head, squinting in the wind, trying to make out the first smudge of land on the horizon. Quirks of fate could determine entire lives; the Wheel never stopped turning. So long as King Henry and his son were alive there was hope for the House of Lancaster's future. As yet another wave broke over the prow of the ship, Jasper vowed to himself that he would do everything he could to secure that future.

II

Part Two

1461–1471

"Jasper was ordained for us, he will draw us out of the net and set us free..."

—Dafydd Llwyd o Fathafarn

16

November 1461

By the time they set foot in Scotland they were title-less and effectively penniless; little more than common fugitives. News of their attainder had surprised no one, least of all the men themselves, though that did little to soften the blow. Yet while Holland raged against the injustice, Jasper sat mute, silently contemplating how Fortune's Wheel could have brought him so low. Rather than the hot anger he might have expected, the loss of his earldom registered like a dull blow on a mind already numbed cold by defeat.

If he thought about it, maybe the reason for the contrast in his and his companion's reaction was that whilst Holland had seen three generations of accrued effort wiped away in a single pen stroke, Jasper had no such legacy to protect. He had come to his earldom unexpectedly, free from any inherited expectation. Pembroke was his alone to use, and his alone to lose. And maybe that was why his real anger was reserved for the name listed below his. Despite his hope for the contrary, not even a four-year-old was exempt from the Pretender's paranoia and greed. The earldom of Richmond, the only gift aside from life that Edmund had ever given his son, stolen away from Henry before he could even acknowledge it. He could imagine Margaret's reaction to the news and it made him hang his head in shame to think how he'd failed both mother and son.

Jasper inhaled unevenly, his throat aching from the effort of suppressing his emotions. His word of honour had pulled him in opposite directions, stretching him to breaking point. On one side, the fealty he owed his king, and on the other, the promise he'd made to a young girl abandoned in the brutal world of men. But that solemn oath echoed hollowly now, taunting him from across the distance of time. He had made his choice. He had walked through Pembroke's gates clear in the knowledge that he may never return, content to leave Henry to the mercy of the man responsible for his father's death. His duty to his king had won the battle that had raged within him. For now, at least, he would have to push Henry to the back of his mind. He could not afford to be distracted. More than their titles would be lost if he was.

Whilst their reduced status may have soured his and Holland's moods, it had done little to diminish the enthusiasm with which they were welcomed to Linlithgow Palace, now home to King Henry's court in exile. Their arrival had provided a much-needed, if only temporary, reprieve from the heavy gloom that enveloped the foreboding fortress and the hearts of those who now called it home. The fires in the magnificent great hall had been piled high and the long tables bedecked with what little finery had been saved after Towton. Marguerite presided over the rag-tag assortment of nobles and knights. As the king had slipped deeper into one of his episodes so she had stepped up to fill his place, her determination and iron-strong will making up for her husband's unresponsiveness. Positioned at Marguerite's right hand, Jasper was reminded of the night at Pembroke many months before when the queen had sought refuge behind his own castle's imposing walls. It had felt then as though their cause could not fall any lower. How wrong he had been. Still, it felt good after months on the road to be within the warmth of a castle and surrounded by people united under a common purpose. Further down the table, Holland was well on his way to intoxication, drowning his sorrows in the endless stream of wine supplied by servants. Despite the time they'd spent together over the last months, he'd never warmed to his travelling companion. The young duke was obnoxious and unpredictable, with a propensity for violence, and Jasper was quietly relieved that their time together had come to an end.

Marguerite had been deep in conversation for much of the evening with John Blacman, a wizened former monk who had recently been appointed as Prince Edward's new tutor. He had been Jasper's tutor once, back in those early days at court. He had been a patient yet firm teacher, one who'd hopefully be up to the task of educating Prince Edward. Adored by Marguerite, from his limited interactions with the boy Jasper thought him to be spoilt and ill-tempered. He did not envy Blacman his task. Absorbed as he was in his thoughts, Jasper was caught slightly off-guard when Marguerite turned her attention abruptly to him.

"What is your relationship like with the new King of France?" she asked without any preamble.

Jasper raised a questioning eyebrow. "Louis? I have not had cause to meet him."

"But he is your cousin?" Marguerite persisted.

"Yes," he replied steadily, still unsure where the queen's train of thought was headed. "But my mother's house is a large one that reaches all corners of Europe. I do not think my familial connection to him is particularly unique. Certainly, it would not afford me any special attention."

"Ah, that is where you are wrong. Louis is also my cousin, we have that in common, yet I have a better insight into his character. The Valois name may be widespread, but he understands the value it holds. When it comes to the ties that bind people together, he is somewhat of an expert. I hear in some quarters he has earned the nickname *L'Universelle Aragne.*"

"The Universal Spider." Jasper paused, taking a sip of wine. "And you wish me to take advantage of such ties?"

Margaret nodded. "You will cultivate our relations with our European cousins in France and Brittany. We need money Jasper, and soon. Men have already started to slip away, we cannot afford to lose any more," she confided. "Once the ground is prepared, Prince Edward and I will join you."

"And the king?"

Sadness flickered across Marguerite's face. "He will stay here in Scotland. I fear the journey will be too taxing for him," she replied, her usual display of strength faltering. The unspoken truth hung between them. No foreign leader would offer their support if they saw Henry in his current state. He was too delicate, too easily manipulated. Yet his face had lit up with recognition when Jasper had visited him in his chambers, drawing him towards him with the unguardedness of a child. With tears in his eyes, he had expressed his profound sorrow for Owen's death and together they had said prayers for the souls of the family they had lost. Yet what had been impossible to ignore was how much older the king had seemed. There were just ten years between them, but with his silver hair and bird-like limbs, it could have been thirty. Jasper placed a comforting hand on Marguerite's and she gave him a small smile in return. "There is no one else I trust other than you to do this."

17

April 1462

As it transpired Marguerite's confidence in their cousin, and in himself, was ill-founded. Two months in Brittany and Jasper had nothing to show for it but a pile of letters politely declining his request for an audience with King Louis. His adeptness at navigating the English court counted for nothing here, and the idea that it ever would have now seemed foolish. Yet the months had not been a complete waste. While the the gates of Château du Plessis-Les-Tours might have remained resolutely shut against his advances, the Breton court was decidedly more welcoming, and Duke Francis II had been more than happy to play the role of generous host. Attached to France like a mussel to a rock, Brittany reminded Jasper of Wales, and over the weeks he had grown fond of its ruler. Roughly his own age, Duke Francis was resourceful and diligent, his desire to maintain his region's quasi-independence from France influencing every decision he made. The two men shared a love of riding, and once Jasper's skill on a horse had been recognised, he had become a regular companion on Francis' daily rides, the two of them galloping hard through the woods surrounding Château de Clisson. Although not what he had planned for, his time in Brittany was not unhelpful. While biased,

Francis was extremely knowledgeable about the inner workings of the French court and Jasper took advantage of their outings together to learn all that he could. As such, he was feeling quietly confident about Marguerite's imminent arrival. He might not have met with Louis, but he had secured a loan of twelve thousand crowns from the duke and laid the foundations for a new alliance. He also had a strong suspicion that it would only be a matter of time before the French king's curiosity got the better of him; they just needed to be patient.

When Marguerite arrived a few days later, she was unusually taciturn and distant. More so than even Jasper's failure concerning Louis warranted. She had been cordial with Francis throughout her first evening in Brittany, yet despite her attempts to convey the contrary, it was clear something was troubling her. It was only after dinner when Francis had excused himself that Jasper was finally able to speak to her in private. He found her sitting with one of her ladies-in-waiting, a slim, fair-haired woman. Anne? Alice? Jasper could not recall her name, and at this particular moment, he did not much care. Without asking, he sat himself down next to the queen.

"What is troubling you, Marguerite? Something has happened, that much is obvious. Is there anything I can do to help?" he asked, his eyes searching the queen's downturned face for some clue.

For a while, she remained silent. Jasper was on the verge of repeating his question when she finally lifted her head to meet his gaze, her eyes full of tears. "The Earl of Oxford is dead."

Jasper's brow furrowed in confusion. John de Vere was a loyal man and a valuable asset, there was no denying his loss was a blow, though not so disastrous as to warrant Marguerite's acute distress. "There's more. What are you not telling me?"

"I will not speak of it," Marguerite replied, standing abruptly, anger breaking through her sadness. "I will not give voice to the barbarity they have committed."

Without another word, she swept from the room. Jasper made to follow but a sharp look from Anne or Alice, who no doubt held him personally responsible for the queen's distress, brought him up short. Looking around the room in bewilderment, his eyes settled on an elderly man standing alone in a corner. Sir John Fortescue, King Henry's former Chief Justice, had accompanied Marguerite from Scotland. Widely respected for his wisdom and integrity, he was a man who would rather see twenty guilty people escape the death penalty than let one innocent suffer capitally. At nearly seventy, the old judge's face was heavily lined yet his eyes remained bright, evidence of the sharp mind that whirred behind them. Jasper made straight for him.

"What happened to Oxford?" he asked, in an urgent whisper, conscious of others who may be listening. "Why is the queen so distressed?"

"He was executed," Fortescue replied, seemingly unsurprised by the intrusion.

"Yes, I gathered as much," Jasper bit back.

Fortescue gave him a withering look that must have made many a criminal's heart stutter. Jasper glanced away, embarrassed by his impertinence. After a beat, the old judge continued. "They uncovered his plot against King Edward. I believe you were a key player in his plans?"

A wave of guilt washed over Jasper. "We had discussed the idea of drawing the Pretender north and then launching simultaneous invasions," he explained slowly, trying to remember details contained in hastily scrawled letters. "I would attack from Wales, the king from Scotland, and Somerset from East Anglia." He sighed. "It certainly had merit, but given our current situation, I did not consider it a viable option. I assumed Oxford thought the same."

Fortescue looked at him as though he was a naive child. "Do you think Edward cared about its viability?" He shook his head. "A plot, however preposterous, is still a threat. They intercepted Oxford's letters to Somerset, after which his fate was sealed. He and his son were brought in front of Sir John Tiptoft, the newly appointed High Lord Constable. Oxford's son was simply beheaded, but the earl himself—" Fortescue trailed off. Jasper waited quietly for him to gather himself. Clearing his throat, he continued. "Executions can be an effective deterrent. Certainly, for an offence such as high treason, it is the only suitable penalty. However, there is a line beyond which judicial punishment tips into gratuitous cruelty. Tiptoft, the brute that he is, acts beyond that line and Oxford, God rest his soul, was on the receiving end. First, they disembowelled him, then they castrated him, and finally, while he was still conscious, they tied him to a stake and burned him."

Jasper swallowed uncomfortably, his mouth suddenly dry. His discomfort did not go unnoticed by Fortescue, who placed a hand on his shoulder. "That is why the queen is so distressed," he continued, more gently. "It speaks to her worst fears about the safety of herself and her family. Give her time to process the news. She will be back to her usual self before long. It is a dangerous game we have chosen to play, yet play we must."

* * *

Fortescue's words continued to echo in Jasper's head, the idea of being an unwitting pawn in a game determined by fate keeping his mind preoccupied on the long ride to France. Marguerite had only been in Brittany for a week or so when Louis' invitation finally arrived. They now found themselves in Amboise, a bustling market town in the centre of France filled with crooked timber-framed buildings. The town's imposing château, confiscated from its original owner by Louis' father, was the French king's favourite residence. As Louis honoured guests, a suite of rooms had been prepared for them, though they had yet to meet the king himself. Apparently he was preoccupied with some local administrative matters, but in Jasper's eyes it was just another tactic designed to wrongfoot them. Not that there was any point in getting frustrated: they had no other choice than to wait till Louis was ready. At least Marguerite seemed in better spirits. Fortescue had been correct in his belief that she would overcome her distress over Oxford, and she was certainly energised about their forthcoming audience. Yet something almost imperceptible had shifted in her. He was not sure exactly what it was, but her demeanour was more guarded, as if she'd erected an emotional barrier to protect herself from further upset. Still, she seemed jovial enough as the cards and counters were laid out for the evening's game of *Brelan*. It had become a sort of nightly ritual between them after Marguerite had introduced him to the game at Linlithgow. The rules themselves were simple enough, with each player aiming to secure a *brelan carre*, a hand with three cards of matching rank to the one dealt face-up. What made it more interesting was the betting. It required discipline and patience, and over many rounds, Jasper had steadily honed his skills. Not that he won every game. As in life, the queen was adept at controlling her emotions and Fortescue, with his lifetime of unearthing the hidden secrets of men, was a formidable opponent whenever he chose to join them. There was a comfortable informality to the time spent around the card table, which allowed for frank conversations. Tonight was no exception, the impending audience with Louis at the forefront of all their minds. So much was dependent on their ability to negotiate advantageous terms, and now that the moment was upon them, the responsibility weighed like a stone.

"How do you intend to win over Louis?" Jasper asked, placing his initial bet on the table as Fortescue began shuffling the deck.

"With honesty," Marguerite replied, adding her counters to the pile.

"I will not try to outwit his intelligence. He is a shrewd ruler who will do whatever he judges to be in his country's best interests. I can use that to our advantage."

"A wise choice, your Grace. Only fools underestimate their opponents," Fortescue commented, continuing to move the cards between his hands. "If I recall correctly, his own route to the throne was not without its difficulties. I imagine he will empathise with your husband's situation."

Jasper nodded in agreement. "It certainly does him no favours to have a usurper succeed in the way Edward has done. It could give his own nobles ideas. And we all know where that ends," he added, with an ironic smile.

The conversation died out as Fortescue began expertly dealing out the cards. Trying to appear nonchalant, Jasper reached for his and discretely glanced at them. An ace, a queen and an eight. Not perfect, but not unsalvageable either. He watched intently as with a flourish, Fortescue dealt the face-up card. A king. It was not to be his night. Next to him, Marguerite pushed forward a handful of counters.

"*Relancer,*" she announced, not even trying to disguise her confidence.

Jasper assessed the pile of counters in the centre of the table. He could call her bluff, but he had nothing to back it up, and he'd already lost enough. With a sigh, he leant back in his chair. "*Filer.*"

Never a man to be hurried, Fortescue took a slow slip of his wine before matching Marguerite's bet. "*Tenir.*" Clearly, he did not fancy risking it all on this particular round. With a nod, they turned over their hands. Fortescue's was strong with three nines but Marguerite's—

"A house of kings," Jasper murmured approvingly.

Marguerite smiled at him triumphantly. "Let us hope it is an omen of what is to come."

* * *

Walking into the throne room, Jasper was suddenly grateful for the clothes Francis had gifted him. He'd only managed to save a few possessions from Pembroke and whilst his sword and garter chain spoke to his status, his clothes had left something to be desired. Francis had taken one look at him on their first evening together and declared he would send for his tailor immediately. "My gift," he'd stressed, as if reading Jasper's mind about the cost of such extravagance. The new doublet and hose were made from a rich dark cloth, with velvet accents. Cut in the Breton fashion, they fitted Jasper perfectly, accentuating his slim, muscular physique. The attention of every courtier in the room was focused on their small group and at least their clothes did not draw any mockery. For her part, Marguerite, dressed in a low-cut, blood-red gown, looked every inch a queen, carrying herself with a self-assuredness Jasper did not share. A hush fell as she stepped towards the dais on which Louis was sitting and swept into a low curtsey, her knees practically touching the floor. Standing, she raised her head, fixing her intense stare on the king.

"*Votre Majesté*, I come to you as your cousin, as a wife, as a mother, and as a queen who has had her divine prerogative stolen away from her. I come to ask for your assistance, one monarch to another. You know what it is to fight for what is yours; help me defeat the Pretender who threatens all that I hold dear."

Her voice rang out clearly without hesitation or uncertain stutter. The words were exactly what they'd discussed the previous night, striking a delicate balance between strength and deference. However, what had not been planned was what the queen did next, and Jasper could only stare in astonishment as she prostrated herself in front of Louis. The gesture also took the French king by surprise, and in the silence that drew out, Jasper was struck by the powerlessness of their

123

position. Laid out on the tiled floor, the vulnerability of Marguerite's prone figure, whilst moving, highlighted the fragility of their cause. They were fooling themselves if they thought they held any bargaining power in this exchange. Their fine clothes and jewellery were nothing more than a borrowed façade, and one Jasper was certain Louis could see straight through.

There was only one thing that they could offer him that had any value, and it made Jasper sick to his stomach to even think of it. Calais. If handing Berwick to the Scots had been shameful enough, the loss of Calais would damn them in the eyes of every Englishman from Cornwall to Cumberland. And yet, however distasteful, they had no choice. It was their only option if they were ever going to set foot on English soil again.

Louis eventually regained his composure, stepping forward to help raise Marguerite from the floor. "Of course I will help you," he said gently, though from the unmistakable glint in his eye it was clear that the Universal Spider's mind was already spinning a new web.

* * *

Jasper scanned the document in front of him. As well as two thousand men and twenty thousand francs, it gave Marguerite the authority to raise men in Normandy. In return, she had committed to a hundred-year truce between their nations and to return Calais to the French. Louis was not naive to the difficulties their campaign faced. As such, there was an added caveat that if Calais was not returned within a year, they would be made to pay double what they'd been given as a penalty. It was plain who the real beneficiary of the treaty was. Jasper glanced up at Marguerite, their eyes locking. She nodded her head. With a resigned sigh, Jasper picked up the quill, adding his mark below that of the king and queen. It angered him to see the smug looks on the faces of the French dignitaries, but they'd got what they had come for. Now they needed to act on it.

18

October 1462

The white crests of the waves broke like wild horses on the beach before being dragged out once more by the relentless undertow in a never-ceasing cycle. The sand that in summer glowed golden against crystal blue skies looked dull and lifeless, merging with the thunderous storm clouds that swirled above. Looming over the sandy bay like a slumbering giant, Bamburgh castle was one of the last Lancastrian strongholds in England. Exposed to the elements, it was only a stone's throw from the churning North Sea, its position allegoric of their fortunes; pushed to the outer extremities of the country, its deep foundations holding fast despite the shifting sands beneath. The raging wind howled around it, hurling waves and gusts of rain against the broad stone walls. Only the mad or truly desperate would brave such conditions, which was why Jasper was standing on the castle's highest promontory, his eyes trained on the horizon looking for the first glimpse of the Royal fleet.

He had arrived a week or so before, the crenellated walls that rose from the gently rolling plain surrounding Bamburgh a welcoming sight after days on the road from Scotland. It had been raining then too. In fact, Jasper struggled to remember a time when the sky had not been a foreboding shade of grey. The castle was one of a trio of strategic Northumberland strongholds within which the admittedly fragile heart of Lancastrian hope continued to beat. Alnwick and Dunstanburgh completed the group. The latter, a bleak fortress on an isolated headland twelve miles down the coast, was held by Sir Ralph Percy. The grandson of Henry Hotspur, death haunted him like a shadow, as it did nearly every man of their generation. His losses charted the conflict's progression. First his father at St Albans and a younger brother at Northampton, and then the triple blow of Towton; two brothers dead, his nephew imprisoned and the family title of Northumberland stolen away. Not even his barely contained anger at Marguerite's decision to hand Berwick over to the Scots could overcome the depths of his hatred of York, the blood feud winning out against historical animosity. The message he sent to the new arrivals had been welcoming but characteristically forthright, promising the full might of the Percy name at their disposal. The situation at Alnwick had the potential to be more complicated. The Duke of Somerset, who had trudged through the seemingly never-ending miles of mud from Scotland at Jasper's side had been quickly dispatched to secure it from the Yorkist sympathiser holding it. He had anticipated a siege, but in the end, the mere sight of the unruly Scots was enough to convince its constable to hand over the keys.

Jasper felt a presence behind him and turned to see Sir William Tunstall ascend the final steps up to the battlements on which he stood. A few years younger than his brother Richard, William was slim with dark hooded eyes that darted nervously.

"Any sign of them, my Lord?" he asked, attempting to bring his breathing under control after the long climb.

"No, not even a glimpse of a sail," Jasper replied, turning his attention back out to sea.

They stood in silence for a while, both pairs of eyes scanning the tempestuous water, the wind whipping their cloaks and tangling their hair.

"Is there a reason that you climbed up all this way?" Jasper asked coolly, with no hint of his usual good humour. While he trusted Richard implicitly, he had never warmed to the younger Tunstall. He did not have the same unwavering commitment as his brother, preferring instead to lend his support to whoever's cause was in ascendance. Just a month before, he had been holding Bamburgh for the Pretender. It was only Richard's fraternal intervention and the threat of the approaching Royal fleet that had convinced William to turn the castle over without resistance. The unreliability of his loyalty made Jasper cautious in his interactions with him, and since arriving at Bamburgh his keen grey eyes had been watching the other man almost constantly, as they were now, making William shift uncomfortably.

"Sorry, my Lord," he mumbled. "The Duke of Somerset has returned from Alnwick and is keen to speak to you."

"And where might I find him?"

"He is in the great hall."

Jasper nodded and with a final glance at the waves, began his descent into the heart of the castle. He moved quickly with little regard for either the steepness or the sound of William's faltering steps behind him, confident that his own feet would find each step. He arrived in the great hall as a fully laden platter was set down on the long table in front of Somerset, who tucked into it hungrily.

"Are you going to save some of that for me?" Jasper asked with a smile as he walked over.

Somerset glanced up from his plate. "Jasper!" he exclaimed, flecks of food flying from his mouth.

Jasper took up his place opposite his friend, accepting the cup of small ale that was poured for him. Raising it, he knocked it against Somerset's. Some of the ale sloshed over the side onto the table, mingling with the other marks and stains that told the story of the countless feasts that had taken place beneath the hall's vaulted ceiling. "So, what news from Alnwick?"

"Very little, if I'm honest. The constable, Sir Ralph Grey, claims it was a shortage of food that made him surrender. In reality, he's just ashamed to admit what he really is – a coward."

"Or a realist," Jasper countered. "With Bamburgh and Dunstanburgh already under our control, he may have thought any resistance would be worthless and simply sought to avoid any unnecessary bloodshed."

"As ever my friend, your consideration for the other side is admirable. Regardless of his reasoning, Alnwick is secured. And most importantly, before the king and queen's arrival. Has there been any sight of the fleet?"

"None." Jasper's brow furrowed with concern. "They were due days ago. Granted, the weather will have made the journey more difficult, but it should not have taken them this long."

If he had hoped his friend would share his unspoken fears then he was mistaken. Somerset waved a chicken leg dismissively. "You worry too much."

"And you too little," Jasper sighed leaning back in his chair. "I pray to God they arrive soon. The Pretender is fully aware of our presence here. I've heard murmurings that Warwick is preparing to march north to confront us. If that's true then we only have a matter of weeks before they are upon us."

"I'm sure Ralph Percy will relish any opportunity to wipe that smug grin off Warwick's face," Somerset said with a laugh that Jasper did not share. "Relax Jasper. The fleet will arrive any day now, along with the soldiers Louis granted her. There are already three hundred men in Bamburgh's garrison alone, not to mention the scores of Scots who marched from Berwick with us. We can withstand whatever Warwick may throw at us."

Jasper nodded. It was impossible not to give in to Somerset's charm, but still, he could not fully shake his creeping sense of doubt.

* * *

The ships arrived the next day as the storm lost its anger and the skies were beginning to clear. One moment the horizon was empty, and the next it was filled with a mass of masts and sails. Relief flooded through Jasper when the shout went up. After weeks of anxious waiting, he relished the frenetic activity that now gripped the castle as the final preparations were made. Somerset gave him a knowing 'I told you so' smile when they passed each other in the corridor, each hurrying in opposite directions. Within a few hours, the first of the new arrivals were being transferred from the ships to the longboats that would ferry them to shore.

Standing on the sand just out of reach of the wash from the breaking waves, Jasper watched as the boat carrying the king and queen navigated the surf. Somerset, standing a few paces ahead of him, unbothered by the seawater soaking through his boots, was the first to greet the royal couple.

"Welcome to Northumberland, your Majesties," he declared, sweeping into a low bow. As he straightened, his eyes took in the king, supported like a child with servants on each side gripping his arms tightly. Marguerite saw the focus of his gaze and her own eyes narrowed in displeasure.

Jasper stepped forward to prevent a confrontation. "We are relieved you were able to negotiate the storm. I admit I was worried it might overcome you," he said quickly.

Marguerite's expression softened. "We have the Captain to thank for our safe passage." Glancing over her shoulder, she waved over a stocky, silver-haired man who had been assisting with the boats.

"Jasper, may I introduce Captain Pierre de Brézé?"

Jasper inclined his head in welcome. "Captain, your reputation precedes you."

"As does yours," the Frenchman replied with a smile, although Jasper had the distinct feeling that behind the amiable façade the old soldier was assessing him.

"And this is Henry Beaufort, the Duke of Somerset," Jasper continued, motioning to his friend in an attempt to dilute the scrutiny of Brézé's gaze.

The Captain bowed briefly to Somerset. "Your Grace."

Marguerite, who had been watching the interaction with the expression of a woman who was all too familiar with the unspoken jostling of men, gave a bored sigh. "I'm not sure about you, sirs, but I would certainly prefer the warmth of a fire to this blustering sea breeze. Shall we?"

* * *

Jasper pinched the bridge of his nose and let out a loud sigh. Captain Pierre de Brézé, who had been in full flow gave him a contemptuous look. "*Pardon* my Lord, was I boring you?"

"What? No, of course not Captain. Please, you were saying?" Jasper replied, straightening himself in his chair and trying to refocus his attention. God only knew how long they had been sitting here locked in debate, and still they were no closer to reaching a consensus.

"I was saying," the Captain said tersely, "that we should push south while we still can."

"Respectfully, I disagree," Somerset countered. "Taking London is not the only way to destabilise Edward. He is reliant on the Nevilles. If we break their hold on the North, the rest will follow."

Brézé shook his head. "You have a personal score to settle with the

Earl of Warwick. I respect that, but it clouds your judgement."

Somerset opened his mouth to respond but Jasper cut across him. "I think you both continue to overlook the central issue. We are vulnerable and already spread too thin. If it comes to it, we do not have enough men to win a pitched battle against Warwick. We need to focus our energies on building support, whether that be here in Northumberland or further afield. Pockets of Wales still hold out for Lancaster. We could achieve more if we coordinated with the commanders at Harlech."

"Despite what you might think, Wales is not the answer to all our problems," Brézé retorted.

Jasper rounded on him, but the queen intervened before he could challenge the Frenchman's insolence. "Sirs," she announced, raising a hand. Sitting alone at the head of the table, the chair next to her was conspicuously vacant, the king having long since retired. The table fell silent. "It is obvious everyone here holds strong opinions, and I commend you for your passion. It makes me proud to know my husband has such men supporting him. Yet, the hour is late. I suggest we retire for the evening. The problems we are wrestling with will still be here in the morning. After a good night's rest, we may all be better equipped to deal with them."

There were mutterings of ascent, and the men around the table began to rise, stretching out limbs that had gone numb from so many hours in one position. Somerset caught Jasper's arm as he made to leave.

"We cannot go on like this," he whispered sharply.

"What do you mean?" Jasper asked, glancing at the others to check no one was in earshot.

"How can we expect to challenge Edward if we cannot even come to an agreement about this?"

Jasper looked back at Somerset, surprised by his friend's sudden pessimism. Normally sanguine, the duke seemed tense and exhausted, devoid of his previous nonchalance. His young face was lined with worry and dark shadows ringed his eyes.

"Go to bed, Henry," Jasper said gently. "The queen is right, it is late. Things will seem better in the morning."

"And what if they aren't?"

"Where has this doubt come from?" Jasper asked, trying to push away a creeping sense of unease. "You were the one who chided me for such thinking just the other day."

Somerset glanced away. "Jasper, I—"

He stopped as the sound of running reached their ears. Instinctively, both men's hands reached for their weapons. There was a loud bang as the chamber doors burst open and William Tunstall came rushing in.

"Warwick is coming!"

19

December 1462

The shock waves reverberated through the walls as another barrage struck the castle. A fortnight of almost constant bombardment had left countless dead and the survivors exhausted. Jasper had ordered those who remained to take shelter in the keep hall. Here in Bamburgh's fortified heart, they continued to wait for the reinforcements Captain Pierre de Brézé had promised and which even now would be marching quickly south. The king and queen had set sail for Berwick a few days before Warwick's bear and ragged staff banners had appeared on the horizon, safely ushered into the same boats that had only recently delivered them. Somerset had headed out for Dunstanburgh shortly after with a few hundred men to reinforce Ralph Percy's garrison. Jasper would have expected to have heard from him by now but it was likely any messengers had been cut off by the enemy's quick approach. It was a frustrating situation and Jasper missed his friend's counsel. Beyond the castle's walls, about twenty-odd miles south, Warwick – or the Kingmaker to use his recently acquired moniker – was overseeing simultaneous sieges against Bamburgh, Dunstanburgh and Alnwick from his base at Warkworth. It seemed as though all the Yorkist nobles had been conscripted into the campaign. All, that is, except the Pretender himself who had been taken ill at Durham. Jasper hoped whatever ailment afflicted him would prove fatal.

The keep hall was not a large room and there was barely enough space for the number of men crammed inside. The low, arched roof added to the sense of claustrophobia, the moans of the injured echoing off the stone. Designed for defence rather than comfort, one corner was dominated by an old well of unknown depth. That thirst would not be the cause of their deaths was of little reassurance to the men sheltering inside the keep. There was only one entrance, a peculiar bottle-shaped door designed to allow a rider to enter without dismounting, not that there was room for a horse amongst all the bodies.

The men nearest it started as three loud knocks sounded on the wood. From the other side, a voice called out, "I have news for the Earl of Pembroke."

Jasper, who had been deep in conversation with the store master about the need for further rationing, looked up at the sound of his former title. He picked his way through the tightly packed room as the door was opened to reveal a weary messenger clutching a note. He thrust it towards Jasper, who snatched it from his outstretched hand and quickly broke through Somerset's seal:

Our cause is lost. The royal fleet has been shipwrecked, all are presumed drowned – the king and queen amongst them. No reinforcements are coming. Warwick has offered a pardon to all those who swear loyalty to York. All, that is, except you; he has sworn he will have your head. I am sorry, my friend.

The news was like two sharp kicks to the gut. The king and queen, dead? Jasper could not believe it, would not believe it. And the

135

second? It was clear enough, though he had not explicitly said what he had done, and the unexpectedness of the betrayal left Jasper breathless. Henry Beaufort, the noble Duke of Somerset, whose hatred for York was so deep-rooted it had seemed unfathomable it could ever be extinguished, had bent the knee to the Pretender. Jasper let out a frustrated roar causing the messenger to take a nervous step backwards.

For a moment it was as though he was back at Hay, on the night he had heard of his father's death, that same sense of suffocating helplessness threatening to overwhelm him again, the ground that had only moments before been stable and certain suddenly giving way. Life over loyalty. That was the choice Somerset had made. A choice Jasper did not have the luxury to make. In a way, he supposed he should be flattered that, out of all those who fought for the true king, it was he alone that Warwick had singled out, but in reality, the thought brought little comfort. Death awaited him, whatever decision he made. Yet it was not only his life he held in his hands; it was also the lives of the men crammed into the keep hall alongside him. Jasper looked around the room. Though some eyes still burned with determination, the bloodied, gaunt and exhausted faces told him all he needed to know.

"Raise the white flag."

* * *

Briefly, Jasper entertained the idea of disguising himself amongst his men, but he quickly shook the thought from his head. He was no coward. He would not shrink away from his fate. He would meet it face-on, with his head held high. Besides, he was almost certain William Tunstall would have given him up if he'd tried; anything to re-ingratiate himself with Warwick. At his signal, the bolts, each thicker than a man's arm, were slid back and Bamburgh's gates slowly swung open.

For a moment, it was as though time slowed, the seconds drawing out. And then in a rush, a mass of men flooded through the gates, blotting out the light from the setting sun and filling the castle's inner ward in an instant. Jasper's vision seemed to narrow, his heartbeat filling his ears and drowning out the sounds of the enemy's triumphant cheers. He watched as if in a dream as one of his own men ran forward, his sword raised. He tried to shout a warning but his tongue felt like lead in his mouth and he could do nothing to prevent the scything blow that cut the man down. In a matter of seconds what remained of Bamburgh's garrison were surrounded, pikes and billhooks levelled at their chests. Tension hung thick in the air, the enemy's thirst for blood palpable. One false move and they would all be dead.

Raising his hands, Jasper took a slow step forward. "My name is Jasper Tudor, Earl of Pembroke, and I have command of this garrison," he began, trying to keep his voice steady, ignoring the enemy's jeers. "I wish to speak with the Earl of Warwick." There was no response, the men in front of him exchanging grins with one another as though sharing in some private joke. And so, he tried again, this time more forcefully. "I wish to speak with the Earl of Warwick." Days of no sleep and eating only scraps had dulled his senses, slowing his reactions. By the time he noticed the club swinging through the air, it was too late. The blow struck his head and the world went dark.

* * *

The sound of water dripping steadily invaded Jasper's unconscious dreams. It intermingled with the soothing images of home parading across his mind until the intrusiveness of the sound was impossible to ignore. When his eyes fluttered open, it was not the rolling hills of

Pembrokeshire that greeted him, but the pitch-black and icy coldness of a prison cell. It took a moment for his eyes to adjust to the gloom. He was alone, save for the rat he could hear scrabbling in the corner, and slumped against a wall opposite a thick cell door. Next to him, the water which had dragged him back to consciousness continued to drip. His head was throbbing, a trickle of blood running slowly down his face. He lifted a hand to wipe it away, but his arm was strangely heavy and unresponsive. Glancing down he saw the reason why. Iron chains bound his wrists and ankles, the rough metal rubbing against his skin.

How long had he been unconscious? A few minutes? An hour? Here in the darkness, it was impossible to know. Was this how Edmund had spent his final days, he wondered, chained and alone, feeling life slip away, sure in the knowledge that no one was coming to save him? An unbidden image of his brother's face rose up in his mind. Yet unlike the Edmund he had known in real life, this ghostly visage was twisted and bloodied, its mouth silently screaming for help that would never come.

Jasper shook his head. "Get a grip of yourself," he muttered. He sucked in a long breath in an attempt to slow his racing heart. Focusing on the door in front of him, he tried to bring order to the thoughts whirring in his head. It was not the idea of dying that scared him. In fact, he imagined that death, when it finally greeted him, would be a swift release, and the thought of being reunited with his parents and brother was not unappealing. No, it was what would come before that made his blood run cold. *Warwick has sworn he will have your head.* Somerset's warning echoed in his mind. He'll want more than that, Jasper thought grimly, remembering the Earl of Oxford's gruesome demise. He closed his eyes against another wave of panic, forcing his thoughts to happier subjects. To Henry and Margaret, and the life they could have lived, if duty had not pulled him away. Would they mourn him? Margaret maybe, but he was fooling himself if he thought his nephew remembered him.

A new sound disrupted Jasper's thoughts. Quiet at first, but getting louder. Footsteps. Death had come knocking at last. He scrambled to his feet, swaying slightly on legs that had gone to sleep. As the key turned in the lock, Jasper steeled himself to face the Earl of Warwick. But when the door swung open, it was not the Kingmaker's scornful face that greeted him. For the first time in weeks, a flicker of hope sparked in Jasper's mind as Sir John Neville stepped into his cell.

The younger Neville took in the scene in front of him; Jasper's bloodied face, his torn clothes and the chains around his limbs. "Fortune is a fickle mistress, is she not?" he sneered, clearly enjoying the change in circumstances. It had been more than four years since they'd held hands during the Loveday parade. Since then, Jasper's luck had gone from bad to worse, while Neville's had seemed to belong to the Devil.

"Sir John." Jasper nodded.

"It's Lord Montagu now," he replied with a smirk, unable to hide his satisfaction with his new title. "Whereas you are nothing but a nobody."

"If I were a nobody, you would not be here," Jasper bit back. Anger flashed in Neville's eyes. Jasper silently cursed his foolishness. It did him no favours to goad the man who had the power to set him free. With a shake of his head, Neville turned to leave. Jasper felt his heart leap into his mouth, but pride prevented him from calling out. At the threshold Neville paused, glancing back at him. "You are fortunate that King Edward is more merciful than my brother. You and your men will be escorted to the Scottish border and released," he drawled. As he left the cell, Jasper's legs gave way from underneath him and he collapsed to the ground, relief flooding his body.

20

January 1463

The return march to Berwick was as arduous as the outward one. Never had twenty miles felt so long. With every step, thick mud sucked at Jasper's boots, while hail pelted him in the face. His only belongings were the clothes he was wearing, and they were now little more than sodden rags. The rest, including his sword, garter chain, and the gifts from Francis, had been either confiscated or stolen by Neville's men, though at least his father's ring still encircled his finger. Hunger gnawed at his stomach, leaving him hollow and light-headed, while an unshakeable paranoia that Neville would renege on his oath pervaded his thoughts. The relief he had felt when Neville had stepped into his cell had given way to an uneasy wariness. He saw no glimmer of the boy he knew from childhood in the hard-faced man riding at the front of the column. In the shadow of his elder brother, John Neville had grown bitter and mean, the reality of always being second souring his character. Rather than being sated by elevation to the peerage, his ambition had increased, making him blinkered and unpredictable. Jasper could only hope that Neville's loyalty to the man who had raised him up would ensure their safe passage, and with every laboured step he took that hope became more solid as they marched ever nearer to safety.

As they crested what felt like the hundredth hill, an excited shout went up amongst his men. Below them, the River Tweed, which marked the long -disputed border between England and Scotland, wound lazily before spreading out into the sea. On the far side, Berwick's town walls seemed to rise out of the water, and Jasper felt his spirits lift at the sight of the Royal standard flying high above the castle. Somerset's source had been mistaken: they were alive.

Without warning the soldiers who had guarded them so closely over the long miles came to a halt. Neville's men would escort them no further. It was all the encouragement the prisoners needed, and as one they began to hurry down the hill, limbs that had only moments before felt heavy and weary suddenly refreshed now that freedom was in sight. Jasper began to follow them, making it a few paces before Neville called out.

"Tudor, wait."

Those nearest Jasper paused but he waved them on. Turning, he watched as Neville reached into his saddle bag, and from its depths, withdrew a sword. He felt his heart falter. Was this truly where his luck ran out? Neville crossed the space between them in a few long strides, swinging the sword in lazy circles as he went. Jasper braced himself for the deadly blow, but it never came. Fear turned to confusion as Neville presented the sword to him.

"I believe this is yours."

Taking it in his hands, Jasper saw the familiar etching of his mother's motto on the blade. "How— I—" he stuttered in disbelief. "Thank you."

Neville nodded. There was nothing more that needed to be said.

* * *

The bells of Berwick's churches tolled out as Jasper and his men made their way through the streets. Whether they sounded in welcome or warning, Jasper did not know; nor did he care. Food and rest were the only things on his mind. Those men who called the town home peeled off one by one, heading for the embrace of loved ones, or a jug of ale. By the time they reached the castle walls, the group had dwindled to a handful of French and Irish mercenaries. To Jasper's surprise, the gates were wide open and the inner ward was alive with activity. Supplies were being loaded into carts, soldiers were sparring and above it, the clang of the blacksmith's hammer rang out unceasingly.

Jasper grabbed a young boy as he rushed past. "What's the reason for all this commotion?"

"The Earl of Angus is marching out with the French captain," the boy replied breathlessly. "They are going to retake Northumberland!"

Jasper released him, his good mood instantly evaporating. What the hell were they thinking? It was little over a month since he had surrendered Bamburgh and already they were planning to return. With a dismayed shrug, he dismissed those men still hanging around him. Hopefully they'd be able to find some respite before they were pressed into service once more. Meanwhile, he headed straight for the armoury, where he was certain he would find Brézé. Sure enough, he found the Frenchman hunched over a large-scale map of Northumberland, next to a broad-shouldered man with a thick ginger beard, who Jasper recognised vaguely as the Earl of Angus. Brézé glanced up at the sound of Jasper's arrival.

"*Mon Dieu*, you're alive!" he exclaimed in disbelief.

"I could say the same of you, Captain. I heard your fleet was destroyed?"

Brézé nodded gravely. "Many lives were lost."

"And now you plan to try again?"

"Aye," Angus confirmed. "That is our intention."

142

"You know Somerset defected?" Jasper challenged. "He bent the knee and already lent his support to the siege at Alnwick. Percy too has sworn loyalty to the Pretender. There may be nothing left for you to salvage when you get there."

Brézé shook his head. "Somerset's betrayal is indeed unfortunate, but Percy is now the constable of Bamburgh as well as Dunstanburgh. We've had word he will turn over the castles as soon as we arrive. And we have surprise on our side. They won't be expecting us to attack again so soon. With the men Angus has provided us," he continued motioning to the burly Scotsman next to him, "victory will be ours."

Jasper was silent for a moment, digesting the information. Whatever Ralph Percy had said must have been extremely convincing for him to still be trusted to such an extent. Either that, or the Pretender was more desperate for support than he had realised. It was more than his sleep-deprived mind could contend with. He rubbed his face with his hand and let out a long sigh.

"If you'll excuse me, sirs, I have had a testing journey and there is much for me to consider. I dare say I am also in dire need of a bathe." With a nod, he turned his back, leaving Brézé and Angus to their map.

* * *

Alone in his chambers, Jasper wrestled with all that had happened over the last few days. He almost felt sick with the speed at which Fortune's Wheel had turned. Try as he might, he could not share in Brézé's enthusiasm for the new campaign. All he could focus on was the seeming futility of their actions. It felt like they were going around in circles, and despite his best efforts, Jasper struggled to shake the disquieting sense of déjà vu nagging at the edges of his mind. He was not sure he could stomach the idea of returning to Northumberland so soon, but ultimately he had no say in the matter. He was at the disposal of his queen and would go wherever she saw fit. The lack of acknowledgement for his close brush with death had left him under no illusion that he was of any more importance than the next man.

* * *

At supper the next evening, he tried not to give into the hopelessness welling up inside him. He kept his voice light and laughed along with Angus' bawdy jokes. In a matter of days, they would set off for Northumberland and Jasper still did not know what his role in the campaign would be. It was with a sense of foreboding, then, that he let Marguerite draw him aside after the others had headed off to bed.

"You will not be coming with us to Northumberland," she informed him. "If this campaign is unsuccessful, I need to know we have options to fall back on. The patience of our Scottish hosts is wearing thin and I have heard whisperings of a truce with the Pretender. It seems we must look elsewhere for support. Reach out to our friends on the continent, my father even. Do what you must, so that if Fortune's Wheel turns against us, there will still be safe havens available where we may take shelter and plan our next move."

21

December 1463

After days spent confined in the château while a storm raged, Jasper welcomed the night's cold and clean air, breathing it in deeply. The wind that had whipped the falling snow into blinding blizzards had finally abated, the soft flakes now drifting lazily downwards. The landscape was almost unrecognisable, disguised under a thick blanket of virginal white. Despite the lateness of the hour, Jasper had no need for a torch. The glow of candlelight flickered in the château's windows and the light from the new moon reflected off the snow, illuminating the grounds and accentuating the shadows.

They had arrived in the Duchy of Bar at Duke Rene's château as summer turned to autumn, exhausted after months of moving from place to place as the castles of Northumberland changed hands back and forth in an endless line of sieges and broken oaths. Marguerite's whispered fears had been realised, and so Jasper's contingency plan had swung into action. The duke was not overly elated at being reunited with his daughter. He'd sent her off to England two decades before with the hope that, in marrying the King of England, she would secure the financial future of their family. Instead, she had returned to him title-less and destitute, with a similarly downtrodden retinue in tow. However, Rene was a proud man, and even if it was only for appearance's sake, he offered his château and assistance without comment.

Their precarious position, dependent on the goodwill of an unpredictable man, added to the claustrophobia Jasper had felt at being cooped up inside. Now he'd been released into the grounds, he relished the sound his feet made as his boots broke through the undisturbed crust of snow. It brought back memories of long winter walks around Pembroke with Ianto bounding excitedly alongside him. A smile played on his lips. Ianto had always loved the snow. He'd launch himself into the drifts, using his head to plough deep furrows, first on one side, then the other. It had always left his fur beautifully soft, and if Jasper closed his eyes, he could still recall the feeling of running his fingers through it. He stood there for a moment, the snow falling around him, letting the memories and the calming silence wash over him.

It had been two years since he had fled Pembroke. In that time he'd had barely any news, gleaning what little he could from the scraps of gossip brought to him by messengers. Henry was under Herbert's guardianship now, despite his mother's protestations. He'd been moved to Raglan and by all accounts was being well cared for. Despite his animosity towards Herbert, Jasper saw no reason to doubt it. Henry would be almost seven by now, the same age as he'd been when his mother had died and he'd been sent to the Abbey. Yet where he'd had Edmund to lean on, Henry had no one. It made Jasper's heart ache to think of his nephew alone in a strange castle. But maybe Ianto had gone with him, the old wolfhound stubbornly refusing to leave Henry's side until Herbert acquiesced. It was an unrealistic thought, but one that brought Jasper comfort, despite the tear that rolled quietly down his cheek.

A sound broke through the stillness. Jasper's eyes snapped open, and he spun around, his hand on the dagger at his belt. A short distance away a shadow detached itself from the darkness and stepped towards him.

"*Qui va là?*" he challenged.

"Peace, my friend," the shadow responded in a familiar voice, its hands raised.

"Beaufort?" Jasper asked incredulously.

"It's good to see you, Jasper," the shadow replied, stepping fully into the moonlight. The Duke of Somerset looked the same as when Jasper had last seen him on the battlements of Bamburgh, though there was an obvious nervousness to his movements instead of the usual charming confidence. A wide smile was spread across his still-youthful face, a smile that was quickly wiped away as Jasper grabbed him and flung him against a stone wall. Somerset went still at the cool touch of the dagger on his throat.

"Tell me, Henry," Jasper hissed through gritted teeth, "why should I not just slit your throat right here?"

"Go on," Somerset replied. "It's no less than I deserve."

He winced as Jasper increased the pressure on his dagger, lifting his chin as the sharp edge bit into his skin. Yet despite his racing heart, his arms remained limply by his sides, the picture of a man who had accepted his fate.

"Why did you do it?" Jasper demanded. "How could you do it?"

Somerset's dark eyes met Jasper's. "Because I saw no other way to end the purgatory I was trapped in," he confessed, his voice conveying the shame that such a truth carried.

They stayed there for a moment, eyes locked, and then with a deep sigh, Jasper lowered his dagger and pushed away from Somerset. Sheathing his weapon, he gazed up at the stars and ran a hand through his snow-dusted hair.

"Do you know what it was like to hear you had deserted us when we were already at our lowest ebb?" he asked, emotion breaking through the hard anger in his voice. "At that moment, I did not think it possible that I would leave that godforsaken fortress alive. Had it been anyone else, Holland even, I would have put it down to reckless ambition, but you? Did I misjudge you to such an extent?"

"I am sorry. Truly, my friend, if I could turn back time, I would. I was a fool and a coward. There was no other reason than that, though it would be easier if there were. My father—" Somerset's voice cracked. "My father, God rest his soul, would hang in his head in shame to know I bent the knee to his murderers."

Jasper stepped closer, compelled by sympathy for his friend's regret. "Why are you here, Henry? Do you really expect Marguerite to welcome you with open arms?"

"No, I do not, but nevertheless I must try. My heart is and has always been with Lancaster, I pray the queen sees that."

Jasper grasped his friend's arm. "I pray she does too."

* * *

Compared to the icy cold night outside, stepping into the queen's private chamber felt like an enveloping embrace. Ornate tapestries hung from the walls, adding to the cocooning warmth of the room. The queen was seated by a large fire surrounded by her ladies-in-waiting. Cards were spread out on a small table between them and the room was alive with the hum of gossip. It was rare to see Marguerite so relaxed. Jasper swallowed uncomfortably and steeled himself to disrupt it, the heat of the room feeling suddenly oppressive.

One of the ladies-in-waiting noted Jasper's arrival and leant in to quietly inform the queen. Marguerite glanced up from her cards, a wide smile spreading across her face. "Ah Jasper, there you are. Join us, we're about to start a new game of *Brelan*." She motioned him over but Jasper remained rooted to the spot.

"Your Highness, I'm sorry to disturb you at such an hour," he began, inclining his head. "But there is someone here to see you."

"Whoever they are, they must be important, if you choose to address me as Your Highness rather than Marguerite," she replied, laughter in her voice.

Jasper raised his head. "Henry Beaufort, the Duke of Somerset."

Marguerite stood in surprise, the smile vanishing from her face as Somerset stepped into the room, his footsteps echoing on the stone. He came to halt next to Jasper and swept into a low bow.

"Your Highness," he said solemnly.

For a moment Marguerite stood frozen, obviously caught off-guard by the new arrival, before anger propelled her forward. She stalked across the room towards Somerset, stopping a pace or so away. Without warning, her hand flew out, striking him hard across his cheek. His head snapped round at the force of the blow, the noise reverberating around the chamber. With some effort Jasper stayed still, his face impassive, while next to him Somerset tried to recover himself. The room was silent now, everyone watching intently as the scene unfolded before them, all wondering what would happen next.

Somerset sank to his knees, his head bowed. "Your Highness," he began nervously. "I know I have no right to ask for forgiveness, yet here I kneel. To beg mercy and once again offer my sword and life in defence of the true king."

Marguerite surveyed him with cold, piercing eyes. With one word she could see him burn; all of them, even, if she so wished, these men who played at life as if it were no more than a game. She felt some satisfaction at the sight of Somerset's cheek glowing red where she had struck him, the marks of her rings visible. Feeling Marguerite's penetrating gaze boring into him, Somerset lowered his bowed head even further. He could feel the sweat prickling his brow, his cheek

149

throbbing in time with his heart, which hammered in his chest.

"You are correct, you have no right to ask such a thing," she replied, letting the words hang in the air, drawing out Somerset's suspense. "Yet your family have always been loyal supporters of my husband's house. The king will be gladdened to know of your return." Jasper felt the tension in his muscles loosen as Marguerite held out her hand. "Let us put the past behind us and instead praise God that, like the Prodigal Son, he has returned you to us."

Somerset kissed the offered hand reverently. He remained on his knees, his head bowed until the queen had swept from the room. Only once the swish of the ladies-in-waiting's skirts had faded did he lift his head and accept Jasper's outstretched hand.

"Well, that went better than I was expecting," Jasper chuckled, pulling his friend up from the floor and slapping him on the back.

"I'd forgotten what a formidable woman she is," Somerset replied, rubbing his cheek. "Remind me never to cross her again."

"You'd have more than the queen to contend with if you did," Jasper replied in mock seriousness. "For now, I think it's time we got a drink."

* * *

Kœur-la-Petite may not have been Duke Rene's largest château, but what it was lacking in size, it made up for with opulence. Jasper's apartments, situated in the east wing, were second only to the queen's in their scale and grandeur. Somerset gave him an approving look as Jasper ushered him into his private study. He poured them both some wine and the two men settled in front of the fire. Now they were alone, Jasper could finally ask the question he had been wanting to ask since Somerset materialised in the snow.

"How is my sister-in-law?"

Somerset smiled. "I wondered how long it would take you to ask about Margaret. She is well. She seems content with her life in Lincolnshire with her husband, though their differing loyalties are sometimes the cause of marital tension. But my cousin is a shrewd woman, she knows Stafford's loyalty to Edward enables a level of freedom she might otherwise be denied. Besides, the game she plays is a long one."

"Did she speak to you of her son?"

"Only briefly. She has not yet been allowed to visit him at Raglan. I think Herbert fears the impact her influence might have on young Henry." He exchanged a knowing glance with Jasper. "She does receive regular updates though. It seems Henry has become part of the family. I believe Herbert intends him for his daughter Maud, when they are both of age of course. It is said he paid almost a thousand pounds for Henry's wardship, an impressive sum that he will want to see a return on."

Jasper took a moment to digest the new information. Margaret's separation from her son was not unexpected though he could well imagine that that did nothing to ease her frustration. As for the idea of Henry's betrothal to Herbert's daughter, he was surprised the arrangement did not vex him. Maybe sentimentality was to be expected, now he was in his thirties. Or maybe it was that, above everything, he wanted Henry to be happy and safe, and if that meant marriage to Maud Herbert, then so be it.

"It is funny, do you not think, to talk of betrothals of children when you and I are still unwed," Somerset commented, as if reading Jasper's mind.

"If my half-brother had had his way, I would have remained as celibate as a monk," Jasper replied, lines creasing at the edges of his eyes. "But there was a woman back in Pembroke who I cared for once," he continued, his smile fading as he gazed into the fire. "Myfanwy. She had a daughter, Helen, who she claimed was mine, though I have never been convinced." He shook his head. "Still, I hope one day I can start a family of my own. When all this madness is behind us," he trailed off, waving a hand.

Somerset nodded. "I have a son back home, little Charlie. His mother is a woman of low standing, yet love is blind to the hierarchies of society." He looked up at Jasper with a smile. "The truth of which your parents were well aware."

Jasper's own face broke into a grin and he raised his cup. "To love, in all its many forms."

"To love."

They were silent for a moment, their minds preoccupied. In a corner, the sputtering of the candle brought them back to reality, reminding them of the lateness of the hour. Jasper leant forward in his chair. "You've not yet told me what you've been planning."

Beaufort looked at him with a confused expression but Jasper was undeterred. "Come now, Henry, give me some credit. You would not have made such a long journey if you did not have a plan for how we might secure our house's future."

Somerset glanced away, taking a slow drink from his cup. When he looked back, the determination Jasper recognised of old shone in his eyes, and there was a new urgency to his voice. "We must strike soon, while Edward's reign is still in its infancy and the people have not grown accustomed to the rule of a false king. His illness last year showed the precariousness of his position. He has no children, no heir, and no wife. I was his bedfellow for a time, and believe me when I say he is but a precocious teenager, desperate to be liked, raised up by Warwick, a man who seeks only to expand his influence on a malleable mind. A fearsome warrior he may be, but when it comes to statecraft he still has much to learn."

"And how do you intend to exploit that scenario?"

"For the past year, my agents have been working to stoke up support for King Henry. One word from me and they will rise up. Ralph Percy has already pledged his support. The banner of Lancaster will soon be raised over Bamburgh and Dunstanburgh once more. Edward is entirely dependent on the Nevilles; once they are out of the way he will be forced to capitulate. If the queen permits it, I will return to Northumberland and prove her faith in me is not unfounded."

"Did Ralph Percy not pledge such support the last time an attempt was made to retake Northumberland? If I remember correctly, Brézé barely crossed the border before he was repelled."

"Yes, that is true, but it was not the plan that was flawed, rather its participants. This time will be different, because I won't be leading the fight against it."

"A fair point," Jasper conceded.

"So you will join me?" Beaufort asked eagerly.

Jasper shook his head, making Somerset's shoulders slump in disappointment. "I'm sorry, my friend, the queen has need of me here."

22

May 1464

In the end, Duke Rene's hospitality had only lasted a few weeks
longer, running out as the festive spirit was beginning to wane
and the harsh reality of another winter set in. And so Jasper had
found himself on the road once more. While Marguerite chose to
re-ingratiate herself with King Louis, he continued to Brittany. Duke
Francis had welcomed him like an old friend, and Jasper had quickly
fallen back into the rhythm of life at the Breton court. As the first
signs of spring had emerged, so the court had moved north, from
Château de Clisson to the Breton coast and the spectacular beauty of
Château de Suscinio. After weeks of driving rain, the sun had finally
emerged and Jasper relished the opportunity to once again join Duke
Francis on his daily rides.

The countryside around Suscinio felt a world away from the woods
of Clission, and as they emerged from a line of dunes, a long, unbroken
beach that stretched for miles revealed itself. Only a few hundred
yards away from the gates they had just ridden out from, it reminded
Jasper of the beach below Bamburgh, though instead of that fortress'
crenellated walls, it was Suscinio's two imposing gatehouse towers
that rose above the landscape. Barely anything moved on the vast

expanse of sand, the only sound the breaking waves and calls of gulls. Francis brought his horse round to stand next to Jasper's.

"Seems like a waste not to take advantage of all this space. What say you to a race, Sir Jasper?" he asked.

"I'd be more than happy to oblige, though only if your Grace does not mind losing," Jasper replied with a mischievous smile.

"Ha, we shall see about that!" Francis pointed to a shadow on the distant horizon. "You see that outcrop of stone? The last one there has to muck out the stables."

"A fair forfeit. Agreed," Jasper confirmed, circling his horse around so that it was in line with the duke's.

Francis adjusted the reins in his hands, his eyes already fixed on the finish line. "Ready? On the count of three. *Trois, Deux, Une—*"

The word had barely left the duke's lips before he launched his horse into a gallop. Caught unawares, Jasper scrabbled for a moment, losing precious ground as his horse found its stride. But it was a fine animal, bred for speed, a world away from Tarn's steady plod, and soon it was racing over the sand. Jasper felt as though he was flying. His grip on the reins was relaxed, his body bent low over his mount's outstretched neck, its mane whipping his face. He had always felt at home in the saddle, relishing the freedom it offered. He let out an exhilarated cry as he thundered along the beach in pursuit of Duke Francis. With every stride, the gap between the two men shrunk. But so too did the distance to the finish line, the outcrop that had started as a smudge on the horizon now a looming, solid wall of rock.

Crouching even lower, Jasper pushed his hands forward, spurring his horse ever faster. It seemed to sense his determination, finding a hidden reserve of power even as the duke's horse began to tire. With only a hundred yards to go, they were neck and neck, both men leaning as far forward as they dared, foam flying from their horses' mouths. Jasper shut his eyes as they flew past the finishing stone.

* * *

"Well raced today, Sir Jasper. I'll admit there were some surprised looks amongst the stable hands when I picked up a shovel and set to. I do not believe I've set foot in there since I was a child!"

"It was a close run thing, your Grace. Had the rock been a few yards earlier, I would have been the one ankle deep in manure. Although by the sounds of it, it is a position with which I am more familiar."

A smile played across the duke's lips. "Well then, thank you for giving me the opportunity to experience it."

The two men fell into an easy silence as their plates were cleared and cups refilled. Jasper felt a presence at his side and turned to see a servant holding out a letter to him. A cold sense of dread washed over him as he recognised Sir Richard Tunstall's seal. Taking his knife, he sliced through the wax and quickly scanned the familiar scrawl.

"More news from England?" Francis inquired.

Jasper looked up at him, unable to hide the shock from his face. The duke put his glass down in concern. "Sir Jasper, are you quite well? What news has affected you so?

"The Duke of Somerset is dead."

"Somerset? I do not believe I know him. Was he a friend of yours?"

"Yes," Jasper replied, taking a deep breath in an attempt to regain his composure. "Forgive me, your Grace. I suppose I should be numb to loss by now, yet still I feel its sharp cut."

Francis waved a hand. "Do not be so hard on yourself. It is so often only when something is lost that we truly realise its importance."

"I feel so distant. It is as though I am cursed to be a bystander, forever watching events unfold through secondhand accounts."

"Exile is cruel like that," Francis replied gently. "I am sure you would appreciate some time to yourself to digest this news." He glanced at the window. "It is late anyway, I will bid you goodnight. In the morning, you shall accompany me on my ride around the nearby villages. I find fresh air, exercise and a bit of local gossip can be the perfect tonic for such news."

* * *

Alone in his room, Jasper slumped into a chair and re-read Richard's letter. Now that the shock had abated, he was better able to absorb the details it contained. What he hadn't divulged to Francis was the full extent of their defeat, though he had no doubt the duke would learn of it soon enough. Somerset's death was just one damning blow in a long line of catastrophes. Twice in the span of a month, John Neville had crushed what little Lancastrian resistance Somerset had been able to muster.

Jasper cursed. If he had been there, he would have cautioned his friend not to underestimate the younger Neville brother. Instead, Somerset found himself exposed and outnumbered, with retreat his only option. Another man may have judged him and his fellow commanders for fleeing, but Jasper knew the impossibility of such a choice and his cheeks still burned with shame to remember his own experience at Mortimer's Cross.

There were some, however, who had ignored Somerset's calls to abandon the field. With characteristic stubbornness, Sir Ralph Percy refused to show his back to a Neville, having long since accepted there would be no second chance for a man who had already forsworn his oath. And so it was, on some nondescript patch of bleak Northumberland moorland, that Death finally caught up with Henry Hotspur's last grandson, and the House of Lancaster lost yet another staunch supporter.

Given the unmitigated disaster of their first meeting, Jasper struggled to understand why Somerset chose to once again engage Montagu, only a few weeks later and this time with King Henry at his side. If he was hoping Richard might shine some light on the decision then he was to be disappointed, and his friend's letter gave no further insight. Whatever Somerset's reason, the decision had cost him his life, those of almost thirty other Lancastrian commanders, and nearly that of the king. The time for taking prisoners had passed with Towton, and without exception, the leaders had been rounded up and executed, a tree stump acting as a crude executioner's block. According to Richard, Somerset was made to watch them all, before, at last, his own neck was stretched out on the log, its bark still wet with the blood of those that had gone before. Though he tried not to, Jasper could imagine Somerset being led out to meet his end, his handsome face bloodied and bruised, yet defiant, staring down Montagu, just as his father had done to Neville's at St Albans; the proverb 'as the father, so the son' gaining new, morbid relevance.

Jasper felt another wave of grief wash over him. In the tumultuous world in which he found himself, there were very few people who he could count as friends, but Henry Beaufort had been one of them. His easy charm and optimism had lifted Jasper from many a dark hole and, his actions at Bamburgh aside, he had been a loyal supporter of Lancaster. Now that he was gone, Jasper was even more grateful for their reconciliation at Kœur-la-Petite. Their short time together had reminded him just how much he valued Beaufort's company and counsel. But there would be no more late-night conversations. For the third time in his life, Jasper was deprived of a confidant; yet another life wasted on an endless conflict.

It had only been thanks to Richard's quick thinking that the king had not joined that list. Feeling the tide of battle turn, Richard had managed to make it to the rear, where Henry had been watching the fighting unfold, and spirit him away before Montagu's men overwhelmed them. They were now in hiding, moving between the houses and villages of trusted loyalists. Unsurprisingly, Richard gave no details as to their current whereabouts, other than to confirm they were safe. Despite the dire situation and lack of information, Jasper still found some small sense of comfort in knowing Richard was watching over his half-brother.

Tossing the letter into the flames, he leant back in his chair and watched as the paper blackened and curled. Whichever way he looked, Lancaster's future seemed bleak, their cause hanging by a thread. The king was God-knows-where in hiding, all their money had been spent or buried to prevent it from falling into enemy hands, and the North, for which they had fought so hard, was lost. Dunstanburgh and Alnwick had surrendered as soon as they'd heard of Somerset's defeat and Bamburgh was currently under siege. Against the barrage of Edward's new cannon, it would only be a matter of time before they too capitulated. Only one castle still held out for Lancaster. Jasper sighed, it was time he returned to Wales.

23

July 1465

Once home to the royal court of giants, the rock of Harlech rose like a beacon from the surrounding landscape. Approaching from the east, it was easy to see why old Longshanks had chosen the dramatic outcrop as the location for one of his most ambitious building projects nearly two centuries before. The resulting foreboding fortress was part of a ring of similarly impressive castles encircling North Wales from Aberystwyth and Builth in the south to Conwy and Beaumaris in the north.

Accessible by sea via a water gate and a steep winding staircase cut into the cliff, Harlech had been designed to withstand any type of siege. This way to the sea was an invaluable asset and, since fleeing Pembroke, Jasper had spent what little money he had on using it to keep the castle supplied by ships from Ireland and Brittany. It was an investment he had not once regretted. As the final Lancastrian stronghold, Harlech's broad walls, which had once protected Owain Glyndŵr from his mother's first husband, now provided a refuge for Jasper and the other exiled Lancastrians. Richard Tunstall was amongst the motley crew of outlaws, having recently arrived from Lancashire where he had been taking care of King Henry, moving him from place to place, always staying a step ahead of their pursuers. Though he was happy to see him, Jasper would have preferred it if he'd stayed with his half-brother, but there was only so long that someone as useful as Richard could remain in hiding. King Henry was now under the care of the Tempest family at their home in Waddington, while Richard was enjoying the greater degree of freedom this isolated corner of Wales offered.

As for Jasper, he had been in Harlech for nearly a year, using it as a base from which to launch attacks on nearby Yorkist outposts. He'd mustered a core group of mercenaries for the task, a few of whom had followed him since Bamburgh. They were loyal men, hardened by the wind and rain, true salt of the earth. After so many months on the road, Jasper felt more at home with them around a campfire than he ever had in the vaulted halls of Westminster. One of the group, Gwil, was a local lad who knew the area like the back of his hand. It was thanks to him that there was always some hidden valley for them to disappear into after a raid. He was also a master storyteller, and Jasper enjoyed getting lost in his tales as they rode along high mountain passes and tree-lined river banks, the boy's sturdy welsh cob plodding alongside Jasper's warhorse.

The disruption their raids inflicted was significant enough for news of them to reach London, and the Pretender had recently placed a bounty on all those sheltering in Harlech. Yet despite Jasper's best attempts to lure him from Raglan, Sir William Herbert had yet to show his face. Still, it felt good to be a thorn in both his and the false king's side. Now in the fourth year of his reign, Edward had become increasingly settled on his stolen throne, taking advantage of the lull in Lancastrian resistance since the loss of Northumberland. Though that was not to say the previous months had passed without incident. Of most interest to Jasper were the small cracks starting to appear in the Pretender's relationship with his closest advisor, the Earl of Warwick. According to his informers, the latter was still furious about the embarrassment of negotiating a European alliance through marriage to Bona of Savoy when Edward was secretly already married. The fallout was not only damaging for Warwick personally, but a political disaster too, and King Louis had still not forgiven either man for shunning his sister-in-law.

Despite his disdain for Warwick, Jasper could understand his anger, and even to him, Edward's choice of wife seemed an odd one. Elizabeth Woodville had been a Lancastrian once, her first husband killed in service to King Henry at the second battle of St Albans. And the family affinity went deeper than that. Her mother, the revered Jacquetta of Luxembourg, had been briefly married to Henry's uncle, the old Duke of Bedford. But clearly, historical ties meant nothing in a conflict characterised by constantly shifting battle lines, and Edward was besotted with his golden-haired wife. There were rumours Elizabeth had used witchcraft to seduce him, not that Jasper held much stock in such things.

As Harlech's familiar outline loomed closer, Jasper's thoughts turned to the small luxuries that awaited him. After days in the saddle, his muscles were crying out for the soothing embrace of a warm bath, while his stomach yearned for something other than dried-out strips of meat and stale bread. He smiled involuntarily at the thought and willed the final few miles to speed past.

Eventually, they passed through Harlech's outer gate, the sound of hooves echoing off the stone. Though he knew they posed no threat to him, he could not help but glance warily at the arrow slits positioned along the narrow entrance passage that lead from the gate into the heart of the castle. Above his head, hidden in channels cut into the masonry hung three portcullises ready to drop on unsuspecting intruders. Dafydd ap Einion, the captain of Harlech, had gleefully shown him how the various mechanisms worked when he'd first arrived at the castle. It was the very definition of a killing alley and Jasper was glad he'd never be the one tasked with attacking it.

As they rode through the final arch into the sun-drenched courtyard it was not the usual hubbub that welcomed them but an uneasy silence. In various places, men stood in groups whispering to each other. No one met Jasper's eye as he dismounted. He threw his reins to Gwil. "Have you heard anything?"

The boy shrugged. "No, my Lord."

Jasper's brow furrowed in concern. "See to the horses will you?" he asked over his shoulder as he strode purposefully away. He swept up the stately staircase that connected the courtyard to the apartments on the first floor of the gatehouse, heading straight for Richard Tunstall's chamber. He found his friend pacing angrily, a letter balled in one fist, a cup of wine in the other, its contents sloshing wildly.

"Richard, what's happened?"

"The king has been captured."

Jasper froze in the doorway unable to process the news. Richard looked up from his pacing.

"Did you hear me? Fucking captured!" he roared, hurling his cup across the room. Jasper flinched as it collided with the wall, wine spraying everywhere. Normally calm and controlled, he had never seen his friend so enraged. He took a step into the chamber, his hands raised placatingly.

"Richard, take a seat, let—" he began, trying to soothe his friend's anger but to no avail.

Richard rounded on him. "Christ's bones, Jasper, do not tell me to sit down! All our efforts, all the years of hardship and sacrifice—" He stabbed at his chest. "I haven't seen my wife in two years. Two years! And for what?" He threw up his hands in exasperation. "To watch helplessly as the king is carted off to the Tower. You know as well as I the dangers that exist behind its walls. It is like sending a lamb to slaughter!"

"Sit, Richard," Jasper repeated with more forcefulness. "Do not mistake my composure for indifference. I assure you, the news is as distressing for me as it is for you. But you told me once it does no good to discuss such matters on an empty stomach. So first we will eat, and then we will talk."

Reluctantly Richard nodded, his shoulders slumping as the fire of anger left him. He collapsed into a chair with a deep sigh, his head in his hands. Jasper retrieved the cup from where it had landed on the floor and refilled it with wine. Richard gave him a weak smile as he gave it to him, along with a small platter of bread and cheese he had found in the corner. Jasper filled his own cup before coming to sit next to him.

"Now," he began once Richard had eaten a few mouthfuls, "let us start from the beginning. How was he discovered?"

"Apparently, he had just sat down for dinner with the Dean of Windsor when men burst into the hall to arrest him. I truly believed the king would be safe with Tempest. He is a kind, loyal man, and Waddington is only a small village; it seemed as good a place as any to hide. What I had not bargained for was Tempest's own brother betraying him." Richard sighed. "That's what this god-forsaken conflict does, put brother against brother, father against son. Is my own family not the same? At Bamburgh, my brother merely watched from afar as I was almost flattened by cannon fire." He shook his head. "I should never have let the king out of my sight."

Jasper leant towards his friend. "Do not blame yourself, Richard, you could not have stayed with him forever. We've known this was coming, ever since Hexham. It was a miracle he remained hidden for so long."

Richard gave a weak smile. "I appreciate your reassurance, but you'll understand that this is a blow that will take some time to get over."

"Of course," Jasper acknowledged, slumping back into his chair. "Though you do realise this leaves us in a precarious situation? Have you any thoughts on what we should do next?"

"I was rather hoping you'd have the answer to that."

Jasper shook his head, laughing quietly at the impossibility of the position they found themselves in. "Honestly, I do not know. I will write to Marguerite, though I'm sure she has already been informed. My gut says our best hope is to continue holding Harlech. Now he has the king, Edward will want to scourge the last remnants of the house of Lancaster. It will only be a matter of time before he sends Herbert to deal with us once and for all. We cannot let him succeed."

24

September 1467

Jasper shifted his weight in an attempt to relieve the cramp
building in his muscles. He had been crouching for what felt like
an age, as still as a statue amongst the wet bracken. A thin layer
of mist hung between the moss-covered tree trunks, proving resistant
to the first probing fingers of sunlight that promised a beautiful day
to come. The early weak rays had yet to warm the air, which was
sharp with the first chill of autumn. It crept up under Jasper's shirt
making him shiver involuntarily.

The forest around him was a living being – its sights, smells and
sounds all-encompassing. Even at this hour, it was not truly silent.
There was a gentle pitter-patter as water droplets, the last remnants
of the previous night's rainstorm, slid from leaves and plummeted to
the forest floor. A few brazen songbirds had started up their dawn
chorus, the noise of their warbling swelling as others lent their voices
to the refrain. Off to his left, Jasper could hear the babble of the River
Artro as it flowed over rocks and through pools. The smell of damp
earth was all around him, filling his nostrils. It was a comforting scent,
one that reminded him of childhood hunting trips with his father and
brother.

He felt a movement behind him but did not turn his head as Gwil settled next to him. "Any luck?"

"A few rabbits, but nothing more. One of my snares had been meddled with."

Jasper shrugged. "It was probably just some local lads looking for an easy meal."

Gwil made to reply but stopped short as a doe emerged through the trees and began to graze about thirty yards from where they were crouched.

"Finally," Jasper breathed softly.

Moving with painful slowness in an attempt to avoid spooking the doe, he pulled an arrow from his quiver and nocked it before raising his bow. Drawing back the arrow, he felt the familiar stretch across his shoulders as his muscles went taught. He took his time lining up the shot, noting the light breeze blowing from the east and the distance to his target. He was about to let the arrow fly when he felt a hand on his arm. Without lowering his bow, he turned his gaze on Gwil who was staring at him, an intense urgency in his eyes, a finger on his lips. Without a word, he stretched out his hand pointing to a gap in the trees a few hundred yards away.

Jasper let out a breath. There in the distance, beyond the edge of the forest, figures were moving. Now he could hear the unmistakable sound of marching men cutting through the other noises in the forest. The doe heard it too, lifting her head, immediately alert to the potential danger. She stood like that for a moment, the only movement the quivering of her nose. Then she fled, and Jasper could only watch as his supper disappeared into the trees. Rabbit stew it was. Still better than being discovered by whoever was beyond the trees.

With a sigh, he returned the arrow to the quiver and slung his bow over his shoulder. Keeping low, he moved carefully through the undergrowth to find a better vantage point, beckoning Gwil to follow him. He came to a halt when he was little more than a spear's throw away from the tree line. From his new position, he could see a line of about two hundred men winding their way along the old dirt track. In their hands, they held a varied array of weapons, from swords and pikes to billhooks and even scythes. Some had armour, but the majority looked as though they had just left their fields. A few wore tabards bearing a red and blue crest, the sight of which made Jasper's blood run cold. Herbert. He grabbed Gwil's arm. "We need to get back to Harlech, now."

* * *

Harlech's great hall was light and spacious. Eight windows, four on each side, added to the sense of grandeur, with those on the far side offering a commanding view out across the Irish Sea. Today the water was calm and Jasper watched as a couple of small fishing boats made their way back to shore, their nets no doubt teeming with the morning's catch. He turned as two other men entered the hall behind him.

"Black William has finally decided to show his face then, has he?" Dafydd ap Einion, Harlech's grizzled captain asked, rubbing his calloused hands together in fiendish delight.

Jasper shook his head. "At first glance I thought it was him, but on reflection I think it was more likely his brother."

Tunstall leant against one of the long tables. "So Sir Richard is mustering an army? And I suppose we can safely assume that William is doing the same in the south?"

"We knew they would come sooner or later. If we're honest with ourselves, we're lucky it's taken this long. They've held the king for, what, two years now?"

"Don't remind me," Tunstall grimaced.

"And it's because of that delay that we've allowed ourselves to be lulled into a false sense of security," Jasper continued. "Today was a valuable reminder of that. I am confident there is no risk of an imminent attack, not with the state those men were in. But it will happen. Whether it be in six months or a year, eventually the enemy will be hammering on those doors."

"I say let them come," Dafydd growled. "In my youth, I held a castle in France for so long, the old women in Wales still talk of it." A crooked grin spread across his face. "I intend to hold Harlech for so long that all the women in France will speak of it."

Despite the situation, Jasper felt a smile tugging at his mouth. "I admire your conviction, Captain. But the men I saw were but a fraction of what the Herbert brothers will send against us, and already they would outnumber us three to one. We need more support. The question is, from where?"

"What about Duke Francis?" Tunstall offered. "He's supported you before, why not again now?"

Jasper shook his head. "He will not be able to help us. Brittany is not the haven it once was. Francis' position is vulnerable. In the face of threats from his neighbours, he has moved closer to Edward."

"Turncoat," Dafydd muttered.

"No, he is a pragmatist, that is all. First and foremost he must act in the interests of his people. If that means creating closer ties with the Pretender then that is what he must do. He is an honourable man, I will not hear a word against him." Dafydd raised his hands in acquiescence.

"So if Brittany is off the table and we've already exhausted the hospitality of our Scottish friends – where does that leave us?" Tunstall asked, a hint of despair creeping into his voice.

"There's always France," Jasper replied.

Tunstall raised his eyebrows in surprise. "I thought King Louis was in league with Edward?"

"That's certainly what Warwick would want but, as seems to be increasingly common at the moment, what Warwick wants is of little concern to the man he made king. From what I can gather, Louis' relationship with Edward, if there ever really was one, is in tatters. The York pup seems intent on favouring Burgundy over France. Whether he does so for true political gain or just to spite Warwick is irrelevant. Such actions only amplify Louis' anger at the way his sister-in-law's hand in marriage was rejected."

Dafydd clapped his hands together. "So France it is."

"When will you leave?" Tunstall asked, coming to stand next to Jasper.

"As soon as a ship can be prepared. Captain, can you see to the arrangements?"

Dafydd nodded before striding out in the autumn sunshine, leaving the other two alone in the long hall.

Tunstall grasped Jasper's arm with one hand while the other gripped his shoulder. "Godspeed, my friend. We will be here when you return."

25

July 1468

Acrid smoke hung in the air, a testament to the fields set alight by Jasper's men. Across the valley, the view from the ridge showed the full extent of the devastation. The whole area had been ravaged by fire – nothing had been spared. The hill on which Denbigh was perched was now little more than a smoking mound, the three octagonal gatehouse towers standing like skeletons amongst the ruined town. Jasper felt a grim sense of satisfaction as he surveyed the destruction. He had tried to take his former castle peacefully, but to no avail, the fiercely loyal Yorkist garrison refusing to even negotiate. Taking it by force would have required cannon, resources he could ill afford. Burning the town around it cost nothing and sent a clear message to those in North Wales who still held out for York. Yet, there was a sadness at seeing Denbigh so reduced. Jasper could remember the pride he had felt when he had been granted the lordship with his father, and the excitement when standing on this very ridge, news of the castle's capitulation reached them. He thought of Arwen, her soft skin and the nights they'd lain tangled together. So much for healing divisions; all that was wasted now. With a sigh, Jasper turned his horse away from the blackened ruins and made his way off the ridge towards camp.

In the end, fifty men and a few hundred pounds were all King Louis had deemed this Welsh endeavour was worth. It seemed that after years of generosity, his cousin's enthusiasm for funding their campaigns was waning. With so little to show for his efforts in France, there had seemed little sense in landing at Harlech. The castle needed food and weapons, not more hungry mouths to feed. And so he had decided to land a few miles down the coast at Barmouth. If he couldn't bolster the garrison with supplies then he would strengthen it in other ways, starting with its resolve.

He had struck out from the small port, marching for sixty miles along valley floors and across moorland, heading for Denbigh. He'd held court sessions and assizes along the way, proclaiming his half-brother as the true king and dispensing justice in his name. The people welcomed him. The bards called him *Y Mab Darogan*, the Son of Prophecy, hailing him as the one who would save Wales, and men flocked to his banner, fifty swelling to two thousand in a matter of days. Even with such an increase, his force still paled in comparison to the number the Herbert brothers had mustered. According to reports, they had nearly ten thousand between them. At the moment, their force was divided. William was headed for Harlech, while Richard was laying waste to the coastline north of the castle, isolating it from its supply networks. The last he'd heard from Tunstall they were having to limit hunting trips to areas still visible from the castle walls to minimise the risk of ambush. It would only be a matter of days before Harlech came under siege. Defensively, it could withstand anything, but if no ships reached the way to the sea then they would be starved into submission before the summer was out. Jasper bunched his reins in frustration. If he could just catch William unawares from behind then there might yet be some hope for the last Lancastrian outpost.

As he arrived into the camp, one of his captains, a lanky man from

Anglesey named Ieuan, came out to greet him. "So they chose to burn?" he asked in Welsh.

Jasper nodded as he slid from the saddle.

"Idiots," Ieuan chuckled. His laugh turned to a cough as he noticed Jasper's stern stare. "*Syr?*"

"Get the word out, we break camp at first light."

* * *

The first evidence of the approaching rider was the dust cloud kicked up by pounding hooves. Jasper reined in his horse and waited as the scout came haring down the track before coming to a skittering halt a few yards away, his mount snorting loudly.

"Richard Herbert's army is waiting for us in the next valley."

"How many?"

"Five thousand, at least."

Jasper cursed. They were so close. Just a few miles more and Harlech's familiar outline would appear on the horizon. They weren't going to make it. He signalled Ieuan over.

"It seems Herbert has sent us a welcoming party."

"Shall I ready the men?"

Jasper looked over his shoulder at those traipsing behind him. They were coated with dust, sweat gleaning on their faces. He'd marched them hard, taking advantage of the long summer days to cover as many miles as possible in a desperate attempt to reach Harlech before the siege began. He'd known it was a gamble and now he was paying the price. He shook his head. "If we engage them now, it will be a bloodbath. Tell the men that those who wish to leave are free to do so. I will stand with any who wish to remain."

"There will be nothing for you if you stay here. What point is there in dying now, when you've survived so long? It's you that Herbert wants, not this rabble of peasants. With you gone, I wager he'll let us all slink back to our villages."

"And those in Harlech?"

"Even if we somehow manage to beat this Herbert brother, do you really think we'll be in any state to meet the other? Harlech's fate is her own, there is nothing more we can do. So go, now, while you still can."

Jasper hesitated, looking again at the Welshmen who had followed him across countless miles, sure in the belief that he would be the one to secure their country's future.

"Do not worry about the men," Ieuan reassured, recognising Jasper's unspoken concerns. "They will melt away into the mountains like snow in spring. By the time Herbert crests that hill, there will be nothing here. Now, go!"

Jasper grasped his captain's arm in gratitude. "*Diolch.*" Wheeling his horse around, he spurred it into a thundering gallop.

He rode hard, retracing the route back towards Denbigh, though he gave the town itself a wide berth in case any of the recently dispossessed townsfolk recognised him. Though his decision to return north rather than make a break for the coast would seem to some to be counter-intuitive, there was reason behind it. After Mortimer's Cross, he'd learnt a valuable lesson in always ensuring there was a viable escape route, or a few people willing to shelter him while the storm passed over. And that was why he was now winding his way down narrow country lanes and across shallow fords, making for the tiny village of Picton. He'd been this way only once before, with his father, on one of their excursions out from Denbigh and, as he turned down another lane indistinguishable from the last, a creeping sense of doubt in his navigational skills entered his mind. But then on the outskirts of the village, just as he was contemplating retracing his steps, he came across a tired-looking longhouse with a candle flickering in the window and relief flooded through him.

The bear of a man who answered his furtive knock took one look at the figure on his doorstep and ushered him quickly inside. Hywel was a cousin of some sort, though Jasper had lost track of the exact details of their familial ties. When he'd tried to press a few gold nobles into his rough hands as a thank-you for his kindness, the old Welshmen had shaken his head sadly. "I told your father I would repay him one day," he said, pushing Jasper's hand away.

At another time, he would have wanted to question Hywel further, to sit with him in front of the fire and ask him about his father and the adventures they'd shared. But fugitives do not have the luxury of reminiscing, so instead he'd gripped his arm and told him his generosity would not be forgotten. Nearly a week had passed since then, the shadows moving across the bare stone floor one of the few indicators of the passage of time.

The interior of the longhouse was as bleak as the landscape in which it sat, the hearth laying cold and dark. In one corner there was a basket filled with blankets, although so far the midsummer evenings had not been cool enough to warrant them. Each morning Hywel would drop a parcel of food by the door as he made his way down to the nearby harbour to see the goods being unloaded. This morning there was also a letter. The ink had run slightly in the rain, but Tunstall's distinctive scrawl was still legible, and it was with a heavy heart that Jasper sliced through the familiar seal:

My friend, this will be my last letter. Herbert has offered terms, and the castle will surrender tomorrow at first light. We did all we could, yet it was not enough. I doubt the outcome would have been different if you had reached us in time. Old fortresses may still make an attacker's blood run cold, but cannon have shifted the balance. I saw the destruction that such power wrought on Bamburgh – it is a small mercy that Harlech will not meet the same fate. Do not fear for me. I am to be taken to the Tower along with Dafydd and the other captains. Herbert has given his word that we will be pardoned. It seems Edward is keen to extend the hand of friendship. I intend to take it. I hope you do not think less of me for accepting such an offer. I do so not because I crave power or coin. I simply wish to see my family, tend my land, and walk through my orchards without fear of reprisals. I have given the best years of my life in defence of Lancaster. There may yet be a reason to give more. For now, though, I intend to rest my sword. I believe you, of all people, will understand that. Godspeed my friend. May His hand guide you on whatever road you find yourself. I look forward to the day when we can meet again.

That the news was expected did little to soften its blow. Just like that, the last Lancastrian foothold was lost. The despair was suffocating, the last ember of hope finally extinguished. Down and down his fortune went. Every time he felt he must surely have reached the bottom of the wheel, it would turn once more, and to his dismay he'd move even lower. The rise when it came would be meteoric, but that depended on him surviving long enough to see it. At least, Jasper reasoned, there was a high probability Tunstall would be safe. He could not have forgiven himself if another person died as a result of his failures. He was pleased that his friend would be reunited with his family, from whom he had been separated for so long. And if he was honest, he was envious too. Envious that Tunstall had something, someone, to return to. It made him wonder, would he have made the same decisions if he'd had a family waiting for him at home – if he knew his death would leave a wife widowed and a child fatherless? He rubbed his chest, feeling the familiar loneliness gnawing at his heart, and tried to focus his mind on more pressing matters.

Within the next few hours, while Herbert and his men were focused on the hand-over of Harlech, he would make his escape, sneaking down to the harbour where a small boat would be waiting. He'd already discarded his armour and cloak. His sword was hidden in a bundle of pea straw that was currently leaning up against the wall, and he'd tied his father's ring on a cord around his neck. On the off-chance, an eagle-eyed guard was patrolling the wharf, all they would see was a peasant carrying supplies for one of the many fishing boats. Once he was aboard, he would chart a course north, circling Anglesey before heading south again, keeping a safe distance from the Welsh shoreline. As to what came after, that was in God's hands. Duty called him back to Amboise, where Marguerite was still hovering around King Louis, grasping at whatever scraps he threw her way. Though he respected him, the idea of seeing his cousin again was not one he relished. He was tired of being looked down upon and begging for charity from people who sought only to advance their own interests.

Hywel poked his head around the door, disrupting his brooding thoughts. "It's time."

Jasper nodded. "Coming."

Standing, he retrieved one of the gold nobles from his pocket. Turning it over in his hand, he ran his finger over the inscription around the edge that declared his half-brother the King of England and France. A moment frozen in time. Jasper smiled ruefully. If only reality was as unchanging. Placing the coin on the mantel beam, he hitched the bundle of pea straw under his arm and, without a backwards glance, made his way out into the uncertainty of a new dawn.

26

July 1469

Victorious shouts echoed across the moor as Richard Herbert's headless body was dragged away. The Earl of Warwick bent to wipe his bloodied sword on the long grass. Above him, his bear and ragged staff banner flapped proudly in the wind. Despite his disdain for the earl, Jasper found himself lending his voice to the chorus of 'a Warwick' as William Herbert was made to kneel before the Kingmaker. He seemed oblivious to those clamouring for his death. His eyes were fixed on his brother's decapitated corpse, his lips moving in silent prayer. Behind him, Warwick stepped up to take the fatal strike, taking care to line up his target. As he drew back his sword, Herbert lifted his gaze, finding Jasper and fixing him with a defiant stare. Jasper simply stared back, triumph shining in his eyes, and watched unflinchingly as his old foe's head was struck from his shoulders. It rolled away over the wet grass, finally coming to rest next to Richard's, the two brothers reunited in death. But Jasper's triumph was short-lived. His brow furrowed in confusion as Warwick waved another prisoner forward. Dwarfed by the men on either side, the prisoner was struggling with all his might against his captors. His face was bloodied and bruised, his slim frame comically exaggerated by the oversized armour he wore. Jasper's eyes widened in horror as realisation dawned on him. Though *he had grown much in the last eight years, Henry looked exactly as Jasper remembered. He cursed. Even in death, Herbert continued to taunt him – what other reason would have compelled him to bring a twelve-year-old to such a place? He tried to take a step towards Henry, but his muscles refused to obey. Suddenly, he was engulfed by the suffocating press of fighting men. Bodies jostled against him, blocking his view. He felt the air move behind him, ducking quickly as a sword passed inches above his head. When he straightened, he saw Warwick force his nephew to his knees. Jasper felt panic rising in his throat, his movements becoming more frenzied as he tried to fight his way through the crush. Above the noise of battle, he could hear Henry screaming his name. Jasper parried yet another blow. He was trapped. With every step he took towards his nephew, a new attacker pushed him back two. An evil smile spread across Warwick's face. Slowly, he lifted his sword, its blade still dripping with Herbert's blood. The two guards held Henry still. The boy had fallen silent now, his eyes wide and terrified, tears streaming down his mud-splattered face. In manic desperation, Jasper sliced and cut at everything in front of him, not waiting to see if his strikes hit home. At last, he broke through the heaving mass. But he was too late. With an anguished roar, he watched as Warwick brought his sword down upon Henry's neck.*

* * *

Jasper sat bolt upright, immediately awake. His heart hammered against his ribcage, his chest heaving as he took in great, gasping breaths. Sweat trickled down the nape of his neck, while around his legs, the sheets were a twisted mess of linen. Disorientated, he struggled to make sense of where he was. With difficulty, he forced himself to focus. In the distance he could hear footsteps on stone and the hum of a tune as a maid passed outside his door; the distinctive noises of Amboise castle waking from slumber.

Jasper collapsed back against the pillows, his heart still beating a tattoo as the adrenaline that had been coursing through his veins slowly drained away. He'd received the news from the battlefield at Edgcote a week before. Since then Herbert had haunted his dreams, while Henry's close brush with death wracked him with the guilt he had repressed since he'd abandoned his nephew in Pembroke.

It was not just Henry and his guardian who had been taken by surprise by the speed and completeness of Warwick's betrayal. The Pretender too had been utterly blindsided. One moment he thought he was dealing with a few rebels, the next his closest advisor had raised an army against him. Warwick's simmering displeasure had been common knowledge, but no one had anticipated such a sudden escalation into violence. Marguerite could barely contain her glee when she'd announced Edward was now under house arrest at Middleham castle. Yet Jasper struggled to share in her excitement. Despite the drastic shift in circumstances, beneath the surface he predicted very little would change. Unlike his usual considered approach, Warwick's actions appeared uncharacteristically rash. No thought seemed to have been spared as to what would happen once Edward was imprisoned. In the days since, Warwick had made no moves to release King Henry from the Tower. Clearly, regardless of Marguerite's hopes to the contrary, the reinstatement of a Lancastrian monarch had not been the earl's intention when he took to the field. Personal ambition was the more probable cause. But if that was the case, then what had Warwick actually achieved, other than biting the hand that fed him? There was only so long the throne could sit vacant. Sooner or later Edward would have to be released. Only once that had happened would the picture become clear. Until then, Jasper's more immediate concern was for his nephew. Henry had been Herbert's ward for the last eight years, and his guardian's death left him in limbo. Even though still a boy, his Beaufort inheritance made him a valuable asset, and there would be many willing to fill Herbert's place. No doubt Margaret would already be petitioning to be reunited with her son, though given his current position there was little chance the Pretender would give his blessing for such a move, especially while Herbert's widow, Anne Devereux, continued to jealously guard her late husband's ward.

Jasper ran a hand through his bed-tousled hair. When he'd first held his nephew in his arms, it had seemed inconceivable there would ever be a time when he wouldn't be there to guide and protect him. How naive he'd been. Though he wanted to deny it, the reality was that, after so long, he was more a stranger than an uncle. Yet the love he had for Henry had never waned; it still burned strong, giving him purpose when all else seemed bleak. Throwing back the tangled sheets in an attempt to dispel the familiar frustration beginning to tug at his mind, Jasper reached his arms up to the ceiling, stretching his fingers higher and higher until he heard a satisfying crack. Sunlight was starting to peak through the gaps in the wooden shutters, creating patterns on the stone floor. Jasper padded across the room and pulled them open to reveal a perfect blue sky. He rubbed his eyes against the brightness. Enough dwelling, time to face another day.

27

July 1470

U nlike the stifling air outside, the inside of Angers cathedral
was soothingly cool. The large oak doors were flung open,
letting the hubbub of nearby market stalls float into the
vaulted hall on a light summer breeze. Leaning against a column,
obscured by shadows, Jasper watched the Earl of Warwick and Duke
of Clarence arrive. While Warwick was all dark hair and sharp angles,
Clarence was fair and, at twenty years old, yet to fill out his gangly
frame. They seemed to be in the middle of a heated exchange, though
at such a distance, it was impossible to make out what they were
saying.

The idea of an alliance with Warwick still left a sour taste in Jasper's
mouth, as it did in Marguerite's. Yet King Louis had been nothing
if not persuasive. Over the course of many long evenings, he had
slowly brought his cousins around to the idea of uniting with their
old enemy to put King Henry back on the throne. He'd pointed
out that Warwick's position was just as desperate, if not more so
than their own. His attempt to imprison Edward after Edgcote had
only lasted a few weeks. Reunited with his throne, Edward showed
surprising leniency, welcoming Warwick and Clarence back to court.

But whatever trust had once existed between them was shattered. In the void left behind, Edward moved even closer to his wife's family, choosing to favour the Woodvilles and their allies over his former favourite. Warwick endured the humiliation for a few months, until his brother being ordered to return his title of Northumberland forced his hand, propelling him across the channel to seek out alternative options.

Despite Louis' assurances, Jasper was unable to shake the nagging thought of what Warwick might do once King Henry was restored. It was clear his ambition knew no limits; his actions at Edgcote the previous year were evidence of the extent to which he was willing to go to protect his interests. While those interests aligned with their own aims the uneasy union might just hold. But at some point, Warwick's ascendance would once again reach its summit. After that, there was no telling what he would do.

Yet, at least Jasper knew Warwick well enough to have a grasp of his character. Clarence, on the other hand, was an unknown entity. He seemed to be little more than a spoilt brat, easily manipulated and hungry for power. The apple of his mother's eye, Duchess Cecily had sown the seed of doubt in his mind when, jealous of Edward's new wife, she had suggested the Pretender may not have been her husband's son. Jasper had met the Duchess many times at Westminster; she had been devoted to Richard in life and continued to be so in his death. The idea she would have betrayed him for some dalliance with a common archer was absurd. Yet, she was a proud woman. Why would she tarnish her name in such a way unless there was some truth in it? In the end he supposed it did not matter. The whisper alone was enough to push George closer to Warwick and destabilise Edward's reign. Jasper struggled to understand what the young duke had to gain from aligning himself with Lancaster. Though Elizabeth had given her husband many golden-haired princesses, she had yet to produce an heir. As it currently stood, Clarence was second-in-line to the throne. Whatever tale Warwick had spun must have been incredibly persuasive for him to surrender such a position. When he'd raised his concerns with Marguerite she had waved a hand dismissively and told him he was indulging his paranoia. But you didn't survive what Jasper had without analysing a decision from every angle, so he made a mental note and continued to watch the teenager closely.

Their argument concluded, Warwick and Clarence began to make their way up to the altar, their family following a short distance behind. Jasper shadowed the unlikely pair while they walked up the long nave. As they drew to a halt a few paces from Marguerite and Prince Edward, Jasper took up his position at the queen's left shoulder. Tension hung thick in the air as the former enemies faced each other.

It was Warwick who broke the deadlock, dropping with an unnecessary flourish onto his knees with his head bent low, the very picture of deference. "Your Majesty, thank you for agreeing to this audience."

"Warwick," Marguerite acknowledged coolly.

The earl kept his head lowered. "I wish to ask for forgiveness for the injuries and wrongs done to you in the past, for which I must share responsibility. My eyes have been opened to the harm the lies and misrule of the usurper Edward have done to the country I love. With your help, I shall see it returned to its former glory with the true king, Henry VI, at its head."

Warwick spoke with such sincerity that Jasper was certain he must have rehearsed it. The earl glanced up, awaiting Marguerite's permission to stand, but it did not come. The queen assessed the figure grovelling before her. Not for the first time she was struck by the ordinary vulnerability of even the most powerful of men. With his pale neck exposed, Warwick was completely at her mercy – the fact of which she knew the earl was all too aware.

The minutes drew out, Warwick's discomfort becoming increasingly acute, and still she refused to let him stand. Warwick's hand brushed his belt. Though the movement was unconsciously done, Marguerite's heart skipped a beat. Jasper saw it too, flexing his grip on his sword in response to the potential threat. They might be on sacred ground, but he had no qualms about killing Warwick, if that was what was required. His action did not go unnoticed by the earl, whose eyes darted towards him in barely concealed panic. The seconds ticked past, the tension palpable as Warwick's life hung in the balance. Even the stones of the cathedral seemed to hold their breath.

Finally, Marguerite's voice rang out. "Only God can truly absolve you of your sins. But we are minded to look favourably upon you and the union you offer." She extended her hand to Warwick who took it in his and kissed it reverently. Satisfied, at last, by Warwick's show of deference, she motioned for him to stand. Jasper bit back a smile as he struggled to his feet, his joints stiff after fifteen minutes knelt on the hard cathedral floor.

Humbled by the humiliation he had endured, Warwick stuttered with uncharacteristic nervousness as he spoke. "Your Grace, may I introduce my daughters, Isabelle and Anne?"

The pair took a hesitant step towards Marguerite before dropping into low curtsies. The eldest, Isabelle, was married to Clarence, and her dark eyes followed her husband wherever he went. She clearly cared for him, but there was little in Clarence's demeanour to suggest it was reciprocated. Though his brother's refusal to allow their union had pushed him further down the path to betrayal, it was wealth not love that had provoked his anger.

Next to her was her sister, the real focus of Marguerite's attention. An agreement between two parties, especially two as historically divided as the queen and Warwick, would need more binding it together than mere words. They needed to be united in the eyes of God, and what better way to achieve it than through marriage?

If Isabelle was tall and striking then Anne was the opposite. Petite with mousy brown hair, she was neither stunningly beautiful nor plain. Her face was open and trusting, reflecting the naivety with which she moved through the world. That such an innocent would soon be married to a man as callous and uncaring as Prince Edward seemed like leading a lamb to slaughter, and it only served to heighten Jasper's dislike of Warwick, who so willingly sold his daughter for political advancement. However, despite her diminutive stature, he was pleased to see she did not look away from Marguerite's piercing gaze. It spoke to a hidden strength that she would no doubt need to draw on in what was to come. As she stood like a statue whilst the queen assessed her potential daughter-in-law as a farmer might do prized cattle, Jasper was reminded of Margaret and just how young she had been when she'd married Edmund. At least in this instance the age gap between bride and groom was only a couple of years, rather than the decade that had separated Margaret and his brother, the thought of which still prompted a wave of disgust. He hoped for Anne's sake that, unlike his brother, the prince would wait before consummating their marriage.

Marguerite looked over at her son. *"Qu'en penses-tu, ma cherie?"*

Prince Edward surveyed Anne with barely concealed indifference. "She will do," he replied, as though purposely choosing to speak in English to further cement Anne's humiliation.

In the face of such coldness from her future husband, she seemed to shrink into herself, the fleeting confidence Jasper had seen melting away along with the romantic dreams she had no doubt clung to on the journey from England.

"Then it is agreed." Marguerite turned to address Warwick. "I give my blessing for the union of your daughter Anne to my son, Edward of Lancaster, the Prince of Wales. Obviously, as they are distant cousins, we will need to wait for the Pope's dispensation. After that, England."

186

A smile spread across Warwick's face. "Your Majesty," he replied, bowing low.

Jasper watched as the earl strode back down the nave, his family trailing behind. It was only once they stepped out into the summer sunshine that he finally relaxed his grip on his sword.

* * *

Supper had been a strained affair. King Louis joined them, the Universal Spider no doubt intrigued to see how his carefully orchestrated plans were playing out. His presence had the benefit of diffusing some of the tension simmering beneath the amicable façade. Just because Marguerite had given her blessing for the marriage did not mean she and Warwick were suddenly bosom friends, and her demeanour remained icy. At the other end of the table, Jasper had been seated between Clarence's wife, Isabelle, and her mother, Anne de Beauchamp. A fiercely proud woman, it was because of her inheritance that Warwick had come to hold his title and the considerable lands that accompanied it. They had exchanged a few pleasantries, but for the most part had passed the meal in silence. Isabelle was still suffering from her ordeal during their channel crossing when she'd gone into early labour. Denied access to Calais, she had given birth in a dank and cramped cabin while a storm buffeted their ship, threatening to drown them all. The baby, a little boy, had been stillborn, and the loss still shadowed her eyes. Once the plates had been cleared, King Louis excused himself, beckoning Prince Edward along with him, shortly followed by the Countess and her daughters. Their departure left Warwick and Clarence on one side of the table and Marguerite and Jasper on the other. The conversation quickly turned to their impending invasion as they tried to thrash out the details. At least an hour had passed since then and tempers were starting to fray.

"Once the ships land at Plymouth, I will head for London," Warwick explained, his fingers sketching an invisible map on the table in front of him. "Prince Edward will accompany me to—"

"No," Marguerite's voice echoed around the room, cutting Warwick short. Next to the earl, Clarence rolled his eyes in a way that made Jasper want to lean across the table and slap him.

"Your highness, we need to present a strong hand," Warwick reasoned. "Bringing the prince will show the people that King Henry's line is secure."

"I will not risk his safety. He will stay with me until it is safe—"

"Your Majesty—" Warwick injected.

"I warn you, Warwick. Do not test me. I will not negotiate on this matter."

But the earl would not back down. "The King has been imprisoned for a long time. It is unclear what state he will be in when he is released. If Prince Edward accompanied the campaign it would help garner support in the eventuality King Henry is unable to rule."

"I have told you no! Sir Jasper will go in Edward's place."

Warwick turned his dark eyes on Jasper, assessing him from across the table. Jasper returned his gaze with an unflinching stare. After a beat, the earl looked away. "And what if the king cannot rule?" he pressed.

"If my husband is incapacitated then you and Jasper will govern in his name until my son is old enough to do so himself. Now enough. It is late and this meeting is over. Goodnight, sirs, we will speak more in the morning."

The men stood as the queen rose from her chair and swept from the room. After exchanging a few whispered words with Warwick, Clarence slunk away in the opposite direction to his chambers, no doubt heading for the town's brothels with which he had become quickly acquainted.

Jasper was almost at the door when Warwick intercepted him. "I must say I'm pleased my brother released you after Bamburgh. Too many lives have been wasted in this unnecessary conflict. It is good yours was not one of them."

"Oh really? As far as I was aware, you wanted my head?"

"Oh come now, Pembroke – my apologies – *Sir* Jasper," Warwick replied, placing unnecessary emphasis on his reduced title. "We've had our differences, but as the queen herself said, we are here to forge a new future. Besides, I'd have thought you'd be thanking me for killing the man you held responsible for your brother's death?"

Jasper looked at him in disbelief. Truly did the earl's arrogance know no bounds? Clearly, whatever humbleness Warwick had shown in the cathedral had been fleeting. Jasper would not let him have the satisfaction of receiving any praise from him. He shrugged in attempted indifference. "Herbert was going to get his comeuppance soon enough. If I am grateful for anything, it is that my nephew did not meet the same end as his guardian. Though that can be more attributed to fate than any of your own actions."

"Ah yes, young Henry, such an amiable boy." Warwick must have seen the flash of emotion in Jasper's eyes because a sly smile spread across his face. "Not that you would know. It's been, what, eight years now since you last saw him?"

"Nine," Jasper corrected tightly.

"Nine, of course – how time flies," Warwick replied with a smirk.

Jasper remained quiet, his face impassive, the muscle jumping in his jaw the only evidence of the effort it was taking to not rise to Warwick's goading. His dagger itched at his side but he ignored it, twisting his father's ring instead. Whether he liked it or not, Warwick was the only hope he had of ever seeing Henry again. If only for his nephew's sake, he needed to stay in control.

Warwick slapped a hand on Jasper's shoulder. "Only a few more weeks now." With a wink, he swaggered away.

Jasper let out a long breath. "Bastard."

28

September 1470

Summer was still stubbornly refusing to release its grip on the county, and the early morning mist that had covered the passing fields like a blanket had given way to a beautiful day. Others may have found the sun beating down oppressive, but it warmed Jasper's soul and soothed his disquieted mind. The journey had been long, but after so many years in exile, he'd been content to take his time winding through lanes and stopping at country inns. He'd landed at Dartmouth a couple of weeks earlier with Warwick and Clarence, having left the queen and her son behind in France. Before they set off, Warwick sent word to his supporters in the north to launch an uprising. Designed to draw Edward away from the capital, they hoped it would allow them to land in relative safety. For once their plans came off without issue. When their boats landed on the Devon coast, Edward and his army were hundreds of miles away dealing with the rebellion. By the time he realised and turned south, it was too late. Pursued by Warwick's brother John, Edward was forced to flee to Flanders, barely escaping with his life. The country was now theirs. Beaming in triumph, Warwick and Clarence made straight for London to release King Henry from the Tower. Jasper, meanwhile, headed for Wales. Herbert had used his time as Earl of Pembroke effectively, turning the loyalties of the Welsh people so that nearly all of the areas that had once been loyal to Jasper and to Lancaster now held Yorkist sympathies. If King Henry was to enjoy any sort of stability on his reclaimed throne, Herbert's work would need to be undone. It would not be an easy task. First, though, Jasper wanted to return home, to feel its comforting familiarity once more.

His heart physically ached when Pembroke's outline appeared on the horizon. Yet as he rode through its gates it was clear it was not the same home he had walked away from nearly a decade before. There was no Ianto bounding out to greet him, and when he led his horse to the stables, Tarn's usual space was empty. The inner ward was eerily quiet, the only activity a few loose chickens scratching at the dirt, and when he looked more closely at the masonry, he could see it was in a poor state of repair, evidence of its neglect since Herbert's death. A creeping sense of disappointment spread through him. Pembroke had always been the place where he felt most at ease, but now he felt like a trespasser. He'd been naive to think it would be otherwise after so long away.

With a sigh, he made his way towards the main hall, memory more than conscious thought propelling his muscles. The thick door creaked on rusty hinges as Jasper pushed it open and stepped across the threshold. It took a moment for his eyes to adjust to the change in light, but when the room finally came into focus Jasper was surprised by what he saw. While Pembroke's exterior may be decaying, it was clear someone was still caring for the castle. The flagstone floor was spotless and the long oak table had been recently polished, the smell of beeswax still hanging in the air. Looking up at the familiar beams above his head, Jasper felt a glimmer of his old self returning. He tensed as he heard a woman's voice behind him.

"If you've come sniffing for gold, you've come to the wrong place.

There's nothing here for you. Now get!"

Jasper remained unmoving. Unseen by the woman, a wide smile started to spread across his face.

"You heard me, away with you!" she repeated with more force.

Slowly, Jasper turned to face the woman, who was holding a broom out in front of her as though it were a weapon. *"Helô,* Joan. *Sut wyt ti?"* he asked, enjoying the sound of Welsh after so long spent speaking French.

Joan almost dropped the broom in surprise. "Jasper?!" She took a few steps towards him. For a moment it seemed as though she might try to embrace him, but then, suddenly remembering who he was, she stopped and bobbed into a curtsey. "I'm sorry, my Lord. I— We—" she stammered, smiling nervously. "As you can tell, you've taken me quite by surprise. I was not told you were returning. I admit I feared you dead."

"Well as you can see, I am very much alive," Jasper replied with a chuckle. "It is good to be home. Thank you for looking after Pembroke while I've been away. I trust the past years have been kinder to you than they were to me?"

"Ach, I don't know about that. Like most folk, there were times when we struggled. But God was kind to us. He saw us through. There aren't many of us left here, mind. Old Black William didn't care much for this place, as you can probably tell, and so one by one people drifted away. That'll change now though. And what about you?"

"I survived."

Joan nodded, and there was something in her eyes that told Jasper she understood the mental and physical toil that one word contained. She did not probe him further. "You must be hungry? If you don't mind waiting, I could bring you something up from the kitchen?"

"No need to traipse there and back, I'll come down to the kitchen with you. I want to revisit every inch of this place."

Joan smiled. "As you wish, my Lord. I trust you remember the way?"

* * *

The kitchen had always been the beating heart of Pembroke, and it seemed that, in that regard, little had changed. Freshly plucked birds hung from hooks and piles of vegetables covered the surfaces. Now was the time of abundance and Joan was making the most of it. In the corner, next to a large fire where pots were simmering, was a boy of about twelve or thirteen. For a fleeting moment, Jasper thought it was Henry, but he dismissed the thought almost as soon as it arose. His nephew was in Hereford, under the care of a man named Sir Richard Corbett, who had been looking after him on behalf of Herbert's widow. Still, there was a striking familiarity about the boy. Jasper was trying to put his finger on it when Joan came bustling into the kitchen behind him.

Catching sight of the boy in the corner, she wagged her finger at him. "David Owen, what do you think you're doing hiding in here?"

"I was just—" David protested.

"I don't want to hear it," Joan interrupted, shaking her head. "Your mother has been looking an age for you. You'd better go find her before she has your guts for garters." With a sheepish look at Jasper, David scurried away out of the room.

"Is that—?" he began, pointing at the door through which the boy had just left.

"Your half-brother? Yes. Bless him, he's a sweet boy really. His mother, Beth, was devastated when she heard about your father. We all were. He was a good man."

Jasper gave a tight smile. He'd lost enough people to know that grief would never truly leave him. Mostly he carried it unconsciously, but then, just when he started to think he had mastered it, it would rise up unbidden to choke his voice and sting his eyes. Talking about Owen while standing in the very place in which they had shared so many happy memories made it do just that, and so he merely nodded in acknowledgement of Joan's words.

Sensing the change, Joan cast around for a different subject. "Speaking of boys, how is my Henry?" she asked, brightly.

Jasper, appreciating her effort, tried to keep his voice light. "I have not had a chance to see him yet. I'm collecting him next week from Hereford on my way to London."

"You're leaving so soon."

"I'll be back. But my presence is required at Westminster, and my nephew needs to be reunited with his mother."

"Ah Margaret, such a brave little girl. Though I imagine she'll be a great lady now."

"Yes," he agreed quietly, a sudden wave of nervousness at the prospect of their reunion coming over him, "I imagine she will be."

* * *

Jasper was not expecting a warm welcome from Sir Richard Corbett, which was just as well as he certainly did not receive one. The man who met him in a once-grand but now-dilapidated hall regarded him with frosty coldness and barely concealed disdain. Still, he managed to begrudgingly lower his head in some semblance of a bow. "Tudor."

"Corbett. I have little desire to exchange pleasantries. I merely wish to collect my nephew and leave as swiftly as possible."

"You'll have no objection from me on that. If you'll come with me," he replied, setting off down the corridor. Jasper followed him, ducking below a low door frame as they entered what he suspected had once been a study.

At the sound of the men entering the room, a boy who had been studying the details of an old tapestry hung on the wall, turned to face them. Jasper let out a breath. Taller than the child who had filled his dreams, Edmund was present in every shadow of Henry's dark features. All, that is, except his eyes. Strikingly blue, they undeniably belonged to his mother, and they watched Jasper with the same uncertainty that Margaret's had in Lamphey's great hall.

Jasper came towards him, smiling broadly. "Hello, Henry."

He knew it was wishful thinking, but deep down Jasper had been hoping his nephew would be overjoyed to see him. Instead, Henry bowed formally. "My Lord, welcome to Hereford."

His voice still had the treble of youth, and he had yet to fill out his gangly frame. In the absence of any conversation from his nephew, Jasper scrabbled to fill the silence. "I've just arrived from Pembroke. I've come to take you to London, to your mother."

Henry nodded. "Sir Richard told me you would be coming. He has been very kind to look after me."

Jasper glanced at Corbett with a tight smile, this wasn't going how he had expected. "Yes, he certainly has. I'm sorry we are unable to stay longer, we have a long journey ahead of us and I am keen to be underway."

"No need to explain," Corbett replied, stepping forward. He grasped Henry's shoulder, the fondest in the gesture taking Jasper by surprise. "Well, I suppose this is goodbye then, boy. Stay safe and be good for your mother."

Henry gave him a small smile. "Thank you."

29

October 1470

Jasper had forgotten how dirty the streets of London were. Mud, sewage and other substances that were best not dwelled upon flowed along open gutters, emitting a putrid smell that he was trying his best not to inhale. Next time, he told himself, he would go by boat, not that the river smelt much better. He stifled a yawn with the back of his hand as he picked his way through the grime. He'd been at Westminster all day, and though it was satisfying to be within its familiar halls once more, he was pleased to have left them behind for the night. He'd hoped to see his half-brother, but the king was still weak from his long imprisonment and so he had had to be content with Warwick's sneering face, the earl's arrogance even more insufferable now his power had been reinstated. Henry had gone straight to his mother as soon as they had arrived in the capital. Given their long separation, Jasper had thought it only right to allow Margaret some time alone with her son before the chaos of court invaded her threshold. Besides, the demands on his time meant that, while they were in London, Jasper was unable to give his nephew the undivided attention he deserved. He remained frustrated by the awkwardness between them. He'd imagined Henry would be talkative and excitable, but instead they'd spent most of their journey from Hereford in silence, occasionally interspersed with stilted conversations in which Jasper did the majority of the talking. He'd quickly realised that for all their physical similarities, Henry was not Edmund, and in his excitement at being reunited, he had lost sight of that. Jasper could tell his eagerness had unnerved his nephew and he could only hope that, in time, he would find a way to overcome Henry's shyness.

He stepped up to the door, hesitating for a moment before rapping his fist against the wood. Why was he so nervous? Exhaling, he lowered his hand and waited, twisting his father's ring round and round. He was about to knock again when the door swung open. Jasper had been expecting a servant, but instead it was Henry Stafford's smiling face that greeted him. His hair was grey and thinning, while the extra weight around his middle confirmed that the previous decade had been far from arduous. Still, his eyes shone with the same kindness that had convinced Jasper that Margaret would be happy with him.

"Tudor!" Stafford exclaimed, gripping Jasper's arm in warm welcome.

His good humour was infectious, and Jasper felt his worries drifting away as he grasped Stafford's arm in return. "Stafford, it truly is good to see you."

"Come in, come in out of the cold," Stafford said, ushering him inside. "Autumn has us in its grip, does it not?"

"The weather has certainly turned," Jasper agreed, although in his opinion it was still relatively mild, certainly not as biting as the October evenings in Harlech.

Stafford shut the door behind them and began guiding Jasper along the hallway. "Goodness, it's been, what, nearly thirteen years since I last saw you?"

"It has indeed."

"Margaret will be thrilled to see you. She'll be through in a moment, but Henry is waiting for us in the solar."

Jasper nodded. He didn't know who he was more nervous about seeing. Rationally, he knew it should be Margaret, so much had happened since they had last been together, but the way Henry held him at arms length pained him. Taking a deep breath, he followed Stafford into the solar. Henry was sitting in one of the high-backed chairs, a book on his lap. He stood as the two men entered and gave the same formal bow he had before.

Jasper felt his heart sink. His mind scrambled for something to say to Henry but Stafford interrupted his thoughts. "So you've been in France these past few years?" he asked.

"France and Brittany, yes, and before that Harlech and Bamburgh," Jasper replied.

"And do you mind me asking how that was?"

Jasper shrugged. "Cold and lonely. There were some difficult moments during the sieges, but as for my time in Europe, I cannot fault my hosts' generosity. It certainly made up for having to escape Wales disguised as a peasant."

Henry stared at him wide-eyed. "You had to disguise yourself as a peasant?"

"Oh yes. I'll tell you more about it one day, maybe when you're slightly older," Jasper replied, secretly pleased to have impressed his nephew.

A voice sounded from the doorway. "There's a sight I feared I might never see again."

Jasper turned as a woman walked into the room. Elegant and serene, she held herself with an unmistakable confidence.

"Margaret," Jasper breathed.

The woman's face broke into a wide smile. "Hello, Jasper."

As though propelled by an invisible force, he crossed the room, reaching out to grip Margaret's arms, as if needing proof she was not just a figment of his imagination. Margaret reached up a slender hand and cupped his cheek, her rings cool against his skin. Her eyes, the twins of Henry's, were brimming with tears. "I prayed every day that God would deliver you back to me."

"Well, you were obviously very persuasive," Jasper chuckled softly, taking her hand and kissing it.

He had worried there would be some awkwardness between them after so long apart. But those fears quickly evaporated as Margaret looped her arm through his. "Come, we have over a decade to catch up on," she said, guiding him along a tapestry-lined hallway into the heart of her home. It felt right to be walking arm in arm with her once more, and Jasper was happy to listen as she talked about how she'd acquired her London home. He noticed she had grown since he had last seen her, on her wedding day, her chin now level with his shoulder, where before the top of her head had only just reached. A sudden thought came to Jasper – they fitted well together.

The room Margaret led him to was designed to impress. Elaborately carved dark wood panels lined the walls, while above their heads the ceiling was painted in opulent shades of blue and red. Running down the centre of the room was a long table that had been tastefully decorated with foliage from the garden and silver candlesticks. Jasper pulled Margaret's chair out for her, waiting for her to settle herself before taking up his position next to her. He noted an empty place setting beside him but was too eager to hear from Margaret to enquire after their absent guest.

"It seems you have adapted well to your life as Lady Stafford," he commented, gesturing at the grandeur of the room.

Margaret smiled modestly. "I consider myself very fortunate. The decision after Towton to swear fealty to York was not an easy one. However, it has afforded us a freedom others were not so lucky to enjoy."

Jasper waved a hand. If he had once cared about it, it troubled him little now. Some things were more important than impossible decisions made years ago. "And you are happy?"

Margaret nodded. "I am. I finally have my family together again. You know, in all the years he was at Raglan, I was only permitted to visit Henry once. The pain of being separated from him was unbearable, though my husband did his best to ease it." She looked over at Stafford. "He is kind and caring, just as you said he would be. Ours is a true partnership. Though it surprised me at first, I have come to love him." She smiled. "Even when he beats me at chess."

"But no children?"

"No. After Henry— Well, God has other plans for me." She took a sip from her cup, the wine staining her lip. "And what about you? Every report I received seemed more outlandish than the one before."

"I can promise you it was not nearly as exciting as those might have made out." Jasper tried to keep his voice light, but the flicker of sadness that darkened his eyes did not go unnoticed by Margaret.

She placed a hand on his. "I was sorry to hear about your father. We mourned him, as we did my cousin Somerset."

Jasper gave a tight smile. "I would be lying if I said the past decade had been without its difficulties. I have found myself at my lowest ebb more times than I ever thought possible. But that is all behind me now."

"I am glad of it."

Margaret smiled again and Jasper noted the faint lines at the corners of her eyes. He calculated she was twenty-seven now, the same age he had been on her wedding day. To think of all the life since then, the years stolen from them. Sensing where his thoughts had wandered to, Margaret squeezed his hand. She opened her mouth to speak but stopped as a man was led into the dining chamber. Jasper stood in surprise. "Richard!"

Tunstall shot a smile in Jasper's direction, before turning to Margaret and bowing. "My apologies, my Lady – I was delayed by business."

Margaret waved a hand. "Not at all. Please, take your seat."

Richard walked round the table to Jasper and grasped his arm. "Christ's bones, aren't you a sight for sore eyes!"

"But after Harlech, I thought—" Jasper stammered, still in shock at his friend's appearance.

"Dead? Me?" Richard shook his head, as he sat down next to him, the mystery of the empty chair now solved. "Never. I was taken to the Tower and then Edward let me go. Like I said in my letter, it seems away from the battlefield he is not nearly as fond of killing. Enough of me though, what of you? What adventuring have you been up to without me?"

"Adventuring? More like begging at Louis' table for scraps."

"It cannot have been that dreadful if you now find yourself here."

"No," Jasper considered. "I suppose I should be grateful for my cousin's interference. And your family – how was it, being reunited?" he asked, keen to turn the attention away from himself.

Richard's face lit up as though illuminated by the sun. "They are the gift I thank God for every day. I know all men say their wives are the most beautiful women in the world, but my Elizabeth truly is something special. And little Lizzie, oh Jasper, I wish you could meet her, she is a wonder. I did not think it was possible to love something so much."

"It warms my heart to hear you speak of it," Jasper replied, unable to stop himself from looking at Henry. It was clear that over the past few weeks, Stafford had won the boy's trust and the two of them were talking animatedly. Jasper felt a pang of jealousy.

Richard noted the direction of his gaze and leant over to him. "Such things are not to be rushed," he observed. "The upheaval of the last few months has been hard enough on us, let alone a thirteen-year-old boy. You will have plenty of time to become reacquainted when you are back in Pembroke."

Stafford sensed the pair watching from across the table and looked up from his conversation with Henry. "I hear you have an audience with the king tomorrow," he called over to Jasper.

He nodded. "I believe it is time young Henry here was introduced to his uncle."

Margaret leant into the conversation. "And Henry's earldom? You must petition the king to return his title to him."

"Certainly I will ask, but Clarence is the Earl of Richmond now. I doubt he will return the title, or its lands, willingly and Warwick will be keen to keep him on side."

"You speak of Warwick as though he is the one sitting on the throne."

"The crown may rest on Henry's head, but do not be fooled as to where the true power lies. This is an uneasy alliance. Only when Marguerite and her son arrive from France will there be the chance to redress the balance."

"And when will that be?" Margaret challenged. From across the table, Stafford watched his wife with an expression that suggested he was quite familiar with her impassioned arguments.

Jasper shrugged. "That is a question I cannot answer. The queen will come when she believes it is safe."

"Safety is relative," Margaret countered. "If Warwick really holds as much power as you say, haven't we simply swapped one tyrant for another? And Clarence? I don't trust him."

"Only a fool would trust that arrogant peacock," Jasper replied dismissively.

Margaret raised an eyebrow. "Oh, so you're a fool now are you, Jasper Tudor?"

Stafford almost choked on his wine, while Richard roared with laughter. "We could have done with you in Harlech, Lady Stafford," he cried. "You would have helped keep this one in check!"

Jasper leant back in his chair with a smile, his hands raised in surrender, genuinely happy for the first time in years.

* * *

Westminster hall was heaving with people, the hum of conversations echoing off the vaulted ceiling. The energy in the room added to the sense of occasion, and though Henry tried to appear nonchalant, Jasper could tell he was slightly awestruck. Keeping a firm grip on his nephew's collar lest he should get lost in the crowd, Jasper wove his way through the throng. A few men nodded their heads in acknowledgement and occasional surprise, but Jasper did not have time to exchange anything more than a few pleasantries; they were there on business, not idle socialising.

The purpose of their visit was seated at one end of the hall, on a throne raised up on a dais. Slowly, Jasper and Henry made their way towards him. There were some other men gathered around the throne, all keen to curry favour, and it was not until the pair in front of them had moved away that Jasper was able to step up to the dais. The king's eyes lit up at the sight of him. "Brother!"

"Your Grace," Jasper replied, bowing low. "It gladdens me to see you so restored. May I introduce my nephew, Henry Tudor?" Next to him, Henry stepped cautiously forward and copied Jasper's low bow.

The king smiled and waved the boy closer. "Come, come – let us see you properly."

With his hand on the small of his back, Jasper pushed Henry forward a few steps so that he was within touching distance of the throne. The king leant towards him, searching his face. "Ah yes, there is much of

Edmund in him," he observed. "Would you not agree, Jasper?"

"Yes, your Grace, I would," Jasper replied quickly, trying to disguise his surprise at his lucidity.

The king nodded with a smile before turning his attention back to his half-nephew. "Welcome to court, Henry. We look forward to getting to know you better. And Jasper," he added, "we request your presence tomorrow – we would benefit from your counsel."

"Of course." With another bow, Jasper and Henry moved away from the dais, melting back into the assembled crowd. Jasper was amazed. It was the most eloquent he had heard his half-brother be since his first collapse. Henry was beaming, clearly ecstatic with how the king had acknowledged him. Jasper squeezed his shoulder. "Well done," he whispered in his ear.

30

December 1470

The official restoration of his earldom had made Jasper happier than he would have thought. Herbert's son, who had inherited the title on his father's death, was kicking up a fuss, but Jasper did not dwell on it. What mattered most was that Pembroke was officially once again his. Frustratingly, his nephew could not enjoy a similar reinstatement. Clarence was refusing to even discuss Henry's right to the earldom of Richmond, let alone negotiate on the matter. It was an irritating impasse but one that, with time, Jasper was certain would come to some sort of resolution.

Despite the favour bestowed by Fortune's Wheel in its most recent turn, Jasper had not fully given himself over to unbridled optimism. Yorkist sympathisers still lurked in the shadows, and for all his clarity at the meeting, it was clear his half-brother lacked the mental capacity to rule independently. He was a puppet king, a mouthpiece for other men's decisions, and vulnerable to their ambitions. It would be different if Queen Marguerite were by his side, but concerningly she showed no sign of making the journey across the Channel. Initially, Jasper had been surprised by her hesitance. Given her fierce defence of Lancaster, he had assumed she would want to be reunited with her husband as soon as possible. But maybe, on reflection, it was not so surprising that all her energy and attention was now directed at her son. Having recently turned eighteen, it was on his youthful shoulders, and not the frail shell of his father, that the hopes of their house rested. The years in exile and countless defeats had made Marguerite more cautious. Now that she had something priceless to lose, this trait had been amplified to the point of inaction. So she remained in France, biding her time. In her absence, Warwick became increasingly paranoid, while Clarence grew ever more sullen. Clearly dissatisfied with the current situation, it would only be a matter of time before he slinked back to his brother, his tail between his legs.

Jasper had confided his fears in Margaret and was relieved to hear she shared them. Her response was predictably pragmatic. Like the queen, the welfare of her own son was her paramount concern and so, even as London celebrated King Henry's reinstatement, the two of them stood in Margaret's solar and planned what they would do when the Pretender returned.

"We need to divide our loyalties. Obviously, you will support King Henry, but when Edward calls, my husband will answer," Margaret began. Even though Jasper had expected it, he still struggled with the idea of them being on opposing sides. "A battle is coming, there is no question about it. If Lancaster were to triumph then I know, because of you, we will be safe. But if Edward were to win, as I fear he might, he will not show the same forgiveness he demonstrated after Towton. Though it pains me to do it, I will continue to feign loyalty."

"And Henry?"

"Will go with you. He has been overlooked so far, but the Beaufort blood that runs in his veins poses a threat to Edward." Though they were alone Margaret's voice had dropped to a hushed whisper.

"You believe he will see Henry as a potential challenger for the throne?" Jasper asked. "I agree he has royal blood, though surely there are many others with superior claims?"

"It is true, there are. But mark my words, when Edward returns it will be with a terrible vengeance. He has suffered the ultimate betrayal, he will not be so careless again. Any and all with a claim will be at risk, my son amongst them. That is why he must go to Pembroke with you."

The pain the thought of being separated from Henry caused her was obvious. Instinctively, Jasper tried to ease it. "There is no rush, he can stay here with you for longer if you wish."

"No!" Margaret burst out. "I cannot protect him here. In Wales, you can. I will not, I cannot lose him. I—" She fell silent, her true fear finally out in the open.

Jasper stepped towards her. "Margaret—" he said gently.

She reached out for him and gripped the front of his doublet. "Swear to me you'll keep him safe."

"You know you never need ask me such a thing."

But Margaret shook her head, some of her long hair falling in front of her face. "Swear to me," she repeated, gripping him more tightly.

Jasper raised a hand and tucked the loose hair behind her ear. "I swear."

Margaret visibly relaxed at his words, wrapping her arms around him. Jasper felt the wetness of her tears as she pressed her cheek against his. "Come back to me," she whispered in his ear. "Both of you."

* * *

By the time it came for them to depart, Margaret had regained her usual composure. Yet tears had still shone in her eyes when she laid her hand in turn on their heads. Kneeling before her to receive her blessing, Jasper had been reminded of when she'd done the same in the great hall of Lamphey Palace. For his part, Henry seemed untroubled by the thought of returning to Pembroke or by being separated once more from his mother. Though he'd enjoyed the weeks spent with Margaret, he was a typical boy on the cusp of adulthood, eager to learn the ways of men and prove his independence. Despite the clear respect he had for his mother, he chafed under her constant attention, and with every mile they rode further from London, the more relaxed the boy became. Jasper felt he was starting to get a better measure of Henry's character. Richard had been right to advise him to take it steadily. There was a reservedness to Henry, a cautiousness that was no doubt a product of his tumultuous childhood. But given time, this soon gave way to a pleasant affability. Certainly, their return journey to Wales had been significantly less strained than the outbound one, laughter, not silence filling the miles of rutted tracks, any awkwardness left long behind. Though Henry professed to never be tired, they stopped regularly. They were in no rush and it gave Jasper the opportunity to attend to matters that had been much neglected in his long absence. Henry sat in on every meeting, conducting himself with a maturity that reminded Jasper of Margaret. From the conversations they shared afterwards, it was clear he had inherited his mother's intelligence as well. Whatever Jasper may have thought of Herbert while he was alive, his care of Henry had been above reproach, and for that he would be forever thankful. The fact that his nephew had been so well looked after soothed the shame he carried for abandoning him all those years before, and as they rode side by side through Pembroke's imposing gate, for the first time in years Jasper felt the disparate parts of his soul slot together once more.

31

May 1471

The room at the top of Chepstow castle's Great Tower offered far-reaching views of rolling green hills basking in the May sunshine. Normally, such a sight would soothe Jasper's soul, but not today. Today, he was restless and nothing, not even a beautiful spring day, could shake it. It was not just the reason for his presence in Chepstow that made him so. There was something about the building itself that he found unsettling. Castles usually held command over the landscape in which they were set, but Chepstow was different. It was not that the castle itself was lacking in grandeur. Indeed, it was as large and imposing as any that Jasper had seen. But yet, despite that, it was the River Wye flowing below it that held sway over the valley. Mirroring the course of the river, the castle's east wall was curved, conveying an unshakeable sense that rather than a conscious architectural decision, the shape had been created by the stone yielding to the sheer force of the water.

Jasper peered down at the inky water below. From such a height, it would be easy to dismiss the Wye's languid meandering as benign, but still waters ran deep, and Jasper could almost sense the ancient power flowing in its current. He watched mesmerised for a few moments before turning his attention back to the table that had been crammed into one corner of the room. Arrayed across its surface were half a dozen letters. Each contained enough bloodshed and misery to make even the most optimistic of men despair. Together, they sounded the death knell of Lancaster and enveloped Jasper in a suffocating black cloud of depression. He'd only managed to enjoy a brief few months of relative peace before the first reports of Edward's landing at Ravenspur reached him. Immediately, he had begun recruiting men. There were still those who saw him as *Y Mab Darogan* and soon hundreds had flocked to his banner. He could have marched out right then, but instead he waited. When Warwick's pleas for men arrived in early April, he ignored them. And he was not the only one.

Of all the Lancastrian lords, only Exeter and Oxford answered the Kingmaker's calls. Yet while Edmund Beaufort, the new Duke of Somerset, refused to lend support purely out of spite and a need to avenge his brother's murder, Jasper's reticence was more calculated. As she'd said he would, Margaret's husband had rallied men to fight for Edward. Given their discussion, it would have been counter-intuitive for him to take the field against Stafford. Queen Marguerite's delayed departure from France further cemented his decision. From the speed he was moving south, it was clear Warwick would be forced to engage Edward before the queen's ships landed. If Jasper committed his men to battle too early, he would be in no position to support Marguerite, should Edward triumph. Better to let Warwick act as an obstacle. If he fell, so be it – Jasper would not mourn him. The delay would enable him to raise more men and meet with the queen before continuing on to deal with whatever remained of Edward's forces.

At least that had been his plan. What he had failed to properly account for was Edward. He had swept through the forces assembled by his former mentor as though they were nothing, leaving the lifeless corpses of both Warwick and his brother, John, behind him. Despite the disastrous consequences his death would have for Lancaster, Jasper could not help feeling there was a fitting sense of irony that the Kingmaker had ultimately been cut down by the man on whose head he had placed the crown. As for Henry Stafford, being on the winning side had not protected him. Dealt a serious injury, Margaret confessed she did not believe her husband was long for this world.

Delayed by the weather, news of the defeat at Barnet reached the queen at Dorchester barely a day after she had landed on England's shores for the first time since fleeing Bamburgh. In an instant, the journey northwards to convene with Jasper's own forces, which had been devised as a royal procession to rally support, became a frantic race to avoid being cut off by Edward. She marched her men hard, at times covering more than thirty miles a day underneath a scorching sun. There was a moment when the two armies came within a hair's breadth of each other, yet Marguerite was able to slip away unnoticed under the cover of darkness.

From the Welsh side of the Severn, Jasper tracked her progress northwards, all the while cursing the expanse of water that separated them. If their luck could hold until Gloucester and its river crossing, there might still be hope for them; Edward was unlikely to pursue Marguerite into Wales, especially given the area's Lancastrian sympathies. But the capriciousness of fate was to burn them yet again, their luck running out at Gloucester's gates, which remained resolutely shut. With the enemy only a few miles behind, there was not enough time to storm the city's defences, and so the queen forced her men on once more, with Edward hunting them down like dogs every step of the way. Exhausted and hungry, she finally called a halt at Tewkesbury and prepared to face the Pretender.

What followed was, in a word, a massacre. In the shadow of Tewkesbury's abbey, streams ran red with blood and fields piled high with bodies. The heat and exhaustion drained morale, caused tempers to fray and discipline, even amongst the commanders, began to wane. Edmund Beaufort, demonstrating none of his elder brother's composure, dashed Lord Wenlock's brains out in response to the latter's delay in committing his men to battle. After that, their fate was sealed.

Distracted by bickering, Edward was able to sweep mercilessly through the queen's forces. The Prince of Wales, leading the centre and experiencing his first taste of battle, was no match for the Pretender, his position quickly engulfed by the enemy. In the mêlée that followed, his young life and the hopes of Lancaster were ended. Even those who managed to escape into the sanctuary of the abbey were not spared. Somerset was dragged from its consecrated grounds and beheaded, just as his brother had been at Hexham. The only one excluded from the purge was Queen Marguerite. Tied to her horse to prevent her falling off from grief, she was returned to London, from where she was to be ransomed back to her father and cousin. Now a shadow of her former self, Jasper doubted he would ever see her again.

As Edward re-entered the capital in triumph, so his attention had turned to the Tower and its newest occupant. King Henry never stood a chance. The proclamation announcing his death blamed his displeasure and melancholy at the loss of his son for his demise. Few believed it. Fewer still were prepared to challenge it. Edward's hold on the throne was absolute. For his part, Jasper had been surprised by the lack of emotion he felt. There was sadness, yes, but given the years he had sacrificed, he'd thought he might feel a more acute sense of grief. Maybe after so many deaths he simply had no more left to give? Or maybe it was because he'd already grieved the loss of his half-brother. Illness had stolen him away long before Edward had stalked into his chamber. And so the overwhelming emotion Jasper felt was an uncomfortable sense of relief. The competing struggle between fealty to his king and his promise to Margaret had been broken. There was no longer a choice to make. His nephew, and him alone, was his priority now. Nothing else mattered. Besides, he did not have the luxury to dwell on his emotions. Margaret's doom-filled prediction had come true, and Jasper could feel the net closing in.

Of the Lancastrian lines in whose veins the blood of old King Edward ran, only three male heirs survived. Exeter, Buckingham and Henry. The first was imprisoned and the second was York's ward. Henry alone remained free from the Pretender's grasp, safe for now behind Pembroke's formidable walls, but danger would soon be pounding on its gates. Indeed, according to Jasper's informants, there was already a man on his way to capture him. Roger Vaughan, like his half-brother William Herbert before him, was a staunch Yorkist. Responsible for the round-up of prisoners after Mortimer's Cross, he had been the one to order Owen's execution. Jasper cracked his knuckles. When Vaughan arrived in the town, he would be waiting for him.

* * *

Fortunately, he did not have to wait long. The men he'd placed on Chepstow's gates seized Vaughan as soon as he appeared, dragging him unceremoniously through the streets. He now stood in front of Jasper in the castle's angular inner ward, held on each side by a guard, not that he required such restraint. Roger Vaughan of Tretower was not a young man. Apparently, he had fought at Agincourt which, if true, would make him around seventy years old. Looking at the wizened man in front of him, Jasper didn't doubt it. A respected warrior he might once have been, but those days were long behind him now. Part of Jasper was mildly offended that one old man was all Edward thought was needed to capture him. Was he really so underestimated, or was this all his track record suggested he deserved? Well, Jasper thought, setting his jaw, Edward would quickly learn that if he wanted to take him, he'd have to try harder.

Jasper spread his arms wide with an ironic smirk. "Welcome to Chepstow, Roger. I would apologise for the reception you've received, but you understand why." The old man nodded warily. "Yes, well, I'm sorry to disappoint you and that York bastard, but I will not be returning to London and nor, it would seem, will you." He paused just long enough for realisation to register on Vaughan's face before he continued. "First though, I wish to discuss your actions at Mortimer's Cross. You were responsible for those rounded up after the battle, correct?"

Vaughan shifted from one foot to the other, unnerved by the sudden change in subject. "Yes, I was."

"And you took them where?" Jasper asked, feigning confusion. "Remind me."

"To Hereford."

"To Hereford. Yes, I remember now. And what did you do with the prisoners once you were in Hereford?

Vaughan shrugged. "Some were ransomed, others were imprisoned."

"And what about Owen Tudor? What did you do to him?" Jasper's voice was now dangerously quiet.

"He was executed. In the market square."

"And you gave the order?"

Vaughan swallowed uncomfortably before nodding.

"What would cause you to do such a thing? He was the king's stepfather. Surely you realised he would have raised a significant ransom?"

"I did. But my orders were clear. The Tudor name commanded too much loyalty. He couldn't be allowed to live. My Lord, you have to understand, I—"

Jasper raised a hand to silence him. He had heard enough. With a nod, the men restraining Vaughan pushed him to his knees. Jasper drew his sword. He weighed the weapon in his hand, feeling its familiar weight. His late half-brother had spared no expense on his gift. Crafted from the finest steel, Jasper had taken the opportunity while in London to have the blade sharpened. At least Vaughan would have that small generosity.

Jasper took a deep breath, his heart surprisingly steady, despite what he was about to do. This was no rage or passion. This was a deliberate, calculated act. Though it went against his notions of gallantry to kill an unarmed man, it was what equity demanded.

Vaughan watched, his eyes wide with fear. "Mercy, my Lord," he pleaded.

"Mercy?" Jasper repeated, harsh anger finally breaking through the controlled exterior. "You wish for me to show you mercy?" He shook his head. "No, Roger. I will show you the same consideration you showed my father."

Vaughan opened his mouth to respond, to beg again for his life, but the words never came. Jasper took a quick step forward and, swinging his sword around in an arc, brought the blade down hard and unwaveringly on Vaughan's neck.

Justice. At last.

32

June 1471

"You can't stay in there forever, Tudor!" the man shouted, the veins on his neck bulging from the effort, spit flying from his mouth.

Crouched behind Pembroke's crenellated battlements with his back against the wet stone, the subject of the man's goading banged his head in frustration, his eyes turned heavenward in a futile prayer for divine intervention.

Eight days he had endured Morgan's shouted threats. Eight days he had remained hidden behind Pembroke's thick walls. Jasper cursed. Once again he hadn't been quick enough. He'd covered the more than a hundred miles from Chepstow as fast as he could, switching horses continuously as they tired, yet even then he'd only just arrived in time. The cold dread he'd felt when he'd seen the torches snaking down the track towards the castle still chilled his bones, intermingling, as the days passed by, with a fathomless sense of despair.

Morgan ap Thomas had been a friend once, but those days were long gone, and Jasper only had himself to blame. If he'd wanted to keep Morgan on his side, decapitating his father-in-law was not the way to do it. Even the strongest of friendships could not survive such violence, and theirs had never been particularly close. Now Morgan was hungry for revenge.

As if he could sense he was being thought about, Morgan shouted up again. "Come out and face me. You'll have to sooner or later, so why delay the inevitable? I might even let your nephew live. Not you though, Tudor. No, I'll have your head, just as you took my father-in-law's."

Threats to his life were one thing, but Henry? That was another thing entirely. Growling, Jasper propelled himself to his feet. "Fuck you, Morgan," he bellowed, too tired to search for more eloquent words. "Lay a hand on my nephew and I swear it will be the last thing you do. Your father-in-law was a murderous bastard who got what he deserved. As for my head, if you want it, come and get it. Or are you too much of a coward?"

Morgan's face turned an alarming shade of red, and even from such a distance, Jasper could feel the hatred radiating off him. Morgan screamed for an archer and Jasper watched defiantly as a wiry man ran over. Pride alone stopped him from ducking for safety as the archer took up position and drew back his bow, aiming directly for him.

The world seemed to slow as the arrow flew through the air but the angle was awkward and rather than hitting home, it clattered harmlessly to Jasper's left. With a triumphant smirk, he turned his back on Morgan, ignoring the renewed barrage of insults, and headed off the battlements. He'd won this round, but Morgan's threats still echoed in his head. They couldn't hide in Pembroke forever.

At the bottom of the stairs, he bumped into Joan, whose arms were full of firewood. He'd tried to send her away when he'd arrived back from Chepstow but she'd stubbornly refused, as had Beth and her son. Their loyalty had warmed Jasper's heart, though now the situation had deteriorated, the added weight of their lives weighed heavy in his hands.

Joan saw the expression on his face. "That bad?"

Jasper grimaced. "Only a miracle will save us now."

* * *

Under siege, the great hall had become the centre of life at Pembroke. The true strength of Morgan's force was unknown, and though tall, the castle's towers would be vulnerable to cannon fire should he have such weapons in his arsenal. Situated in the north-east corner of the inner ward, the great hall offered greater protection if Morgan grew restless of waiting. Straw beds had been set up on the upper level, not that Jasper had slept much since the siege began.

He was constantly on edge and whenever he attempted to sleep, he was plagued with nightmares of Bamburgh and an unshakeable sense of déjà vu – not that he confided in anyone. All those within the castle were looking to him for leadership; he couldn't show any weakness, not even for a moment. Despite the dire situation, life inside the castle continued to run smoothly. Joan had taken command of the hall, her strength and level-headedness reminding Jasper of Queen Marguerite, before grief had left her a hollow shell. Under Joan's watchful eye, chores were shared out and rations were equally divided, though Jasper knew full well that she was slipping her own portion to Henry when she thought no one was looking. Despite their best efforts, there was a limit to how long they could draw out the supplies, and after more than a week, the shortages were becoming increasingly obvious. Jasper estimated they had another week, ten days at most, before they ran out completely. He needed to think of something, and fast.

It was while he was sitting by the fire thrashing out possible ideas in his mind that one of Pembroke's few remaining guards came hurrying over to him. "My Lord, this was shot over the wall," he explained breathlessly, handing over an arrow to which a piece of paper had been crudely attached. A seal was visible, but it was not one Jasper recognised.

Henry, who had been sitting nearby, wandered over. "What is it, Uncle?"

"I'm not sure," Jasper replied. "It would seem someone wants our attention." Carefully, he removed the letter from the arrow and unfolded it. The note itself was hastily scrawled, though still legible, and Jasper read it aloud:

"My right worthy Lord, I have heard of the siege that has been laid upon your castle at Pembroke. I write to offer my assistance. If you can make it to the north bank, I will be waiting with horses to convey you to Tenby. I have spoken with our mutual friend Thomas White. He will have a boat ready. By the grace of God, your friend, David ap Thomas."

"Ap Thomas. Is that not the name of the man attacking us?" Henry asked, his brow furrowed in confusion.

"Yes, it would seem our miracle is to be in the form of the brother of the man who has put us in this situation," Jasper replied, smiling wearily at the irony.

"But how do we know we can trust him?"

"We don't."

Silence fell. Jasper looked at Henry, unsure of how he might react. He need not have worried. Henry scanned the letter once more. "How do we get out without Morgan seeing?" he asked.

"Meet me in the kitchens. I have a plan."

***

For the second time, he was being made to flee his home in fear for his life. But at least this time there was one important difference: this time Henry would be coming too.

When he had first left Pembroke a decade before, the idea of exile, of being isolated from all those he held dear, filled him with an almost inconsolable level of despair. In the years since, he had become immune to its sting. He had come to accept his life would always be that of a fugitive, constantly yearning for yet never reaching home. The previous months had been a wonderful reprieve but Jasper had always known it would not, could not, last. Edward was too strong, his late half-brother too weak. It was always going to end up this way – Margaret had been right about that. There was no point dwelling on it now, no point raking through his memories wondering what might have been if he'd done things differently. What was done, was done.

Jasper pulled the strings of his bag tightly shut. With a sigh, he took in the familiar surroundings of Pembroke's solar. It had never felt quite the same without Ianto and his father sitting by the fire, or Margaret playing chess. Yet it was the place where he had felt the happiest. Who knew if he would ever experience such a feeling again. Certainly he doubted he would ever see Pembroke again.

The Beaufort blood running in Henry's veins might give him a claim to the throne, but it also put him, and by extension Jasper, in danger. Edward had returned from exile with a vengeance. Incensed by his brief fall from power, it was clear he would not show the same leniency as before. No longer a York pup, Edward had grown into a formidable ruler, one whose position was stronger than ever. As if crushing the Lancastrians hadn't been enough, the birth of a son had quelled any remaining doubts. The news of the new prince's arrival was met with widespread rejoicing, the people grateful for the stability little Edward's birth promised. Though he did not share in their enthusiasm, Jasper could not blame them for such a reaction.

After so many years, even he had grown weary of conflict, and he understood their desire for peace.

The same, however, could not be said of Margaret. Rather than being resigned to the new order, King Henry's demise had given her a greater sense of purpose. Whereas before she had only wished to be reunited with her son, now she harboured hopes of seeing him upon the throne. In Jasper's mind, such an idea was nigh on impossible, and too far ahead of them to give it any attention. His immediate priority was keeping Henry alive to see another sunrise. Anything beyond that was at the mercy of fate.

Jasper took one final look at the solar, then shut the door firmly behind him and headed for the kitchens, where the others were waiting for him. Beth was putting the last of Henry's belongings in a pack while David looked on with obvious envy.

Joan meanwhile was busy wrapping crusts of bread in a cloth. "For your journey," she explained when Jasper entered.

"There's no need. Keep it for yourselves."

Joan shook her head and continued to wrap the little parcel.

"I said keep it," Jasper repeated, but she continued to ignore him. Coming closer, he noticed the tears rolling down her cheeks. "Joan," he said gently, reaching out a hand.

The touch on her arm broke the last of Joan's defences, and she began to weep. "I already mourned you once, I cannot do it again."

Jasper pulled her into a tight embrace. "Who said anything about mourning? What do you think I've been doing for the last ten years, sitting in a library?" he teased her gently. "There's no need to be scared, I've escaped tighter situations than this."

Joan wiped her tears with the corner of her apron. "You must think me a silly old maid," she said, attempting a smile.

"Never."

He looked at Beth. "Take care of her, won't you? Even the strongest

222

people need friends to lean on."

Beth walked over to Joan and put her arm around the older woman. "Of course, the three of us will be just fine."

David spun around. "Three of us?" he exclaimed. "I'm not staying here!" He looked pleadingly at Jasper. "Please, I want to come with you. I want to go to France."

"And someday you might, but not today. Today, I need you here." David opened his mouth to protest but Jasper raised a silencing hand. "I need you to keep the Tudor flame burning in Wales, so that we may one day return. Can you do that for me?"

David's eyes widened at the gravity of what he was being tasked with. "I swear I will," he replied earnestly. "I swear it on—" he scanned the room as if trying to find something suitably solemn. After a moment, he turned back to Jasper. His eyes which had been filled with surprise now shone with determination. "On our father's grave."

Jasper felt a sharp pang of grief. He looked down at his hand and began to work his father's ring from his finger. It had become a comforting talisman in the decade since he had received it, that devastating night at Hay. The skin underneath was paler than the rest of his hand, leaving a ghost of it imprinted on his skin. He turned it over in his hand, before offering it to David.

"Here. This was our father's. It has brought me comfort through many trials. I hope it does the same for you." The boy took the ring reverently. It was too big for his little finger so he slipped it onto his middle one instead. "Keep your head down. Do as your mother and Joan tell you," Jasper continued, motioning to Beth who had come to stand by her son. "We will return. Be ready when we do."

Glancing out of the window, he saw the last slivers of sunlight had drained from the sky. Walking over to the corner by the fire, he moved aside a sack to reveal a low, plain door. With a sharp tug, he yanked it open, letting a cold draught rush into the room. He turned to Henry.

"It's time."

33

June 1471

The steep stairs were treacherously slick, covered in a slimy substance that seemed to seep from the very stone into which the passageway had been carved. Down and down they went, descending deep below the earth's surface. The route was narrow, and as they went ever lower it seemed to constrict tighter and tighter until Jasper's shoulders rubbed painfully against the sides. Then suddenly, when it felt as though they could go no further, they emerged into a gigantic cavern. The Wogan. Long forgotten to history, it was the only flaw in Pembroke's impenetrable defences, though tonight it was escape, not attack that drew them into its darkness. Their lanterns illuminated the Wogan's moss-covered walls, casting eerie shadows and disturbing some bats who had made the ancient cavern their home.

"What is this place?" Henry whispered.

"Our way out of here," Jasper replied. Cautiously, he made his way over to the old water gate, where a small rowing boat was moored. Crossing the mill pond would be the most dangerous part. Once they pushed away from the cavern's walls they'd be completely exposed. The darkness would offer them some protection, but if Morgan had any sense he would have men watching the water. They'd need to be quick and silent, and pray that David could keep his brother suitably distracted. It made Jasper uneasy to place both his and Henry's lives in the hands of a relative stranger, but he had no choice. David had promised he would be waiting with horses on the other side. There was little point wondering whether he'd stay true to his word. Either he would, and they'd be able to slip away into the night, or he would not, and they would be dead before morning. The thought brought a wave of trepidation crashing over him and he pulled Henry close.

"Whatever happens do not look back. Do you understand me? Keep going. Ride hard to Tenby – my friend Thomas White has a boat waiting. From there, get yourself to France."

"But, Uncle, I—"

"No, you listen to me, Henry. I swore to your mother I'd keep you safe, and I will do so by whatever means necessary. Promise me you will not stop."

The fiery intensity in Jasper's eyes made any further protests fall silent on Henry's lips. "I promise," he whispered.

"Good. In you get then. Steadily now."

Once Henry was settled in the prow of the boat, Jasper climbed in after him. Moving slowly and with as much care as he could, he gently slipped the oars into the water, cringing at the splash that echoed in the still night. Taking a composing breath, he pulled on the oars and they began to move. Mercifully, the moon was obscured by thick clouds, and as they drifted out into the mill pond they were soon enveloped by darkness. Jasper tried to minimise the number of strokes he took, letting the current do the work instead. He strained his eyes and ears, keeping alert to any movement or sound. Through the gloom, he could make out a few shadowed figures milling around the base of Pembroke's walls. They were too far away to pose any threat, but nevertheless, Jasper whispered at Henry to keep his head down.

After what seemed like an age, the boat finally bumped into the north bank. Using the reeds as handholds, Henry began to climb up the bank. Suddenly, a man materialised from the darkness. Before Jasper could react, the stranger grabbed Henry, hauling him to his feet. Jasper fumbled with the dagger in his belt, fingers numbed by the water. A hand reached out for him. Instinctively, Jasper flinched away before realising there was no weapon held in its grip. Instead, it was offered palm up to steady him.

"Careful," the man cautioned in a low voice. "We don't want to lose you in the water now. Not when you've already done the hard part!"

Jasper felt relief wash over him. "David ap Thomas, I presume?" he asked, accepting the offered hand.

The man nodded. "I'm sorry about my brother, he can be a right bastard when he wants to be. I blame his wife. Never did warm to the woman, and now she's put Morgan on the warpath to avenge her father's death." He shook his head. "Love – don't ever fall for it, boy," he said with a wink at Henry. "Anyway, no time to hang about. Come on."

With a wave of his hand, David led them into the trees, where some horses had been tethered. They were fine animals, sure-footed and fast, and soon they were racing through the countryside, the distance to safety closing with every stride. They did not stop to rest, did not once look back, not even when horns sounded the alarm of their escape and the barks of hunting dogs echoed in the night. As the first hues of light bled into the horizon, Tenby's walls, still strong and thick from Jasper's improvements, appeared before them. At this hour the small town was still asleep, the only signs of life a few smoke columns drifting lazily upward. Above the uneven roofs rose the spire of St Mary's Church, calling the small group towards it like a beacon. Jasper swallowed down the hope that bubbled in his throat. They weren't safe yet. The riders slowed as they neared Tenby's south-west gate, one of four controlling access into the town. There were no men standing guard, and the gate itself was slightly ajar – the advantage of having the mayor onside already paying dividends.

"This is as far as I go with you," David explained, as Jasper and Henry jumped down from their horses. "Thomas is expecting you. I'll do my best to keep my brother occupied, but I will not be able to hold him off forever."

"You have already done more than enough," Jasper replied, grasping the other man's arm in thanks. "We owe you our lives."

"And don't you forget it." David winked before wheeling his horse around and heading back towards Pembroke, leaving uncle and nephew alone.

Jasper looked at Henry. "Ready?"

Henry nodded. "Ready."

"Stay close."

With a final glance at David's retreating figure, Jasper slipped through the gate, navigating the sharp right-angle turn designed to negate the threat of battering rams. Once through the inner-gate, he set off at a run along the cobbled streets, his feet remembering the way even as his mind scrambled to find its bearings in the early morning haze.

The town had changed little in the years since he had last visited, and as he swung left past St Mary's Church, the familiar frontage of Thomas White's home came into view. It was a handsome town house with large mullion windows that looked out onto the churchyard opposite. Its central location on Tenby's main street reflected not only Thomas' success as a merchant but also the high regard in which he was held by the townspeople. Even at this hour, it was too risky to use the main entrance, so they continued along the street before diving down a side alley. A low unassuming doorway opened in front of them, candlelight slipping through the crack.

"Quickly, in here," a silhouetted figure whispered, ushering the pair inside and shutting the door firmly behind them.

Once the bolts had been firmly drawn, the figure spun round to face them, a wide smile plastered across his face. "Praise God, you made it!"

"Thomas! It is good to see you, my friend." Jasper turned to his nephew. "Henry, may I introduce Thomas White, the mayor of Tenby and an old friend. Thomas, this is my nephew, Henry."

Thomas reached out a hand. "A pleasure to meet you, Henry. The last time I saw you, you were just a babe in arms."

"Thank you, sir, for opening your home to us," Henry replied, shaking the offered hand.

"It is my pleasure, and the least I can do given the circumstances."

Jasper stepped closer to his friend. "You'll forgive us, Thomas, if we do not linger too long. David mentioned a boat?"

"Yes, yes, absolutely," Thomas nodded "One of my ships is waiting for you just off St Catherine's Island. The captain is a trusted friend. You must wait for the tide to turn though. It won't be more than an hour or so from now, and you'll still be away before it is fully light. I would offer you my rooms to rest in, but it is too dangerous. As mayor, I may be afforded some leeway, but our friendship is well known; it will not be long before Morgan's men are knocking at my door. I'm afraid I must ask you to hide in the cellar. Once night has fallen, you can take the old tunnels down to the beach. There will be men waiting there to ferry you to the ship."

"I always thought those tunnels might come in useful one day," Jasper replied. "I just didn't imagine this would be the reason. Do not worry about us, my friend. I'll send word once we land in France." He reached out and grasped Thomas' arm. "Thank you."

"Godspeed."

* * *

The cellar beneath Thomas' house was primarily used to store wine, with barrels piled up against the walls. Jasper found a space between two particularly large containers which would hide them if anyone was to make a cursory search. Settling on the cold floor, he leant his head against the wood, exhausted by their escape. His body was crying out for sleep but he couldn't give in to it. Thomas had given them a large candle, marked at inch intervals so they could monitor the passing of time. If he fell asleep they might miss their opportunity. It was a thought not worth contemplating. Next to him, he felt Henry shiver. There had not been time to worry whether Henry would be able to keep up, and as it transpired, there was no need for him to do so. Jasper was proud of how his nephew had handled himself. In the frantic hours since they'd left the warmth of Pembroke's kitchen, he had not once complained nor hesitated to follow an instruction. But now, as they sat in the dark, eerie quiet, Jasper imagined it was more than just cold making him shake.

Henry shivered again. "Oh, come here boy," Jasper sighed, pulling his nephew close so that they were huddled together. He unbuckled his cloak and wrapped it tightly around Henry's thin shoulders. He held him close, for comfort as much as warmth, and after a while Henry's shivers subsided. "Is that better?" he asked.

From within the folds of Jasper's cloak, Henry nodded. "It won't be long now. We just need to wait for the tide to turn in our favour. Once that happens, we'll be away."

"Who built these tunnels?" Henry asked, poking his head out of the cloak, his usual curiosity returning now that he was warm.

"Merchants, smugglers, maybe even pirates. Nobody knows. They've been here for as long as anyone can remember. They run all the way down to the beach, which is how we will get to the boat undetected."

"If the tunnels are really that long, how will we find our way out?"

"Ah," Jasper said with a smile. "That's the clever part." He pointed to a rope that was affixed to the wall and ran off into the darkness. "Have you ever heard of Theseus and the Minotaur?"

Henry shook his head.

"Well, long ago on the island of Crete, there lived a terrible monster. Half-man, half-bull, the Minotaur struck terror into the hearts of men all across Greece. Unable to control it, King Minos, the ruler of Crete, ordered the construction of a vast underground labyrinth, and within it he imprisoned the beast. But even trapped beneath the earth, the Minotaur still posed a threat. And so, every few years, seven young men and women were sent from Athens as sacrifices."

"But why would Athens send its people to their deaths?"

"That is a good question. A few years before, Athens had gone to war against Crete. They were defeated, and as punishment they were forced to send their sons and daughters into the Labyrinth. Now, Theseus was a Prince of Athens, and he grew tired and angry with watching his countrymen sent to slaughter. So when the time came, he volunteered to go to Crete, promising to slay the Minotaur and end his people's suffering. Theseus was a great warrior, capable of bringing down even the most ferocious of monsters. But the prison in which the Minotaur roamed was a complex maze of passages. Even if he managed to kill the beast, he would still most likely die before he managed to escape the Labyrinth."

"What did he do?" Henry asked in wide-eyed fascination.

"I'm getting to that. King Minos had a beautiful daughter called Ariadne, and luckily for Theseus, she took pity on him. She gave him a ball of string, tied at one end to the exit, so that he might find his way out of the suffocating darkness."

"And did he?"

"Yes. Theseus killed the Minotaur, escaped the Labyrinth, and went on to have many more adventures."

"Just as we will."

Jasper smiled in the darkness. "Exactly, Henry. Just like we will."

* * *

Jasper woke with a start, panic coursing through his veins. Despite his best efforts, he'd been unable to resist the seductive lure of sleep. He looked around frantically for the candle, releasing a long breath when he saw it had not quite burnt to a stub. He'd been lucky. Reaching out a hand, he gently shook Henry awake. The boy's eyes fluttered open, his brow furrowed in confusion as his brain worked to remember where he was.

"It's time to go," Jasper said softly. "And remember what I said – whatever happens, don't stop."

Slowly they picked their way along the tunnels, following the rope that ran along the wall beside them. Thankfully the prolonged dry weather over the preceding weeks had dried out the often-flooded tunnels, and they were able to make their way through them faster than Jasper had anticipated. As they neared the jagged entrance where the tunnel met the beach, Jasper heard muffled voices through the darkness. He put a finger to his lips, motioning for Henry to stay quiet, and then continued to edge his way forward. As he got closer, the sounds became more distinct and he was able to distinguish individual words. He felt a wave of relief at the realisation that the men were speaking French. They'd found their contacts. He gave a low whistle and the talking broke off.

"*Seigneur?*" a voice called out.

"*Oui,*" Jasper replied, emerging from the tunnel, keeping Henry behind him just in case. There were four men in total waiting for them. The one that had called out to them was clearly the leader and he stepped forward.

"*Il faut y aller maintenant*," he said, glancing at the sky, which was growing lighter with every passing moment.

"*D'accord*," Jasper nodded.

Taking their packs from them, the sailors lead the way across the beach to a boat that was being held steady by two burly men. Beyond it, ship lanterns blinked in the waning darkness off the shadowed outline of St Catherine's island. They splashed through the surf, the icy sea water soaking their clothes. One of the sailors lifted Henry up into the boat as if he was as light as a feather. Jasper, meanwhile, helped to push the boat further out to sea, only hauling himself in once the freezing water reached above his knees. The exertion left him more exhausted than he'd care to admit, but there was still more to do. He took up his place in the middle of the boat, next to one of the sailors. Once the other men were aboard, he placed both hands on the oar in front of him, and with a groan, hauled on it with all his might. He kept pulling, over and over again, until his shoulders screamed in protest.

Minute by excruciating minute, they edged towards the glowing orbs of the ship's lanterns, the waves prolonging their agony. But the tide was in their favour, and eventually they drew level with the ship. Heads appeared over the side and a rickety ladder was thrown down to them. The other sailors held the boat steady as Henry stepped up to begin his climb. Jasper was right behind him, ready to catch him should he slip. He need not have worried. Henry climbed nimbly up the ladder like a monkey. Jasper's own ascent was decidedly less effortless, but soon he too was standing on the ship's deck. He looked back at Tenby. In the lightening gloom, he could see torches and the smudged silhouettes of dozens of men winding their way through the streets. Jasper gave a sigh of relief. At last, fate had turned in their favour.

Behind him, someone cleared their throat. He turned to face the captain, a surprisingly youthful man with thick, golden curls. "The heading, my Lord?"

"Southwest. Once we've cleared Lands End, we make for France. It seems I must call on my cousin's generosity one more time."

With a nod the captain hurried away, shouting orders that had men scurrying up the rigging and pulling hard on ropes. The wind quickly filled the sails, and with a lurch they were away. Jasper found Henry clinging to the ship's rail. His long hair was being whipped by the wind and it was clear from his expression that he had yet to find his sea legs.

"You'll get used to it soon enough," Jasper chuckled, slapping a hand on Henry's back. "I remember the first time I went to sea, I spent the whole voyage with my head over the side."

Henry managed a weak smile before leaning out over the edge once again. Jasper remained by his side, watching the retreating outline of Tenby. The beach was now teeming with figures, the scale of the force sent to hunt them and how close they had come to capture suddenly apparent. In his head, Jasper said a prayer of thanks for their safe delivery.

"When do you think we'll be back?" Henry asked.

It was an innocent question, one that should have had a simple answer. Part of Jasper wanted to reassure Henry, to give him a response that would soothe his anxiety. But sheltering his nephew from the stark reality facing them would do him no favours. The truth, however brutal, was what was needed. "I don't know. I wish I did, but I don't," he sighed. "I won't lie to you, it is likely to be a long time."

Jasper watched Henry carefully as he digested the news, worried that this might be the blow that finally broke his nephew's remarkably mature composure.

Henry was silent for a moment before he turned to his uncle. "If that is the case, then I am pleased I have you with me."

Jasper felt tears sting his eyes. Reaching out, he pulled his nephew towards him. "So am I, Henry. So am I."

III

Part Three

1476–1485

"The only impe now left of King Henry the Sixth's blood..."

— *Edward IV*

34

November 1476

Through a small window, Jasper watched the clouds' slow march across a dreary autumn sky. All seemed peaceful enough, yet in the distance, a bank of darkness was rolling in. A storm was coming. He glanced down at the market square below, where, sure enough, the sellers were hurrying around dismantling their stalls, constantly keeping one eye on the horizon.

Sheltered within Château Josselin's thick walls, the impending storm did not concern Jasper, though it did remind him of the fateful journey from Tenby. Just as the sails had been filled with wind, so he had been filled with confidence, his mind already planning for their arrival in France, and what life might look like in his cousin's court with Henry at his side. But fate, as always, had other ideas. As they had rounded Land's End, the wind had whipped up a mighty tempest, churning the sea and tossing their little boat as if it were a toy. The skill of their golden-haired captain had seen them safely through, but bruised and battered, they were forced to take shelter in the first port they found. Which was how they ended up in Brittany.

Duke Francis had welcomed the unexpected arrivals with open arms and his usual generous hospitality. Château Suscino's towers had become home once more, and Jasper had enjoyed taking Henry for rides along the beach, though at a steadier pace than the races he and Francis had shared. But despite the warm welcome, it quickly became clear that the situation was very different from when Jasper had last been a guest. Whereas before he had had independence and autonomy, now he and Henry were valuable pawns in a game of diplomatic chess. Having come tantalisingly close to obliterating the entire Lancastrian line, Edward was not content to let Henry VI's last remaining relatives enjoy a peaceful exile. Henry's claim to the throne needed to be extinguished, and as for Jasper, Edward had regretted not having him killed at Bamburgh ever since he'd been released from that castle's dank cell. And the Pretender was not the only monarch who wanted them under his control. King Louis had also been petitioning Francis, arguing that, given their kinship, Jasper and Henry should be under his care. There were many words Jasper could use to describe the French king, but sentimental was not one of them; no doubt the Universal Spider had ulterior reasons for wanting them at his court. And so, the long rides along the beach became short trips around the curtilage of the Château, which in turn became walks through the gardens – their world gradually shrinking as the pressure on Francis built. Whilst the duke had been explicit in his reassurances that he harboured no intention of handing them over, the constant pestering from England and France wore on him. The longer he refused to cooperate, the greater the risk of an attack to re-capture them increased. Meanwhile, whispers from those in his own court grew bolder.

In the end, Francis had been forced to compromise – nephew and uncle would be moved inland and separated. Ostensibly intended to make it harder for agents to seize both of them, Jasper knew it was also designed to weaken his influence over Henry. He had begged Francis not to go through with the decision. It would be painfully cruel, he had pleaded, to be torn apart after so little time reunited. But Francis would not be swayed, and so Jasper had watched helplessly as Henry was taken away to Tours d'Elven and its colossal octagonal tower, while he was sent to Josselin, thirty miles further north.

Two years had passed since then. Two years of monotonous solitude. Of having nothing to fill his time save reading and thinking. The town below his window offered a tantalising glimpse of freedom, a constant reminder of a world with which he was not permitted to engage. Still, there were many things to be thankful for. Chief amongst them was the fact he was alive, which was more than could be said for many of his contemporaries. Each morning, he ran through the names of those who had paid the ultimate price. It had become a ritual, like saying the Hail Mary, a reminder of the odds he had survived. Three Dukes of Somerset, two Northumberlands, Buckingham, Wiltshire, Exeter. Even the kind and ever-dutiful Henry Stafford had not avoided Death's purge, finally succumbing to the wounds he had received at Barnet, leaving Margaret alone once more. And so the list went on. Jasper could count eighteen with ease. Some he'd considered friends, others mentors, and some he'd only known as faces around council tables, thrown together by a common goal. There were enemies too, like York, Herbert, Montagu and the indomitable Warwick – men who he'd trusted once, before the world was turned upside down. And then of course there were those with whom he had been closest of all; his brother, his father and his king. He would not let his nephew join that list. Though cathartic, running through the names also served as a painful and stark reminder that he was one of only a handful of Lancastrian nobles remaining after decades of conflict, and the only one to have witnessed the first unravelling of the fragile threads binding the country together at the battle at St Albans.

Jasper shook his head, banishing the faces of men long since departed. It did him no good to dwell on the past. If he allowed himself, he could spend hours lost in his thoughts and memories, content to drift away from reality and the oppressiveness of captivity. Instead, he pushed himself out of his chair and, after removing his shirt, set to with his daily exercises, punching the air in quick succession before dropping to the floor and propelling his body up and down, over and over again until his upper arms burned from the exertion. After so many years in exile, it would have been easy to give in to hopelessness and the aches and pains of an ageing body. But something had always burned inside him, deep in his very soul, driving him forward even when all seemed turned against him. A desire to keep striving, not for himself but for his family. His father had always said loyalty was his greatest virtue, and all these decades later he still believed it to be true. There had been times when he'd questioned the course they had taken, but never had his commitment to his house wavered, and now the hopes of Lancaster rested on his nephew's shoulders, his resolve had never been stronger.

With a final grunt, he pushed himself off the floor. Straightening, he regarded himself in the window. With no need to maintain appearances he had let his hair and beard grow long, a few grey hairs intermingling with the brown. Casting his eyes downwards, he continued his assessment. His shoulders and arms were still strong and muscular, testament to the hour he set aside each day for sword training. On his bicep, a long silver line was all that was left of the wound he'd sustained at St Albans, a mark mirrored by the one snaking around the curve of his calf, from that opportunistic dagger thrust at Mortimer's Cross. His stomach which had once been hard and rippled like a washboard had grown softer with the passing years, but he was still trim, and a far cry from the pot bellies of many men his age. It was a thought which pleased his small kernel of vanity, especially when he considered the recent reports from England. Apparently, in the absence of war and violence, the Pretender had turned to drink, food, and whores to sate his insatiable appetites, and was now paying the price. The fact did not surprise Jasper, and though he would not consider himself prone to maliciousness, it nonetheless pleased him to know the man who forced him into exile was suffering in some small way.

Splashing his face with water, he retrieved his shirt and headed through a low arched door frame into the adjoining room. Large enough for a desk, a small dining table and a selection of mismatched chairs, this miniature solar, as he'd come to think of it, was where he spent most of his time. Despite the fire crackling gently in the hearth, there was still a chill to the air, a feeling exacerbated by the rain now pelting the window. He'd left his thickly padded doublet slung over the back of one of the chairs and he pulled it on before settling in front of the desk. Its surface was covered with an assortment of papers and letters, typical of every desk he had ever used, and he rummaged through them till he found what he was searching for.

Despite their enforced separation, he and Henry kept in constant contact, letters flying back and forth, keeping each other up to date with their daily lives and hopes for the future. Henry's guardian was a man named Jean de Rieux, the marshal of Brittany. He had a son, Francoise, who was a few years younger than Henry, and he had included his unexpected guest in his son's lessons from the moment he had arrived at Tour d'Elven. As such, while Jasper endured a mostly solitary existence, his nephew had much to divert his attention. His mornings were devoted to study while his afternoons were given over to training, his letters excitedly relaying his practice fights with Francoise. But beneath the youthful exuberance, there was a more solemn tone, a despondency that spoke to a youth spent in exile. Jasper scanned Henry's most recent letter and sighed; he needed to address his nephew's pessimism before it became all-encompassing. Selecting a new piece of parchment, he took up his quill. Dipping the nib into the ink pot, he paused a moment to collect his thoughts before setting pen to paper:

Well-beloved nephew, I greet you well, he began, dipping his quill once more into the ink. *I received your last letter and wish to counsel you on matters mentioned within. It—* A knock at the door made him start, causing ink to smudge across the paper. He growled in annoyance. The knock came again.

"Coming," he called irritably, putting down his quill. He stalked across the room and yanked the door open, ready to berate the person who had interrupted his thoughts. But his retort died on his lips as he saw who was standing on his threshold.

"Your Grace," Jasper exclaimed in surprise. "I was not informed you would be visiting."

Duke Francis smiled, lines appearing at the corners of his eyes. "It was a last-minute decision. I'm not interrupting am I?"

"No, not at all. Please, come in," Jasper replied, moving aside to allow the duke to enter. As Francis stepped into the room, his eyes took in the scene before him. For a fleeting moment, Jasper was conscious of the modesty of his rooms, but he pushed it aside. Was it not the duke himself who had placed him here? If anyone was to be embarrassed about the state of his accommodation, it should be Francis. "To what do I owe this honour?" Jasper asked, shutting the door.

Francis turned to him. "I bring news of your nephew."

"Of Henry? I was just writing to him." Jasper's brow furrowed in concern. "Has something happened? Is he hurt?"

"No, no. Henry is quite well. No. I have come to tell you that he is returning to England."

Though he said the words lightly, they hit like punches – swift and painful – and Jasper could only stare open-mouthed at Francis as his mind emptied of all logical thought.

"I can see you are shocked, but you need not be concerned. King

Edward has personally assured me of Henry's safety. In fact, he intends to restore him to his rightful title of Richmond."

"How can you be so naive?" Jasper burst out, his anger outweighing any sense of propriety. "Edward intends nothing of the sort. It is merely a ploy to get his hands on him."

Francis bristled at Jasper's rudeness. "You forget yourself, Sir Jasper. Have I not protected you these past years, even when it would have been easier for me to concede to those who clamoured for you? After all this time, do you think I would cede control on a whim? No, Edward has changed, he is keen to put the violence of the past behind him. With two sons of his own, he is more secure than he has ever been. What possible reason would he have to harm Henry?"

"Because he is a threat! Twenty years of conflict cannot be forgotten just like that."

"Well, his mother would seemingly disagree," Francis countered.

"What?" Jasper asked incredulously, the sudden mention of Margaret knocking him off balance.

"Edward has informed me that Lady Margaret has been petitioning for her son's safety." Jasper made to interject but Francis held up a hand. "You may shake your head, but by all accounts, she is keen to have him home."

"She would never," Jasper replied forcefully. "I don't know what lies Edward has spun for you. I promised Margaret that I would protect Henry. If this was truly what she wanted, she would have found a way to tell me herself. You cannot let them take him."

Francis shook his head. "I'm sorry, Sir Jasper, but he has already been taken from Tour d'Elven by Edward's ambassadors. They are on the road to Saint-Malo as we speak. From there, they will embark for England."

Jasper bunched his fists in frustration. He had offended Francis with his impertinence, and anger was getting him nowhere; he needed to change tack.

"Then send someone after them," Jasper implored. "If Henry steps aboard that ship, he is as good as dead. Trust me on that. Please, your Grace," he continued, appealing to Francis' emotions. "I'm begging you. You know how much this conflict has taken from me. If our years of friendship mean anything to you, do not let them take my nephew from me too."

Francis hesitated and Jasper felt a flicker of hope. Grasping the opportunity, he ploughed on.

"What harm is there in delaying? Send someone to negotiate, say there's been some mistake. See how Edward responds. From his reaction, you will know if his assurances were genuine. If he truly has no ulterior motive for wanting my nephew then he will understand your reluctance to give him up. If he responds with threats and anger, then you will know he has tried to play you."

"There is merit to what you say," Francis replied slowly, weighing up the options in his mind. Jasper held his breath, not even daring to move. "Fine, Sir Jasper, you have persuaded me. I will send my treasurer to Saint-Malo to discuss matters, but I cannot promise anything."

"Thank you, thank you, your Grace," Jasper cried, taking Francis' hand and kissing his ring. "God will reward your kindness."

35

December 1476

The wait had been unbearable. With nothing else to distract him, Jasper had spent every moment worrying. Even sleep, when it finally came, had offered no reprieve, his dreams cruelly taunting him. He'd considered writing to Margaret, but in the end thought better of it. She would know the outcome long before he did. Had Francis not said that she supported Henry's return to England? The idea of his former sister-in-law in league with the Pretender troubled him. It seemed uncharacteristically rash and he remained adamant she would not take such a risk. But then again, much had changed in the five years since they had last seen each other. She was Lady Margaret Stanley now, married to one of Edward's closest advisors. Maybe her position at the very heart of the Yorkist court had given her a perspective that he, confined to his glorified prison cell in the heart of Brittany, could only guess at. And so, he had tried to turn his thoughts to something else, to anything that would distract him from reality – but to no avail. Henry was all his mind could focus on.

The days dragged past, Christmas creeping ever closer, and still he heard nothing. Despite himself, he could feel the small kernel of hope he held in his heart shrinking. Then finally, just when he thought he might wear through the soles of his boots from pacing, the news arrived. Henry was safe. He could have practically kissed the messenger who delivered Francis' letter, so strong was his feeling of elation. Henry was now heading south towards Vannes, where they would be reunited. The duke, no doubt trying to atone for breaking his vow, had decided uncle and nephew had been separated for long enough.

* * *

Built by Francis' grandfather, Château de l'Hermine was amongst the most beautiful of the duke's residences, with immaculate gardens that backed onto the city's wall, not that Jasper paid them much attention when he arrived. His only thought was finding Henry. The walk to the main hall seemed to take an age, but finally he found himself outside its thick doors. A courtier tried to delay his entrance so that he could be properly introduced, but Jasper barged past him; protocol be damned, he would not be kept from his nephew a moment longer.

If he'd hoped for a private reunion, he was to be disappointed; the hall was filled with people. But despite the crowd, Jasper spotted Henry immediately, standing in the middle of the room, surrounded by eager members of the Breton court. Taller than many of those around him, the ungainly lankiness that had characterised his adolescence had given way to a lean and muscular physique, one that epitomised the youthful vigour of a man on the cusp of twenty. Like Jasper, Henry had let his hair grow long, and from behind it struck him just how like Edmund his nephew had become. Yet, when he turned to see who the new arrival was, it was Margaret who Jasper saw reflected in his blue eyes.

A wide grin broke across Henry's face. "Uncle!" he called, pushing through the throng. He strode across the room, and when he reached Jasper, the pair threw themselves into a strong embrace.

"I thought I'd lost you," Jasper said, gripping his nephew tightly.

"For a moment, Uncle, so did I," Henry confided.

* * *

Sitting in a well-worn chair, Henry watched, mesmerised, as flames danced in the fireplace. It filled the room with comforting warmth, and stretching out his arms, he gave a contented sigh, finally letting himself relax after weeks of tense uncertainty. Down below in the hall, the banquet Francis had thrown to celebrate his return was still in full swing, though thankfully he had managed to sneak away to snatch a moment of quiet. He glanced up as his uncle walked into the chamber, holding a glass filled with amber liquid in each hand. Taking one of them, Henry waited as Jasper settled himself in front of the fire.

"I hope I have not pulled you away from the revelry too early?"

Jasper smiled. "Not at all. I'm not as young as I once was, and in any case, there is no one I would rather spend time with than you."

Henry looked across at his uncle. He opened his mouth to speak but stopped, taking a sip of his drink instead, feeling its warmth spread through his body. There was so much he wanted to say, yet he was struggling to find the words.

In the end, it was Jasper who broke the silence. "Forgive me," he said quietly.

Henry frowned, shaking his head. "No, you don't—"

Jasper cut across him. "Yes, I do. I should never have let them separate us. I should have fought harder. I promised your mother. And to think I almost lost you." Jasper shook his head, words failing him. He'd always loved Henry, ever since he was a newborn mewling in his arms, but it was only now that he realised the strength of his feelings.

Henry reached out a hand and gripped his uncle's shoulder. "There was nothing you could have done. We are pawns in a game played by men far above our sphere of influence. You have already done and sacrificed so much for me. I need to start taking responsibility for my own life, I'm a child no longer."

Jasper gave a small smile. "No, you are not. You look more and more like your father with every passing day."

"I often wonder what he would have made of me."

"He would have been prouder than you could have possibly known," Jasper replied, tears springing to his eyes. But he did not want to dwell on sadness, especially not tonight. "Anyway," he continued more brightly, "tell me about it. How did you escape Edward's clutches?"

Henry leant back in his chair and swirled the liquid in his glass. "I'm still not entirely sure how I managed it. God must have been on my side, that's for sure. Even before I knew where I was being taken, I felt something was wrong. Maybe it was the speed with which we left; there was no chance to say goodbye to Francoise and his father, let alone you. Or maybe it was the men themselves." Henry shrugged. "Regardless, something in my gut told me not to trust the situation. But I felt so helpless, and as we got closer to the coast I could feel the noose tightening around my neck."

He was relaxing into his story, the alcohol that warmed his veins helping him find the words that had been eluding him. "I knew I somehow needed to delay them – feigning illness seemed like the only viable option. But there's only so long one can pretend, and as the days wore on, I could tell they were getting suspicious. Who knows what I would have done if Landais had not arrived? You know, Francis' treasurer? It was as though he was heaven-sent. Naively, I thought his arrival signalled the end of my ordeal. Instead, it marked the start of the negotiations. They went on and on, long into the night, and in the morning they started up once more. The Englishmen were stubborn, but Landais was relentless. Yet still there seemed to be no end in sight, and so I decided to take matters into my own hands and channel some of your daring."

Jasper raised an eyebrow. "Some of my daring?"

"Oh yes," Henry chuckled. "You must have realised your stories would rub off on me somehow? It was deep into the third day when I saw my opportunity. I persuaded one of the servants to lend me their clothes, and then, when everyone was distracted by the negotiations, I slipped out of the door and into the street. Dressed as I was, no one gave me a second glance. I'd noticed the cathedral when we'd arrived and I made straight for it. I ran the whole way – I must have looked like a dishevelled mess when I arrived at the doors. But when I explained the situation, the monks ushered me in without a moment's hesitation. Thank goodness they did, because the English agents were right on my tail. They tried their best to lure me out, but with no luck. There may be little regard for the principle of sanctuary in England, but not so in Brittany. It is still a sacred right, and one that the people of Saint-Malo were determined to defend. In the face of their anger, the Englishmen gave up and slunk back to their boats."

Jasper slapped a hand on Henry's leg. "Well, I'd say that far outdoes any of my so-called feats of daring! It is an impressive tale, and one that is considerably more enjoyable to hear when its subject is the one telling it. The determination you showed also has cause to give me heart. I admit, when I was first informed of your being taken, I was concerned you might have gone with them willingly."

"Why would you think such a thing?" Henry asked incredulously.

"Your recent letters made me think that you might have lost faith in our cause," Jasper began to explain.

"Never," Henry interjected vehemently. "I know my destiny. Yet I also knew my letters were most likely being read. Jean de Rieux is an honourable man and a kind guardian, but he is loyal to his country and his duke above all else. Better for them to think me a depressed adolescent than to know the truth."

Jasper nodded, struck by his nephew's instinct. "I should have trusted you more. I'm sorry."

Henry waved a hand dismissively. "It is in the past now."

"Speaking of the past," Jasper said more brightly, "I think that is where Francis intends to leave this whole episode. He went against his word of honour, it will take time for that harm to be repaired, but your safe return will certainly have helped."

Henry frowned. "Is it wrong that I feel sorry for him? He apologised profusely when I arrived in the city. I do not believe he made the decision with any malice. He told me the Pretender had been very convincing, and that my mother had been one of those wishing for my return."

"It is never wrong to try and see the good in people. In any case, I believe you are right, he told me much the same."

"Could it be true?" Henry asked, leaning forward. "About my mother, I mean. Would she really believe Edward to such an extent?"

Jasper considered the question for a moment. "Truthfully, I do not know. I thought I knew your mother's character, but really I only know her as a frightened teenager, not the formidable woman she has become. It may be that she does desire your return. She is one of the cleverest people I know; she would not lend her support to anything if she believed you were at risk. But even so, I cannot shake the thought she has placed too much trust in the Pretender."

"Maybe it was my new stepfather who convinced her," Henry commented with an uncharacteristic hint of bitterness.

"Maybe," Jasper shrugged. "Whatever the truth, I will write to her. No doubt she has already been informed of your escape. But there needs to be more communication between us, we have been isolated from events at home for far too long."

"How do you know they won't be intercepted?"

Jasper smiled. "Oh your mother will find a way – of that, I am certain."

36

April 1483

T he sound of swords clashing rang out in the calm spring
morning, causing some birds who had been resting nearby
to rise up in alarm. In a roughly outlined ring, Henry was
sparring with a member of Francis' bodyguard. Though the man had
skill, it was clear Henry was dominating the fight. His strikes were
unrelenting, the strength of them sending his opponent stumbling
backwards. From a distance, Jasper regarded Henry's fluid movements
with a pride that was tempered by envy. He could remember a time
when he had spent whole days sparring, never feeling fatigued, and
then waking up in the morning ready to do it all again without a
second thought. Those days were long gone now, but the prospect of
a duel still excited him. In the ring, Henry's opponent was tiring, his
movements becoming slow and heavy, and after a few more minutes
he held up his hand in defeat. Henry stepped back breathing heavily,
a wide grin spread across his face. Looking up, he noticed Jasper
watching and raised a hand in welcome. "What did you think of that,
Uncle?" he called.

"You have some skill, but now let me show you how it's really done,"
Jasper replied, walking over to the ring.

"Be my guest," Henry smiled with a mock bow.

Jasper pulled his sword from its scabbard, surveying it for a moment as it glinted in the sunlight. The only item of value he possessed from his old life, it felt like an extension of his body, so familiar was its weight. Almost unconsciously, he spun it lazily around in his hand as he'd done a million times before.

"Don't go hurting yourself now, Uncle," Henry commented.

Jasper raised an eyebrow. "Careful boy, I've been fighting with this very sword since before you were born."

Taking up position opposite Henry, he extended his sword in front of him with both hands gripping the hilt. Slowly, Henry began to stalk towards him, the gap between them shrinking with every step. But Jasper did not move. He stood as still as a statue, his grey eyes trained on his nephew. When there were only a few yards between them, Henry lunged. Jasper parried the blow easily, immediately moving to the left to re-establish the distance between them. The sequence repeated itself again and again. Every time Henry attacked, Jasper reacted defensively and then moved away, biding his time while he got the measure of his nephew.

Even after a whole morning spent practising, there was no hint of tiredness in Henry's sharp, precise movements. His technique was good, though he had a tendency to plant his back foot. For the most part, his height and reach compensated for it, but it was a flaw that an enemy could easily exploit – as Jasper intended to do now.

Parrying another blow, he darted quickly forward. Henry, who had been expecting him to move sideways like before, was taken by surprise. It forced him awkwardly back onto his planted foot and, caught off-balance, he only just managed to get his sword up to deflect the strike. It left his side unprotected, a fact that did not go unnoticed by Jasper, who delivered a swift punch that made Henry gasp as he staggered back.

"Never let your guard down, not even for a moment," Jasper schooled. "If that had been a dagger, you'd be dead. Keep moving. Any brute can swing hard, it takes skill to stay balanced."

Henry nodded, his teeth gritted in concentration. Beads of sweat coated his brow, but otherwise he still looked as fresh as when they had started. Jasper meanwhile could feel exhaustion setting in, his breath coming out in short, painful gasps. There was no doubt that Henry would soon be easily beating him, but for now, that was in the future. Today, Jasper's pride was on the line, and he would be damned if he was going to concede. But Henry's blows continued to come thick and fast, and Jasper grunted against the force of them. His whole body felt like it was on fire – if he didn't stop soon, he thought he might collapse. Grimacing against the pain, he readied himself to finish the fight. Deftly deflecting another of Henry's lunges, he forced his nephew back a few steps with a swift combination of thrusts. Frustrated, Henry swung his sword wildly. Jasper watched as the blade arced through the air. Then, at the last moment, he feinted to the side. Unable to slow his momentum, Henry stumbled and Jasper saw his opportunity. He swung his own sword around, finishing with the blade inches from his nephew's neck.

Henry froze, his eyes wide in surprise at the speed with which the fight had turned against him. For a moment, Jasper thought he might be angry, but instead a wide grin spread across his face.

Jasper lowered his weapon. "Better luck next time, Henry," he chuckled, slapping a hand on his shoulder.

* * *

By the time they arrived in Château de l'Hermine's great hall for supper, news of Henry's defeat at the hands of a man twice his age had spread. There were a few jokes made at his expense as they wove their way to their places, but for his part Henry endured them all with good humour. As usual, the hall was filled with the hum of dozens of conversations. It might make it difficult to hear one's neighbour, but Jasper relished the frenetic energy after so long in his own company. In the years since the Saint-Malo incident, Francis had gradually relaxed the conditions of their imprisonment. Though they were still not allowed beyond the Château grounds, they had been permitted to dine with the rest of the household. By anyone's standard, five years was a long time to eat in the solitude of one's room, and this small but significant change had transformed their daily lives, providing an opportunity to socialise and hear about events beyond the city walls.

Settling into his seat, Jasper poured himself a flagon of small ale. Taking a sip, he scanned the room and frowned.

"Is it my imagination or are people watching us?" he asked Henry, who was already hungrily helping himself to a portion of spiced stew from the communal platter in front of him.

"Maybe they've heard of your triumph in the ring!" Henry chuckled.

"No, it's something else." Jasper leant over to the man across from him. "Has something happened?"

"You haven't heard?"

"No..." Jasper replied warily.

The man paused dramatically. "King Edward of England is dead," he announced.

Jasper felt his mouth fall open in surprise. Glancing at Henry, he saw the same look of shock mirrored on his face.

"That's got you, hasn't it!" the man cried, clearly delighted at their reactions. "Apparently, the fat bastard just keeled over. Might be an opportunity for you, hey Tudor," he continued, nudging Henry with an elbow.

From across the table, Jasper gave his nephew a sharp look, with an almost imperceptible shake of his head. Here, amongst loose tongues and flagons of ale, was not the place to discuss such matters. Who knew who could be listening?

Henry gave a non-committal shrug. The man opened his mouth to probe further but was distracted by the arrival of fresh jugs of ale.

As the men around them greedily refilled their cups, Jasper quietly stood up from the table and signalled Henry to follow him. He walked purposefully out of the hall and down the corridor without a backward glance. Light from the full moon filtered through the windows, fracturing the passageway into pools of shadow and light.

"Where are you going?" Henry asked with a hint of exasperation, quickening his stride to keep up with his uncle.

Jasper looked furtively over his shoulder to check no one had followed them before pulling Henry further into the shadows.

"This changes everything," he said, his voice barely above a whisper.

"But he has a son and a spare," Henry countered.

"Children," Jasper replied dismissively. "That is all they are. And Woodville children at that!"

"What does that matter?"

"Edward may have been besotted with his golden-haired wife and her extended family, but the other nobles are not. They endured the humiliation of mismatched marriages and lost positions of influence only because of their respect for Edward. Now he's gone, they will show no such deference to his widow. I wouldn't be surprised if they haven't already started spreading rumours that their marriage was never legally binding."

"So what do we do?"

"For now, nothing. We need to wait for the dust to settle. But fate has started to spin her wheel once more, let us hope she moves it in our favour."

37

June 1483

Intricately designed, the glow of the summer sun only served to heighten the beauty of Château de l'Hermine's gardens. Walking amongst the flowers and plants was one of Jasper's small daily pleasures, a time to reflect in undisturbed peace. Henry often joined him, as he had today, the two of them walking side by side, occasionally talking, but for the most part enjoying a comfortable silence. As they turned to make their way back to the château, Henry stopped.

"Someone's coming."

Lifting a hand to shield the sun's glare, Jasper watched as a messenger hurried along the paths towards them. He bobbed into a quick bow as he reached them.

"A letter for you my Lord, from England," he puffed, thrusting it towards Jasper. With a nod of thanks, Jasper took it from his outstretched hand and watched as the messenger scurried away again.

"Who is it from?" Henry asked, peering over his uncle's shoulder.

"Your mother," Jasper replied quietly, running his fingers over Margaret's portcullis seal. "This might be the news we've been waiting for."

"Well open it then!" Henry exclaimed impatiently.

Jasper gave him a look and Henry fell silent. Taking his knife, he sliced through the seal and slowly unfolded the paper. Letters from Margaret were more common now than they had been in the first years of exile, but sending them was risky, and even with a trusted network of messengers, they were still only sent when absolutely necessary. From the number of pages across which Margaret's elegant hand flowed, it was clear something significant had happened. Clearing his throat he began to read:

"To my well-beloved brother, Jasper Tudor, rightful Earl of Pembroke, and my cherished son, Henry, Earl of Richmond. I greet you well, though with urgent news. All is in disarray and England is in the grip of a dangerous coup. On the Pretender's death, the kingdom demised to his son, Edward. Yet, he is just a boy, still many years shy of his majority. And so, Richard of Gloucester was named Protector. The youngest of the old Duke of York's sons, he had been unquestioning in his devotion to his eldest brother. Even when Edward ordered Clarence's execution, Richard's fidelity to his king did not waver, remaining silent while his brother was drowned. Yet, no sooner had Edward taken his last breath, did the schemes start. Under the guise of Protector, Richard began to steadily and systematically isolate his nephew from his Woodville relatives. His uncle, Earl Rivers, who had been the boy's guardian at Ludlow, was captured and executed, and his mother fled into sanctuary at Westminster Abbey in fear for her life.

When Richard entered London in early May, with his nephew, it was to the sounds of jubilation and excitement. That the original coronation date had been postponed did not seem suspicious, given the turmoil of the previous month. In any case, a new date for the boy's coronation was immediately set for the middle of June and the Royal council granted Richard Protectorship for the period until this time. Shortly afterwards, Edward was placed in the Tower, ostensibly to prepare for his coronation, as every monarch before him has done. He was soon joined by his brother and Gloucester's namesake, Prince Richard. Unsurprisingly, it took much effort and eventually the gentle coaxing of Archbishop Bourchier, who is now in his ninth decade, to convince Elizabeth to give up her son.

Planning for the coronation continued, but as the day itself grew closer a sense of unease set in. At council meetings, the atmosphere was often tense, especially between Hastings and Gloucester. Then one evening, my husband dreamt he was attacked and killed by a boar. It left him badly shaken. He told Hastings of his fears but the duke would not listen. He was so focused on settling his own personal score against the Woodvilles that he failed to recognise Richard's true intentions until it was too late. Still, he did not deserve his fate. He devoted his life to the Yorkist cause and for what? To be dragged from the council meeting as a traitor and immediately executed without trial or process. His death was the final confirmation of fears that before had only been whispered. When the day of Edward's coronation arrived it was not bells that rang out but declarations of his illegitimacy. With that mark against them, there was no need for Richard to pretend any longer, and a date for his own coronation has now been announced. As for the Princes, they remain in the Tower, from where I fear they may never emerge."

"Only a monster would order the death of his nephews," Henry, who until this point had been listening in silence, exclaimed.

Jasper gave a small smile. "While I appreciate the esteem with which you hold the position of uncle, he wouldn't be the first man to commit nepoticide. Even if he doesn't order it himself, court is full of sycophants willing to do anything to get ahead. One might easily take the situation into their own hands, if they felt it might please their new king."

"But what of the other nobles? Surely they will not just sit by and let this happen?"

"You underestimate the hatred they harboured for the Woodville family, and the power Richard wields. You just heard what happened to Hastings. Why would the other nobles risk their neck for a child that has just been declared a bastard?" Jasper challenged. "Now, where was I?" he asked, turning his attention back to Margaret's letter:

"Given the paranoia at court, it is hard to know anyone's true feelings, and thus one must tread carefully. Despite his wariness towards Richard, my husband remains committed to his cause, but not everyone feels the same. So far, Buckingham has publicly supported Richard's quest for the throne. He even lent his voice to the declaration of the Princes' illegitimacy, but in private, it is a different story. Though it is early days yet, I believe he intends to move against him —"

"See!" Henry exclaimed.

"Christ's bones, you're as bad as your grandfather," Jasper sighed in exasperation.

"Sorry," Henry mumbled.

Jasper shook his head as he scanned the page, picking up from where he had been interrupted:

"I have known him since he was a child. Like Henry, royal blood runs through his veins. Given the people's current confusion and anger, it may just be enough to convince them to follow him. This could be the chance we've been waiting for – a way to finally bring you home. I will send more information when I have it. For now, look to the water. Edward Woodville escaped to the Channel when he heard of his brother's capture and is headed for Brittany – I would not be surprised if others follow him in the coming weeks. May God guide and protect you both. Your loving sister and mother, Margaret."

They stood in silence for a moment digesting the magnitude of what they had just learnt. Then Henry lifted a hand and gripped Jasper's shoulder. His blue eyes shone with determination. "This is it, Uncle."

38

October 1483

The feeling of the wind in his hair and the tang of salt on his tongue made Jasper shout in exhilaration. For the first time in twelve years, he felt truly alive. Looking out to his right, the other ships of their little flotilla stretched into the distance. There were seven of them in total, each carrying sixty-odd men. It was not a large number, but the chest of gold crowns in the hold would go a long way to make up for any shortcomings. As always, Jasper had been struck by Francis' generosity. Yet he had seen the flicker of hesitation when the duke had agreed to their latest request, and could not help feeling that after so many years his saint-like patience might finally be wearing thin. But, Jasper thought more brightly, such a thing did not matter any more. If everything went to plan, there would be no need to call on Francis' hospitality any longer – though if he was honest with himself, he was still unclear as to the aim of their campaign. Margaret had tried to make it as clear as possible in her letters, and the sentiment had been echoed by Buckingham himself when he'd written at the end of September. Yet it was difficult to see how their interests aligned, beyond the immediate goal of defeating Richard, and there seemed to be little reason why the young duke would choose to turn on the very people who had raised him and the man he had helped to steal the crown. Ambition is a powerful motivator, but when it came down to it, Jasper doubted Buckingham would have the resolve to see it through. But that was a problem for the future. All that mattered now was that the duke had given them a lifeline, and Jasper intended to make the most of it.

Scanning the deck, he spied Henry standing at the helm beside the captain, a weather-beaten man named Jean Dufour. Though they had been granted the ships and men by Francis, overall command of the flotilla was in Dufour's capable hands, and his experience and calm demeanour gave Jasper considerably more confidence than some of the other captains he had sailed with. Next to him, Henry looked self-assured and relaxed. There was no hint of the seasickness he had suffered on their crossing from Tenby, and not for the first time Jasper was struck by a simultaneous sadness for the lost boy, and pride in the man who now stood in his place.

"How does it feel knowing that we will soon be home?" Jasper asked, coming to stand beside his nephew.

"We've been in exile for half my life; I'm not sure I know what home is any longer, beyond being with you," Henry replied, surveying the expanse of sea before them. "But standing here, I feel a sense of freedom I have not felt in a long time."

Jasper smiled. "I admit it does feel good to be on the open water once more. And what say you, Captain? How is our progress?"

Dufour considered his question. "For now, good. However, the sea is an unpredictable beast, and never more so than in the Channel. Many an unwary sailor has been lulled into a false sense of security by the tantalising proximity of land. Conditions can change in an instant, as I'm sure you are aware, my Lord."

Jasper gave a wry smile. "Indeed I am."

Next to him, Henry regarded Jasper with his piercing blue eyes.

"You look tired, Uncle. Maybe you should get some rest while you can? There will be little time for it once we arrive."

Jasper raised an eyebrow. "I do not know whether to be offended by the implication about my appearance or grateful for the suggestion."

"I only—" Henry began.

Jasper shook his head. "I am teasing you. Let me know when we sight land."

Leaving the two of them at the helm, he made his way steadily down into the belly of the ship, doing his best to avoid the various obstacles in his way. Most of the available space had been given over to horses and supplies, leaving just one cramped, dark cabin right at the stern. Despite its size, the bunk within it was comfortable enough, and after a few moments, Jasper felt his eyes grow heavy as the gentle movement of the ship eased him into sleep.

* * *

An indeterminable time later, panicked shouts pulled him from his slumber. Stumbling bleary-eyed, Jasper emerged onto the deck, where he was shocked to find the bright October sky had grown dark and oppressive. Above his head, the sails, which had been filled with a soft autumn breeze, now flapped wildly. The violent gusts whipped up the sea, crashing waves against the ship, causing it to pitch alarmingly. Down below the deck, the horses stamped and snorted in protest.

Squinting against the sea spray that stung his eyes, Jasper looked across towards the other ships. They had spread out in an attempt to reduce the risk of a collision, and from such a distance the sailors frantically rushing around the decks were little more than shadows. Suddenly, one of them was flung overboard by the force of the waves. If the sailor had managed to cry for help then his screams were lost on the wind, his body instantly swallowed by the raging sea. The other shadows seemed to barely register their shipmate's fate, so preoccupied were they with trying to secure their ship. But it was all to be for nothing. With a mighty crack, the mast of their vessel was finally overwhelmed by the violence of the wind. It broke clean in half, one end plunging into the sea in a tangle of rigging while the sails covered the deck, and the souls aboard, like a shroud. The weight of the broken mast unbalanced the ship, and it began to list. In calmer conditions, they might have been able to help, but as it was, Jasper could only watch on in detached horror as men began to desperately launch themselves into the sea in a vain attempt to escape their fate. Even those few that could actually swim did not make it far, the waves were too strong, and eventually, they too were dragged down into the depths to join their shipmates in a watery grave. The sight was all the motivation the sailors aboard Jasper's own ship needed. With grunts of effort, they heaved on their ropes, ignoring how the coarse fibres cut into their hands. Inch by agonising inch, the sails were hauled away. The storm continued to rage around them, tossing them one way then the other, but with the sails safely stowed it lost some of its ferocity. When at last the outline of the Dorset coast appeared through the clouds, Jasper did not know whether to trust his exhausted eyes. It was only when Henry came over and quietly murmured, "God has seen us through" that fear released its icy grip on his heart.

* * *

With the conditions still ominous, and with no sign of the rest of the flotilla, Dufour made for Poole Harbour. A natural refuge from the unpredictability of the Channel, it had a narrow mouth that opened up into a wide bay. Henry Beaufort had owned land in these parts at one time, and Jasper could remember being told about the harbour's deceptive shallowness, and how it had been the downfall of many an unsuspecting captain. As such, they did not venture too far in, choosing instead to drop anchor near a small island on which a monastery was perched. It was the perfect spot, one that shielded them from the storm but still enabled them to see out into the Channel should any of the other ships make an appearance. And so they waited. And waited. Above their heads, the storm clouds dispersed, the night sky filled with stars, and when the sun rose once more, they found their situation unchanged. With hope fading, Henry gave the order to make for Plymouth, further down the coast, from where they could better attempt to make contact with Buckingham. It seemed to prove the right decision as, although there was still no sign of the other ships when the town came into view, figures were visible on the headland.

"Look!" Henry exclaimed, "those must be Buckingham's men sent to greet us. Make ready a boat."

Jasper caught Henry's arm. "I don't like this. How do we know they're Buckingham's men?" he whispered urgently.

Henry shrugged his arm free. "You're too cautious, Uncle," he replied dismissively.

"Caution is the reason I'm alive when the men that started this whole mess are dead. Watching and waiting, that is how to survive. You need to learn when to listen to that whisper of doubt in your mind, just like you did in Saint-Malo. This is another such time. By all means send a forward party ashore, but not you, you're too valuable. Wait to see what they say first and then we'll take it from there."

Henry hesitated. After so long in exile, Jasper could understand his nephew's eagerness, but reason had always been Henry's greatest strength, and it was this that won out. "It will be as you say, Uncle."

And so the two of them remained together on the ship as a small rowing boat manned by a handful of Breton sailors set out to make contact with the men, whoever they might prove to be. As the little boat drew up to the harbour wall, its occupants were waved enthusiastically ashore. It was hard to see the details of the exchange from such a distance, but it seemed amicable enough. Yet when the boat pushed away from the wall once more, it only had half the number of occupants as on its outbound trip.

Henry looked at Jasper in concern. "Something isn't right."

After what felt like an age, the boat arrived back and the remaining sailors clambered back onto the ship. No sooner had they made it over the guardrail than Henry began interrogating them. "What happened? Who are they?"

The man who had been first over the rail straightened up. "Nothing happened," he replied with a shrug. "They just welcomed us ashore. They said Buckingham had sent them to bring you to him. They were disappointed you weren't with us, but cheered up when I said you'd be coming in the next boat."

"And what of the other sailors?"

"Buckingham's men made them stay behind. Said it would make the process of getting everyone off the ship too long if we all went back."

"Did they say anything else?"

"No, just what I've told you – it wasn't a long conversation, though one of them did slip this to me when the others weren't looking," the man added, handing over a tightly folded note. Henry scanned it before passing it to Jasper, his face set. The message was short but damning:

It is a trap. Buckingham is dead. Richard is coming. Leave while you can.

"Jesu," Jasper breathed, his mind whirring at the magnitude of the news.

Henry remained silent, though, from the muscle jumping in his jaw, Jasper could guess the anger and disappointment he was grappling with. Then with a resigned expression, he turned to Dufour. "Give the order to weigh anchor – there's nothing for us here."

The man who had delivered the note looked aghast as realisation dawned. "What about the others?" he demanded.

Caught off-guard Henry struggled to find the words to respond with. At the sight of his uncertainty, a spiteful sneer began to spread across the man's face. Noting the change, Jasper stepped forward and assessed the man with his grey, impassive eyes. "Leave them," he said coldly.

"What?" the man burst out incredulously, sizing Jasper up.

Instinctively, Jasper's hand went for his dagger but Dufour placed a restraining hand on the man's chest.

"They'll be fine. Now, you heard what he said. Return to your station and be ready to weigh anchor," the captain ordered.

Jasper watched as the man slunk away to the other end of the ship, his hand still on the dagger at his side. When he was certain the man no longer posed a threat, Jasper relaxed his grip and turned back to his nephew. "You know what this means?" he asked.

"That we've failed," Henry replied despondently.

Jasper shook his head. "No, you're not seeing the larger picture. With Buckingham dead, you are the only man left with a claim that can challenge Richard."

"You mean—?" Henry stuttered, his eyes widening in comprehension.

"It is time for you to claim your birthright, Henry. We've waited long enough – it's time to claim your throne."

"But how?" Henry spread his arms. "Look around us, we have nothing."

Jasper shrugged. "For now, maybe, but trust me, that will all change. If we play our cards right, you can be the one to unite the factions that have divided this country for the last three decades." Henry gave his uncle a quizzical look. With a small chuckle, Jasper threw an arm around Henry's shoulders. "Tell me, nephew, have you given any thought to marriage?"

39

December 1483

Vannes Cathedral was a vast, magnificent building, and, just as he had been at St Paul's, Jasper was mesmerised by its architecture. He stood gazing at the broad columns that rose up towards the heavens before splaying out like fingers to support the vaulted ceiling, marvelling at how such beauty could belie such strength. Following the line of one of the columns down to its base, Jasper refocused his attention on those that had gathered within this holy place, on this the anniversary of Christ's birth. Hundreds of people were packed into the nave. Margaret had intimated in her letters how deeply the dissatisfaction with Richard ran, yet even with that knowledge Jasper had still been shocked by the sheer number of those who had joined them in Brittany. There were almost five hundred of them now; a small enclave of exiles forced to find a home in a foreign land. Many were a similar age to Henry, their youth and vigour making Jasper run a hand through his greying hair self-consciously. The majority had arrived penniless and the city was struggling to support them all. Jasper was not blind to the strain the new arrivals were placing on Duke Francis, but even if he wanted to, there was little he could do to stem the tide. With every day that passed, more exiles arrived, each drawn to Brittany by the hope that in Henry, there was a challenger who could topple Richard.

Chief amongst the arrivals was Edward Woodville, the recently created Lord Scales and former Admiral of the Fleet. He had been waiting in the city for them when they finally returned, by way of France, from their ordeal in Plymouth. Far from the arrogant, self-entitled man Jasper might have expected, Queen Elizabeth's youngest brother was surprisingly modest and utterly devoted to the ideals of chivalry. He was never far from the other members of his family and indeed, as Jasper cast his eyes over the congregation, there he was, standing between his two elder brothers with his nephew, the Marquess of Dorset just behind (though it would be easy to mistake the pair for twins, given their shared age). The presence of this Woodville quartet epitomised just how far the Wheel of Fortune had turned and provided proof, to whoever might require it, that the plan to unite York and Lancaster had both houses' full support.

It was not only the exiles that had gathered within the cathedral. Off to one side was the Duchess of Brittany, seated on a delicate chair that had been brought along especially for her. At her shoulder stood Pierre Landais, her husband's treasurer and the reason Henry had been able to escape Edward's clutches at Saint-Malo. The duke himself was notably absent; his declining health keeping him away. Jasper could only hope he would hold on long enough to see their cause triumph. France had already been plunged into uncertainty with the recent death of Louis XI, and their position in Brittany was precarious enough without the added disruption of a succession crisis. Jasper's response to his cousin's passing had been mixed. He'd come to respect the French king, but his constant schemes to keep his country ahead had prevented a true friendship from blossoming between them. Still, it was a shame to see the webs Louis had so carefully laid begin to unravel. He may have been adept at controlling everything around him in life, but even the Universal Spider could not defeat death.

Turning his attention back to the event at hand, Jasper looked over to the reason for the assembly, who was raised above the rest of the congregation on a dais. Though the chair on which Henry sat was not a throne, its commanding position left no doubt as to the message being conveyed. With his long arms resting on the sides of the chair, he cut a casual yet confident figure. He was wearing a simple, unadorned doublet in his preferred colour of black, the dark cloth emphasising the brightness of his eyes. There was no hint of nervousness in the way he held himself, though he had confided in Jasper just that morning of his lingering apprehension.

"What if they see me as an imposter?" he'd whispered, as if speaking the question aloud would cause his fears to come to fruition.

Jasper had pulled him close and placed a hand on his shoulder, just as his father had done when seeking to reassure him. "Your blood gives you the right to stand above them, but it is your actions that will distinguish you. Respect is not automatic, it is earned. As it stands, these men are far from home and lack purpose – give them something to believe in and they will willingly follow you."

"But how do I do that?"

"By believing in yourself first."

Henry had been visibly reassured by his words, squaring his shoulders and drawing himself up to his full height. It was that poised version of himself who now acknowledged the bishop stepping up towards him.

"Do you swear to unite the noble houses of Lancaster and York by marriage to Princess Elizabeth, eldest daughter of the late King, Edward IV?" the bishop asked.

"I swear," Henry promised, his voice ringing out clear and true. With a nod, the bishop retreated from the dais as Henry stood to address the exiles.

"Sirs, for too long our great houses have been bitterly divided. But looking out across this congregation on this holy day, I believe that those dark days will soon be behind us. It is time for us to look forward to a future free from conflict and grief. I swear to you now, in this sacred house of God, that we will drive the tyrant Gloucester back into the hole from which he has crawled and reclaim what has been stolen from us. And so, I humbly stand before you and ask for your loyalty." Henry raised his chin and his voice. "United we will conquer, and before the Boar has soured our homeland, we will cross the water and restore our country's honour!"

His final words were nearly drowned out by the thunderous roars of approval that filled the cathedral. The crowd swelled forward, and one by one the exiles made their way up to the dais. Dropping to their knees at Henry's feet, they each paid homage to him as if he were already king. Scales, Dorset, Rivers – all bowed their heads to him and swore their loyalty. From where he stood, Jasper silently watched the procession.

The image of so many men submitting to Henry was a powerful one. And with that image came the sudden realisation that the bards had got it all wrong. It was not he who would be the saviour of Wales, but Henry. His nephew was the true *Y Mab Darogan*, the Son of Prophecy who would restore their homeland's glory. It was a realisation that made his heart swell with pride, and solidified his resolve. His destiny was not to be the dragon that conquered the English lion, but to raise the one who would, and he would not rest until that day was upon them.

Whatever the oaths made by the men before him, Jasper knew that they would only hold while Henry offered something in return. He had seen, far too frequently, the fickleness of men once danger was upon them. Self-preservation was a fact of life and Jasper did not judge them for it, but he was different. He loved Henry with a ferocity he had never thought possible. As such, he was not giving his oath to the figure of Henry as king, but rather to the babe he had cradled, the child he had played with, and the boy he had guided. When things turned bad and all others had abandoned him, Jasper would remain. He would stand by his nephew and fight Death himself if necessary, to ensure Henry survived. And so, when it was finally his turn to step up to the dais and the bishop opened his mouth to recite the same words the scores of men before him had sworn, Jasper waved a hand dismissively. This was a turning point in his and Henry's relationship – he would not let it be marked by generic, meaningless words.

Nodding at Henry, he dropped to his knees with his head bowed. His voice, when he spoke, was strong and unwavering.

"I, Jasper Tudor, Earl of Pembroke, pledge, in the sight of almighty God, my life and my sword to your service. Kneeling before you here, I commit to continue the promise I made to your mother." Lifting his head, Jasper's eyes met Henry's. "I will protect you and serve you in whatever way I am able, till Death comes to claim me."

40

September 1484

S ummer was waning, and the colours of the trees were beginning to change. The evenings were closing in and there was a chill to the morning air that had been absent for many months. Yet there were still days when the sun beat down from a spotless blue sky, fooling those beneath into believing autumn would never come. Today was one such day. The doors to the solar had been flung open and Jasper was thankful for the cool breeze flowing through the room. He was seated at an ornately carved table alongside his nephew. Across from them sat Edward Woodville and John Cheyne, a giant of a man who had arrived with the first wave of exiles and had immediately become one of Henry's closest friends. Strewn across the table between them were coins, counters and cards, evidence of the rounds of *Brelan* they had been playing for much of the afternoon. Even after so many years, it was still a favourite of Jasper's, and he'd enjoyed introducing the others to its addictive twists and turns, though some had taken to it better than others. Henry's considered approach reminded him of Sir John Fortescue, and his nephew was certainly as formidable an opponent as the old judge had been. Cheyne meanwhile was more blasé, throwing his coins down with seeming reckless abandon. As for Woodville, it appeared his chivalric character did not lend itself to such a game. He was too easy to read, his face too open. Needless to say, there were only a few coins left in front of him.

"I don't think this game suits me," he said with an exasperated sigh, leaning back in his chair.

"You can't be good at everything, Woodville," Cheyne chuckled, clearly pleased to have beaten the golden-haired knight at something.

Henry shook his head at the pair, a smile playing on his lips. It made Jasper happy to see his nephew so relaxed in the company of the other men. He'd become more self-assured over the past months, growing increasingly comfortable with the expectation that weighed on his shoulders.

Woodville and Cheyne continued their gentle ribbing of each other as a servant hurried into the room and bent low to Henry's ear. He listened intently, and then with a nod dismissed the servant. "I'm afraid, my friends, we will have to adjourn our fun for the time being. There is business I must attend to."

"Say no more," Woodville replied as he stood. "Cheyne, shall we?"

"I'd had enough of sitting around anyway," Cheyne said, stretching out his long legs which had been awkwardly bent underneath the table. "But I'll see you in the morning for training?" he asked Henry pointedly.

Henry groaned. "And there I was hoping I might be allowed to rest."

"Don't pretend – you secretly love the torture I put you through!" Cheyne called over his shoulder as he left.

"Who—?" Jasper began as a short, dour-looking man, who was certainly younger than he seemed, shuffled into the room.

"Thank you for seeing me, my Lord," the man said softly. "My name is Christopher Urswick, I am a chaplain in your mother's service."

Henry, charming as ever, greeted the man warmly. "You are a long way from home. I hope my mother is not the reason for your visit?" he asked, his expression turning serious.

"No, my Lord. She is well and sends her fondest wishes. She—" Urswick hesitated and glanced at Jasper who had remained in his seat at the table. "Forgive me, I cannot continue until we are alone."

Jasper glowered at the chaplain, offended by the implication of his untrustworthiness. Henry caught the change in his uncle's demeanour and spoke quickly to calm the situation. "Anything you have to say, you can say in front of my uncle – I trust him implicitly," he explained.

Urswick nodded but did not apologise to Jasper, addressing only Henry when he spoke. "You are aware of Duke Francis' illness?"

"Yes, we pray for him daily," Henry replied with genuine concern.

"Yes, and while he is incapacitated his treasurer Pierre Landais rules in his stead—"

Jasper stood up abruptly, interrupting the chaplain's speech. "If you've come all this way to inform us of this country's current ruling arrangements then you have had a wasted journey," he said tersely. Urswick's earlier rudeness had irked him and he would not be lectured about Brittany by someone who had only just arrived. "We are well aware that Landais is acting on Francis' behalf, as is every other person in this country." Jasper turned to his nephew. "Come, Henry, we have better things to be doing than listening to things we already know."

Henry held up a calming hand and Jasper fell silent. "Patience, Uncle. My mother trusts this man, and for that reason we shall hear him out. But Urswick," Henry added, "my uncle is right: I am a busy man. You had better make your case, and quickly."

"Thank you, my Lord," the chaplain replied, glancing warily at Jasper, who had settled back into his chair. "I agree it is common knowledge that Landais currently wields power, but what is much less known is what he is doing with that power."

Henry frowned. "I know Landais. He saved me at Saint-Malo; he is not a man obsessed with power."

"No, my Lord, he is not. Yet while he may not crave power for himself, he does crave it for his country. He may have saved you once, but that was eight years ago. He is frustrated by the position his country finds itself in. He believes your continued presence here threatens Brittany's future, and thinks the money Francis has lavished on you could have been better used to build defences against France."

"I would not say 'lavished' is the right word, though I agree that over the years the duke has been generous," Henry conceded.

"Precisely. Brittany is isolated on the diplomatic stage and Landais has had enough. He approached Richard." Urswick took a breath. "He has agreed to hand you over."

A shocked silence descended on the room. Jasper, who had been lounging in his chair was suddenly alert, his attention utterly focused. "What?" he asked sharply.

"Landais has made a deal with King Richard. He will hand both of you over in return for two thousand archers."

"When?"

Urswick shrugged his shoulders. "I cannot be certain. But soon. A couple of weeks, a month at the most."

Henry's eyes narrowed. "How do you know this?"

"Your mother," Urswick replied simply.

Jasper stood, shaking his head. "That's not possible. Margaret is under house arrest for her suspected involvement in Buckingham's rebellion. She is not permitted to leave her chambers. There is no way she could have found out about this."

"You forget who her husband is. Besides, Lady Margaret is not a woman who would let something as inconvenient as house arrest get in between her and her son—"

"I do not need someone like you telling me what type of woman my sister-in-law is," Jasper seethed.

Urswick blanched. "What I mean to say is, she has a network of agents working for her," he scrambled. "One of them, Bishop Morton, is in exile in Flanders, and it was he who received word of Richard's plans, I believe from Stanley himself. I had only recently arrived when Morton bade me make haste and inform you."

Henry turned to Jasper. "What do we do?"

"We will seek refuge in France."

"France? But how do we know they will accept us? What if they also decide to hand us over to Richard?"

"We don't know if they will accept us, though I cannot see why they would not. As for whether we can trust them, that is in fate's hands. My cousin was a shrewd ruler and would have seen it for the opportunity it is – we can only hope his son and daughter are the same."

Jasper turned to Urswick, who still looked uneasy at being directly addressed by him. "You will ride to the French court in Angers immediately. Inform them of our predicament and request permission for us to enter. Do not return until you have secured it. We will depart as soon as we receive word from you."

"How will you leave Vannes undetected?" Urswick asked.

"That is not for you to know," Jasper replied coolly.

For a moment, Urswick stood awkwardly, unsure of what to do next, before Henry rescued him from his indecision. "Thank you for bringing this news to us. My mother is lucky to have men such as you in her service. Godspeed."

With an inelegant bow, Urswick left the room. Henry looked over at Jasper. "Did you have to be so short with him? You're normally more considerate."

"I do not appreciate having my integrity called into question by a man I have never met. In any case, at this precise moment, my behaviour is not our biggest concern."

"No, our main concern is how in God's name we are going to make it to France without being detected!" Henry cried, throwing himself dejectedly into a chair.

Despite his nephew's despair, Jasper could not help the smile that spread across his face. "I might have a plan for that."

* * *

"No!" Henry exclaimed. "I will not leave the others. I will not dishonour the oath they made to me."

Jasper rubbed his face in his hands. Normally, he loved Henry's fierce loyalty to the exiles who had made Vannes their home, but right now it was causing no end of frustration. They did not have the time to argue and yet, here they were. Previously, he would have simply overruled his nephew, but after the oath he had sworn, he needed to take a less domineering approach.

"We must do everything we can to avoid suspicion," he explained placatingly. "Secrecy is key. If Landais has even an inkling something is afoot, he will act. As such, only you and I can leave. Why can't you accept that?"

"Because they've risked so much to be here," Henry replied, his voice losing some of its fiery passion. "I can't just abandon them. They'll think me a coward."

"At first they might," Jasper admitted. "But you are no use to them dead. If they are to have any hope of ever returning home then they need you alive. If that means leaving them in Vannes then they will understand."

Henry closed his eyes and took a deep breath. "So how do you propose we escape?"

Jasper sighed in relief. Finally, they were getting somewhere. "Leaving together would be too suspicious, and they will shut this city down the moment they realise you are gone," he began, speaking at a measured pace, the plan forming in his head as he spoke. "I will leave first. Francis is recuperating near Rieux, just a stone's throw from the border. I will say I am visiting him; our friendship is such that no one would question it. And then, just before I reach him, I will make a dive for France."

Henry considered Jasper's plan. "It could work. Certainly, I agree your visiting Francis would not raise any suspicion. But what about me? If you're expected at Rieux, there won't be too much time before your absence is noted, and if I'm not leaving with you then when am I?"

"It is a tight window, I grant you, but we must make do with the hand we've been dealt. Two days after me, you will leave Vannes, together with a small group of men – I'd say no more than five. Ostensibly, you are visiting a friend in the countryside—"

"Who?" Henry interjected.

"It doesn't matter," Jasper shrugged. "If anything, it is better you don't specify. The vaguer you are, the better. It will make it harder for them to track you down. Once you're a fair distance from the city, you will slip off the main road. Send most of the men on, but keep one with you. It will need to be someone you trust, a servant perhaps, and they must have good knowledge of the country and the safest routes to take to the border. You won't tell him any of this in advance, mind, only when the moment is upon you will you reveal the plan. Once the others have left, you will change your clothes. To a passer-by you will look like a servant, accompanying his master on a day's outing. After that, make for the border."

"Simple yet effective. It might just work. And when do you propose we leave?"

"As soon as we get word from Urswick."

"And what if the new French king does not agree to grant us safe haven?" Henry challenged.

"Then we will go anyway." Jasper gazed around the room. "Either way, before the month is out, we will be gone from here."

41

October 1484

Sens was a peaceful city huddled around an imposing cathedral with the Yonne river to the east. Conveniently positioned a reasonable seventy miles from Paris, the young Charles VIII, or more accurately, his elder sister Anne de Beaujeau, had deemed it an acceptable location for their English guests. By some miracle, their escape plan had come off without a hitch, though that was not to say it hadn't been touch and go at points. Jasper's wait at the border had been predictably stressful, though not as fraught as Henry's journey. It transpired later that Landais' men had reached the border not an hour after he'd crossed. If safety had been a few miles further on, it could have been a very different outcome; one that Jasper could not bear thinking about.

They'd settled into their new lives in Sens remarkably easily. After thirteen years in Brittany, Jasper had feared it might take Henry a while to adjust to French culture, but his nephew adapted quickly to his new environment. His command of the language was flawless, arguably better than his English, and the locals welcomed him as if he were one of their own. By the time Edward Woodville and the first of the exiles arrived from Brittany a few weeks later, a stranger would have been forgiven for mistaking Henry for a Frenchman.

The news from Vannes was better than they could have hoped for. Francis had recovered from his illness shortly after Jasper and Henry fled, and had been horrified to learn of Landais' treachery. Embarrassed by his treasurer's actions, he had immediately sought to rectify the situation, willingly giving permission for the exiles to leave for France, and even going so far as to cover the cost of their journeys. The letters he sent to Henry and Jasper reiterated his disappointment at how they had parted and spoke of his ardent wish for there to be no bad blood between them. Given his final display of generosity, Henry was more than happy to reassure Francis that he held no grudge against him. That they were even alive today was testament to the duke's generosity, and in his own letter to Francis, Jasper had been profuse in his thanks. Yet it felt right that that period in their lives had come to an end. He only had to look at his nephew to see how much had changed since they'd arrived at Francis' court, lost and frightened. Witnessing how Henry had grown into the expectations placed on him gave Jasper an unshakeable sense that they now stood on the cusp of the final chapter of their saga, the ceaseless revolutions of the Wheel of Fortune unrelentingly propelling them forward to meet their destiny.

It took a while for all the exiles to make their way from Brittany, arriving in dribs and drabs as autumn steadily gave way to winter. Henry individually greeted every single one, eager to remedy any simmering anger they might be harbouring from their recent abandonment. For the most part, they had been content to let the episode slide. Woodville himself had been particularly pragmatic, expressing only sadness that Henry had not felt he could trust him, whilst also admitting he would have done the same if the situation had been reversed. Jasper had noted that he'd lost some of his usual brightness, the recent death of his brother Lionel no doubt weighing on his mind. Hopefully, the move to France would re-energise him. Edward commanded significant respect amongst the exiles and they could not afford for him to be distracted. Concerningly, the Marquess of Dorset had been much less forgiving than his uncle, berating Henry for his actions in a way that almost bordered on impropriety.

"We will need to watch him," Jasper had warned his nephew after the embittered Dorset had left. "He chafes under the disappointment of his reduced position. If the opportunity presents itself, I have no doubt he will be the first to break rank."

Henry studied the door through which the Marquess had departed with a resigned expression. "I had been thinking the same," he confided. "Yet is it not strange that he would harbour such resentment when his uncles are committed to our cause?"

"I agree, it is surprising. However, a son's devotion to his mother often far exceeds other familial loyalty. If there is even a suggestion that Elizabeth Woodville might be reconciled with Richard, he will turn against us."

Henry made to respond but was interrupted by a servant who materialised by the door. "Excuse me, my Lord. Two men have arrived and are requesting to see you."

Henry groaned. "Just once I would like to enjoy an evening without interruption. Who are these new arrivals?" he asked the servant with a sigh.

"The Earl of Oxford, my Lord, and James Blount, the captain of Hammes."

Henry stood quickly. "Why didn't you start with that? Send them in!"

"Yes, my Lord," the servant replied with a quick bow before scurrying away.

Henry grinned at Jasper excitedly, while self-consciously smoothing the creases from his doublet. He stopped as the door re-opened and the new arrivals walked in. There was no mistaking who was who out of the pair. Oxford, dressed plainly yet undimmed by a decade of imprisonment, took the lead. Just behind came James Blount. A handful of years younger and a good few inches taller than the earl, he held himself with the easy confidence of a professional soldier.

"Sirs, welcome to Sens," Henry announced, greeting both men warmly. "I believe you know my uncle?"

"Pembroke," Oxford smiled. "I am grateful fate saw fit to cross our paths once more."

"As am I," Jasper replied, grasping the earl's hand in welcome.

"Thank you for receiving us," Oxford continued, turning back to Henry. "We do not wish to disturb you, I know the hour is late."

"Not at all, it is never too late to receive friends," Henry replied, waving a hand. "Your reputation precedes you, Oxford, and I was delighted to hear of your escape from Hammes."

"It took me long enough," the earl replied with a wry grin. "My previous attempt was distinctly less successful – some broken bones and a mouthful of moat water was all I had to show for it." Oxford motioned to the broad-shouldered man standing next to him. "If not for Blount and his wife, I would not be here. Having your captor on your side does make things considerably easier."

"What can I say, my Lord? You're very convincing when you want to be," Blount replied in a deep voice that hinted at his Derbyshire origins. "In any case, I owe no loyalty to Richard. He is a murderer and a tyrant. After what he did to Hastings, he deserves what's coming for him."

"And your wife, is she here with you?" Henry enquired, turning to Blount, who straightened himself at being addressed directly.

"No, she was required to stay at Hammes, my Lord."

"Oh, to look after your children I presume?" Henry ventured.

Blount shook his head. "No, my Lord, to hold the castle."

There was a beat as Henry digested what he had just been told. "I'm sorry, your wife is currently holding Hammes?" he stammered in disbelief. "But has Richard not sent men to attack it?"

"Yes, I believe he has," Blount replied nonchalantly.

"Then are you not concerned for your wife's safety?" Henry asked incredulously.

Blount smiled. "You clearly haven't met my wife," he chuckled. "Elizabeth has been waiting for a moment like this for years. She will hold the castle, my Lord, for as long as is required – have no doubt about that."

"You are fortunate, sir, to have such a wife," Jasper commented.

"Thank you, my Lord, indeed I am," Blount smiled, the pride in his voice obvious.

"In any case, Elizabeth will not be on her own for long," Oxford added. "We intend to relieve the garrison and return here with them. The men who guard that castle are professional soldiers, every single one, and we will need their skills if we are to triumph against Richard."

"So you will support our cause?" Henry asked, grinning broadly.

Oxford assessed Henry. "Did you ask the same of your uncle?"

Henry's smile faltered as he glanced uncertainly at Jasper. "No."

"Then you need not ask me. We are cut from the same cloth, he and I," Oxford replied, motioning to Jasper. "I may not have been there at the very beginning like him, but I've been fighting for Lancaster since I was old enough to hold a sword. And I've suffered for it. My father and brother were brutally killed, my lands were confiscated, and for the last decade, I have been imprisoned, left to rot in Calais while York's sons reaped the benefits of his treachery. But no more. I will see their hopes snuffed out and a Lancastrian once again upon the throne of England."

* * *

289

"I'm amazed Blount left Hammes under his wife's control," Henry remarked, settling into a chair next to his uncle. The two of them were alone once more, and he was thankful for the respite from being on show.

Jasper raised an eyebrow. "Are you? I cannot say I am. I have been fortunate to know several women whose bravery would bring many men to shame. Your mother for instance. She would have relished commanding a garrison, if she had ever been given the chance. And if she's inherited even a thimbleful of her father's spirit, then I expect your intended will be equally formidable."

Henry considered Jasper's comment about his future wife. For a long time, he had assumed he would never marry. His life was too restricted, too uncertain and he had made peace with the fact that it would be like his uncle's: nomadic and solitary. All that had now changed. Though he had not discussed the planned marriage much since the service last Christmas, he was surprised by his excitement at the prospect. After so long alone, the companionship of marriage appealed to him, and while he may not have met Princess Elizabeth, by all accounts she was astute, kind and beautiful. And yet, despite his anticipation, he could not escape the knowledge that many of his supporters only regarded him as a credible leader because of his promised union with the York heiress. When the time came, he would need to ensure that the people saw him as ruling in his own right, not only through marriage. But that was for the future; for now, there were more pressing matters.

"Speaking of formidable, Oxford has obviously not let imprisonment dim his resolve," Henry observed.

"No, he has not," Jasper agreed. "What happened to his father was unspeakably horrific. It makes me grateful that at least my own father's death was quick." There was a pause as Jasper's mind was filled with images of Owen, before, with a deep breath to suppress the spike of grief, he refocused on the conversation at hand. "It will be good to have Oxford here with us," he continued. "I was beginning to feel somewhat isolated with all the Yorkists who have joined us. They are motivated by overthrowing Richard, and that alone. The idea of your rise being a triumph for Lancaster has likely not even crossed their minds, and it is important it continues not to. In such circumstances, it is valuable to be surrounded by commanders whom you can implicitly trust, and Oxford is such a man."

Henry nodded in agreement. "With the two of you at my side I feel as though I can conquer the world," he confessed.

"Let's start with England first, we'll get to the rest of the world once I've had time to rest!" Jasper replied, leaning his head on the back of his chair, a smile playing on his lips.

42

July 1485

I n reality, conquering England was going to be much harder than simply having a few good men supporting their campaign, and it was not going to happen quickly; after all, they only had one chance to get it right. The Buckingham debacle had taught them the perils of rushing into such an undertaking, as well as the dangers of launching a campaign in winter. Better to bide their time and wait for the perfect moment. And so the months ticked past, each day filled with training and planning. Meanwhile, underneath the surface, imperceptible at first, things began to change, and then, as the new year found its feet, the pieces finally started to fall into place.

In England, Richard lost his son and wife in quick succession. One death would have been unfortunate, but to the superstitious the loss of both suggested he was cursed. Even the more rational recognised it for the disaster it was. With no heir, Richard was exposed. He offered his subjects little by way of security, and the rumours he intended to take Elizabeth of York as his wife only served to alienate him further. The obvious incest aside, Richard had based his entire claim to the throne on the invalidity of her parent's marriage. If that were true, why then would he choose to marry her? Across the water in France,

Henry and Jasper watched the situation unfold with bated breath. If Richard went through with the marriage, it would be disastrous for their campaign. After all, so much hinged on Henry's promise to take the York heiress as his wife. It was therefore a huge relief when, in response to the public outcry against the union, Richard released a statement declaring he had no intention of marrying his niece. And just like that, a weakness became an advantage. Richard was the most vulnerable he had been since he'd first seized power. The Wheel of Fortune was turning and their time was coming.

Which was how they came to find themselves in Harfleur, a town on the banks of the Seine a few miles from where it opened into the sea. It was here that the fleet that would carry them across the Channel was being assembled. Every day, Jasper made his way down to the river's edge to check on the progress being made. Half a dozen ships sat moored alongside the quay, bobbing gently as they were loaded with supplies. A similar number were anchored further offshore in the middle of the Seine where the river was at its deepest. In total, they had thirty ships capable of transporting over two thousand men. It was considerably more than when they'd last attempted to cross the Channel, but Jasper was careful to temper his excitement; they would need to recruit many more if they were to successfully challenge Richard.

He was not the only one who made the daily pilgrimage to the quay. Edward Woodville and his brother, Richard, were often there too, the former putting his experience as admiral of the fleet to good use. To observers accustomed to seeing the two of them together with their nephew, it appeared as though they were waiting for the final member of their trio. But the Marquess of Dorset would not be joining them. Jasper and Henry's wariness of Elizabeth's last remaining son had been well founded, his loyalty to his mother finally tipping the balance within him. Strong in the belief that Richard intended to reconcile

with his sister-in-law, Dorset had snuck away from the makeshift
court at Sens, heading for the coast and a boat that would take him
home. Oxford had been only too happy to hunt him down and return
him to the city, seeing his desertion as proof of Yorkist deceit. Henry
had been more forgiving. He, more than anyone, understood a son's
devotion to his mother, even one who was hundreds of miles away,
and Dorset was suitably contrite about his actions. Yet the episode
had confirmed that he could have no place in their campaign – the
bond of trust had been broken and there was no way to repair it. So,
when surety was required to secure a sizable private loan from one of
Charles VIII's councillors when the king's own generosity had fallen
short of expectations, it was Dorset who stepped forward. Swearing
on his honour as a Knight of the Garter, he agreed to stay behind in
Paris until the loan was repaid. Thankfully, the Woodville brothers
understood Henry's reasoning. They were ashamed by their nephew's
dishonesty and grateful for Henry's magnanimous response.

The one downside to the arrangement was that, with the removal
of Dorset, they had also lost the option of landing in the west country.
Wherever they landed, they needed to be certain of the ability to
quickly recruit new men whilst avoiding any localised resistance.
Having the landowner on side was therefore crucial. With Dorset and
Devon now out of play, various other options had been put forward.
There had been some support for the proposal of landing in North
Wales. The rugged landscape would deter Richard from venturing to
meet them, and it had the added advantage of being under Thomas
Stanley's control. But Henry had been quick to dismiss the idea. His
stepfather's standing with Richard was too precarious. As it stood,
Richard only suspected Stanley of aiding his enemies. If they landed
on his doorstep, he would know it for sure. Though Henry did not
mention it, Jasper knew the other reason was the danger it would put
his mother in. Margaret had been lucky not to end up with her head

in a noose after her involvement with Buckingham. There was no question it was Richard's reliance on her husband that saved her, and Henry would explore every other option to avoid her being put in such a position a second time.

For his part, Jasper had quietly listened as the commanders of Henry's force debated the merits of different locations. Oxford, Woodville, Cheyne, Blount; all had their own opinions. To Jasper, the solution was blindingly obvious, but he was conscious the others needed to feel included in the decision. The years with no one to rely on, save each other, had made he and Henry incredibly close. But a ruler is only as strong as the support he has around him; it would not serve Henry to be over-reliant on just one person. And so, bit by bit, Jasper had begun to take a step back, to let other men fill the space he had occupied for the last fourteen years. Yet despite that, even he had his limits on how long he could remain silent.

"There is only one viable option," Jasper announced abruptly, speaking over a heated discussion about whether Woodville's prior connections to Portsmouth would be sufficient to secure that port's support. "We will land in Pembrokeshire."

Henry looked up, surprised by his uncle's sudden interruption – though from the look on his face, Jasper could tell his suggestion had caught his nephew's imagination. "Tenby?"

Jasper shook his head. "No, it is too conspicuous. Thirty ships arriving unannounced would set the alarm bells ringing and terrify the locals before we had the opportunity to state our intentions. And in any case, we need to keep away from Pembroke – the current steward would willingly ride all the way to Scotland if he thought it would help Richard. No, it needs to be somewhere more secluded yet not so remote as to add unnecessary days to our march."

"Then where do you suggest?" Henry asked.

Jasper was silent for a moment, scanning an imagined map in his head, selecting and then dismissing various options. And then it came to him. "There is a bay to the south of the Dale peninsular that could accommodate our numbers with ease. It is at the mouth of the Milford Sound, but on the opposite side to Pembroke. The nearest town is Haverfordwest, some fifteen miles to the north-east. If we move quickly, we should be able to reach it before news of our landing has time to spread."

Oxford scratched his chin. "What about opposition? It has been a long time since the Tudor name has held any power in those parts. How can you be confident we will receive the support we need?"

Jasper smiled ruefully. "It has been a long time, I grant you. But Welshmen have long memories, and their loyalties are not as easily swayed as those of the English. I already warned my half-brother of the possibility of us landing in the area, and he has been discretely canvassing support in and around Pembrokeshire. As for opposition, Rhys ap Thomas is Richard's principal lieutenant in South Wales. He will be able to amass a significant force, though I do not believe he will have any intention of using it against us. His grandfather fought alongside me at Mortimer's Cross and his father and brothers' opposition to York is well known. David has been speaking to him. He has not yet committed himself. I am confident that when the time comes, he will join us."

Jasper fell silent, waiting in anticipation for the response from the others. He hoped he'd done enough to convince them and certainly, none seemed overtly opposed, but in the end, it was only his nephew's opinion that mattered. He therefore felt a sense of satisfied relief when Henry came to stand at his side, a wide smile on his face.

"Pembrokeshire it is," he announced. "It is fitting that our route to victory will begin in the county in which I was born."

There was little time to revel in the achievement of a decision finally being made before the next barrage of questions was upon them. "And after we've landed? What then?" Woodville asked.

Oxford, who was still uncomfortable at being in such close proximity to his former enemy, shook his head. "It is not something we can plan in detail. We need to remain reactive, ready to adapt to situations as they arise. Much will also depend on where Richard is staying when we land. According to the last reports, he is currently in Nottingham, but this may change."

"I think we can be confident the battle will not take place in Wales," Blount commented.

Next to him, Cheyne nodded in agreement. "Yes, Richard would not risk being drawn into a fight in an area where he cannot guarantee the loyalty of the locals. Wherever he is when we land, he will wait to meet us in England."

Woodville turned back to Henry and Jasper. "So if we work on that assumption, what route should we aim to take through Wales – recognising it may need to change," he added, noticing Oxford's frown.

Jasper considered the question. "It depends on Rhys ap Thomas, though I would suggest we stay close to the coast for as long as possible. It would give us the option of sending a few ships ahead with supplies to save time. But we can only take that approach for so long. Once we are past Aberystwyth we will need to start moving inland. After that, we'll just have to see."

"So then, when do we leave?" Cheyne, ever eager for the next challenge, asked.

Jasper made to reply but held his tongue. It was Henry, not him, who was entitled to make that call. He glanced at his nephew, who squared his shoulders, already mentally preparing for what was to come.

"On the next favourable wind," he declared. Scanning the room, he looked intently at each man in turn. "Prepare yourselves. The greatest opportunity of our lifetimes is nearly upon us. Be ready to grasp it, for there is no coming back."

IV

Part Four

August 1485

"There is a longing for Harry, there is hope for our race. His name comes down from the mountains as a two-edged sword ... And the city of England will be reduced under thee; the world will be driven, the Boar made cold and the Mole will flee."

—*Dafydd Llwyd o Fathafarn*

43

7–16 August 1485

Twisting around in his saddle, Jasper surveyed the train of men that stretched all the way down the narrow, winding lane back towards Mill Bay and their landing site. It was impossible to make out the end of the line thanks to the haze of dust kicked up by thousands of marching feet. Positioned at the front of the column, Jasper was little troubled by it but still, he spared a thought for the poor souls at the rear who were no doubt coughing and spluttering.

There was nothing subtle about their advance through Pembrokeshire. If the dust cloud didn't draw attention, then the hundreds of colourful banners fluttering above the train certainly would. To the untrained eye, it would seem like a confusing, unorganised mass of flags, but nothing could be further from the truth. Each banner had its purpose. Some, like the one flying above Jasper, identified individual commanders. Interspersed along the line, they helped the men beneath locate their respective companies, though it was really in battle where their true purpose lay. When chaos descended, it was often only these squares of cloth that ensured some semblance of order was retained, their bright colours standing proud against a canvas of mud and blood. Jasper could remember the hours he'd spent as a young boy learning to identify the different crests. At the time he'd thought it inordinately dull, but the knowledge stayed with him, and looking over the train he could make out the yellow and red of Oxford, and the blue and white of the Woodville brothers with ease. Yet, not all the banners were meant for identification. Some were more symbolic, designed to stir up loyalties and entice men to join them. Of these, the Beaufort portcullis signalled Henry's claim to the throne through his mother's line, while the image of St George on horseback conjured images of chivalrous valour triumphing over evil. But most important of all was the standard that flew at the very head of the column: *Y Ddraig Goch*, the red dragon of Cadwaladr. Held proudly aloft by the strong arms of Sir William Brandon and set upon the Tudor colours of green and white, it proclaimed to all who saw it that, at last, the Son of Prophecy had returned. Though they had only covered a few miles, it had already worked its magic, enticing people out of their low thatched cottages to gawp and stare as they paraded past. Every now and again a few men, encouraged by the soldiers filing past, would stop what they were doing, grab the closest thing to a weapon they possessed, and then with a quick kiss goodbye to their families allow themselves to be swept up into the ranks. Before long Jasper began to hear Welsh voices amongst the French and English, the language like music to his ears.

For a moment, he allowed his head to tip back, turning his face up to the cloudless blue sky to relish the warmth of the Welsh sunshine. Riding across this ancient landscape, it felt as though his soul, starved for so long, was at last being replenished. He was home. For the first time in fourteen years, he felt a contented peace settle upon him, filling his heart with an unbridled happiness that made him want to whoop with joy. Pembroke was so close he could almost touch it. How he longed to walk along its walls once more as its rightful owner. But that dream would have to wait just a little longer. The course they were set on left no space for his desires. His nephew was the priority, and in comparison, everything else came second. Yet he did not begrudge the situation. True, he had sacrificed more than he ever thought possible to see Henry succeed, but he'd give it all again without a second's hesitation. The Welsh sun might soothe his soul, but it was the three oaths he had sworn, one each for the stages of Henry's life, that gave him purpose. The first, given at Lamphey, to the unborn child and the brave mother who carried him. The second, given in London, to the uncertain boy on the cusp of adolescence. And the third, most poignant of all, given in the sight of God to the true *Y Mab Darogan* and the man who would be king. He prayed fate would give him the chance to make a fourth, kneeling in front of the coronation chair as the crown was placed on Henry's head.

From beside him, a voice broke him from his reverie. "It must feel good, Brother, to be walking amongst Pembrokeshire's hills once more?"

Opening his eyes, Jasper turned to see his half-brother bringing his horse alongside his own. David looked exactly like Jasper imagined his father had done at a similar age, with an unruly mop of hair and an easy smile.

"It is like food to a starved man, though it feels almost cruel to be so close to Pembroke yet unable to see it once more," he replied, gazing out across the surrounding countryside.

David nodded. "I can well imagine, but just think how much sweeter your return will be when it finally comes. Pembroke is not going anywhere. When all this is over," he continued, spreading his arm, "it will be waiting for you – Joan and my mother as well."

The motion made the ring on his brother's little finger glint as it caught the sunlight. Jasper's eyes widened in recognition. "You kept it? After all this time?"

303

David smiled down at the signet ring where Owen's crest, though slightly worn with age, was still clear. "I have never been parted from it, not since the day you gave it to me. I promised, did I not, to keep the Tudor flame burning, and here we are."

"And how proud our father would have been. If only he could be with us today." Jasper sighed. "Now that I am home, I feel his absence most keenly."

"But he is with us – in here," David countered, placing a hand on his heart. "And even now, he is guiding us."

Jasper considered his half-brother, as if seeing him properly for the first time. "I remember his happiness at your birth; how the light that had died with Edmund returned to his eyes. It was as though he knew the man you would become. I am grateful fate has given me the opportunity to know it too."

* * *

They'd been on the road for over five hours by the time the outline of Haverfordwest came into view. The scouts that had been sent on ahead had returned excitedly to inform them that a man named Arnold Butler and roughly eighty men were waiting for them at the castle. Jasper and the other commanders had gathered around to hear the reports, and it was to them that Henry turned.

"Do you think it's a trap?" he asked.

Jasper shook his head. "I recognise the name, he's a local landowner. In any case, if he intended to challenge us he would have done so on the open road."

"And with more than eighty men," Oxford added.

Henry smiled with relief. "In that case, we will see what this Butler has to say. Oxford, stay with the men. Uncle, Woodville – come with me."

Just as the scouts had reported, they found Butler and his retinue of men in the ward of Haverfordwest's somewhat dilapidated castle. Jasper vaguely recognised the man who stepped forward to greet them from meetings at Pembroke a lifetime before.

"Your Grace." Butler bowed to Henry, quickly dispelling, with the use of the higher form of address, any remaining fears that he might have been sent to resist them. "I have come here from the camp of Rhys ap Thomas with eighty men to assist in your campaign."

"Thank you. Your support, and that of your men, is much appreciated," Henry replied smoothly, clearly pleased that the man on whom so much hinged regarded them favourably. "You say you have come from Rhys ap Thomas; when can we expect to meet him? Is he on his way?"

"No, your Grace, he is not. He remains in Carmarthen."

Henry's brow furrowed in confusion. "Did you act without his blessing in coming here?"

A shadow passed over Butler's face at the insinuation of his disloyalty. "No, it was he who sent me."

"Then why does he not make his way here to join us?" Henry pressed.

"He believes it is better to wait. As far as Richard is concerned, he is utterly loyal and will deal swiftly with any threat that arises in Wales. Why not make him believe that for a little longer? If Rhys were to declare himself now, Richard would be forced to act. In contrast, by remaining silent, Richard will continue to sit idly in Nottingham, thereby bettering our chances of catching him unawares."

"Respectfully, I disagree," Henry replied, shaking his head. "If he were to join us now, it would send a message throughout the whole of Wales that we stand together against a common enemy. It would enable us to amass an even greater force. Does he not care for the banner under which we march?"

Butler's eyes took in the blood-red dragon hanging behind Henry.

"He has heard what the bards are calling you, and he knows it is Cadwaladr's badge that flies proudly above you. But it will not make him move before he is ready. He knows this country and the way things work, and you do not. Your uncle maybe," he considered, nodding at Jasper, "but not you. You can claim all the history and heritage you want, yet it won't change the fact that you are the stranger here."

Jasper inhaled sharply. Up until now, Henry had had to deal with little by way of opposition. Even the most headstrong of the exiles were reluctant to challenge him, their desperation to return home making them bury their feelings. But they weren't in Brittany any more. Though every fibre in his being made Jasper want to leap to his nephew's defence, he held his tongue. If they were to succeed and Henry was to sit on the throne then he needed to learn how to deal with men such as Butler. And so Jasper waited, watching his nephew closely to see how he would respond.

A muscle jumped in Henry's jaw as he fixed his piercing eyes on the man before him. "Then why are you here?" he challenged. Though his voice was still low, it was edged with anger. "If that is truly what you think of me, why have you bothered to come all this way?"

Butler assessed Henry. He seemed pleased with the flicker of passion, as though it were the final confirmation he needed. Raising his head he met Henry's stare. "Because you may be a stranger, but your blood sings with the legacy of Llywelyn the Great, and it is time for the sons of Cadwaladr to triumph once more."

* * *

Turning away from the coast had felt like a door being locked shut behind them. For more than a week they had hugged the rugged coastline, knowing that while they stayed close to the sea, the option of escape remained open to them. But they couldn't stay by it forever. The inevitable move inland took away that escape route, committing them fully to whatever lay ahead. So far, their journey had been remarkably uneventful, almost to the point of being unsettling. They'd been allowed to wind their way north without any opposition. Rhys ap Thomas had continued to keep his distance, though the constant trickle of men from his camp was unspoken confirmation of his continued support. He was also marching north, his own route mirroring theirs. Judging by the scouts' most recent reports the two forces would converge near the town of Welshpool. As the miles ticked past, Jasper could only hope that the meeting, when it finally came, would be amicable. He could remember Rhys ap Thomas only as a boy, hanging around his father and grandfather, eager for adventure. He had no idea what the man that boy had become would be like, though he took heart from David's conviction that everything would work out smoothly.

Jasper had thought he and Henry would have hours together to discuss their plans, but the reality was very different. His nephew was constantly tracking back and forth along the line, catching up with different commanders and checking in on the new arrivals. For those used to only seeing their leader as a remote figure, Henry's personality came as a welcome surprise, and his actions had cemented his popularity amongst the men. Yet, when Henry did finally bring his horse alongside Jasper's, there was an unexpected insecurity to his demeanour.

"I need your counsel, Uncle," he confided.

Jasper smiled quietly to himself. That Henry still turned to him for advice when there were many others just as capable was a source of satisfaction. "What is it that troubles you? You're popular with the men and we're making good progress."

"It is neither of those things. No, I'm nervous about our meeting with Rhys ap Thomas. We are nothing without his support, what if I fail to secure it?"

"Firstly, you won't," Jasper replied, matter of factly. "Look how you've captivated the men. I've seen many far more experienced leaders fail to command the respect you have so effortlessly won. As for your second concern, while it may be true we are dependent on Rhys' support, he does not know that. It is a game, Henry, nothing more. As long as he believes we are a force to be reckoned with then it will be so."

"But how do we make him believe it?"

"As I said to you in Vannes, by believing it yourself."

"I think it might take more than that," Henry said dejectedly.

"Well, if that's the case, then I see no harm in playing a few mind games," Jasper replied mischievously. "Choose the right meeting location and most of the work will be done for you."

Henry raised an eyebrow. "And what is this magical location that will woo Rhys?" Henry asked, his scepticism obvious. "I defer to your greater knowledge of the area. After all, I'm the stranger here."

Jasper shook his head. "You are many things Henry, but a stranger is not one of them," he replied, his voice turning serious for a moment. "Though I will agree that when it comes to knowledge of the Welsh landscape, I might have a slight advantage," he continued with a wink. "There is a hill not far from here, *Cefn Digoll* as the locals call it, or Long Mountain. The old Roman road runs along the plateau at the top and it boasts commanding views across into England. More importantly though, it will require Rhys to climb up to meet us. If we are not enough to convince him, then the physical exertion required to reach us certainly will be."

* * *

There was a palpable feeling of relief when the town of Welshpool came into view. The men had been marched hard across unforgiving terrain and it was clear they were exhausted. The groan, therefore, when the order went out that they were to continue a few miles further on up to the nearby summit of Long Mountain was audible. But the afternoon was bright, with a gentle breeze that cooled the air, and it did not take long before camp was set and the men were able to rest.

Within Henry's tent, the remnants of the evening meal were just being cleared away when the first scout raced in to inform them that Rhys ap Thomas was close at hand. With minimal fuss, the order went out to form up. The majority of the men would remain hidden amongst the tents, ready to react if the situation were to suddenly deteriorate. Meanwhile, Henry, flanked on either side by his commanders, took up position at the entrance to the camp.

Jasper stood at his nephew's right hand, and together they waited for Rhys ap Thomas to finally make his appearance. As it was, they heard the approaching force before they saw them, the unmistakable sound of thousands of marching feet echoing across the still summer night. Even though they were friends not foes, Jasper still felt the familiar wave of unease come over him. His throat felt tight and he could feel a trickle of sweat travelling down the nape of his neck. Almost unconsciously, he flexed his grip on his sword. Next to him, he felt Oxford respond to the movement, but the earl said nothing, and even in the darkening gloom, Jasper could see the tension in the younger man's jaw. The topography meant it sounded as though the force was closer than they actually were. As such, it took longer than Jasper had expected for the first shadows to crest the hill. The scouts had given a rough estimate of the numbers they could expect, yet even equipped with that knowledge, the reality seemed even greater. The shadows kept coming until the edge of the plateau was a dark mass, pin-pricked with torches. Trumpets signalled a halt as a small group detached itself and began to make its way across the plain towards them.

Rhys ap Thomas was not a tall man, but while his stature might not speak to his status, his demeanour left no doubt as to his authority. He walked at the head of the small group, relaxed and noticeably unarmed, seemingly unaffected by the climb to reach them. As he drew closer, his dark eyes took in the weapons at their belts, and a small smile tugged at the corners of his lips.

Keen to take control of the interaction, Henry stepped forward. "Well met, sir," he announced.

Rhys inclined his head. "So you are the man who comes to challenge Richard?"

"I am," Henry confirmed.

"Then I must congratulate you, my Lord, on your progress thus far."

Henry smiled charmingly. "I believe we have you to thank for that. I do not doubt our journey through Wales would have been much livelier without your guiding hand. However," he continued, "you have remained in the shadows for long enough; it is time for you to step into the light and for us to march from this place together, united under a common cause."

From next to his nephew, Jasper watched Rhys intently, waiting to see how he would respond. The Welshman assessed Henry for a moment before replying. "It would appear the reports about you are true. You know what you want, and are not afraid to grasp it. I admit there is something about your character that is hard to resist."

Henry shook his head dismissively. "You flatter me, sir. I merely wish to see our country delivered from the evil force that holds it. And for that, I need men such as you by my side. So what say you? Will you join us?"

A smile spread across Rhys' face. With a brief glance left and right at his men, he dropped to one knee. Behind him, the others in the group did the same. He fixed Henry with his dark eyes. "I, Rhys ap Thomas, Lieutenant of South Wales, hereby pledge, in the sight of those assembled here, my support and sword, and those of my men, to your service. May God guide my blade and keep my heart true."

Henry reached out a hand and pulled Rhys to his feet as Jasper lent his voice to the cheers echoing around the camp. "Come, let us celebrate your most welcomed arrival."

44

17–18 August 1485

Riding high on their success at Long Mountain, there was a feeling of invincibility as the distinctive outline of Shrewsbury appeared on the horizon. That feeling alone should have been enough to warn Jasper that something would soon go awry. Their journey had been too easy. That they actually believed they could make it to England without facing any opposition proved just how far they had been lulled into a false sense of security. The first indication that something was wrong was the ripple of uneasy murmuring that travelled like a wave through the ranks. Immediately, Jasper had an inkling of what it might be, but he waited for the scout rushing over to him and Oxford to confirm it before he spoke his fears aloud.

"The gates, my Lords – they have been closed against us," the boy announced breathlessly.

"It is an oversight, nothing more," Oxford replied dismissively. "I'm sure we'll have them open in no time."

Jasper nodded in support of the earl's assertion – there was no need to spread further panic through the men – but privately he remained unconvinced. Closing a city's gates was not a small undertaking, and certainly not something regularly done in the middle of a Wednesday afternoon. As he watched the news spread to the other commanders an unbidden image of Queen Marguerite frantically banging on the gates of Gloucester while the Pretender bore down on her like a rabid dog filled Jasper's mind. It had taken more than a month for Tewkesbury's abbey to be purified and re-consecrated after the brutal atrocities that took place there – would Shrewsbury's cathedral experience the same fate? He shook his head. The past would not repeat itself. Yet even with that conviction, he felt a sense of pessimism creeping over him, the first since they had landed at Mill Bay.

Next to him, Oxford spurred his horse forward to join Henry, who was standing close to the walls. "Open the gates!" he bellowed.

His shout was met with silence, the flags fluttering in the wind the only movement on top of the high walls. And so he tried again. "I said open the gates in the name of the true king!"

There was a beat and then a face appeared, peering down from the battlements. "I see no king amongst your number," it retorted.

"How dare—" Oxford began, bristling at the affront, but Henry held up a silencing hand.

"Who is it that shouts down to us?" he called.

"Thomas Mitton, the warden of this city," the man replied.

Henry smiled up at him, using a hand to shield his eyes from the sun's glare. "Well met, sir. I am Henry Tudor, Earl of Richmond. I have come—"

"I know why you are here," Mitton interrupted. "And little good will it do you. I hold this city in the name of King Richard."

"I appreciate that sir, but why don't you come down here and let us talk, man to man."

Mitton shook his head. "Not likely, my Lord. I swore an oath to the king – you will have to step over my body before I forsake it."

"There will be no need for that. Our quarrel is not with you, sir, nor with your city. We merely wish to cross the river."

"There are plenty of other places you can do so. May I suggest you go and bother them?" Mitton shot back, before disappearing from the battlements.

Jasper was impressed that Henry was able to keep his calm in the face of such impudence. He was aware of Rhys' eyes on his nephew. He was standing alongside Butler, their heads bent together in conversation. Only a day into their alliance and already there was an obstacle. He watched as Rhys signalled over a messenger. Intrigued, Jasper made his way over to them.

"I hope you are not losing faith in us so soon," he joked lightly.

"Not at all, Sir Jasper. Your nephew seems to have the situation well in hand, though the longer we stay here, the more vulnerable we are. I have just ordered the number of scouts to be increased and for their range to be widened – we don't need anyone creeping up on us while we are distracted. If a farmer even so much as moves his cattle, we will hear about it."

"A wise idea – thank you."

"Not at all. The histories of our families are closely intertwined, and I intend to see us triumph. I'm sure my grandfather is smiling at the sight of the two of us standing here together, united once more."

"As I'm sure is my father," Jasper replied, looking up to the sky. The light was draining from it, the shadow of the moon already visible, and beneath it he could feel the men growing restless. He turned back to Rhys and Butler. "If you'll excuse me, sirs, I need to speak with my nephew."

Though Mitton had not reappeared, Henry was still standing in the same position with Oxford at his side. He smiled grimly when he saw Jasper approaching. "This is not the situation we wanted, Uncle."

"It's certainly far from ideal."

"Yet, I believe Mitton could be brought around if only he would come out and talk to me," Henry continued earnestly.

"That may be so, but it's getting late. We cannot wait here, we're too exposed. Let us retire back to Forton. We need to regroup and consider the best course of action."

Henry nodded reluctantly and turned to Oxford. "Give the order, and tell the commanders I want them in my tent as soon as the men are settled. I would have their counsel."

* * *

Positioned in the centre of the camp to protect it from potential ambushes, Henry's tent was considerably larger than those surrounding it, and usually very spacious, though tonight it was struggling to accommodate the number of men crammed beneath the canvas. The air felt thick and despite a side panel being rolled up to allow a breeze to circulate, there seemed to be little change in the temperature within the tent. All of Henry's commanders were assembled, from the stalwarts like Blount and Cheyne, to new arrivals like Rhys and Butler. It was a complete assortment of men that reflected the diversity of Henry's support base. All of them were crowded around a large table on which a map of the Marches had been spread. Someone, Jasper suspected Oxford, had placed a counter near Shrewsbury to indicate their current position.

"How long would it take to go around?" Philibert de Chandée asked. Personally appointed by the King of France, he was responsible for the mercenary force that had travelled with them from Harfleur.

"If memory serves me right, there's a crossing not far from here at Buildwas?" Jasper replied, turning to Rhys for confirmation.

"Yes, it's around fifteen or so miles south, near the abbey," the Welshman confirmed, pointing to the location on the map.

"The monks would probably give us less trouble than Mitton,"

Cheyne chuckled.

"I imagine they would, but it would add at least another day onto our journey," Butler countered.

"And time is not a luxury we can afford," Woodville added gravely.

"Could we not storm the city?" Blount, ever eager for a challenge, suggested.

Oxford shook his head at his former captor. "We don't have the resources, and even if we did, it would hardly endear us to the people."

"We might not have a choice," Earl Rivers stated matter of factly. "If we cannot cross the Severn then we are doomed."

Woodville turned to his elder brother. "Yes, thank you, Richard – we are all aware of what failure here would mean."

Rivers held up his hands. "I'm just making the point," he argued.

Jasper glanced at his nephew. "You've been unusually quiet, Henry. Pray, tell, what is on your mind?"

"Just something Mitton said when he was discussing his oath."

"A foolish oath given to a tyrant," Oxford spat. "What good does it do him to stand by it?"

Henry looked up at the earl. "We may debate the merits of his choices at another time, but for now, I believe I have an idea."

* * *

"You would have me do what?" Mitton shouted. Even from such a distance, the look of incredulity on his face was clear.

"You said yourself that I'd have to step over your body before you would renege on your oath to Richard," Henry reasoned. "Well, that is exactly what I'm proposing to do. I admire your loyalty, and I have no interest in reducing this great city to ashes."

Though Henry delivered the line as if it were an afterthought, the threat was clear. Behind him unobserved, Jasper shared a glance with

Oxford, and hoped the fact they had nowhere near the resources to follow up such an ultimatum would go uncommented upon. Judging from how the colour drained from Mitton's face, it seemed to have had the intended impact.

Taking advantage of the other man's shock, Henry pressed on. "Contrary to the lies Richard has spread, I am not here to ravage, but rather to rebuild. It is not in my nature to make threats; all I want is to return this country to its former glory. Unlike Richard, I am no tyrant. I will not force any man to submit to me, nor will he be punished for the refusal. But what I won't allow is for that refusal to jeopardise my campaign. And so I am offering you an alternative. If you let me walk over you, your oath is preserved, my men and I can continue our progress and the people of Shrewsbury will remain untouched."

Mitton's head disappeared from the battlements. Henry glanced at Jasper who shrugged his shoulders. There was no movement along the walls, no indication of what might be going on inside the city. And so they waited, the minutes ticking slowly past and the sun creeping ever higher in the sky. Just when Jasper thought they might be forced to consider marching to Buildwas, Shrewsbury's great gates began to open. Once the gap between them was wide enough, Mitton strode out of the city, accompanied by a handful of guards. There was no look of jubilation on his face, merely the resigned expression of a man worn down by reason who had lost any desire to argue the matter further.

He gave a perfunctory bow when he reached Henry before launching into his speech. "I have heard your entreaty, my Lord, and I agree to your terms. I will lie down here on the ground and allow you to step over me. After you have done so, you will be permitted entry into the city and my men will escort you through the streets to the bridge. You must not dawdle or delay, and if so much as a market stall is damaged,

I will be forced to act."

"Of course, sir," Henry replied. "You have my word."

"Very well. Let us get this over with then," Mitton grumbled, and just like that, without any further preamble, he lay down on his back in the dust at Henry's feet.

With a slight moment of hesitation, Henry stepped over his chest, before turning around and helping the older man to his feet. "History will praise you, sir," he said.

"We'll see about that," Mitton replied, sounding unconvinced. "More importantly, God will know I am not a man to forsake his oath."

318

45

19–21 August 1485

The column seemed as if it would never end. Used to riding near the front, Henry had not paid much attention to the supply carts and servants that brought up the rear. An army marches on its stomach, that was what Herbert had told him as they'd made their fateful journey to Edgcote. At such a young age it had been impossible to grasp the scale of what that actually meant; now he had some idea. Thousands of men meant hundreds of carts, and given his explicit orders that no farm or village was to be ransacked, the number was even greater. Why his uncle wanted to meet him at the very back, Henry could not fathom, yet nevertheless, here he was, weaving past heavily laden wagons and dodging small herds of sheep. The air this far back in the column was so thick with dust and manure that he could taste it, and no amount of spitting would rid his mouth of the acidic tang. He was close to losing his patience with the whole charade when at last he spotted the final few carts, and beside them, a broad warhorse with his uncle sat on top.

"There you are, Uncle. Why are you hiding back here?" Henry asked. "Your note said you wanted to speak with me?"

"Henry," Jasper smiled. "I was wondering when you would finally appear."

"In my defence, it's quite a distance from the front to back here, and it's never easy going against the tide," Henry replied, steering his horse around a wagon trundling in the opposite direction.

"Well, thank you for making the effort. Apple?" Jasper asked, pulling one from his saddle bag.

Henry nodded, deftly catching the fruit Jasper tossed his way. After a quick polish on his jerkin, he took a large bite, the sweetness of the juice banishing any lingering taste of manure. Jasper made no move to follow the column, so Henry relaxed into his saddle and watched as the last of the carts rounded the corner, leaving them completely alone in the lane, with only songbirds for company.

"You know, you could've just talked to me up at the front of the line," he said, as the sounds of the army faded into the distance. "Why the need for such secrecy?"

Jasper did not immediately answer, instead turning his horse to one side and a small gap in the hedgerow that led into a clump of trees. "Follow me."

Henry shot him an unconvinced look. "Won't we get lost? How will we find the others again?"

"Oh, give me some credit, Henry," Jasper chuckled, spurring his horse into the undergrowth.

Shaking his head, Henry tossed the apple core away before following his uncle into the trees. The path, if it could be called that, was little more than a winding dark line, broken by the occasional tree root and low-hanging branch. It was cooler beneath the canopy than out in the lane and Henry welcomed the reprieve from the heat. "So why did you want to speak to me?"

Jasper glanced over his shoulder. "We need to discuss our contingency plan, should Fortune's Wheel not turn in our favour."

Henry brought his horse to a halt, forcing his uncle to do the same.

"You think we are going to lose?"

"I did not say that," Jasper replied with a hint of exasperation, turning his horse to face Henry. "But I haven't survived this long without having options to fall back on."

Henry shook his head. "There's no need to make any secondary plans."

Jasper looked at his nephew in surprise. "Why not?"

"Because if we should lose, I intend to go down fighting with my men."

"That is a noble wish indeed Henry, but be serious now," Jasper replied, just about stopping himself from rolling his eyes at his nephew's naivety.

"I am being serious," Henry shot back. "We did not come all this way just to flee at the slightest hint of danger."

"That is not what—" Jasper began to protest.

"And what would we even be fleeing to?" Henry challenged, speaking over him. "A lifetime of exile and the slow decline into obscurity?" He shook his head. "No. I am tired of hiding, Uncle. I want to live my destiny, and if that means meeting my end on the battlefield then so be it."

"Spoken with the single-mindedness of youth, and the confidence of one who has not known the brutality of battle," Jasper sighed.

"Do not belittle me," Henry spat in annoyance. "I am disappointed in you, Uncle. I did not believe you to be someone to shy away from a fight. Of all people, I thought you would be the first to grasp an opportunity to end this conflict."

With a sudden flurry of movement, Jasper brought his horse forward so that he was knee to knee with his nephew. He fixed his grey eyes on Henry, who noted the anger shining in them. "Save your lecture, boy. You know full well I think little of my own desires beyond how they can serve you. From the moment I took you away from Hereford,

I have done nothing but consider your well-being. Do not mistake my desire to protect you for cowardice. If you had said to me now that you wanted an escape route, I would have moved heaven and earth to secure it. But don't you dare believe that means I won't stand with you till the bitter end if that is what you require of me." He paused for a moment, letting his impassioned words hang in the air. When he continued, his voice had lost its edge, the anger softening to something more gentle. "I brought you back here to give you the opportunity to speak candidly, as you have not been able to do since we were at Josselin. I am not just another one of your commanders, Henry, I am your family and I love you – you need never hide anything from me."

Henry hung his head, ashamed of his rash insolence. "Forgive me, I'm tired. I did not mean what I said." He waved a hand. "I just—"

"You don't need to apologise," Jasper replied quietly. Moving his reins into one hand, he dismounted and motioned for Henry to do the same. "Come, let us put aside our worries for a moment. There's a small river just down there, the water will soothe you."

Together the two of them led their horses through the trees until they came upon a peacefully meandering stream. The water was completely clear and Henry could see fish darting about beneath its surface. Leaving Jasper to secure the horses, he eagerly stripped off his clothes and launched himself into the stream's cool embrace. The feeling of the water on his skin made him groan in pleasure and once he had rid himself of the day's dust, he flipped over to float on his back with a contented smile on his face.

"This is more like it," Jasper sighed as he joined Henry in the water.

The two of them stayed like that for a while, their eyes shut against the sun, enjoying the soothing motion of the stream and the sound of the breeze through the leaves. Eventually, Henry coaxed his eyes open and turned his head to face his uncle.

"Speaking candidly then, how do you rate our chances?"

"Hmm, it depends," Jasper replied, pulling himself from the doze he had been lulled into.

"On what?"

"On the Stanleys. If we can secure their support, the battle will be ours, of that I am confident. If not—" Jasper trailed off with a shrug.

"It is a coincidence you should mention them. I received a letter not more than a few hours ago from Sir William, requesting a meeting."

"And you tell me that now?" Jasper cried, propelling himself upright so that his feet were planted on the river bed.

"It's not my fault you were hanging back here. I couldn't find you!" Henry exclaimed in exasperation.

"What did it say?"

"It said that he and my stepfather wish to meet with me to discuss matters. I believe they intend to defect."

"I would not be so sure," Jasper cautioned.

"Why not? What other reason could they have for wanting to meet me?"

"The Stanley brothers are renowned for their ability to always end up on the right side of history, and it's important you remember that. *Sans Changer* may be their motto, but *Semper Changer* would be more accurate. Probability of success, not loyalty, dictates their decisions, and they will not commit their forces until they know how the die has been cast. So whatever your stepfather says, take it with a grain of salt."

"Argh, why must everyone have an agenda? I am sick of it," Henry groaned, dunking his head under the water as if he wanted to drown out the world.

Jasper smiled at his nephew's uncharacteristic display of immaturity, and waited for him to reappear. Once the need for air eventually propelled Henry to the surface, he continued with his questions.

"When did they propose this meeting take place?"

"The day after tomorrow, at the abbey in Merevale. Richard departed Nottingham and is now in Leicester. Once Northumberland arrives, he will set out to meet us. Sir William believes by Monday we will have our battle."

"Well then," Jasper announced, making his way to the edge of the stream. "We'd better get back to the others."

* * *

It was well past midnight by the time they arrived back in camp, the army having travelled much further than they had anticipated. If they had hoped their absence had gone unnoticed, they were to be disappointed. Oxford was waiting for them in Henry's tent with a face like thunder.

"You cannot just disappear like that," he berated as soon as they stepped through the entrance. "You must speak with us before doing such things. You're gone for hours to God-knows-where, and now you return as if nothing has happened."

Henry held up his hands in acquiescence. "Forgive me, it was never my intention to cause any distress."

"It might not have been your intention, but that does not change the result. What did you expect would happen? That your absence would not be noticed?"

Jasper stepped forward. "This was my fault, John. I merely sought to have a moment alone with my nephew," he explained placatingly. "I'm afraid we quite lost track of time."

"Well, you could have chosen a better moment to do so," Oxford grumbled, though the heat of his anger had dissipated. "While you were gone, Hungerford and Talbot arrived, bringing with them another few hundred men, and I had to lie and say you'd been forced to retire to your bed. Fortunately, they did not press me on the matter. It seems Richard is haemorrhaging men quicker than he can recruit them. Speaking of which, what of these rumours about the Stanleys?"

"Oh, so you've heard about that?" Henry replied, taking a seat and kicking off his boots. "I received word that my stepfather wishes to meet with me."

"To what end?"

"The message did not say, but his brother, William, will be with him. I can only assume they intend to pledge their support. Or at the very least, confirm their planned inaction," he added with a glance at Jasper remembering their earlier conversation.

"So that's the slippery bastard's intention."

Jasper frowned. "What do you mean?"

"Jesu, did you lose your minds back there as well as your way? The Stanley brothers have been playing cat and mouse with us for miles. According to the scouts, Thomas has his men in permanent battle formation, yet he makes no effort to attack. No sooner do we move forward to meet him than he retreats back once again. I had wondered what the hell he was doing, but now I figure it a ploy to fool Richard. I look forward to meeting with him so I can ask him myself."

Henry shook his head. "You won't be joining us at the meeting."

"I'm sorry?"

"Stanley has requested it be limited to just my uncle and I. In any case, I need you here, John. I need your experience and your leadership to keep this assorted rabble in check."

For a moment, Jasper thought Oxford might challenge the matter further, but in the end, he let it slide. "As you wish, your Grace. Just make sure you don't get lost on the way back."

* * *

Light filtered through Merevale Abbey's magnificent Jesse window, fracturing into hundreds of miniature rainbows that danced on the flagstones. It was impossible to enter such a place and not feel a sense of spiritual calm descend, and Jasper enjoyed taking a moment to let the feeling wash over him before being ushered along into the heart of the abbey. The Stanley brothers were already waiting for them in the abbot's private office, standing together by the empty fireplace. Both men had close-cropped hair and thick beards, though while Sir William kept his neatly trimmed, Thomas had allowed his to grow long. They broke off their murmured conversation as Henry and Jasper entered.

"Henry!" Thomas exclaimed, striding over. "It is a pleasure to finally meet you."

"My Lord Stanley," Henry replied, taking his stepfather's offered hand.

"Thomas, please, we are family after all. Speaking of which, your mother sends her love," Thomas smiled. "To both of you," he added, nodding at Jasper who inclined his head in response. "And this is my brother, William – I believe the two of you have been in correspondence."

"Indeed we have. Sir William," Henry smiled.

"Your Grace," the younger Stanley replied with a bow. "How has your journey been thus far? I admit to having been impressed by your progress."

"We have my uncle, and the long memories of the Welsh people, to thank for that," Henry replied, shifting the focus onto Jasper.

"It must feel good, Pembroke, to be home once more after all this time?" Thomas inquired, addressing his wife's former brother-in-law directly for the first time.

Jasper gave a tight smile, unimpressed by Stanley's overt display of friendliness. "It will be all the sweeter once I see my nephew safely on the throne."

"Of course."

Henry stepped forward. "And if you pledge your support to me now, that day could soon be upon us."

"Now, let's not get ahead of ourselves, Henry," Thomas cautioned.

Henry raised his eyebrows in surprise. "Ahead of ourselves? Richard is marching here as we speak, and you expect me to do what? Devise a battle plan that leaves a gap for if you should join me at the last moment? Either you are with me or against me."

"It need not be so black and white," Sir William countered.

Henry shot him a look. "Does it not? If you combined your forces with mine, we could stop this battle before it even begins."

Thomas gave a small smile. "You flatter me to think I command such an impressive number."

"Well then, tell us, how many do you have?" Henry asked, clearly beginning to lose patience with his stepfather's games.

Thomas glanced at his brother. "Between us? Four thousand or so."

Henry shook his head. "I do not consider that a small number, Lord Stanley. And Richard, what are his numbers?"

"Now that Northumberland has reached him, close to fifteen," Thomas replied, in an off-hand manner that was most certainly designed to shock.

Jasper struggled to keep his features neutral, swallowing against a throat that felt suddenly constricted. Fifteen thousand. God help them, that was at least three times their own force. He couldn't see Henry's face from where he was standing, but judging from his body language, his nephew had done well to remain impassive.

A flicker of disappointment at the lack of reaction passed across Stanley's face. "Provided Percy allows them to be put to use, that is," he added.

Desperate to avoid dwelling on how hopelessly outnumbered they were, Henry latched onto this small scrap of information. "You say that as though it is not a certainty?"

Sir William smiled knowingly. "Nothing is a certainty in war, not least the loyalties of men."

"So what makes you doubt Northumberland's to Richard?"

Thomas' eyes glinted in the candlelight. "Intuition. If he truly cared about his king it would not have taken him this long to rally his men."

"And what of your loyalty?" Jasper probed, looking at the two brothers.

"Ours?" Thomas replied, feigning confusion.

"Come now, Thomas, you are a clever man, your family is renowned for its ability to choose the winning side. You speak of loyalties, yet you come here today to meet us. I can only imagine the risks such an action raises. But in spite of that, and I have no doubt, your wife's pleas for you to support her son, you remain reluctant to commit." Jasper fixed his grey eyes on the elder Stanley, his voice hardening. "I want to know why."

In the moment of silence that followed, Jasper caught the almost imperceptible look that passed between the brothers. "What is Richard holding over you?" he pressed, suddenly conscious this whole display could be a trap.

"I don't see why—" Sir William began to bluster, but he fell silent when his elder brother raised a hand.

"My son. He has my son," Thomas replied simply, the admission hanging heavy in the room.

"That's quite significant collateral, Stanley. Why should we trust you?"

"Richard will not harm him, not if there remains a chance I will support him. Uncertainty will keep him safe."

Jasper narrowed his eyes. "That does not answer my question."

"You can trust me, Pembroke. Margaret does. And as you say, I've risked much by even coming here today. I could have crushed you the moment you set foot in England, but instead I hung back. I sent false reports to Richard and allowed you time to strengthen your forces. If that is not proof enough then I do not know what is."

It was now Henry's turn to press his stepfather. "And what of during the battle itself? What then? By keeping your son, Richard intends to force your hand."

Thomas shook his head dismissively. "It will not come to that."

"But what if it does?" Henry challenged.

Thomas fixed his stare on Henry. "I have other sons," he replied, dispassionately. And with that, he strode from the room.

Sir William watched his brother leave before turning his attention back to Jasper and Henry. "The royal force is almost here. It would seem that before the sun sets tomorrow, we will know the outcome of all of this."

"And on what side will you be standing, Sir William?" Henry asked.

The younger Stanley smiled at the attempt to make him admit something his elder brother would not. "I think Thomas has made our position clear. In the meantime, though, there is someone eager to see you both. I will bid you good day, sirs – may God keep you safe in what is to come." With a bow, he left the room, nodding his head to someone in the corridor as he passed by.

For a brief moment, Jasper thought it might be Margaret, but he quickly dismissed the idea. Thomas might be accommodating of his wife's strong will, but allowing her to visit the most wanted men in the country on the eve of battle, even if they were family, was too much even for him. Still, he did not expect the man who did walk through the door. Though grey hair now framed his softly lined face, Jasper would have recognised him anywhere.

"Richard," he spluttered. "What in God's name are you doing here?"

A broad grin broke across Tunstall's face, deepening the creases that fanned out from the edges of his eyes. "You didn't think I'd let you have all the fun on your own now did you?"

"Jesu! This is the second time you've done this to me, my friend," Jasper admonished, pulling him into a tight embrace.

"Let us hope that there is no cause for there to be a third," Tunstall chuckled. "I don't think your heart could cope with the shock, old man."

"*Touché*," Jasper shot back with a smile.

Pulling away from Jasper, Tunstall turned his attention to the other person in the room. "And Henry, look at you! Christ's bones, has it really been so long since I saw you?"

Henry frowned in mock seriousness. "I'm afraid it has."

Tunstall considered the man before him, who had changed so much from the fresh-faced boy he remembered from London. "I suppose I should really be calling you *your Grace*."

"You've known my uncle and me too long for such formalities," Henry replied, shaking his head.

"Though after such an absence, we must seem little more than strangers," Jasper added.

Tunstall slapped a hand on Jasper's shoulder. "You could never be such to me, my friend. But there is much to catch up on. Come, you can tell me all about it on our ride back to your camp."

46

22 August 1485

J asper sat hunched over the desk in his tent with a blanket wrapped tightly around his shoulders. It was so early that even the songbirds had yet to start up their dawn chorus and the only light came from the gently flickering candles. He had never slept well before a battle, and this time was no different. He'd tossed and turned through most of the night in a vain attempt to chase the sleep that eluded him. The small snatches he was able to steal were plagued by the memory of friends lost in battle, their grotesquely warped faces parading through his dreams. They called out to him, his father and Somerset in particular, cruelly taunting him while carrying their heads in their arms, their necks nothing more than bloodied stumps. But of all of them, it was the image of Edward of Lancaster that was hardest to shake. Though his ghostly hands gripped his stomach in an attempt to hold back the organs threatening to spill out, his face had been filled with excitement, his eyes shining with the same eagerness to claim his birthright that Jasper had seen in Henry's. The similarities were not lost on Jasper, and he had forced himself awake before Edward's face could morph into his nephew's.

Laying on the desk in front of him was a piece of parchment on which he had written a brief message:

To my most beloved sister. I pray you will never have cause to read this but if you are, then know I did everything I could for our boy. I loved him as if he were my own and I gave my life willingly in defence of his. My only regret is that doing so took me away from you. Pray for me. Forever yours, Jasper.

Re-reading it, the note seemed woefully incapable of conveying the depth of emotion he felt, but it would have to do. Folding it tightly, he dripped some melted wax onto the paper and, for what could well be the last time, pressed his seal into it.

A voice called quietly behind him. "You asked for me, Brother."

Jasper spun in his chair and smiled. "David. Thank you for coming. It's time for me to don my armour. I will need your help."

David frowned. "Would one of your squires not be better?"

"They might, but I do not want them. Not now. I want you."

David's face brightened. "I'll see what I can do then. It's been a while since I last did this."

Jasper's armour was hanging on a stand in one corner. It was a thing of beauty, given to him by King Charles before they had left Sens. It had been crafted in Germany by the skilled armourers that worked there. It was only the second suit he had ever owned and whether or not he lived to see tomorrow, he knew it would be his last. David took care when positioning the plates, making sure Jasper's movement remained as unrestricted as possible. When he was satisfied, he stepped back to allow Jasper to move his arms back and forth to check the fit.

"As good as any squire," Jasper smiled.

"I'm not sure about that," David laughed. "Is there anything else I can do for you?"

"Yes, there is one thing," Jasper said, walking over to the desk and picking up the letter. He handed it to David. "If the battle does not go our way, make sure this gets to Margaret."

"But how will I do that if I'm fighting alongside you?" David asked. "Unless," he continued, realisation dawning. "Unless, I won't be fighting."

"David—" Jasper began gently, but his brother pushed away from him.

"No, you can't do this to me again. I won't let you. Please, don't order me to stay behind."

"I'm not ordering you, David. I'm asking, as your brother. I need to know you're safe. I can't protect both you and Henry at the same time."

"I don't need your protection," David protested.

"No, maybe you don't, but I will not let your mother lose you like she lost our father. You are Henry's uncle, just as much as I am. If I should fall—" David made to interject. "No, listen. If I should fall, I need you to promise me you'll keep him safe. Keep the Tudor flame—"

"Keep the Tudor flame burning," David sighed. "Yes, I know."

Jasper gripped his shoulder. "Thank you."

"Wait," David said, working their father's ring from his finger. "You'll need this."

"No," Jasper replied, shaking his head. "I gave it to you, remember?"

David shrugged. "It was never really mine. I was just looking after it until you could reclaim it." He offered it to Jasper. "Take it, please." After a moment's hesitation, he took the ring and slid it onto his finger. David smiled at the sight. "I'll see you on the other side, Brother," he said before leaving the tent.

On his way out, he passed Tunstall coming the other way, who, like Jasper, was also dressed for battle.

"Impressive," he said approvingly, taking in Jasper's new suit of

333

armour. "How come I don't get one?"

Jasper raised an eyebrow. "Because you are not a cousin of the King of France."

"Damn it, I knew it would be something like that," Tunstall replied in mock annoyance. He watched as Jasper retrieved his helmet and gauntlets from their stand. "So this is it, my friend."

"This is it," Jasper echoed, picking up his sword. He studied it for a moment before sheathing it. With his mother's motto etched along its blade, it had been the one constant through all the years from St Albans till now. It might not have brought him luck, but it had brought comfort, and that was enough for him.

Tunstall smiled as Jasper walked over to him. "I can think of no one I would rather fight alongside."

"Nor I," Jasper admitted.

"Well then," Tunstall announced, clapping his armoured hands together, "let's get your nephew his crown."

* * *

Jasper and Tunstall found Henry outside his tent with his commanders arrayed in front of him. He nodded when he caught sight of his uncle before turning back to the man in front of him, a knight that Jasper did not recognise.

"And your name is?" Henry enquired.

"Sir John Savage, your Grace," the man replied with a bow. "Lord Stanley sent me here with my men to support you."

Henry straightened at the mention of his stepfather. "You are most welcome, sir, but what of Stanley himself?"

"He says he and his brother will wait until the fighting has commenced before committing their troops."

"Surprise, surprise," Tunstall muttered to Jasper, as an uneasy murmur ran through the group. They were all aware of how much they needed the Stanleys' support. The idea of going into battle without them was not something any of them relished.

Henry sucked his teeth in frustration. "I will not wait on the whims of one man. The Stanleys may do as they wish, I for one will not be cowed into submission." Looking past Savage, he focused his attention on the Earl of Oxford. "John, you will have control of the vanguard. I trust your judgement; you may arrange the men as you see fit."

With a nod the earl stepped forward, allowing Savage to shrink back into the group. "Thank you, your Grace. Given the disparity in numbers, I suggest forming a single battle line with two wings. Archers will be arranged at the front with the main force just behind. As for the wings, Chandée and the French mercenaries will take the left, while our recent arrivals, Talbot and Savage, will lead the right. Given their time with the Stanley brothers, I feel it best they take the side closest to them, in the eventuality that they choose to lend their support. There is a marsh on that side which should prevent any attempt to flank us, though it will also present an added challenge while fighting."

Henry nodded. "And what do we know of Richard's plans?"

"I believe Scales has knowledge of those," Oxford replied, searching for the golden-haired admiral amongst the crowd.

Edward Woodville cleared his throat as he stepped forward to address the group. "Norfolk leads the centre and my scouts report that Northumberland remains at the rear. He has made little preparation to join the battle, but that could change. The lay of the land will pose its own challenges. As Oxford mentioned, there is a marsh on the right side, and indeed much of the land below us is interspersed with small water channels. As you can see, the plain is surrounded on all sides by hills. Richard has claimed the rise opposite, while Stanley has positioned himself off to the right. We will need to entice the enemy down to meet us if we are to avoid fighting uphill. I should also mention, it is not just numbers that Richard has to his advantage. Brackenbury has brought the cannon from the Tower, but they are clumsy pieces and will be of little use once we move past their range."

"We had better move quickly then," Henry joked, and laughter rippled through the crowd.

Oxford let it subside before continuing on from where Woodville had left off. "I have a score to settle with Norfolk. He bested me once before, I will not let there be a second. I will lead the first attack with Blount and attempt to spin his forces so that they are fighting into the sun. Once I have done so, Rhys and his men will launch a hammer strike straight through his centre. The confusion and panic should fracture his force into disarray. By that point, I imagine Stanley will have stepped in, after which the field will be ours."

Henry smiled. "Well then, what are we waiting for?"

* * *

The dawn of battle, when fate held your life in the balance, was not the time for dawdling. Every man knew what was expected of him and as a result, they were ready and in position within the hour. Though they might not have the numbers Richard did, it was still an impressive sight to see them arrayed in battle formation. The two thousand that had travelled with them from France had swelled to nearly five, each addition evidence of Henry's popularity. He had worked hard to be seen by the people, not as a foreign stranger, but as the rightful king, and Jasper was proud of the man his nephew had become in the process. He watched on with a full heart as Henry rode up and down the line, checking in on the men while underneath him his bay destrier snorted in anticipation. Towards the centre, near where Oxford's banners fluttered in the breeze, he reined in his horse and called out to those around him.

"Do not be intimidated by their numbers. Though there might be more of them, they are merely farmers and stable boys – men forced into battle by their overlords. But not you. You may come from different countries and different backgrounds yet each of you, down to a man, chose to be here today. That makes you worth at least ten of anyone pressed into service. As I look out over you now, I see only the cold, determined faces of skilled fighters staring up at me. There is no going back from here, only forward. Take heart and may God guide us to victory."

A loud cheer went up in response to his words, travelling like a wave down the entire length of the line. Even those who had not heard Henry's speech found themselves lending their voices to the shouts as an anticipatory frenzy gripped them. With a final glance at Oxford, Henry made his way through the front line to the rear where Jasper, Tunstall and Sir John Cheyne waited with a few hundred foot soldiers. To Jasper's surprise, Henry dismounted when he reached them. He gave his nephew a questioning look.

"I would fight on my feet, Uncle, shoulder to shoulder with my men."

"As you wish," Jasper replied, dismounting. Next to him, Tunstall and Cheyne shared a glance before following suit.

"I did not mean for you to do the same," Henry exclaimed as their horses were led away.

"Jesu, Henry, how many times must I tell you, I will fight at your side until the very end. If you are to forgo your horse, do you really believe I will not do the same?"

"Thank you, Uncle."

Jasper shook his head. "Save your thanks for when this is over."

Henry stared out over the plain that would either raise him high or leave him cold. An involuntary shiver ran over him at the thought.

The nervous twisting of his stomach made him want to vomit, but he swallowed against the rising bile. Inhaling deeply, he tried to emulate his uncle's confident stance "So what now?" he asked.

"Now, we wait."

* * *

"What the hell is he playing at?" Jasper muttered, looking up to the top of the hill on which the Stanleys sat unmoving.

There was no way they could have missed the battle raging below them. Despite their inferior numbers, Oxford's men had made surprisingly good progress, gradually starting to spin Norfolk's troops around. For those fighting in the mêlée, it would be impossible to recognise what was happening, but from his vantage point, Jasper could see how much the two lines had moved. Why then the Stanleys remained stationary was a mystery. If they were ever going to commit their troops then surely this was the moment, unless it was never their intention to do so.

Back on the field, Jasper watched as a pack of men led by Rhys ap Thomas' black raven banner charged at Norfolk's centre, the hammer blow Oxford had promised about to hit home. He could almost see the panic ripple through the enemy as they realised they were now defending on two fronts. In places, men began to throw down their weapons, and as he continued to watch he saw Norfolk's banner waver, then fall, with the duke himself no doubt joining it in the mud. But while they might have enjoyed an early advantage, there was no getting around the fact that, even with Northumberland standing idle, Richard's forces still outnumbered Henry's two to one. If they were to claim victory, they would need to use every man they had.

Jasper turned to his nephew. "The momentum is shifting, Henry. If we are to join this fight, the time is now, but it must be your choice. I will not make it for you."

"What about Stanley?"

Jasper shook his head.

"Then we will do it without him," Henry announced. Drawing his sword, he called out to Sir William Brandon. "Raise the banner as high as you can, I want Richard to know I'm coming." He glanced back at Jasper. "Stay close to me," he whispered.

On Henry's command, they began to make their way out onto the battlefield, moving with purpose and ignoring the desperate cries of injured men. As they passed by the edge of the marsh, Jasper made a mental note of its position; should they be forced back, he had no intention of meeting his end in its copper-coloured pools. Up ahead, they could see Oxford's men still hammering away at the enemy line, forcing them back up the rise. As the earl moved further forward, it opened up the field behind him. On a horse, the space would have been covered in a few moments, but it was a different story on foot. It put them in a vulnerable position, and he called out to Henry to increase the pace. Yet no sooner had he done so than a loud trumpet blast cut through the air. With a cold sense of dread, Jasper looked up to the ridge where Richard had been standing, his eyes widening in shock as a black mass of knights began streaming towards them. He was suddenly acutely aware of the still-significant distance separating them from Oxford. And with that awareness came the realisation that there was no one close enough to help them. As the galloping figures grew more distinct, he bellowed the order to form up, ignoring the fact that it should have been Henry, not him, doing so. The foot soldiers did not need to be told twice, those of them who had already seen the approaching threat shoving the others into position. Almost unconsciously, Jasper moved in front of Henry to shield him from danger, while fighting every sinew in his body that screamed at him to run.

Time seemed to slow as Richard and his cavalry bore down on them like horsemen of the apocalypse. As they reached the bottom of the hill, Jasper saw a small band of men sporting Talbot's colours attempt to disrupt the charge, but they were smashed aside like rag dolls; their heroic sacrifice doing nothing to slow the enemy's advance. By now Jasper's ears were filled with the thundering of hooves and he struggled against the urge to shut his eyes and surrender to the incoming onslaught.

The noise when the charge finally hit was deafening, the screams of men and horses combining together into one horrendous sound. The cavalry had gouged a great gash in the first few ranks of men, but remarkably the core of Henry's unit remained relatively unscathed. They were afforded a crucial moment to regroup as the knights either jumped from injured horses or circled back for another pass.

Sir John Cheyne was one of the first to engage the enemy. Putting his height to good use, he swung his mace around with deadly force. His phenomenal reach caught many a man off-guard, their final thoughts one of utter surprise as the spiked ball buried itself into their skulls. Cheyne's armour accentuated his size and Jasper could see men shrinking back from him in fear. All, that is, except Richard. Easily identified by the gold coronet encircling his helmet, he paced towards Cheyne like a lion. He'd obviously lost his horse in the charge, though he still held his broken lance in one hand. Cheyne noted the identity of his opponent and called out to Richard, goading him, while at the same time deflecting opportunistic strikes from his men. As Jasper had seen far too often, in battle, skill and strength only counted for so much. Chaos was the true determiner, and as another man darted forward, Richard seized his opportunity. Swinging his lance around, he brought it crashing onto Cheyne's head. The knight had always seemed invincible, but even he could not withstand such a blow. He fell like a piece of timber and remained unmoving in the dirt.

Richard stepped back triumphantly and then turned his focus to Henry's banner. Of all the ones he could have picked, Henry had purposely chosen the royal colours to antagonise Richard, and it certainly seemed to have had the desired effect. He stalked towards it with deadly intent. Though Jasper couldn't see Richard's eyes, he could imagine the fury burning in them, and at that moment knew he needed to get his nephew as far away from the banner as possible.

Grabbing the front of Henry's breastplate, Jasper dragged him deeper into the tangle of bodies, hoping to hide him amongst the mayhem. Henry looked questioningly at Jasper but did not resist him, clearly unaware of what prompted his uncle's actions, and there was no time to explain. Richard was but one of a multitude of threats facing Henry, and with him now at a safe distance, Jasper was able to turn his attention to the others.

Nearly a quarter of a century had passed since he had last experienced the heat of battle, atop that godforsaken hill outside Caernarfon, and Jasper felt every single year of it as he put his sword to use. Time lost its meaning, minutes drawing out till his lungs burnt and the metallic tang of blood filled his mouth. Yet the pain he felt was irrelevant, and though his body cried out for rest, he could not allow himself to stop, not for a moment. Kill or be killed, that was the reality, and so he continued to slash and stab at everything in front of him until his mother's motto was completely obscured by blood.

Squinting against the sweat that stung his eyes, he glanced up to where the Stanleys remained unmoving on the hill, and thought he saw a group dressed in the colours of Rhys ap Thomas racing up it. A small flicker of hope fluttered in his chest, only to be extinguished a moment later by a violent lunge of a sword. Jasper knocked it harmlessly away and plunged his own blade into his attacker's stomach. Who was he fooling? Even if help was on its way, it would be too late. He needed only to look around him to see the evidence of their inevitable defeat. Brandon's lifeless corpse lay face down in the mud, his hand still stretching for the broken standard he had given his life for. Not far from him, Cheyne's giant frame lay awkwardly twisted. Richard meanwhile stalked the marsh's edge, dispatching any man that strayed too close. Jasper tried to push his way towards him but he made it no more than a few feet, the crush of men making it impossible to move. If Richard was to die today, it was unlikely to be at his hand. In any case, Jasper had other, more important people, on his mind.

Over to his left, Tunstall was still fighting valiantly, though from his laboured movements, Jasper could tell that his friend wouldn't be able to keep it up for much longer. Next to him, Henry was putting the skills they'd practised at Château de l'Hermine to good use, but even he was tiring, and Jasper could see the fear shining in his eyes. Suddenly, a soldier appeared behind Henry, his weapon drawn back ready to strike. Jasper shouted out a warning but his nephew did not hear him. With a roar, he dived between them and felt the blow make contact. But there was no weight behind it and it glanced harmlessly off his new armour. For a brief moment, Jasper saw his attacker's eyes widen in panic before he ran his blade across his throat, his mind closed to the horror. Moving away, his ears picked up the sound of distant rumbling.

"Uncle, look!" Henry shouted.

Spinning quickly, in fear of another attacker, Jasper had just enough time to register the banners of Rhys ap Thomas and Sir William Stanley before four thousand fresh men swept onto the field. It was like watching Fortune's Wheel spin in real time, and if he'd had the energy, Jasper would have punched the air in joy. All around him, Richard's men began to fall back, pulling each other over in their futile attempts to escape. Few made it more than a couple of yards before they were cut down.

Taken completely off-guard by Stanley's attack, Richard struggled to maintain control of his rapidly depleting force. He tried to call out to those of his supporters who remained, but a savage blow across his head silenced his cries. It knocked his helmet clear off, sending the crown that had been affixed on top tumbling into the reeds; the symbol of that for which so many had died reduced to worthlessness in the frantic scramble for life. Richard flailed about in the mud, desperately reaching for some sort of weapon. Those around him seemed oblivious to their king's struggle, continuing to fight even as their reason for doing so was dragged ever closer towards Death's cold embrace. From across the marsh, Jasper watched as Richard clambered to his feet. He looked around wildly, screaming words that, from such a distance, Jasper had no possibility of hearing. He seemed to be in a daze, unaware of the fighting around him, and as such, unable to prevent the terrible blow that sent him sprawling to the ground once more, this time into the midst of Thomas' blood-crazed men. It would seem that death for the last of the Duke of York's sons would come at the hands of a Welshman, and the last thing Jasper saw before the world stopped was Rhys ap Thomas swinging his halberd round with lethal force as Richard, bare-headed and bloodied, cowered before him.

47

The Aftermath

Rationally, Jasper knew that silence was not a quality associated with battles. Yet as the death blow hit home, he could have sworn that was what descended on the field. Even as he watched the jubilant celebrations of Rhys' men, the world still seemed devoid of noise. It was only when he felt someone shaking him that the sounds came rushing back. Blinking rapidly, his eyes re-focused on the person in front of him – Henry, grinning wildly.

"We've done it, Uncle!" he exclaimed excitedly. "The field is ours!"

Jasper reached out a hand to touch his nephew's face, not daring to trust his eyes. "Henry," he gasped. "You're alive?"

"Yes, Uncle, I'm alive," Henry chuckled. "As are you!"

"But— I— Richard—?" Jasper stammered.

"Dead, and already forgotten."

"And Tunstall?" he asked, dread filling his heart.

"Just here, my friend," Tunstall replied, walking up behind Jasper and placing a hand on his shoulder. "Honestly, you need to stop believing I've died every time you miss me, otherwise I might start to think you don't rate my skills as a swordsman."

Jasper shook his head. "I pray you won't have to put them to use ever

344

again. You and I have experienced enough fighting to last a lifetime."

"I'll drink to that," Tunstall replied. "If I can find a bloody drink that is!"

Laughing more in relief than humour, Jasper looked around. From all corners of the battlefield, men were making their way over to them. Amongst the soldiers, Jasper spotted many of the loyal commanders who had followed them since Brittany. There was Oxford, still grinning despite the blood running down his face, walking with his arm around James Blount who, though suffering from a slight limp, seemed in similarly good spirits. Close behind came the Woodville brothers, almost indistinguishable in their armour. They paused next to what Jasper assumed was a body until Edward reached out a hand and, with his brother's help, pulled Sir John Cheyne gently to his feet. It seemed it would take more than a lance to kill the giant after all.

Off to the side, Sir William Stanley was talking animatedly with Rhys ap Thomas, no doubt reliving their decisive charge. He broke off when he caught sight of his elder brother riding over. Lord Stanley might have waited until the last possible moment to send in his forces but the decision, once made, had been decisive, and Jasper had no desire to hold the delay against him.

"How fares your son, Lord Stanley?" he called out.

"His neck remains intact if that is what you are wondering," Stanley replied, jumping down from his horse and embracing his brother. As he began to walk over to where Jasper stood with Henry, something on the ground caught his eye. Bending down, he reached into the reeds to retrieve it. Straightening, Jasper's gaze was drawn to the gold coronet he now gripped in his hand. Richard's crown. It was such a small, unassuming thing, yet Stanley held it almost reverently. Gently wiping a clump of mud from one of its points, he made his way over to Henry.

A hush descended on the assembled crowd. Henry glanced at his uncle, but Jasper merely smiled as he moved away before dropping onto his knee. All around him, the others did the same until it was just Henry and his stepfather standing amongst a sea of bowed heads.

Stanley regarded his stepson. "Your mother always knew this day would come," he said softly. Raising the coronet up high, he placed it solemnly on Henry's head before taking a step back and joining everyone else on bended knee. Then, with a deep breath, he roared, "God save the king," and Henry's face broke into a wide, disbelieving grin as hundreds of voices answered the call, Jasper's shout the loudest of all.

"God save the king. God save the king," Jasper kept saying it, over and over, until emotion overwhelmed him and choked his words. Closing his eyes, he let the cheers echoing around the battlefield wash over him as the weight of thirty years lifted from his soul. It was over. Against all odds, they had triumphed. Fortune's Wheel had, at last, raised them high.

* * *

Historical Note

In the British Museum, amongst the countless treasures, there is a simple ring in an unassuming display cabinet in the corner of room 46. Few visitors pause long enough to register it. But if they did, they might remark on the proud lion stamped across its face, or debate the meaning of the now-indecipherable motto inscribed on its inside edge. If they stayed a little longer, they might notice how the worn yet still-bright gold glints under the museum spotlights. And if they took the time to read the card beside it, they might begin to imagine how it might have done the same on Henry Percy's finger that fateful morning of the battle of Towton, had the sun, not snow, filled the sky.

It is within that space, where fact gives way to imagination, that *The Sons of Prophecy* sits. It is true that history needs no embellishment, but five and half centuries is a long distance to reach across, and history hides her secrets well. We will never know the content of conversations shared by firesides on long winter nights, but we do know the actions those discussions led to. Those events; the battles, weddings, births and deaths are the anchor points in a sea of unknown. I have used these points as stepping stones, relying on the wisdom of a multitude of historians to plot a course between them. I would argue that complete accuracy is impossible to achieve. Nonetheless, I have endeavoured to try.

Acknowledgements

My fascination with Jasper Tudor started over a decade ago in 2013 when I was searching for a topic for my school's essay competition. I had recently devoured the BBC's adaptation of Philippa Gregory's *The White Queen* and amongst all the intriguingly complex characters, one stood out in particular. When I told my history teacher about my idea, I was afraid he might dismiss it. But instead, Keith Hay, the wonderful teacher that he was, smiled at me knowingly. "Ah," he said, with a characteristic mischievous twinkle in his eyes. "Uncle Jasper." And the rest, as they say, is history.

From the beginning this has always been a passion project, but that doesn't mean it has been a solo endeavour. There would be no Tudor dynasty without the loyalty and support Henry VII received from his Uncle Jasper, and there would be no *Sons of Prophecy* without my Uncle Chris. Thank you for your insight, enthusiasm and, most importantly, your love.

To my father, Mark, who approached this book as he has done with all other things I have tried my hand at, with genuine excitement and an infectious sense that anything is possible, thank you for making me believe it could be more than a Google Docs file!

To Mummy, Phoebe, and the rest of Project Happiness, thank you for being constructive with your criticism and for keeping me accountable. Special mention to my grandma, or SMG as she is more fondly known, who has done more to spread the word of this book than any marketing campaign ever could. After all, what's TikTok compared to the local church group and art society?

To Paul, for your keen eye, and to Mark, for the beautiful designs, thank you for polishing this into something of which I can be immensely proud.

To those of you who have variously endured my random ramblings into obscure 15th century history, thank you for your patience. To Lily for her help with my questionable Welsh and for letting me steal Ianto's name. And to Ed for lending me his laptop so I could get this across the finish line.

Finally, to the other half of the egg, my twin sister Liberty, I lava ewe.

East Sussex, December 2024.

About the Author

Tabitha Tennant grew up in East Sussex. She studied Anthropology at the University of Exeter and is now a solicitor. Long fascinated by the drama and intrigue of the War of the Roses, *The Sons of Prophecy* is her debut novel.